Undercover Tales

Blayne Cooper

KG MacGregor

SX Meagher

ISBN 1-932667-32-6
PUBLISHER: BOOKENDS PRESS, GAINSVILLE, FL
COVER DESIGN BY CAROLYN NORMAN

FIRST PRINTING: JUNE 2005

SECOND PRINTING: OCTOBER 2005

Acknowledgements

I'd like to acknowledge and offer my gratitude to those behind-the-scenes technicians whose assistance with matters of grammar and proofing was greatly appreciated. I bow to your superior knowledge and keen eyes.

SX and KG, it's an honor to share a book cover with you.

Finally, this story is dedicated to my Aunt Charlotte. Your support and love have always meant more than you'll know.

Blayne Cooper

I thank Tami for her excellent story notes, and Jenny for her sharp eye. A big thanks also to my co-conspirators in this endeavor for letting me play too. I'm saying yes already to doing this again.

KG MacGregor

I owe a massive debt of gratitude to my partner, Carrie. She's an integral part of my writing career, and neither my books nor my life would be the same without her.

Contrary to popular opinion, it's not always a bad idea to work with your friends. It was fun doing this, and we're all still speaking!

SX Meagher

Contents

Narc 9

SX Meagher

Quicksand 43

Blayne Cooper

Stolen Souls 209

KG MacGregor

Narc Redux 275

SX Meagher

Narc

SX Meagher

Yesterday was the worst best day of my life. Or maybe it was the best worst day of my life. Either way, it sucked. But it was also fan-fuckin'-tastic.

Okay. Let's take a deep breath. You're confused. But so am I. Why should you get to feel comfortable when I'm sitting here on pins and needles?

Oh, never mind. You don't know me well enough to care about my comfort. But I am a decorated officer of the Chicago Police Department, and that should count for something. Yeah, this is another story of a cop finding that the road to hell—or at least purgatory—is paved with surprises. I know that's not the actual saying, but police work has nothing to do with intentions. Intentions don't matter for squat.

THE SET-UP

Here's the backstory, as they say in Hollywood. About two years ago, my captain, Bill Washington, put me in charge of a very big sting operation. I'm not one for overstatements. When I say very big, I mean very, very big.

We've been nosing around Sonny Kokoris for twenty years. Everybody in town knows he's as dirty as the sidewalks on Waveland Avenue after a double-header. We'd nibbled around him, picking off little guys—guys that Sonny put on the front lines 'cause he didn't care if they got picked off. But we'd never gotten close to busting anyone that mattered.

Captain Washington told me point-blank that he'd do whatever it took to get me kicked up to lieutenant if I could crack the Kokoris gang. He couldn't take the exam for me, but we both knew I didn't need help there. I've always been blessed in the brains department. I didn't get through U. of I. on my looks. But I probably could've.

I was stunned when Washington told me how much support he'd give me to get the job done. I tried to sound matter-of-fact, but I almost cried when he gave me the details. And I never cry at work. Ever.

I do cry at home, though. I'm a sensitive woman, and I get PMS and get my feelings hurt and worry about things, just like every other woman. Just ask my girlfriend. Yeah, I said girlfriend.

No, it's not cool to be a lesbian on the force, but it's no worse than being a woman. Really. That's the pisser. Once the guys accept you as a real cop, it almost doesn't matter that you're a dyke. I get teased about it, but it's not that bad. The fact that I'm black makes the guys even more careful. If they can't make nigger jokes or fag jokes, they're reduced to jokes about wives. I don't mind those, since I have the best wife of anyone—and everybody knows it. Everybody who "knows" I'm gay, that is. I haven't told a lot of people, only those I really trust. I told my partner when I was a patrol cop, and I've told everyone I like enough to invite to my house for dinner. I'm sure a lot of people know ... but they don't officially know, if that makes any sense.

A minute ago I said I was black. I am, but I'm also white. I tend to refer to myself as black, even though my mom is a white woman from Italy. It doesn't matter a whole hell of a lot to me what other people call me, but I don't really look very black. I'm one of those women who makes you wonder: is she ... Brazilian ... Italian ... Greek ... Puerto Rican? So I call myself black to avoid the stilted conversation where acquaintances try to figure me out. "Is your family from ... America?" *No, we're immigrants*, I want to say. *One side of my family came voluntarily, the other was ... shall we say ... conscripted?*

But life's too short to focus much on what strangers think of me. As long as the people I love love me—I'm doing great.

So ... I've been working on this sting for two years. I got nearly everything I asked for: extra cops, extra overtime, extra equipment ... the works. And everything went well, maybe too well. My pops was in the Navy, and he always says that the only time he hated being at sea was when the weather was too good. That always meant all hell was about to break loose. My pops is a smart man.

It took a lot of work—a whole hell of a lot of work—but as of yesterday, I had people working in nearly every level of Sonny's operation. For being such a slick guy, he sure didn't seem too smart to me.

I got in by making small buys, building up my rep, letting the low-level guys know I was reliable. But I always dressed well and drove a very nice car. I wanted the chumps to know I could've bought more if I'd wanted to. I wanted them to know I was testing them while I was being tested.

Over time, I was buying a lot of dope, mostly crystal meth. But no matter how much I wanted to buy, I got the okay. That was my weekly reminder that my entire career rested on this bust.

The big payoff was yesterday, as you might have gathered. I was set to buy $250,000 worth of crystal. That's not the kind of money the Chicago Police Department likes to lose.

The buy was supposed to go down in a warehouse on the South Side. Sonny's third-in-command was gonna be there, and he's a very big fish. I felt good about it. But two days ago, I got a call from Sonny. He said he wanted me to go to his restaurant for the drop. I was sure I was hallucinating. I almost wet myself, but he seemed cool as a cucumber. My team ran around like lunatics for forty-eight hours—checking and rechecking that we had a plan for every possible scenario. I thought we did; I honestly did. But Sonny didn't get to be Sonny by playing fair.

The Bust

I hope I haven't bored you to death, 'cause here's where things get interesting. I was supposed to be at the restaurant at ten-thirty a.m. with my suitcase full of hundred-dollar bills. I got the okay from Washington, with one big hitch. I had to wear a wire.

That might not seem like a big deal to you. You might even agree that it's crazy not to wear one with a buy like this. But Sonny is a very nasty guy, and one of the things he hates is cops. There was no way I was gonna breeze in there, drop my bag, pick up my crystal and sashay outta there like I was buying the souvlaki platter. Sonny was gonna make sure I wasn't wired. I knew that as well as I knew anything. But it took half the day to convince the brass that I had a better chance of coming out alive if I went naked. No, not that kind of naked. We argued so much that I started to think they cared about the $250,000 more than me. Hurt my feelings.

Anyway, they finally gave in, and I got permission to go. I was as nervous as a Mormon bride, but I couldn't show it. I had to be as cool as Sonny and his goons. And they're so stupid, they don't know they should be worried.

I've gone over the whole scene so many times that I have the damned thing memorized. Here ya go:

I showed up on time and parked right in front of the restaurant. Sonny has three spaces reserved for himself and special guests. When I say "reserved," I mean that he ripped the meters out of the sidewalk. I figured my $250,000 merited a prime spot, so I bulked up my attitude and slid out of my lovely ride, the blackout windows completely illegal, but really nice when your nose itches.

I walked inside the restaurant, amazed at how ... normal it looked. The white stucco walls, the travel posters from Greece, a bouzouki playing softly in the background. The older man who looked like he colored his hair with a black magic-marker, sharing a table with two younger men. They might be a father with his sons, having a late breakfast. But it was Sonny with Chris and Spiro, two of his mid-level guys.

I was surprised to see Chris and Spiro. Chris is set to marry Sonny's daughter soon, and we've been puzzled as to why he hasn't been given more responsibility. Maybe today was the day he got promoted.

Spiro's presence bothered me more. He's a nasty fucker. The kind of guy you'd like to kick in the ass just because. He's also believed to be the guy Sonny uses to dispose of bodies. I hoped he had nothing on his to-do list.

"Athena," Sonny said when he spotted me. I'd picked the name to give the impression I was Greek. Like I said, I can pass for almost anything.

"Sonny," I said. "Good to see you again." I'd spoken to him once ... for about two seconds.

All three of them stood, and Spiro moved towards me. He gave me one of those awkward hugs that bad guys give each other to determine if the other guy is packing. I wasn't. He was. Then Chris did the same. Also packing. Then Sonny. Ditto. So all three guys knew I was armed with only a cell phone, and that my breasts were real. I learned that all of them needed new aftershave with a smaller spritzer. Damn! Working girls wore less perfume than these guys did.

I didn't have a whole hell of a lot to say to my friends other than, *Gee, I feel naked when I'm the only one at the party without some steel*, so I thought I'd start working. "Are we ready to do business?"

Sonny made a dismissive gesture with his ring-laden hand. "Don't be in such a rush. Let's have coffee."

I needed more coffee like they needed more cologne, but you don't say no to Sonny. If he tells you to jump, you hope you've got a spring in your step.

I sat down on the available seat ... the one that left my back to the door. It's not just a myth. Cops hate to sit with their backs to the door. We like a nice corner table, with a view of the whole place. But I didn't think I could suggest a change, so I sat.

"How is business?" Sonny asked.

"Good. Very good," I said. "That's why I'm buying a little more. If things go as well as they have been, I'll do all of my business with you." Yeah. That's a good one. If this bust doesn't go down, the only business I'm gonna have is with Spiro.

"Good, good," he said, smiling at me. He stared at me for a long time, long enough to make me twitch. "Is it true what I've heard about you, Athena?"

This is never a good question. Never. But I kept my cool and said, "Depends on who said it."

"I forget," he said, "but it was someone reliable." He stared at me again, and I could feel the sweat running down my arms and back. His head cocked, and he said, "I didn't believe it. You don't look the type. But now that I look at you close, I think they might be right."

I wanted to take a sip of the coffee the waitress had put in front of me, but I knew my hands would be shaking too much. I wiped them on my slacks and shrugged. “A lot of people say a lot of things.”

“Yes, yes, they do,” he agreed. “But this particular thing intrigues me.” He leaned close and said, “You’re not Greek.” It wasn’t a question, but I could tell he wanted an answer.

“No. Never said I was.” I tried to control the sigh of relief that my lungs begged for. I didn’t think he’d kill me for having a Greek first name.

“What are you?”

Hmm ... I hadn’t thought of that. “I’m Sicilian,” I said, even though my mother is Genovese. I thought being Sicilian would better fit into the mobster stereotype.

He nodded, looking avuncular and sage. “That makes sense. A Greek girl would never do what I’ve heard about you.”

Oh, fuck. Now what? “I can try to read your mind, or you can ask me a question, Sonny. But I’m not very good at mind-reading.”

A sly smile turned the corners of his mouth up. “I’ve heard,” he said, lowering his voice, “that you have sex with women.”

Shit! Is that all? I smiled back, even though I wasn’t sure I was supposed to. “That’s true,” I said, partly because it was and partly because I’d told one of his low-level dopes that I only did women when he kept trying to hump me.

“I’m puzzled by this,” he said with Chris and Spiro snickering. “You’re a beautiful woman. Why do you want to sleep with women?”

“The same reason you do, I guess,” I said, hoping he had a sense of humor.

The look on his face said that he wasn’t a regular at the comedy clubs. “What kind of an answer is that?” A vein on his temple pulsed.

“The truth,” I said. “I don’t know why I like women. I’m just attracted to them. I always have been. For me to sleep with a man would be like ... Chris or Spiro sleeping with one.” I decided to not use Sonny as an illustration any more.

Sonny looked at his henchmen, who both looked like they'd been sprayed with eau de shit. Spiro grabbed the lapel of my very expensive jacket, but Sonny put up a hand to stop him. "Calm down," he said. "She didn't say you were a faggot."

"No, no," I agreed. "Furthest thing from my mind." But now that he mentioned it, Spiro looked like he could be up for a little Greek-passive. "I just used you as an example of how ridiculous it would be for me to have sex with a man."

Both of the hulks settled down, but I could tell they'd taken a dislike to me. Sonny looked puzzled and a little annoyed. "I'm not happy about this. I don't know if I can trust you."

It clicked for me when he said that. Sonny had a reputation for being a real ladies' man. Talking with him, I could sense that his problem wasn't that I was gay, it was that he didn't know how or if he could use his charm on me. I put my hand over his and tried to use all of the womanly wiles I'd picked up along the way. "Sonny, you can trust me. We have a lot in common. After all, we both appreciate a beautiful woman, right?"

He gave me a grudging smile. "I suppose so."

"But we're also very different."

"How's that?"

"I also appreciate a beautiful man. I don't sleep with them, but I love men." I blinked my big brown eyes at him.

His smile grew bigger. "I don't love men," he said, "but I like to do business with them."

"I do, too," I said emphatically.

He leaned back in his chair and looked at me again. I couldn't read him right then, but he didn't look like he was gonna throw me out. "Were you surprised when I asked you to meet me here?"

"Ahh ... yeah, I was. I didn't know you got involved in the details of your business."

"I do," he said. "If I'm going to do *big* business with someone, I have to trust them enough to welcome them to my home."

I hoped he didn't mean that literally. The restaurant was decent enough, but if this was the only crib he could afford, he needed a good money manager. "I'm honored," I said, trying to sound humble.

"I don't trust you yet, Athena." He sat quietly for a moment then said, "I have to be careful."

"Of course you do."

"My main concern, of course, is that you're working with the police."

I didn't jump to defend myself. I thought it was better to let him talk.

"We've learned the hard way that it's very difficult to tell if someone is a traitor. You may have heard about some of our problems."

Did I mention that one of the reasons the department was so intent on getting Sonny was because we'd lost two undercover cops to him? Oops. I should have.

Three years ago, one of our guys lost his cover. No one knows how it happened, but he took a three-month dip in the lake, showing up in Michigan once the weather got warm. That sucked.

The year before that, during a drug buy, one of Sonny's grunts had forced one of our detectives to shoot another member of Sonny's family—a guy who had obviously fallen out of favor. The cop killed him. He went on trial for the shooting and did some time. That sucked, too. I don't know what I would have done in his place, but I think I might have spent a little time in the pen. If it came down to me staying alive versus one of Sonny's guys being dead ... Well, you do what you have to do. Anyway, even though our guy went down, the bust was still good. Sonny was obviously still pissed about that.

"I know it's hard to trust people in this business," I said. "Especially with the way the government's breathing down everybody's neck."

"Don't get me started," he said. "The damned government won't let a man make a living anymore." He smiled at me. "At least we still have friends in the department. And when we meet someone who isn't a friend ... we've been successful in making them friends."

Uh-oh. I didn't like the way that sounded. There had been some very unsuccessful sting operations over the last ten years, and the most unsuccessful of all had been with Sonny's operation. A lot of people thought that the cops might have gotten dirty during some of those failed busts. I hated to get dirty. I can wear a white shirt to a blueberry pie-eating contest and not get a mark on me.

"It's always nice to have friends," I said, hoping I didn't become one of his.

"You'd be amazed at the secrets some police officers have. They'd do anything to avoid letting the department know about certain things. Of course, some of the things people do can be very embarrassing." He laughed, a rather unattractive sound, with a funny little hiccup at the end. "I was suspicious about one man," he said thoughtfully. "Before we did business, I brought him a very attractive girl. I think she was ... oh, fourteen at the time." He looked at Chris. "Do you remember that girl?"

"Yeah," Chris said. "Died of an overdose."

Sonny looked genuinely sad. "That's a shame." He looked back at me. "Anyway, our friend has sex with the girl. But after the buy ... poof! We never saw him again. My suspicions about him were right. He obviously didn't want to go to jail for rape." His smile turned feral. "I wonder what he did with the drugs we sold him that day?"

"Maybe he was genuine," I said. "Maybe he got dead or something."

"No, that's not true. After we showed the tape to one of our friends in the department, he confirmed he was a cop."

Ohh ... that's bad. That's very bad. I hope this isn't the day I have to have sex with a fourteen-year-old boy. My girlfriend would kill me. And I might embarrass myself. *Now ... this goes where?*

"I hope you don't take offense," he said, "but I'm going to have to give you a little test, Athena."

I smiled, even though I felt like whimpering. "I'm pretty good at tests."

"I hope you are," he said. "This one is pass or fail." He laughed. "I learned that from my grandson. He's always trying to take classes pass or fail."

"That *is* funny," I said. God, you've got to laugh at a lot of stupid jokes in this business.

"The first little test is to make sure you're not wearing a wire. You'd think that people wouldn't be so stupid, but you'd be surprised."

He's talking about you, Captain Washington. Too bad you can't hear him.

"I'm clean, Sonny," I said in my best Catholic-schoolgirl voice.

"I'm sure you are. But we have to be careful. We check everyone, Athena. Everyone." He twitched his head at Spiro, and the big guy put his furry paw on my arm and pulled.

"Let's go," Spiro said.

I hoped he'd pat me down right there, but there were six or seven patrons in the place, and it probably wasn't good for business to see people frisking each other. Nonetheless, I didn't like having to go anywhere with Spiro. There's something about being pulled into a back room by a known killer that gives a woman pause.

He opened the door to what looked like a break room/coat closet. There was an old oak table, four wooden chairs, a battered, fake-leather sofa, a week-old *Sun-Times,* and a couple of gym lockers. By the door was another door labeled "Toilet." Nice. I guess they couldn't find a sign that said "Shitter."

"Jacket," he said.

I took that to mean I was to remove mine, so I did. I draped it over one of the chair backs because it's twenty-five percent silk, and I hate to be wrinkled. Spiro put his hands around my waist and yanked my shirt from my slacks. I scowled at him. It takes me a good five minutes to get my shirt tucked in properly every morning. Now I was gonna have to do it again.

He put those big, hot hands under my shirt and slid them all over my body. I giggled a little when his fingers poked out from my collar. I can't help it. My neck is a seven on the Richter tickle scale.

I thought we were finished, but he put his hands on my waistband and started to undo the button. Reflexively, I grabbed his hand and glared at him. "I'm not wearing a wire in my ass," I snapped.

He pushed my hand away like he would a gnat and started to slide the zipper down. Just when he was gonna drop my pants, Chris opened the door. "Sonny says that's enough." He looked like the little brother telling the older brother that their mom is pissed. I swear, being childish is a requirement for being a thug.

Spiro let my pants drop just to get back at me, even though it was his mom, I mean Sonny, who was mad. Both Chris and Spiro got a quick look at my bare legs, since my rather attractive panties were covered by my long shirt-tail. It pays to buy quality.

It's hard to pick your pants up from the floor with two big guys leering at you, but I did my best. I shortened my shirt-tuck procedure to two minutes, just to keep things moving. Once I was decent, the three of us walked back to the table. Sonny leaned over and slapped Spiro across the cheek before the big guy could sit down. It didn't look like it hurt much, but I've never met a guy who likes to be slapped. It's undignified.

"You think you're a gynecologist?" Sonny demanded. "You never take a man's clothes off. Show some respect!"

Spiro looked furious ... with me! What did I do? "I thought she might have something hidden ... down there."

Sonny slapped him again, this time leaving fingerprints. "When they make a microphone that works in a woman's pussy, I'll let you know." He nodded at me. "Forgive my language."

"No problem," I said, smiling. Ahh ... an old-fashioned gentleman. A gentleman who had a camera hooked up in the break room. No doubt with a tape recorder attached to it. Nice.

"Now, about that little test."

I was hoping that getting a breast exam and dropping my pants might do the trick. No such luck.

"Chris. Take Athena into the back and let her sample the product."

"No need," I said magnanimously. "I trust you."

"I insist," he said. "I want to make sure you're satisfied."

"I never touch the stuff," I said. "Never have."

His gaze narrowed. "I insist."

"But I've always wanted to see what all the fuss was about," I said, getting to my feet.

Chris followed me to the little room again. I wondered what kind of person would work at a restaurant where large quantities of drugs were sold in the break room. Other than addicts, it seemed like one could find a more appealing place to work. One with fewer guns lying around, too.

He opened a case that was sitting on the floor and placed it on the table. He had a nice little sample all ready for me. How thoughtful. I hadn't been lying. I'd never done crystal or coke or LSD or any of the biggies. I'd smoked grass in high school and college, but stopped before I decided to go into criminal justice. Life was confusing enough without having my senses altered. A couple of drinks is as fucked-up as I can stand being, and I don't do that very often. But I was gonna get a nice, big snort of crystal today, and I was scared shitless.

I'd seen enough films and taken enough seminars on drug use to know the common effects of methamphetamines. But I have a funny metabolism. Drugs that are supposed to make me sleep, like Tylenol PM, keep me up for hours. But Sudafed, which is speedy for most people, puts me out like a light. So I was worried ... mostly because I hate to be out of control ... especially when my life is in danger. I had exactly twenty-three officers within a two-block area, ready to storm the place when I gave the signal, and I didn't want to fall flat on my face on the sidewalk when I walked out. They would be justifiably confused.

I didn't have a choice. Chris neatly laid out two lines, smiled at me and said, "I don't have a pipe. You'll have to snort it."

I took the tiny straw he handed me and sniffed one line into my right nostril and the other into my left. The stuff was nearly pure white, and I knew it was high-quality. My heart goes out to the people who've snorted shit. My eyes watered, my nose burned, and my head felt like it was expanding and contracting with each beat of my heart.

I've never done it, so I'm not sure of the comparison, but it felt like snorting Drano. My God! Why would a sane person do this?

"How is it?" Chris asked, snickering.

"Fucked if I know. Could be the worst or the best shit in the world. All I know is that my nose feels like it's on fire."

Chris thought that was funny. At least one guy had a sense of humor.

We went back to our table, and damned if I wasn't starting to feel the effects. It's hard to describe, but the feeling came over me slowly. Kinda like the sun coming out from behind the clouds. I felt damned good. Really damned good. As good as I've ever felt. Like I could put on my red cape, save the world and be home in time for dinner.

I guess now is a good time to tell you a little secret. Even though I don't do street drugs, a lot of us use prescription drugs in ways we really shouldn't. I know it's not a great idea, but I'd been up for more than two days, and I had to be sharp. So I took a drug called Provigil. It was designed for people with narcolepsy, but it works great when you need to feel like you've slept—even though you haven't. One of the side-effects of the drug is that it dulls the effects of stimulants. I like to read up on things I take ... even if it's just so I know how stupid I'm being. But I hoped the Provigil worked the way it was supposed to—'cause I really needed to be clear-headed.

So far, so good. My mind felt razor-sharp. But my mood was already out-of-whack. I could tell because I wasn't afraid anymore. Fear can be your friend in a bust. I liked being a little bit afraid. Feeling too comfortable makes you take stupid risks.

I also felt a little twitchy and itchy. Kinda like I had on mohair underwear. I looked at Sonny. "I know those are real drugs," I said. "That's about all I can tell."

"Oh, they're real," he said. "You'll see just how real when you take your little test."

Another fucking test? Christ! I'm not trying to join the FBI! I'm just trying to buy some drugs!

Sonny snapped his fingers, and both waitresses looked up. I bet waitresses love that. Nothing better than being called like a dog. The woman who'd brought the coffee was fifty-something, a little on the doughy side and wore her hair like she was getting ready for an Elvis concert. The other one; young, blond, and sweet-faced, looked like a deer in the taillights—balefully staring at the car that'd just hit her. "You," Sonny said, pointing.

The blonde put down her tray and approached the table ... very, very tentatively. "What's your name, honey?"

"Brittany."

Sonny smiled at the other men. "That's a nice name, isn't it?"

Chris and Spiro nodded, their stock response.

"Why are you working here, honey?"

Brittany blinked. "To make money," she said.

Sonny laughed. "There are thousands of restaurants in Chicago. Do you live around here?"

"Uhm ... no. I live near Printer's Row."

"Restaurants over there pay a lot more than I do."

Brittany nodded her agreement. "But I go to school at UIC. I was in the neighborhood one day and saw a sign in your window saying you had a job available. I thought it made sense to be closer to school than home."

"And how do you like it here?" Sonny asked. "You've been here a while, right?"

"Six months," she said. "It's fine. Nice people. Regular crowd."

"Notice anything funny?" he asked, looking into her eyes.

"Uhm ... like what?" Brittany looked like she was gonna piss herself, and I didn't blame her. As I'd found out, Sonny's pop quizzes sucked.

"Oh, I don't know. You look like a smart girl. Perceptive. A young girl like you would probably only work here if she wanted something."

"Wanted something?"

"Yeah. Like an introduction into the business, or to meet a guy with a load of cash or to ... get information." His smile darkened.

"I, uhm ... I ... guess I did notice some funny things going on," she admitted.

"Like what?" Sonny asked, just like he was making idle conversation.

"Like ..." She looked at Spiro. "I've seen Spiro grab a towel and put ice in it and wrap it around his hand. He looked like he'd been in a fight or something."

"Uh-huh. What else?"

"Well ... like you said ... some of the guys have a lot of money on 'em. Sometimes they'll give me a really big tip, even when I haven't waited on 'em." She cast a quick glance at Chris, who colored slightly.

"So ... men in fights ... lots of cash ... big tips. What do you think? Is this just a regular restaurant?"

"Probably not," Brittany said, looking at the floor. "I think it's a front."

Sonny laughed and slapped both Chris and me on the arms. "A front!"

Brittany nodded.

"What kinda front?"

"Probably drugs or some other kinda crime."

"But you'd still rather work here than near Printer's Row."

Brittany nodded again.

"Why is that? Shouldn't a nice girl like you wanna work someplace full of young lawyers and legitimate businessmen?"

"I wanna have money," the young woman said, sticking her chin out. "Sometimes you've gotta take risks to get it."

"Ah-ha!" Sonny cried. "Look what we have here! A little entrepreneur."

"I spent a few months stripping," Brittany said. "The money isn't as good here, but I don't get pawed as much."

He looked her up and down, obviously admiring her body, which was, I had to admit from a purely aesthetic viewpoint, sizzling hot in a nasty girl-next-door kinda way. "You get pawed here?"

"Not much," she said, clearly lying. "Some guys pat my ass or put tips down my blouse."

Sonny looked at Chris. "I'd better never find you doing anything like that. I'll cut your nuts off."

A lot of blowhards said things like that. Chris looked like he knew that Sonny meant it. I couldn't see where his hands went when they left the table, but I had a suspicion they were holding onto his little friends for dear life.

Brittany interrupted. "Chris has always been a perfect gentleman." I could tell she was lying, but it was hard to tell if Sonny could. Guys tended to understand that it was hard to keep your hands off a sexy woman who didn't object.

"Well, Brittany, how would you like to make a quick thou?"

She blinked. Hard. "A thousand dollars?"

"Yep. And I bet it won't take you more than fifteen minutes. Twenty, tops."

"What do I have to do?" she asked, looking suspicious.

"All you have to do," he said, speaking softly so she had to lean in to hear, "is to take my lady friend here into the back room and make her come."

Brittany shot up like she'd been goosed. "Make her come?"

"Yeah. Give her a little head. You ever muff-dived?"

The woman shook her head violently. "Never!"

"Well," Sonny said, "You don't have to do it. But if you don't, you don't need to come back anymore. If I'm gonna have a good-looking young girl around here, she's gotta be willing to do me a favor once in a while."

Brittany snuck a quick glance at the other waitress. "She's the wife of a former associate," Sonny said. "Her husband screwed up, but I don't want her to starve."

God, this guy was a prince! He kills her husband and then lets her slop tables for the rest of her life.

I thought it was time to voice my opinion, even though no one had asked for it. "What's the point, Sonny? I've told you I'm a dyke. Why waste a thou trying to make me prove it?"

He gave me a look that was almost sympathetic. "The drugs are making you stupid. This isn't to prove that you're a dyke. Who would lie about something so embarrassing? This is just my little insurance policy. If you are a cop, you're not gonna want everybody in the department to know you're a bulldagger. And even if you don't care about that, you're not gonna want the tape put on the Internet."

Ooo ... yeah, I'm beginning to see why some of my predecessors decided to blow a bust rather than have Sonny show them doing something embarrassing. I mean, having the whole department know I was a dyke was bad enough ... but having them watch someone going down on me was hard to even get my mind around. Too bad for Sonny I was committed to nailing his ass. Too bad for me, too. My mother's not gonna like this. It's one thing to know your daughter's gay. It's another to have all of the neighbors watch her getting head. Now I know how Paris Hilton felt.

Brittany cleared her throat. "I'll do it." She looked sick to her stomach, which was just the tiniest bit insulting, but I tried not to take offense. I wouldn't wanna blow a guy ... no matter how stunning he was. Truth is, I didn't wanna get blown, and believe me, I don't say that very often. Call me old-fashioned, but I like to make love. I love my woman and she makes me hot. I don't go sniffing around other women. I don't need to, and I don't want to. But this was another one of those tough questions. Would you rather have a good-looking woman go down on you, or take a bullet? Truth be told, I'd rather have a Rottweiler go down on me than take a bullet. So I stood, ready to go to that damned back room again.

Brittany walked in front of me, and I found myself staring at her ass. I'm not above checking out a woman, but I'm usually not so damned obvious about it. But I honestly couldn't stop myself. Brittany was wearing a short, red skirt, and her ass swayed sexily with every step. Her skirt was so tight that I could see she was wearing a thong. One of God's great creations in my book. A tiny indentation at the crest of her sublimely-curved ass outlined the garment, and I had to suck my lower lip in to avoid drooling.

She opened the door, and I did a quick scan, looking for the cameras. Sonny wasn't very subtle. There were two, and they were right in plain sight, in the north and northeast corners of the room. He probably would have used all four corners, but a big air-conditioning duct filled one, and water and sewer pipes occupied the other. I stood so that the cameras were at my back and mouthed, "I'm sorry."

Brittany looked like she wanted to kick me in the groin, so I surmised my apology was declined. "How do you wanna do this?" she asked.

"Uhm ..." I smiled dumbly. "Isn't it obvious?"

"Where do you wanna be? How do you like to come?"

"Oh! Right!" God, I was an idiot. This drug was making me a total moron! I looked around the room. I didn't think I could come standing up. I mean, I can do that at home if I'm really worked up, but I was sure I couldn't pull it off today. So I either had to sit on one of the wooden chairs or the sofa.

Brittany was getting tired of my indecision. I could tell when she said, "Would you make up your fucking mind!"

"I'm trying," I said, feeling flustered and confused.

She moved closer and looked into my eyes. "Are you high?"

"Very," I said. "Crystal."

"Good," she said, letting out a relieved sigh. "Are you turned on?"

"No," I said, neglecting the fact that her ass almost made me dive for her.

"Okay, I'll take care of that first. I don't want to be here all day."

"That's not the best seduction line I've ever heard," I said.

Ignoring my comment, she reached up and took off my jacket, surprising me by neatly hanging it on one of the chairs. Then she started to unbutton my shirt. This time I didn't mind so much. Her hand was small and soft and gentle. She reached behind my head and pulled me down, kissing me hard and rough while she reached into my shirt and squeezed my breast.

Oh! Not so gentle! I don't usually like rough play, but today seemed to be an exception. My nipples got so hard that I could actually feel the skin puckering. Actually, I could feel everything ... everything was so clear ... so vivid. Every sensation was magnified, sharpened.

Brittany grasped my head with both of her hands and really let me have it. She kissed me so hungrily that I was afraid she'd swallow me. Then I was afraid she wouldn't. I've kissed and been kissed more times than I could count, but I couldn't recall ever feeling a kiss like that one. It was completely devoid of all of the things I thought I liked about kissing. Tenderness, love, sensuality, affection, playfulness, teasing, connection. This kiss was almost brutal; clearly intended to do only one thing ... make me hot. And damned if it didn't work!

I let out a gut-groan and cupped her ass cheeks with my hands, but she quickly grasped my hands and pushed them behind my back. She held them there with a surprisingly firm grip. The beautiful thing about this was that she had to press against me to hold my hands. Brittany had a great pair of tits. Not too big, not too small. Juuuust right. Soft, but still firm, they pressed against my belly, just under my bra. I wished she'd take my damned bra off and give me a little attention, but I didn't think I'd get the whole package.

I was surprised and pleased when she seemed to sense my need. She let me take over on the kissing front, while she snuck her free hand between us and played with my tits. She might have been telling Sonny the truth. She might never have muff-dived, but she knew how to work-over a pair of breasts.

If the guys watching this weren't hard, they needed a shot of testosterone. Brittany was quite the little dom, rendering me nearly helpless while she pinched my nipples until I thought I'd scream from pleasure. I was kissing her so hungrily and sloppily that I must have looked like a dog licking ice cream from a baby's face.

Okay. Time out. I know what you're thinking. You're thinking I'm full of crap. Either I don't love my woman, or I wasn't really getting stupendously turned on. "How could she get hot having sex with a stranger, when a bunch of guys are watching her?" Or, "This idiot's career is on the line, she thinks the whole world is gonna see this video, and she's still enjoying herself?" Maybe even, "What kinda sicko exhibitionist is she?"

All valid comments. Ones that I might make if I were in your position. In my defense, I can only say that the crystal took down a lot ... a whole lot ... of my normal boundaries. I will also admit that one of the things I love about police work is the thrill of danger. Having to have sex in order to save your life is pretty thrilling. I know that doesn't make sense to some of you, but the thrill-seekers out there will know just what I mean.

Now I might as well admit to something that I'm not proud of. As I said, my girlfriend and I have been together for six years. Complete monogamy. I like it that way, and so does she. We have a very good sex life because we work at it. We both try to keep things interesting. We're still finding new ways to please each other.

But, being realistic, there are only so many tricks two dogs can do. We have certain ways of approaching each other, if you know what I mean. I'm usually the one humping her leg, asking for sex. I'm usually a little more aggressive than she is. I'm not a stone-butch or anything, and she's not a lie back and take it femme, but I'm a little more dominant.

Having the tables turned on me was nice. It was different. It made me hot. There. I said it. Getting a little strange made me hot. So shoot me. No matter how many symphonies we write, how many great works of literature we pen, breathtaking paintings we create, we're still animals. And animals like to fuck. I'm not saying that's good or bad. I'm just saying it is.

So, here I was, getting hot performing for a bunch of slime-balls. I'm here to tell you, animal instincts are powerful shit.

Brittany didn't seem to like my kissing style. Or maybe I was taking over too much. But she leaned back a little so I couldn't get much leverage. I didn't mind, though, since that pushed her breasts into mine a little harder. Have I mentioned how much I like breasts? I couldn't tell if Brittany liked mine, but she sure knew how to handle 'em. She realized that I responded best when she kept me off kilter. So she'd palm one of my breasts and move it gently, the fabric of my bra giving just enough friction. Then she'd give me a little squeeze, gentle and almost loving. When I started to plunge my tongue into her mouth she'd squeeze me hard, or pinch my nipple. I had my doubts about her lack of experience, but if she was telling the truth, she was just a fantastic fuck. Some people have a gift. She knew how to read me ... how to tell what I needed before I knew myself. That's a very handy talent in the bedroom. Or the break room, in this case.

There was no doubt that I was ready to move on. You could have told that by standing outside the door and listening to me moan. Brittany let go of my hands and grabbed my ass, grinding me against her until I thought I might come in my pants. Then she grabbed my head again and gave me some more of those "I'm gonna suck your face off" kisses while she worked the button on my pants. Once again, I found this far preferable to Spiro's big ham-hands. I reached up and held my waistband taut while she lowered the zipper. She dropped my slacks, and I didn't so much care that they'd get wrinkled. Funny how circumstances change your perspective.

Her hands reached under my long shirt and palmed my lace-clad ass. I was so glad I wore new undies today. If my life is gonna be ruined by letting the world see me have sex, at least people in Malta won't be saying, "Where did she get those ugly-ass panties?"

Brittany slipped her hands inside and squeezed my ass-cheeks. God, I love that. Then she slipped the panties off and tossed them and my slacks aside. I was wearing a very nice pair of black Ferragamo shoes. Italian shoes are the best. It's just a fact. Now, as I said, the shoes were nice, but I also had on black trouser socks. There's nothing attractive about trouser socks. So, mindful of my place in Internet history, I shucked my shoes and socks. Hey, as my mother says, "It doesn't cost anything to care about how you look."

She'd obviously changed her mind about letting me decide how I got done. Brittany shoved me onto the sturdy table, sat on one of the chairs and said, "Spread your legs."

Yes, ma'am! I leaned back on my hands and spread 'em, as we say. She unbuttoned the bottom couple of buttons on my shirt and pushed it aside. Now that she was nearly eye-level with my business end, she didn't look so confident. *Damn!* I started to feel sorry for her. Pity and sex don't mix well. I could feel my rock-hard clit start to wilt.

She looked up at me and asked, "Wanna be fucked while I go down on you?"

Hmm ... my clit liked that question. "Optional," I said. In fact, I always came better with a couple of fingers inside me. But I didn't like to really be fucked. Don't even think about coming at me with a big strap-on. The old in-and-out didn't do it for me. I like to be filled up and feel just a little movement. My girlfriend has this trick where she turns her hand over right when I'm about to come. Makes me see stars. But I didn't wanna be greedy, or make her do more than the minimum. Even though she was getting paid, this wasn't really voluntary for her, either.

She spread me open and got close, looking me over carefully. She laughed a little, probably at how wet I was. That was embarrassing, but I plead the animal defense. She held me open with her fingers, and used her thumbs to spread some of my juices around my clit. Relating this, I probably sound matter-of-fact. But there was nothing ordinary about the experience. If pleasure came in a liquid, she was pouring it over my clit like there was no tomorrow. I can't express how every nerve ending reacted to her touch. I'm sure it was mostly from the crystal, but God damn, my clit has never felt so fantastic. I could feel the blood pulsing through it, and she used the perfect amount of pressure. My pussy felt hot and heavy, and when she'd slide a little more moisture onto it, it felt like the coolest unguent known to man.

My head had dropped and I was staring, glassy-eyed at the ceiling. She still hadn't touched me with her mouth, and I was already in heaven. "Put your legs on my shoulders," Brittany said, partially tearing me from my private nirvana.

Oh, boy! Oh, boy! Oh, boy! Is there anything better than being sizzling hot and having your partner put her mouth on you for the first time? If there is ... I haven't felt it.

I complied, then had to adjust my hands to stay upright. I'm not sure why I wanted to, but it seemed more dignified than lying on the table, squirming.

I could hear her take in a breath, then I felt her lips on me. She was perfectly still for a moment, almost like she was kissing me. Then her lips parted, and her warm, wet tongue lapped me from bottom to top. I've never come from a first touch, but I was damned close that time. I spread my legs to let her get closer, then let her work. She kept her tongue soft and licked me lazily—like a popsicle. That was nice. Very nice. Then she pointed her tongue and worked it in and around and over every fold of skin. She literally investigated me with her tongue, leaving no skin untouched.

I was about to groan or cry or beg or scream, when I came. No warning. None. I just stiffened and came, the sensation so unexpected that I barely made a noise. But she knew I'd finished, since my knees were now touching her ears, and my cunt was pulsing like crazy.

"Fuck," I managed to pant.

To my surprise, she didn't get up. She spread my legs apart and started to lick me again. I had no earthly idea why she did it, but I wasn't gonna argue. It took a little longer this time, maybe two minutes, but I had a better build-up. That first one was too quick for me to prepare for. Damn, I hate to come before I'm ready. But this time, I was good and ready, and my moans and entreaties to her to keep it up ... just like that ... gave her a nice warning, too.

I almost swallowed my tongue when she tried to enter me. I was still locked-up from my last orgasm, but she played around my opening until I relaxed. Shamelessly, I dropped to the table and let her fuck me, my hips moving like a wanton hussy's. She didn't do it too hard or too fast. She just filled me up and moved in and out until I was whimpering in that pleasure/pain state where you want to say, "Stop! Fuck me harder! Stop!"

She didn't wanna stop, so she fucked me harder. I was squirming around on the table when I came again, holding onto her arm with both of my hands, and crying out so loudly the lunch crowd had to think someone was being tortured. Luckily, the regulars were probably used to that.

Brittany sat up and waited for a few seconds so I could compose myself enough to stop rolling around like I'd been hit on the funny bone. She delicately withdrew, then walked over to the corner and held her fingers up to the camera. When she turned them upside down, a big drop of my cunt juices slid off her fingers. Nice touch, Brittany. Classy.

Without a word, she walked into the bathroom, and I could hear her running the water. In a few seconds she came out, and I could see that she'd rubbed her mouth hard with one of the paper towels. I was about to suggest she use some of the stuff they cleaned the grease-trap with, but I decided I was being too sensitive.

I got up, my knees wobbly, and collected my clothes. I went into the bathroom and tried to freshen up, but there was just something about me that said, "Fucked hard and put away wet." I'd have to go to the station house and take a shower or two before I could be in polite company.

When I left the bathroom, Brittany was gone. Trying to find a shred of dignity, I walked back into the restaurant to find Sonny, Chris and Spiro staring into space like they'd been hit with ball-peen hammers. None of the gents stood to welcome me, and I had the impression that they couldn't have if they'd wanted to. It was nice to know I could make a buck as a porn star when I was hounded out of my job. I had to wonder how they got back to the table from wherever the monitor was. I had this mental image of them walking in a little line, all bent at the waist, looking like three guys impersonating Groucho Marx. The patrons had to wonder what in the hell went on in this place.

"Chris," Sonny said, his voice sounding tight. "Make the deal."

Chris gave him a rather insubordinate look, and I realized why when he stood. He'd made the mistake of wearing tan pants, and the front was now decorated with what the fellows call "pecker tracks" if what I'm told is correct. Boy, I'm glad you can't see a trail of pre-cum on my pants when I'm getting excited. Being a man isn't all fun and games. Chris' dick was standing straight up, and I allowed myself to stare at it pointedly, just to give him a taste for what it felt like to be on public display.

"Nice tent," Spiro said, chortling.

"If you don't have one, maybe you *are* a faggot," Chris growled.

"Break it up," Sonny said. "Let's try to get some business done today, okay?"

Chris walked ... or shuffled ... into the back room. I handed him my briefcase and he handed me his. He didn't count the money and I didn't weigh the drugs. We both knew where to find each other. Well, that wasn't true, but I knew where to find them. They thought I did business out of a little office in Bucktown. I did, but it wasn't selling drugs. It was keeping track of them.

Still feeling euphoric, I hefted the case and shook his hand. Then we walked into the restaurant and I shook both Sonny and Spiro's.

"Stay for lunch," Sonny said. "On the house!"

"No, I've got to get back to the office. I was here longer than I thought I'd be."

Sonny grabbed my arm and shook it playfully. "You've had worse mornings, right?"

"Far worse," I said, being perfectly honest.

I waved and started to walk out, taking a quick look for Brittany. She wasn't around. I hoped she was in the bathroom, taking care of business. I've been wrong before, but she seemed to enjoy herself more than she claimed. Of course, every john probably tells himself that. Prostitutes are all money-grubbing whores until they do you. They get off with *you*. Yeah. Right.

I stepped out into the sun, the fine summer day making me glad I'd never left home. Chicago was truly my kinda town. And my kinda cops were all waiting for me to walk two doors to the right and set the case on the sidewalk. I did that, and was surrounded by a sea of men and women wearing T-shirts over bullet-proof vests. The T-shirts all said "Narcotics" in big, yellow letters. I had a feeling Sonny wasn't gonna like to see them. Just to check, I walked back in, watching my guys secure the crime scene.

We had a full team. Detectives, forensics ... everyone. I saw one of my officers patting Brittany down. He turned her around as I walked up. She made a funny face, then hit me right in the puss with a big wad of spit. My guy turned her around and got her cuffed faster than you can blink. He looked like he'd like to teach her a little lesson, but I warned him off. "Leave her alone. She's had a tough day." I grabbed some napkins from a metal dispenser and wiped my face. If I'd let myself, I could have barfed. I hate spit where it doesn't belong.

I looked around and saw Sonny, Chris and Spiro facing the back wall. I could tell by their red necks that they were furious. I could have gone over and harassed them a little bit. But that's classless. I don't like cops who get all power-happy after they make a bust. My dad always told me that whenever I went somewhere that was a little intimidating, I should act like I've been there before. Same thing for busts. I've made 'em before, I'll make 'em again. It's just another day at the office.

But, in reality, this wasn't just another day at the office. This was a big day. The day I'd be recognized for two years of hard work. The day before everybody in the department got a bootleg copy of my multi-orgasmic performance. Oh, well, at least Sonny wouldn't get to put it on the Internet.

I saw an evidence technician sorting through a big load of videotapes. I could have gone over and told him to give me the one that had been in the machine. But if I did that, he'd know I was hiding something. My reputation as an honest cop is worth more to me than my pride.

Captain Washington showed up and congratulated me. That felt nice. I told him about being high.

"Did you have a choice?"

"Hell, no," I said, insulted that he'd even ask.

"Then enjoy it. Just don't make it a habit."

Yeah. Like that would happen. Although, I did have to admit that I had a new appreciation for how easy it is to get hooked. I was already thinking about how it felt to have Brittany's tongue on my clit. I knew it would never feel exactly like that again, and that made me a little sad. But I know that your brain chemistry can start to change after just a couple of exposures to meth. I like my brain just like it is. That study they did where lab rats chose meth over everything else ... sleep, food, sex ... hitting the little rat crank pipe until they starved to death, impressed me. I like having peak experiences as much as the next girl, and I'd love to feel that euphoria again. But, as Ray Milland said in *The Lost Weekend*, "One's too many, and a thousand's not enough." He was talking about booze, and crank is a thousand times more addictive. I'll just have to keep this experience stored in my memory bank and wish I could have had it in the privacy of my own home with my own wife. Oh, well, them's the breaks.

After The Bust

I couldn't sleep last night, so after tossing and turning for hours I got up. Luckily, Aliyah is used to my wriggling around like a kid itching with poison ivy, so she didn't stir when I got out of bed. If I'm completely honest, I felt a little distant around her last night. It's always like this when I have to hide something. She always knows when I'm hiding something, too, but she knows I never reveal anything confidential, so she stopped asking me years ago. Ideally, I'd take a few days off and we'd go somewhere fun and concentrate on each other. But I'm gonna be too busy to take any time off for a while. Making sure a big bust like this is handled by the book is very time-consuming. So instead of taking time off to connect with my girl, I'll probably be taking more Provigil. That's the bargain you make when you become a cop. The job takes over your life. It does for everyone, and if you don't want that kind of commitment, you'd better get a job as a security guard. The pay isn't as good, but you get to wear a uniform and carry a gun, if that's a turn-on for you.

Anyway, it was only four a.m., but I figured I'd go face my execution. I knew the evidence techs had worked on the lists all day, and there would be an exhibit marked something like, "Sergeant Randolph engaging in an act of oral sex with one Brittany Whosits." There would also be another saying, "Sergeant Randolph snorting white powder, possibly methamphetamine." I'd look over the list, try not to cry in front of the evidence tech, and go to my desk, waiting for Captain Washington to come in. He liked to learn about things as soon as possible. I should have told him the whole story at the scene, but I wanted one day where he was proud of me. I know he won't care about the gay thing, I'm sure he knows. But he will be disappointed in me.

Why couldn't my parents have whipped me when I was bad? I can still hear my father telling me he was disappointed in me. It doesn't seem like a big deal, but I'd rather be yelled at any day.

The captain won't be disappointed that I had to go with Brittany. He *will* be disappointed that I obviously enjoyed myself so much. You're not supposed to enjoy disgracing the image of the department. And any way you looked at it, I had done just that. In vivid, living color I had snorted crystal and had three mind-blowing orgasms while drug dealers watched. That's not really the image we like to project to the public.

There's a chance the tape won't get out to the public. There's also a chance it won't get out to the rest of the force. But I'm not counting on that. No matter how tight we try to keep the evidence trail, things go missing. Especially things involving sex or anything else worthy of the tabloids. It's just human nature.

I walked into the station house and went directly to the evidence book. The officer handed it to me after I signed for it, and he looked completely normal. No trying to hide a laugh, no averting his eyes. I took the book and thumbed through it. I read every entry twice. There was nothing ... nothing about my doing the crank or getting done. There *was* an interesting entry about a video monitor on Sonny's table that had been hidden by a hollowed-out napkin dispenser. Pretty smart. "Is this everything?" I asked.

"Yes, ma'am."

"Were you the tech on the scene?"

"No, ma'am. That was Gonzales. But this is his final report. It's all here."

"Sure?"

"Yes, ma'am."

I handed the book back, and he initialed that I had returned it. Befuddled, I went to my desk and started working on the mountain of paperwork that I'd have to complete before I could take a day off. I wasn't working at my normal rate. Not sleeping for three days isn't good for a person's brain, and being worried about something you have no control over doesn't help either. But I kept slogging away until Captain Washington came in.

I saw him enter his office, and I stared after him in a state of total indecision. I knew I should go tell him what happened. The tape was gonna show up. It had probably been mislabeled. Hell, maybe the front of the tape was something innocuous. There were a lot of them labeled, "Chris Tselios having lunch." The camera wouldn't have been on just to watch the guy eat.

I was staring at the captain so intently that I didn't notice anyone walk by my cubicle. But a folded piece of paper fluttered into my lap, startling the hell out of me. I opened it and read, "Meet me in the ladies' room."

Huh? Not the usual interoffice memo. I got up and went to the only ladies' room on our floor. There are only four women in our section, so it was a nice place to have a quiet conversation if you needed a little girl talk. I opened the door and saw ... Brittany. *Fuck.* I didn't even know her name. I just knew she was one of the new people in narcotics. I hadn't even arranged for her to work at Sonny's, one of my team leaders had done that. I mean, I knew we had someone there, but I didn't pay a lot of attention to who it was since we hadn't learned much in the six months she'd been there. Her reports were a snooze-fest, and I barely scanned them. The only thing I remembered was how high her tips were. She had to turn her salary and all of her tips in to the department. You don't get credit for working a job while you're undercover. Now that I'd seen her in action, I understood why she was raking in the dough. I also knew that she was honest. We'd never have known she was cheating the department if she'd turned in twenty dollars a day.

"Hi," I said. What do you say to a co-worker who's forced to give you head?

She put an envelope on the sink. “I know I committed a crime, but I don’t want this to ruin my career.”

“You got the tape?” My heart was beating so hard I thought I’d hyperventilate.

She gave me a half smile. “I had to learn something. God, I never want to be a waitress again.”

I picked up the envelope. “Are you giving this to me?”

She nodded. “You can decide what to do with it. You’re the lead officer. If you want to turn me in for tampering with evidence ... that’s your call.”

We were both a little shy about making eye contact. “I wouldn’t do that to you,” I said. “I could just say I found it. Stuff like that happens all the time.”

She looked somewhere in the vicinity of my left ear. “Will you turn it in? ’Cause if you’re going to, I’ve gotta do some damage control.”

“At home?” I asked, even though it was none of my business.

“Yeah. My husband doesn’t like me working Narcotics. If he finds out about the tape ...”

“Why would he find out?”

She looked like she was about to cry. “He’s a lieutenant in the police commissioner’s office. He knows everything.”

That caught me by surprise. I had no idea what to say, so I tried to reassure her that we were both in this together. “My girlfriend wouldn’t be very happy about it, either.” Coming out to a junior officer had to count for something, right?

But the young detective gave me a challenging look right in the eye. “Would she divorce you?”

My stomach dropped. She looked so sure of what the repercussions would be for her. “I don’t think so. But I guess I’m not sure. It would definitely put a strain on our relationship.”

“I was with a woman in college and I told my husband about it. Big mistake.”

Ouch. At least I hadn’t fucked some guy three times and looked like I was having a great time doing it. I held the tape in my hand, weighing it. Something so insignificant, with the potential to do so much harm.

I looked at the woman again, holding her gaze for a moment. "If I was the only one on this tape, I'd probably turn it in. I'm a strong believer in following the rules. That's the only thing that separates us from scum like Sonny."

She nodded, and I could see a flicker of hope in her eyes.

"Do you know what else is on here?"

"Nothing," she said without a second's hesitation. "I saw Chris put in a new tape right before you got to the restaurant. The machine was right by the storeroom. I was filling all of the sugar shakers. I've still got his fingerprints on my ass," she said, a look of disgust on her pretty face. "That bastard never walked by me that he didn't grab something."

"What about the buy? It's on here, isn't it?"

"No." She shook her head quickly. "Spiro got up and turned the recorder off before the buy." She gave me a sly smile. "They're not dumb enough to record that."

Now that I looked at her in normal clothes I decided she didn't look like the nasty girl-next-door. She was a lovely, sweet-looking woman who'd put up with six months of shit for nothing but a bust she wouldn't get a speck of recognition for.

"Wanna go out for breakfast?" I asked.

She blinked in surprise. "Uhm ... why?"

I didn't blame her for being suspicious. For all she knew, I wanted another blow job. "I wanna go to that crappy little hardware store down the street and buy a magnet. Then I wanna pull this tape out and run that magnet over every inch. Then I thought we could burn it, and then ..."

She gave me a fantastically lovely smile and said, "Can I put the ashes in the river?"

"With a lead weight," I replied, smiling at the thought of sending them to the site of final repose for so many of Chicago's most infamous.

Quicksand

Blayne Cooper

Chapter One

My two o'clock appointment, okay, my *only* appointment of the day, was late. Even though I was grateful that at least someone in this city might want to hire me, I was annoyed, and I showed it by rapidly tapping my pencil on my desk. Rat-tat-tat-tat. Rat-tat-tat-tat. Tat.

Deciding to do something more productive than scuff my desk, I tossed my pencil down and scanned my modest office, making sure everything was tidy. You should know that I'm not neat by nature. Not by a long shot. People find out if they see my apartment. Or my closet. Or my car. Or ... Well, you get the idea. But the point is, I can fake it if I have the proper incentive, and today I did.

My stomach fluttered as I stood and made my way to a small closet located at the back corner of the room. The previous tenants, a now-defunct real estate company, had used it to hold a couple of rusty file cabinets. I know this because they left them here when their lease expired and now I use them to hold my own paperwork, along with a few emergency changes of clothes, gloves, hoods, leashes, and wax.

I was wearing an expensive linen suit instead of my normal jeans and Hawaiian print shirt. I gazed into the full length mirror that I'd tacked to the back of the closet door and checked my teeth for lipstick by running my tongue over them and making a weird, vampire-like face. When I saw only pearly white, I dragged my fingers through my hair, smoothing it. My sandy-blond hair is streaked from the sun and irrepressibly wavy. Usually I pull it up in a ponytail to keep it out of my face while I'm working. But when I do, I look like I could pass for nineteen, which sucks on about a million different levels. I've been meaning to get my hair cut up off my shoulders.

But I guess my heart wasn't in it, because I kept canceling the appointment.

I'm thirty-two years old, and looking like a teenager when you're a grown woman is an enormous pain in the ass. Most of the men who ask me out are either years too young for me, or San Diego's finest geezers trolling for jailbait.

Years ago, during my first week as a private detective, a prospective client came into my office, took one look at me, and starting spinning in circles like a dog looking for a spot to pee. I could tell that he expected someone else to pop out of the woodwork and introduce herself as the real detective. When that didn't happen, he asked me where my daddy was. That pissed me off, but it also taught me a valuable lesson. Who wants to hire someone who looks like they still use Clearasil?

So today I'm wearing my hair up in a sedate clip, stud diamond earrings, my nicest business duds, and to further assist me in my quest to look like I've had boobs for more than six months, a pair of stylish glasses. I don't really need glasses, but I think they make me look more sophisticated. Sure, that's about as smart as a teenager thinking smoking a cigarette makes her look older. But nobody's perfect. And I quit smoking years ago.

I smiled into the mirror. I looked at least twenty-three and a little less like the beach rat that I am at heart. I know that might not sound like much of a victory, but over the years I've learned to take them wherever I can get them.

The knock at my office door made me jump, and with one last glance in the mirror, I shut the closet door and dashed to my desk as quickly as my high heels would allow. I don't know how Stephanie Zimbalist did it for all those years on *Remington Steele*. My butt would be kissing carpet if I tried to run right now.

"Come in," I called out evenly, positioning myself behind my desk and squaring my shoulders. I glanced down at my calendar and tried to look as though I was pondering something very important as I flipped through the pages.

The door opened and in walked the richest people I was likely to ever meet—Kale and Lokelani Poppenhouse. Russ Wilkens, a P.I. and friend I know from the beach ... and a lot more ... had referred them to me.

Russ and I are both avid surfers and see each other several times a week at Black's Beach at sunrise, the most peaceful time to ride the waves. In between those times, we occasionally hang out. He's as close as I have to a best friend and we toss business each other's way whenever we can. Russ wouldn't tell me why he'd referred the Poppenhouses to me, saying it would just be easier for them to explain what they needed themselves.

They'd only been in my office for five seconds, but I figured they must have liked what they saw so far, because Kale and Lokelani Poppenhouse were both staring at me and grinning like idiots. I gestured to the leather club chairs in front of my desk. "Won't you sit down?"

As they began to step around the seats, I remembered that I hadn't introduced myself yet. Stupid. "I'm Belinda Blaisdell," I said, beaming my most winning smile in their direction.

Mr. Poppenhouse held the bottom of his necktie flat against his bulging stomach as he leaned forward to shake my hand, his enormous paw completely engulfing mine. "Kale Poppenhouse." He glanced sideways and nodded once. "And this is my wife Lokelani." I tried not to stare, but the amused, slightly resigned smiles on both their faces told me I wasn't very successful.

He was wearing a beautiful, gray Italian suit and it contrasted sharply with his wife's bright floral muumuu and ivory-colored silk blazer. Their features were bigger than life, just like they were, but not ugly. Cartoonish would be a better word to describe them. I knew that they were Hawaiian from a life-style magazine article Russ had sent over that included headshots. Stereotypical thinking, I suppose, but I thought they'd be small people. How wrong I was. Even Lokelani was well over six feet tall and her husband dwarfed her. At five feet, five inches tall, I had the brief, and admittedly weird urge to jump up and start yelling "Da plane! Da plane, boss! Da plane!"

The Poppenhouses' features were so similar they could have been brother and sister except for one thing. His bronze skin was several shades lighter than his wife's and hinted at a partial European heritage and the likely source of their rather unusual last name.

"The man at the other agency was right, Kale," Mrs. Poppenhouse enthused. Her smile was blinding. "Look at her freckles and that tan! She'll be perfect."

"The suit and the glasses are wrong though," he commented sourly, appraising me as though I was available for purchase. Which, in a way, I guess I was. "And the hair could be a little trendier."

Lokelani nodded and waved a large hand in the air in front of her. "All easily corrected."

I frowned. What did my freckles have to do with anything? Unconsciously, my hand went to my head. And sure as shit nobody was going to touch my hair. I cleared my throat softly and tried to move things along. "I spoke with Mr. Wilkens on the phone on Monday. He indicated that you might be in need of my services?" This is where I usually stop talking and let the client pick up the ball and run. But instead of pouring out their guts, Mr. and Mrs. Poppenhouse suddenly clammed up, looking very uncomfortable.

My curiosity was piqued. I could smell a good case like a dog could smell a juicy bone. I actually started to salivate and I subtly swallowed before gentling my voice. "I can't help you unless I know what you need. I can, however, assure you that I'm good at what I do and I'm very discreet. I can probably help if you'll give me the chance."

I wasn't kidding. Even though I'm not as busy as the detectives in the big agencies, I was slowly, very slowly, building a solid reputation as a quality private investigator. Most of my cases nowadays are referrals from previous clients or from other detectives who are either too busy to take on a certain case or unsuited for something the job would require.

What I said must have made Mr. Poppenhouse feel better, because he licked his thick lips, his deep voice filling the room as he said, "We are a very traditional family, Ms. Blaisdell."

I inclined my head as I listened.

"Our daughter Keilana is a student at Madonna Del Mar College in Santa Medina. And she ... she is ..." he hesitated and his wife quickly moved to fill the void.

"She is *not* traditional." Mrs. Poppenhouse sighed. "In fact, she's rather spirited." Then she stopped as though that explained everything. I grunted encouragingly, but found it a little hard to begrudge a college kid for wanting to kick up her heels a little.

"Keilana's had a rather difficult life in some respects," Mrs. Poppenhouse continued reluctantly. "She's always lived in a world of privilege, reveled in it, really. But that hasn't kept her from facing her share of discrimination. Hawaii can be a very enlightened environment." Her heavy brows furrowed. "But I'm afraid that even paradise isn't immune to racial prejudice. It hasn't been easy being our daughter." There was real worry in her voice and it caused my stomach to lurch. Being a parent must be hell sometimes.

"So you think she's in trouble?" I wondered aloud.

"We think so," Mr. Poppenhouse said firmly, his gaze sharpening as his eyes locked on mine. "She's not the same girl that left Oahu three years ago. Her grades have dropped. She never calls home. And she broke her engagement to one of Hawaii's most eligible bachelors last Christmas." His expression darkened. "That was stupid, not to mention bad for business. His family owns half the pineapple farms on Lanai."

Without my permission, my eyebrows lifted. His daughter had broken her engagement and his biggest concern is business? Not nice. Not nice at all.

Mrs. Poppenhouse's lips edged downward. "Keilana uses every bit of her substantial cash allowance, but doesn't seem to have anything to show for it. To make matters more frustrating, she won't use the credit cards we've given her so we have no record of what she buys. She never travels anymore and she didn't even come home this summer. She said she wanted to stay here and work instead."

"Could she be pregnant?" I had no doubt that Keilana was every bit the mountain of a woman her mother was. But let's be honest, college is nothing if not full of willing explorers.

Mr. Poppenhouse's eyes flashed dangerously and I dropped that line of questioning like a hot rock. I wanted to live.

"Alcohol or drugs?" I inquired carefully, crossing my fingers that Lokelani wouldn't decide to crush me like a bug for suggesting the mere possibility. No parent liked to think about it, but I've seen enough families destroyed by drugs to know it was never something I could ignore. Surprisingly, neither Mr. nor Mrs. Poppenhouse's expression changed with my question.

"We've had a spot ready for her at Betty Ford for the past year," Mr. Poppenhouse said. He steepled his thick fingers. "Should she need it, of course."

I could hear the impatience in his voice that he was trying so hard to hide. He and his wife almost looked as though they hoped that narcotics or booze was Keilana's problem. I supposed that such a revelation might not rock their world the way something else could. Keilana wouldn't be the first poor little rich girl whose experimentation had gotten her into more trouble than she could handle.

"Her behavior toward us has gone from respectful to indifferent in the course of a year. Her actions, what little I know of them, seem erratic. But technically we don't know that she's abusing drugs or alcohol," Mrs. Poppenhouse added, her gaze sliding sideways to her husband.

"Of course," I said soothingly. Yeah, right.

She wrung her hands. "There's more." She glanced down. "She might be ... well ..."

I leaned forward even further in my chair and felt my pulse jump. We were about to get to something juicy. God, I love my job.

"She might be involved in some sort of criminal activity. Gambling maybe. Or selling drugs if not using them," Mr. Poppenhouse ground out, finishing his wife's sentence with ease. Then he sneered. "Or worse, she might be involved with some mainlander scum who's after her money." He slammed his fist down on my desk and I did my best not to wet myself in surprise. When would I learn not to drink a 44-ounce Diet Mountain Dew minutes before a client meeting? "Why else would she go to the places she goes?"

The way he said "mainlander" made me bristle. I was one, after all, and I was really beginning to think that Daddy was an asshole. But he was a rich asshole and I didn't want to screw up this job. The recession has been hell on the private investigation industry. Still, I needed to know as many of the facts as I could before I would agree to take the case. Picking my own jobs was one of the biggest perks of being self-employed. I was never one for schlepping to some stuffy office where they had a dress code, performance evaluations, and fancy water coolers. Okay, I admit it. A water cooler would be totally cool. But that fact aside, my little business suits me just fine. It allows me to head to the beach when the surfing is primo and really enjoy life.

"What makes you think that she's involved with anything more sinister than outgrowing her parents?" I asked, forcing my mind back to business.

He shifted in his chair, his face a mixture of unease and embarrassment. "We hired an investigator to follow Keilana early this summer when she refused to come home on her school break. He told us that she was spending a lot of time with some unsavory types in and around some of San Diego's worst neighborhoods. Once she even went to a strip—" he glanced sideways and seemed to stumble over his words before he hit upon—"gentlemen's club." His wife patted his beefy arm and he placed his hand on hers. "But Keilana somehow found out that he was following her and he wasn't able to provide us with any other information after that. She hasn't spoken to us since."

My brow creased as the wheels in my head spun. They must have guessed what I was thinking.

Mr. Poppenhouse said, "The investigator we hired was Russ Wilkens."

"Hmm," I hummed noncommittally and tried not to show my surprise. Somehow I had trouble believing that some kid had spotted Russ spying on her. He was good at what he did and I couldn't help but ask, "And after that you still took his recommendation to come and speak with me?"

"It's not his fault," Mrs. Poppenhouse assured me. "Keilana is very, *very* smart. And she's not going to be easy to fool after our earlier mishap. That's why we waited several months before contacting you. We want to escalate things and you'll blend in with her surroundings in a way that Mr. Wilkens never could."

Ah ... They wanted me to tail Keilana. No problem. I had practically turned being a Peeping Tom into a new art form.

Mrs. Poppenhouse smiled a little. "We need a woman for the job."

They had really thought this through. And I couldn't help but think they were right. Even in this day and age, and despite the occasional Sue Grafton novel or *Charlie's Angels* flick, there aren't very many female private investigators. The kid would probably expect a private detective to wear cheap suits and smoke cigars. Come to think of it, that did describe Russ when he wasn't wearing a short wetsuit. What the hell was I thinking when I'd slept with him?

"So you'd like me to follow her?" I crossed my arms over my chest, already counting my easy money. The first thing I was going to buy was a water cooler. Then a new wetsuit. Then a bigger bed. Then ... "I can do that."

"We don't want you to merely follow her." Mr. Poppenhouse tugged a fat checkbook from his inside suit coat pocket. "We want you to move in with our daughter, find out what's going on with her and why, then report back to us."

My eyebrows crawled up my forehead, getting higher and higher as he spoke.

"If she's seeing someone," he growled, "break them up. I want her to graduate and I want to bring her back into the fold still speaking to me. I have no more patience for this nonsense."

"What?" I sputtered, truly insulted. Yeah, I could use the work. But what the Poppenhouses wanted was bullshit.

I didn't do things like that. My hands balled into fists and I forced myself to lay them calmly on my desk. I knew, however, that I couldn't get the spark from my eyes. "I don't move in with the people I'm spying on. And I don't break people's relationships. I watch and take notes. I take pictures and do a damn nice report of what I find out. I ask questions and I dig and I ask more questions. But that's *all* I do." There. Crystal clear.

Spying was one thing, but tricking some girl and then breaking her heart was just disgusting. "California is full of unemployed actors, Mr. and Mrs. Poppenhouse. Maybe one of them will be able to help you." I was steaming and I wanted to kick Russ in the balls. I'd been so excited about what he said was a "big" job and then the client had to go and make things complicated. Dammit. There went my water cooler.

Mrs. Poppenhouse cocked her head to the side. "What we're asking isn't illegal, is it?"

I let out a long breath. "No, I guess it isn't." Illegal, no. Immoral, oh yeah. Okay, I could be a grown up. I could let them down gently. I'd get my satisfaction from cracking one of Russ's nuts instead. "I'm sorry to say that I don't do the type of work you require." I did my best to smile politely. "Anyway, I'd never pass for some college kid." Uh-oh. I knew that was a lie before I'd even finished saying it. And, apparently, so did the Poppenhouses. They didn't even dignify my statement with a reply.

Why were they still in my office? They looked so unmoved by what I'd just said, that I tried again. "Won't Keilana be suspicious if I just show up and move in with her? You said she was smart." That's it. Sucking up never hurts. They might have something decent for me to do in the future.

Mr. Poppenhouse snorted. "I'm paying you to make sure that she won't. Besides, I've never done business directly with a woman. She knows I don't believe in it and that should keep her from suspecting you."

My gaze sharpened and he held up a forestalling hand.

"I told you, Ms. Blaisdell, our family is very traditional. We do business in the traditional way and I'm not ashamed that I believe that men and women have very distinct roles. In this one instance, however, I've allowed Russ Wilkens and my wife to convince me that extraordinary measures are required. I'm not above admitting that women do have their uses."

My nostrils flared. There went Russ's other nut.

Either unaware or unconcerned that he'd been so insulting, Mr. Poppenhouse said, "Luckily, Keilana's roommate Pamela was awarded an unexpected scholarship to a college all the way on the east coast. She won't be coming back to campus housing next week and Keilana will need a new roommate."

The way he said that made the hairs on the back of my neck stand at attention. I got the distinct impression that the timing of Pamela's out-of-state scholarship wasn't just good luck. This was a powerful, no, make that ruthless, man.

"We offered to set her up in an apartment, but she wanted to be like the other students," Mrs. Poppenhouse said, clearly embarrassed. "There's no accounting for taste, I suppose, and we've made sure to make her dorm room as comfortable as possible."

I didn't like the way she was so quick to explain away her daughter's pedestrian living accommodations. Some people can't afford college at all, much less the dorms or a fancy private school. Snobs.

Mr. Poppenhouse pulled out a pen and began scribbling on a check. "Keilana will graduate at the end of fall semester and I'm afraid that what little influence we still have over her will disappear then. I'm willing to pay you ten thousand a week plus expenses, including your tuition and room and board, etc., etc."

My mouth dropped open and stayed that way so long my tongue began to feel dry. If there had been a breeze in the room, my own jaw would have swung up and given me a black eye.

His intense stare went even more serious. "And I'll do it for how ever long it takes. But I expect results," he warned.

I swallowed hard. I didn't want this job. I didn't want to screw with some enormous kid's life. But ten-fucking-thousand a week was huge!

"Ms. Blaisdell, do we have a deal?" Tantalizingly, he held out the check and I detected the faint scent of wet ink.

I couldn't think. I couldn't breathe. And I sure as hell couldn't see. I was blinded by the dancing dollar signs flashing behind my eyes. I was only vaguely aware of the Poppenhouses gazing at each other with something that approached concern.

"Ms. Blaisdell?"

Mrs. Poppenhouse was talking now and I sucked in a deep breath of air as I struggled to compose myself. Either the dollar signs were starting to get all sparkly or I was about to pass out from lack of oxygen. "Yes?" I managed to say.

She smiled. "You'll have no trouble passing for a student. Several of Keilana's friends had that dazed look you're wearing all through high school."

"I umm ..." I finally shook myself out of my stupor and nibbled on my lower lip. Could my dignity really be rented out for ten large a week? What if Keilana really was in the clutches of some mainlander scum who only wanted her for her money? Getting her to dump him would really be helping her, right? I visibly cringed at the mental gymnastics I was forcing myself through to justify this job.

"Let's take her car shopping too, Lokelani," Mr. Poppenhouse said. "She needs to look like her family can afford Madonna Del Mar College." He seemed to realize what he said and was quick to add, "No offense. I'm sure your car is very nice."

I held in a whimper. I drove an old Mustang convertible. And not a cool one either. A rusty, junky one. This was just too much. Weakly, I made one last bid for my self-respect. "I'm sorry, but I'll never get accepted into your daughter's college." There. I said it. I hadn't even made it through a year of junior college myself before my sucky grades and lack of money forced me to drop out and go to work full time.

"That's not a problem." Mrs. Poppenhouse pulled a piece of paper from her purse.

I took the paper and read it with stunned eyes. It was my college acceptance. The admissions office even admitted me under a quasi-alias, which just so happened to be my middle name. It seemed that the Poppenhouses had, indeed, thought of everything.

The Poppenhouses exchanged smug smiles. I was hooked and they knew it. "Now," Mrs. Poppenhouse said. "About your clothes and those glasses..."

"Maybe they'll add amber streaks to your hair. That would bring out the honey-colored undertones in your eyes."

I stopped walking and stared at Russ. "*What?*"

He sniffed and gave me a superior look. "I saw that on *Queer Eye for the Straight Guy.*"

"Queer what for the what? Christ, Russ, I have no idea what you're talking about."

"It's a show where gay guys makeover a straight guy."

I sighed and started walking again. I was an avid late night television watcher, but I tried to restrict my viewing to shows that weren't utter crap. That left out nearly everything Russ watched. "Your wife has turned you gay."

"She has not!" he spluttered, his face turning a splotchy red.

Russ was the straightest man on the planet, but I still liked teasing him. "Uh-huh."

Russ and I are friends now, but once upon a time, we were lovers. I guess you could say we share a tempestuous history. Our affair was short and hot and we parted as friends when it became clear that neither of us had made a true love connection. At least that's what we told our mutual friends. And that's mostly true. But the other part of the truth is that Russ cheated on me with a waitress from the Clam Shack. During one of our dates.

Oddly enough, though, that wasn't the part about the date that freaked me out. What really got my head spinning was the realization that I lusted after our waitress every bit as much as Russ did. Maybe more. That night opened my eyes to a whole new world. But I felt as though Russ had kicked me in the teeth. For now, it's enough to know that when it comes to Russ and me, all's well that ends well. We worked things out later. I honestly think he looks more rugged with that chipped front tooth.

As we got closer to the salon, Russ scowled and had enough sense to at least hesitate for a few seconds before admitting, "My wife says I'm a renaissance man who is in touch with his feminine side."

"I think she was calling you a pussy, Russ."

"Ya think?" He made a face and scratched his square jaw. "I wondered that myself."

"Definitely. In fact, are you sure you can handle Smelly?" We stepped off the curb. "He's sort of a macho dog." I glanced down at Smelly, my fifteen-pound mutt that Russ was tugging along on a leash.

I found him underweight and smelling to high heaven, lying in a pile of washed up fish at the beach. When he tried to follow me home, I accidentally ran over him. I got out of my Mustang to assess the damage and looked into those sad, helpless eyes and couldn't help but take him in. Russ, not Smelly. Smelly I got from the pound for twenty-five bucks.

Russ had just gone through a nasty breakup, been kicked out of his girlfriend's apartment, and was coming off a three-day, pity party, bender. I decided to help. I'd been there myself ... well, not the smelly part. Or the sleeping in putrid fish part. Or ... okay, I hadn't exactly been *there*. But I'd broken his arm when I ran him over and didn't want to get sued.

"I can handle your mucho macho dog," Russ insisted, rolling his eyes. "Smelly and I understand each other."

Now *that* I believed. On occasion they both had gas that could fell a rhino, they were lovable in an annoying sort of way, and each would rather spend the day at the beach than anywhere else. That was more in common than many human best friends had.

"Tomorrow's the big day, right?" he asked.

I nodded. "Yep. You sure you can keep him out of trouble while I work this new bizarre case?" I was talking to Smelly and I could tell Russ knew that when he stuck his tongue out at me. When he abruptly stopped walking and starting licking his own crotch—Smelly, not Russ—I took that as his agreement.

I had finished the few odds and ends from my last case three days ago. Lord help me, just in time for the first day of school. I had already received a new wardrobe, which I hated and would give to my eighteen-year-old niece when this job was over, and I had promised not to wear my fake glasses. Today we were walking from my office to one of the most expensive hair salons in San Diego. This was the last step in my little makeover. Thank God I wasn't paying for this.

Russ reached down and petted Smelly's curly brown head as he spoke to me. "I can't believe we're walking when you own brand new wheels."

"That car is on lease in the Poppenhouses' name. I don't own it. Besides, the salon is only another two blocks."

He made a low clucking noise. "I noticed you bought a sports car that you could put your board in."

"That's not why I picked a convertible," I lied. Like I would get new wheels and not take my surf board into consideration?

A thought seemed to suddenly occur to Russ and he turned his head and frowned at me. "For someone who is going to make a quick score with this job, you don't seem too happy about it. What gives?"

I shrugged and stuck my hands in the pockets of my denim shorts. How could I explain to a guy like Russ that I felt like I'd sold myself out? A man who I once saw eat twenty-seven hotdogs in twelve minutes just to win an Igloo cooler that was worth all of about seven bucks. "I'm happy," I said weakly.

"Sure you are." He gave me a meaningful look. "You're thinking too much, that's what you're doing. I'd shave my head bald for ten thousand a week. Hell, I'd shave *your* head for that much."

"Gee, thanks."

"I told the Poppenhouses that I would dress in drag and move in with their daughter myself. But Mr. Poppenhouse looked like he was about to blow a gasket and so I offered up your name rather than be murdered in my office."

I socked Russ lightly on the bicep, thinking that he was more like a sibling to me than my own brother, who I rarely see. "And here I thought I got the referral because you thought I was such a good detective." I pantomimed stabbing myself. "You cut me, Russ. You cut me deep."

"Aw, Belinda." He had the grace to look at least a little chagrined. "You know I think you're good."

"Yeah, yeah." I cupped my hands over my eyes to shield them from the bright afternoon sun and glanced up at a green canvas awning that simply read "Gregory's." I swallowed hard, hoping that Mrs. Poppenhouse's instructions to the stylist weren't going to leave me looking like a blond version of that demented fucker Carrot Top. God, I hate my job. "Oh, boy."

Russ slapped me on the back, ignoring Smelly's protective growl. "Good luck."

I rocked back on the heels of my huarache sandals and gathered my nerve. "Time to go get beautiful, I guess."

Russ's gaze softened as I stepped inside the salon. As the door closed behind me, leaving my two friends to wait in the late summer breeze, I heard him mumble, "Too late."

Chapter Two

After driving through Santa Medina, a sleepy tourist community consisting mostly of shops and small eateries that serviced the industrious day hikers who walked the Topa Topa Mountains, I pulled up outside St. Bridgid's Residence Village. It was Saturday and school would start in just two days. But that wasn't much time to move in, get books and look like a real student, and most importantly, start making inroads with Keilana.

I glanced around. This is what they were calling campus housing? Where were the piles of discarded boxes? Where were the blaring radios and half-clad guys rushing by on skateboards?

I took off my sunglasses and slid them into the pocket of a pair of jeans that cost nearly as much as my first car. I sat there, waiting to be accosted by some slimy-looking guy offering me a MasterCard at twenty-one percent interest and a free Frisbee and T-shirt just for applying. But it never happened. I spun in a circle, feeling the breeze on the base of the back of my newly-exposed neck. "We're not in Kansas anymore, Toto."

I grunted my approval at the series of tiny, stucco, red-roofed cottages that comprised this part of campus housing. They were linked together by a network of stone paths that all intersected at a large fountain. In the center of the fountain was a statue of a fat, bald guy dressed in long robes and holding a bible. Moses, maybe? He didn't look like Charleston Heston, though, so I figured it had to be someone else.

Short, but lush trees planted around each cottage added a sense of privacy to the property. "Nice." I craned my head, looking down one of the paths, but could only see as far as cottage 11. Keilana Poppenhouse lived in cottage number 12.

I exited my new Jaguar convertible, still taking in my surroundings with a note of awe. I'd seen places like this on television, but that hadn't prepared me for the pristine, collegiate atmosphere I was experiencing first hand. There was one thing out of place in this Norman Rockwell campus though. The place was practically crawling with nuns and priests. I'd heard once there was a shortage of nuns and priests. And looking around today, I knew why. They were all here.

I could only hope that they sensed that I was an unchaste, unrepentant sinner at heart and they'd stay far, far away from me during my time here. I was supposed to be a senior and by now I should have been brainwashed ... err ... I mean instructed on religion for years and years now. I was a little worried that my ecclesiastical ignorance was going to blow my cover so I resolved to keep as low a profile as possible.

Most of the students, who were huddled in small groups, their heads tilted together in conversation, were clean-cut and reeked of old money. And despite my new duds and expensive haircut, I couldn't have felt more out of place.

"Hey." A group of girls walked over to me, obviously checking out my new car.

"Hi," I said brightly, reminding myself to be sociable and do my best to try and fit in. It was breezy and I ran my fingers through my now-shaggy hair, smoothing it self-consciously.

A short blonde stepped forward from the group. "Do you need help with your bags?" She inclined her head toward my passenger seat and back seats, which were loaded down with two suitcases and a few medium-sized boxes that were packed ridiculously full.

She and her friends looked just like the girls in high school who wouldn't have spit on me if I were on fire. And a sense of wariness borne of experience washed over me. I glanced at how far the buildings were from the parking lot. Then I breathed a fake sigh of relief. "That would be great. Thanks." I extended my hand, half expecting to be snubbed. "I'm ... Bel—" Okay, try that again. "I'm Cadie."

"I'm Shauna." The girl cocked her head to the side, her eyes sweeping up and down my clothes. I cursed inwardly when I found myself straightening my posture in pure reflex. Despite the women we all eventually become, I guess a little part of us will always be sixteen. Bleck.

"You're new, right?" Shauna asked absently. She popped her gum and waved at another girl who was just pulling into the parking lot. The campus had only about four hundred students, so I figured that everyone pretty much knew everyone else.

I nodded and dutifully repeated part of the history I'd made up for myself. "A transfer student from UC Irvine, yeah. This is my first day here."

"Cool." The girls standing behind Shauna echoed her words. They had yet to speak to me directly.

I grappled for something to say. "Do you live here?"

She gave me a strange look. "Duh. But not in St. Bridgid's. I live in the St. Catherine's complex over there." She pointed over her shoulder and winked at me. "That one is co-ed. Here, let me help."

I had to keep from bursting out laughing when she began picking up my boxes and bags and distributing them to her pack of friends. When she was through, her own hands were left empty and she wiped her forehead as though she'd just run a marathon.

"Okay, which house are you in?" she asked quickly. Her generous spirit, it seemed, was on a short timer.

"I tugged a tattered piece of paper from my glove box and made a show of looking confused. I think I'm in 10, no 12. Yeah, 12. Maybe you know my roommate? Ke.. Ke.. Keilana Poppenhouse."

My words were met with a round of gasps, then pale, sour faces. I heard the word "bitch" and worse mumbled by several of the girls. Well, well, Keilana, it seems, wasn't Ms. Popularity.

"You can't be living in 12," a pudgy Asian girl blurted. "Pamela Anderson lives with Keilana. They've been roommates since freshman year. There is no way—"

Shauna glared at the suddenly verbose girl and slapped a hand over her mouth. "I thought we agreed that *her* name would never be spoken again?"

My eyes widened at Shauna's rigid tone.

"Sorry," Pudgy squeaked contritely, looking as though she might burst into tears. "I forgot."

"So long as you don't do it again," Shauna reminded, enunciating every word with deliberate slowness.

I lifted my eyebrows at the display of dominance. I hadn't seen one so blatant since my last trip to the zoo. "I umm ... I think I remember them telling me at the admissions office that one of the girls living in number 12 got an out-of-state- scholarship. Now that you mention it, the name Pamela Anderson does sound familiar." Okay, everything about Pamela Anderson was familiar. I'd accidentally seen the Pam/Tommy Lee porn video online. Six or sevens times. What? Like you weren't curious.

"Lucky Pam," Shauna ground out, her lips thin. Imperiously, she began marching down one of the paths and her friends were quick to follow.

I had to jog to catch up. "What do you mean, lucky Pam?" I fell in step alongside her as we passed the fountain. "Is there something about my roommate that I should know?"

Shauna smirked. "You'll see."

"Do you know Keilana?" I persisted; I was on the clock.

Shauna's eyes narrowed. "Oh, I know the *whore* all right! You should stay far away from her."

I blinked. "How can I do that? She's my roommate."

Shauna stopped dead in her tracks and gave me an incredulous look. "Be that way then." She pointed to a spot on the grass. "Here, girls. We don't need to waste any more of my time. Let's go."

In less than five seconds my boxes and bags were unceremoniously dumped on the ground and the she-pack, including Shauna, was halfway back to the fountain. I frowned at their sudden departure. With them left my first chance at being able to pump someone who knew Keilana for information.

"See ya," I called out and couldn't stop myself from adding, "assholes" in a voice loud enough to get half of campus looking my way. A few nuns crossed themselves and I felt a mixture of juvenile pride and chagrin at my antics. I knew I was acting like a big baby, but in only a few moments those girls had managed to bring a million bad feelings to the surface. I sighed. Thank God I wasn't actually going through all this again. Growing up was bad enough the first time.

When my stuff had been carelessly dumped on the lawn, one of my cardboard boxes had burst open and the breeze was now tossing some of my clothes around. Nothing like having to chase your bra down the street in front of the God squad and a bunch of snotty kids.

Bra in hand, I tucked a lock of my hair behind my ear and made my way back to my boxes. I dropped to my knees and began gathering my things. At least nobody had stolen anything while I was chasing my undies across the lawn. That was one good thing about an expensive school. No one wanted to steal used panties.

Suddenly another set of hands appeared in front of my face and lifted up one of my intact boxes. "Want some help?" I heard from somewhere above me. The voice was velvety smooth and deep and I might have found it nice if I wasn't already in such a crappy mood.

"No thanks," I muttered, grabbing a tank top and stuffing it down into the box. I didn't bother to look up. The last thing I needed was to square off against some snobby member of the Welcome Wagon.

A gentle laugh. "You must be a pretty big klutz to have made such a mess."

I continued my repacking, stuffing a pair of jeans into a box with a little more force than was necessary. "Thank you for noticing."

"You're new here."

No shit. "Really?"

She laughed again and adjusted the box in her hands so she could dangle a pair of my black panties before my eyes. I reached for them, but she pulled them away at the last second, just the way that Lucy always yanked the football away from Charlie Brown. I fought the urge to bare my teeth and growl, then I caught sight of exactly which panties they were and had to bite back a groan instead. Oh, crap. They were a pair that Russ had given me a couple of years ago as a joke. They were so raunchy that I'd refused to wear them. I didn't know I still had them. I'd just grabbed a few handfuls of underwear while I was packing.

"Slutty undies." She hummed something that sounded suspiciously like approval. "You're not a hooker by chance?"

"Do you need a hooker?"

"Is that a yes?"

I'd had enough. "Do I look like a fuckin' hooker, Rich-Bitch Betty co-ed?"

"I dunno." I could hear the smirk in her voice and it set my teeth on edge. "Maybe."

I finally successfully snatched the panties from her hand and glanced up to see what the next version of Shauna would look like. But the sun was setting directly behind her and I had to shield my eyes.

"You look like you have all the right parts for the job," she continued blithely.

This girl was a real piece of work. My words hadn't had any impact on her at all.

"You might not be a working girl," she chuckled, "but you certainly could be."

"My parents would be so proud. In fact, maybe I'll drop out of school today and call Heidi Fleiss. What's her number? I'm sure you have it handy."

"Are you going to cottage 12?" She didn't sound happy about that prospect. Great, another fan of Keilana. And this one was changing subjects so quickly that my head was starting to spin.

I picked up a few pairs of socks, holding one in my teeth as I tried to get one side of the lid on the box closed again. "If you must know, the answer is yes. But I'll save you the trouble of telling me that my new roommate, Keilana Poppenwhatever, is a whore-bitch. Because I've already heard." I spat out my socks and stood up to tell whomever this annoying person was to get lost once and for all.

When I rose, I was greeted by a pair of icy blue eyes that actually sent a shiver down my spine. Uh-oh. I realized that I must have been wrong about her feelings for Keilana. Maybe the subject of my investigation actually had a friend. If that was true, then it was time to get serious.

The girl was burning holes through my body with her glare that could smelt copper. She was thin and a few inches taller than me with thick dark brown hair. She had skin so fair that I doubted she'd been outside for more than ten minutes the entire summer. Her face was heart-shaped and she had a stronger jaw than most women. She wasn't as conventionally beautiful as she was striking, and despite the haphazard way she had her hair twisted on top of her head, all I could think was how hot she was.

"You're staring," she said, clearly annoyed.

Oops. "About what I just said ..." I motioned to my things on the ground. "I'm afraid my first day here isn't going very well. So ... you're a friend of Keilana's, right?" I stuck out my hand. "I'm Cadie Blaisdell." It's really true that the more lies you tell, the easier it gets.

The young woman's back straightened and she hefted the box she was holding high above her head. In disbelief, I watched her turn the box upside down and dump my clothes and a handful of CDs all over me. "What the fuck?" I batted away a pair of shorts that was hanging from my shoulder. "Jesus Christ!"

"Wrong both times," she said, her voice low and angry. "My name is Keilana Poppenwhatever. Most folks call me Lana. *You* can just call me whore-bitch."

I didn't know quite what to say as Keilana stormed into what was supposed to be "our" cottage. There was no way that this person could be the subject of my investigation. None! She wasn't "spirited," as Mrs. Poppenhouse had said. She was clearly evil. And she wasn't huge or close to being Hawaiian. "Fuck. Fuck. Fuck."

A woman walking by shot me an evil look for my potty mouth. "Hi, Sister," I said a touch sheepishly.

Did that nun just flip me the bird?

I refocused on why I was here and then hung my head. What the hell was wrong with me? I tried to look on the bright side, but so far there wasn't one. Well, except for the fact that at least I knew where the evil Keilana

Poppenhouse was. In fact, I mused, not liking Keilana might make me feel less guilty about breaking up her and her boyfriend. Yeah. I could live with that big fat lie for at least as long as it took for me to play homewrecker.

I repacked the rest of my things and hefted the boxes onto cottage 12's small front porch. As I was straightening from setting down the last box, I heard the lock to the front door slide into place. "I have a key," I gloated loudly. "You can't lock me out." Then I turned the doorknob and to my surprise, it wasn't locked. "Huh." Maybe Keilana wasn't as difficult as she first appeared. God knows I'd been wrong about enough people in my life to know better than to judge someone too quickly. I began to regret the bad names I'd called her.

I stepped forward and pushed the door open ... only to smash my face against the solid wood. "God!" I screeched, and grabbed my now-bleeding nose. The burglar chain had been fastened. "Crap!"

"Still wrong. It's whore-bitch, remember?" Keilana yelled from somewhere in the cottage.

I hit the door with my fist. "Bitch!"

"You're ... getting ... closer," she said in a sing-song voice.

My God, what kind of twisted bitch was she? I was pretty sure I could bust the chain on the door if I wanted to. But I didn't want some do-gooder priest calling the cops on me. I had to save something for day two, didn't I?

My voice was deep and dangerous when I said, "Open the door, Keilana."

Silence.

"Open it."

More silence.

"Open the Goddamn door!" I roared, banging the wood with my fist until my hand ached. Finally, I stepped away from the door and swallowed hard.

My heart was racing. My face was flushed. My palms were sweating and my chest was rising and falling far faster than normal. Isn't it confusing that being furious and being turned-on-as-hell have the exact same symptoms?

"Have it your way, Keilana." I twisted my face and slurred her name the way Seinfeld did when saying "Newman." She was already shaping up to be *my* Newman.

I opened one of my suitcases and took out a washcloth to press to my nose. I held it to my face as I checked the front windows. Both were locked. I could pick them, of course, but it was broad daylight and I'd already attracted enough unwarranted attention. As it was, I'd be lucky not to be fired or expelled.

I walked behind the cottage and found two more windows. The second window was even unlocked, but after giving it a couple of moment's thought, I decided not to try to climb through it. It was a little smaller than the others and getting stuck with my ass hanging out was not on my agenda today.

Finally, on the fourth wall, I struck pay dirt. Stuffing the bloodied washcloth in my pocket, I growled like a cat on the prowl. I *was* getting inside. I tightened my hands around the sill. Despite what you see on TV, it's much harder to pull up all your body weight than it looks. But I was in relatively good shape and after a few huffs and puffs I was propped up on the ledge and staring inside. I glanced around awkwardly, but I couldn't see Keilana. I was sure, however, that the satanic brat was somewhere inside, laughing at me.

The windowsill was digging into my gut and I looked down. Figures there'd be no way to twist my legs inside. I'd have to go in headfirst. Slowly, I leaned forward to ease inside, and suddenly I was flying down the wall! I tried to break my fall with my arms and ended up doing a somersault that would make Mary Lou Retton weep with envy. Well, except for the part where I screamed like a sissy girl when my butt thumped hard against the tile floor.

"Holy—?" Disoriented, I sat there for a few seconds. What had just happened? I saw a piece of paper on the floor, partially hidden by my ass. I pulled it free and it read "Don't fall." I closed my eyes and whimpered. Was there anything more annoying than someone saying don't fall after you'd already fallen?

After a few seconds of wondering what on earth I'd gotten myself into, I stood up on wobbly feet. My tailbone was throbbing, my nose was aching, and I wanted to kill Keilana. I even know a few people who, for a Corona and two fish tacos, would help me dispose of her worthless carcass. God, I love my job!

"Oh, Keilana?" I said in a sickeningly sweet voice. "He-e-e-e-re's Johnny!" She was too young to have seen *The Shining* but it made me happy just saying it.

Of course, there was no answer. I turned my head and saw that the front door was wide open, mocking me. Okay, I admit it, I underestimated my opponent in this twisted little game. That was a mistake I wouldn't make again.

If I'd only known then just what the coming months would bring ... I would have ... I would have ... . What *would* I have done? I guess I would still be me, which means I'd probably do most of it the same way, taking my lumps and all. But it would have been nice to have been just the teensiest bit prepared.

Since I was alone and had no clue where Keilana had gone, I took a moment to look around my new, if temporary, digs. I whistled softly, glad that I'd only bloodied my nose instead of knocking out my front teeth.

The cottage was nice. Really nice. Better than my apartment, actually. Which made me all the more resentful. I was sure that the students here didn't appreciate just how lucky they were.

The furnishings were sparse, but first class all the way, and not surprisingly, the décor was California Mission. There was a tiny kitchen and living area just off a single bedroom that was separated from the rest of the house by a half wall. I walked over to the bedroom and saw that my bags and boxes were neatly stacked next to a naked mattress and box springs. "What did you do, Keilana?" On one of my bags sat a can of soda, beads of condensation attesting to the fact that it was icy cold.

How did she know that I was thirsty? Was she a witch? I didn't know what to think, but one thing was certain. Keilana clearly could not be trusted. And yet, this appeared to be a tiny bit of kindness from the person who had called me a klutz, embarrassed me by making me reach for my panties, locked me out of the house, and sent me careening ass over tea kettle down the wall. Scowling, I rubbed my butt again and tried not to breathe through my tender nose.

Then something on top of the suitcase caught my eye and I was tugged forward by the same unseen force that had shaped most of my adult life—rampant curiosity. The kind that gave the cat a slow and painful death, and would, most likely, do the same to me one day.

On my suitcase was another note.

> Klutz,
>
> You can use your own bed sheets or check some out at the campus laundry for $3. I suggest the former. Too bad you're not a hooker. You'd be worth every penny. You have a spectacular ass.
>
> Your new bestest buddy,

My eyes narrowed. She had signed the note Whore-bitch. I read it again just to make sure I wasn't losing my mind. I tried not to laugh. What was wrong with me? And how could I find her note funny, even though it was clearly meant to torture me? And most curious of all, why had she been looking at my ass? Thinking about asses made me rub mine. Again. It was still sore.

True, my butt was covered in expensive jeans, and she'd recognize that, which was the entire point. But she seemed to be checking out what was under the pants. Was she a lesbian? I thought about that for a bit as I examined my can of 7-UP. Frankly, I was thrilled with even the possibility it could be true. There can never, *ever* be too many good-looking women batting for my team. That said, this wasn't about me, and so I did my best to think about the case.

Keilana's parents were worried about some mainlander scum being after her money. But would they know if the mainlander scum was a woman? Absolutely not. Then again, if she really wanted to rebel, wouldn't the easiest way be to tell mommy and daddy that she liked pussy? After a bit more pondering, I figured it was too early to tell whether she was into chicks, or whether she'd just been yanking my chain.

I cracked open my 7-Up—not the diet, but the honest to goodness, teeth-rotting, sugar elixir—half expecting it to explode or for a big snake to pop out. When it didn't, I tentatively took a sip. Ahhh ... cold bubbles chased their way down my throat. Heaven.

So the subject of my investigation was a nutcase, sometimes-hospitable, maybe-lesbian? Lovely. I'd been in her presence for all of five minutes and she'd already given me the slip. Lovely again. I lifted my soda in salute to Ms. Poppenhouse, wherever she was. "Round one to Keilana," I conceded as my eyes took on a determined glint. "Too bad for you, this battle of the wits is just getting started."

Chapter Three

The cottage was dark except for a small bedside lamp that provided more than enough light for me to write up my case notes. I was lying on my stomach on my bed and doing my damnedest to stay awake as I wrote. A couple of years ago I'd tried to use a Palm Pilot, and then a laptop, but there is something about writing things out longhand that jump-starts my thinking process. At some point during every case, I bow to modern technology and transfer things onto my office desktop for archival purposes and so I can email reports to clients. Until that point, however, I don't feel bad about doing things the old fashioned way and working them out on paper.

But so far this report was boring even me. I tucked my pen behind my ear and yawned, wishing that Keilana would hurry up and get home. It was a little past two a.m. and I was starting to get worried. Yeah, she's a big girl. But after working dozens of missing persons cases, I understood better than most that the world was full of scummy, devouring bastards who would do horrible things to you if given half the chance.

Have I mentioned that really late at night I tend to be a glass-half-empty sort of gal?

I propped my head up on my hands and decided it was best to keep myself occupied by rifling through her things. I know that seems slimy. Okay, it *is* slimy. But now wasn't the time for the faint of heart. Besides, I had to find out as much as I could about Keilana in as short a time as possible. That way I would reduce the amount of lies I had to tell her and the amount of time I had to spend in her presence. Not that it wouldn't be fun to linger on the Poppenhouses' more-than-generous payroll, but because there was always a chance my cover would be blown before the job was finished, I was racing the clock.

Speaking of clocks, underneath one on the wall were three short bookshelves lined with dozens of paperback adventure, true-life crime, and reality stories. I began thumbing through them, their well-worn covers testifying to the fact that Keilana was an avid reader with eclectic tastes. I pulled one of the few hardcover books off her shelf. *Children of Adoption: A Lifetime of Adapting.* Well, that answered one of my questions. Keilana was about as Hawaiian as I was.

Then I ransacked her dresser. A chocolate bar in the top drawer. Hershey's Kisses in with her socks. Tootsie Rolls mixed with her undies. M&Ms in the third drawer by her bras. What a sicko! I popped a Hershey's Kiss into my mouth and acknowledged wryly that this could be love.

Still chewing, I checked the short file cabinet next to her desk. She was actually pretty organized for a college student and everything was laid out neatly in manila folders. Her parents were right about her grades, which since the end of last year, have resembled something that should be flushed down the toilet. Another file contained three letters of warning from her advisor and one from the Dean. I was actually a little surprised that the school hadn't given her the boot. Then I remembered who her parents were. She'd probably have to kill someone to actually get expelled. But that didn't mean they'd just hand her a degree.

I shoved that file back and selected another.

Ooo … I chuckled. Keilana had been a very bad girl. She had a half dozen parking ticket receipts, all showing her illegal parking in and right around one neighborhood. Unfortunately, the area covered several blocks. Even more unfortunate was the fact that I had a passing familiarity with that part of town. I couldn't believe Keilana would drive through it, much less park her fancy BMW there.

I quickly jotted down the addresses from the tickets in my journal, mindful that my roomie could be home any minute. As I wrote, I couldn't help but think about what I *hadn't* found on my little fishing expedition. No address book. No diary or love letters. No photographs. She didn't seem to own a single personal thing beyond her clothing. And despite what her parents had hinted at, I hadn't found any drugs, booze, or even cigarettes. By all accounts, Keilana was living a helluva lot cleaner life than I had in college.

I also couldn't find whatever it was she used for birth control. Then I remembered she had her personality for that.

I glanced over at the clock. It read 3:37 AM. "Where the hell are you, Keilana? You'd better not be out doing something I'd want to know about!"

Murmuring to myself and yawning, I locked my own journal in the desk provided by the college and picked my blue jeans up off the floor so I could stuff the key in the front pocket. You couldn't be too careful with people.

The sound of a key in the front door lock sent me scurrying back to bed, where I lay down, looked up at the ceiling, and did my best to appear nonchalant. Thank God she was home. Staying awake had been torture.

As she walked past me I got a better look at her than I had earlier that afternoon. She had long limbs and the graceful stride that reminded me of a slender jungle cat. Her eyes were heavy-lidded and instead of being the devastating blue I remembered, they appeared almost purple in the muted light. Her gaze flickered my way and I felt my belly tighten in response.

Uh-oh. I could *not* be attracted to her. There were a million reasons why having the hots for Keilana would be a bad idea, and I mentally started listing each and every one of them when she let her purse slide to the floor and stripped out of her blouse and bra in one swift motion. Sweet mother of God! Her skin was milky white and invitingly smooth. And her breasts swayed gently as she moved.

Unconsciously, I licked my lips. I knew that I should look away and give her a modicum of privacy by turning my head, but honestly I was too stunned to do more than gape and collect drool.

Surely the weight of my stare was palpable, but if Keilana noticed it, she didn't say. I groaned inwardly when she presented me with her back. Show's over, pervert, I thought a little resentfully. Even though I hated it to end, I was grateful for the reprieve as she tugged a T-shirt from her dresser and slipped it on.

Unable to ogle her, my other senses kicked into high gear and my nose twitched as I detected the scent of cigarette smoke. Interesting. Who were you with, Keilana? I didn't want to appear overly nosy by asking outright, so I schooled myself in patience.

"Hey," I said softly. I had been looking forward to being snotty to her when she got back, but it was so late that most of my anger over what had happened earlier had already burned away.

Her eyes slowly rolled sideways. "Hi," she murmured. Then she really focused on me and a tiny furrow appeared between her brows. Was she missing her old roommate? For a second I thought she didn't recognize me, but then I glimpsed what I hoped was a spark of recognition.

When she said nothing, I sighed.

"You don't remember my name, do you?" I gave her a lopsided grin that I hope covered my bruised ego. "Am I that forgettable?"

"Hardly," she said seriously and collapsed onto her bed. "And I do too remember your name." Her pillow muffled her voice. "It's whore-bitch." A pause. "No wait. That's me."

I rolled my eyes. "So nice to see you're not the type to hold a grudge. I said I was sorry, didn't I?"

"No."

"Oh." Oops. "Well, I thought it for a fleeting second or two. That should count for something, right?"

Keilana fought it, but in the end, the corners of her mouth turned upward. "You're Katy." She kicked off her sneakers, wiggled out of her jeans, and snuggled under her bed sheets with an enormous yawn.

I frowned. "It's Cadie."

She rolled over to face me and looked at me for a good minute before saying a word. My heart pounded wildly the entire time. Was she sizing me up? Or worse, was she on to me?

Even through my impending panic, I took the opportunity to give her a less lascivious examination. She looked mortally tired and now that she wasn't moving, I could see that her eyes were bloodshot and surrounded by dark circles. Still, she didn't have that glazed-over look that came with being stoned, or the slurred speech and sloppy movements of someone who was drunk.

"Hi Cadie," she finally said, gently. And to my amazement, for just a split second, every trace of smugness was gone from her voice, her expression painfully open. She looked so young and sweet that I felt my heart lurch. "That's such a pretty name."

I blinked and to my amazement felt my face flush with pleasure. Jesus Christ, what was wrong with me? "It ... um ... I mean, thank—"

"Good night."

Then she rolled over and instantly fell asleep, her light snores filling the room so quickly that for a moment I thought she was pulling my leg. It's part of my job to look after this intriguing, annoying young woman. With the kind of money I was making, that's the least I could do, right? So I padded over to her bedside and carefully lifted a thin blanket over her sleeping body, tucking the edges around her shoulders. She didn't even stir. Whatever she'd been doing tonight had exhausted her.

I only wished I knew what it was.

The next morning the ringing of my cell phone awakened me. "'Lo," I rasped, pressing it to my ear, and slowly licking dry lips. "I mean, hello."

"Hey, Belinda, the surf is cookin'! Get your butt down here!"

"Russ?" I scrubbed my face and heard Keilana let out few choice words over being awoken at just past dawn. "Why the hell are you calling me so early?"

"Huh?"

Oh, right. We always called each other when it looked like the waves were going to be excellent. I thought of the hot sun drenching my skin and the cool water lashing against me, and suddenly longed for the rightness and solitude of a perfect wave. I can't explain to a hodad the nearly religious experience of flying on water. You'll just have to take my word for the fact that there are few things better in life.

"Belinda?"

Drats. I promised myself I would be quick about this case and not drag out my duplicity. I couldn't go play. I needed to stay and work. "I can't, Russ."

"Why not?"

"Russ," I warned, my gaze slipping sideways. Keilana had put her pillow over her head to block out our conversation.

"Oh, shit," he said, whispering as though Keilana could somehow hear his voice. "Are you working?"

"Uh-huh."

"Right now?"

"Hopefully."

"But it's Sunday," he complained. "The Poppenhouses don't expect you to break this case in two days, Belinda. Jesus! With what you're being paid, you'd think you'd slow down and take your time."

A little insulted, I said, "You know I'm not like that." I never cheated my clients. Never.

He groaned and I just knew he was rolling his eyes at me. "I wasn't suggesting that you pad your billing. Just take the time you need to do this right. You won't learn everything you need to know about Keilana in a weekend. Besides, school doesn't even start until tomorrow. C'mon," he coaxed, knowing I was a wave-slut. "You know you want to."

I laughed softly. "You're incorrigible."

"I learned it from you." There was a long pause. "Hey, Belinda, I know you're feeling guilty about this job. And when you're feeling guilty about something you tend to push things. Go easy, all right?"

I blew out a long breath.

"You know I'm right," he persisted.

He was right. I hated it when that happened. "Go away, Russ."

He chuckled. "Smelly and I *are* going away. Away to the beach, as a matter of fact. I'll call you later in the week and check on you. See if you need anything, that sort of thing, okay? We can meet someplace off campus and I'll bring your runt dog for a visit."

Russ, I acknowledged not for the first time, despite our checkered past, had turned into a friend that I could count on. I lowered my voice, "I looooooove you, Russ."

Silence.

I had to work hard not to spoil the effect and burst out laughing.

"God, you're evil," he finally spluttered.

I smiled broadly. "I learned it from you. Give Smelly a hug for me, okay?"

"Will do." Then he cleared his throat ominously. "Belinda? There's something important I have to tell you."

Oh, God, he wasn't going to get all sensitive on me, was he? "Yeah?" I croaked, horrified at what my own demonic streak might have started.

"Don't get caught staring at a bunch of eighteen-year-old girls' asses. You'll get a reputation and then nobody will want to take you to the homecoming dance." He started laughing hysterically at his own joke and with a vicious finger, I shut off my phone without saying goodbye. I thought of how I'd stared at Keilana's half-naked body the night before and a wave of guilt crashed over me. She wasn't eighteen years old, but twenty-one wasn't a helluva lot better.

"Jerk," I mumbled, and tossed the phone to the foot of my bed.

Keilana tugged the pillow off her face and gave me a concerned look that fully captured my attention. "Boyfriend troubles?"

She had a serious case of bed-head and her face was creased with a crisscross pattern from her bedspread. I bit back a grin. It is my not-so-humble opinion that good-looking women are at their most appealing first thing in the morning when they're adorably mussed and truly natural. Seeing Keilana painted in early morning sunshine did nothing to dissuade me of that notion.

"Cadie, if you're in any trouble or if ... well, if you need help or something." Shyly, she tried to express herself, charming me in the process. "I can ... I can help."

I was relieved that for the first time since we'd met, I'd be able to tell her the truth. "He's a former boyfriend, but there's no trouble. Honest." Then I had an idea. What would work better than to get to know my subject on my home turf? We couldn't go to my favorite beach, but we could pick up Russ and go someplace else. "He wants me to come to the beach today. Wanna come?" Of course, I'd have to call Russ and have him shave his head so there'd be no chance of Keilana recognizing him. But that was a small price to pay for surfing!

I could tell she was surprised that I had asked. Her eyes narrowed just a little as she tried to gauge my sincerity. Lord, Keilana is even more suspicious than I am. My general mistrust of people was a by-product of my work. There are only so many cheating husbands and wives you can tail before you become jaded. I wondered briefly what had caused her skepticism.

She sat up and cocked her head to the side, her hair falling down around her shoulders. "With you and your ex?" She made a face. "No way." Suddenly, she seemed to realize she was being a little rude. "But ... umm ... thanks for asking."

"Come on," I coaxed, flipping over onto my belly, crawling to the foot of my bed, and propping my head on my fists. Our beds were only about six feet apart and this put me a little closer to her. "It's going to be a beautiful day and Russ really is an okay guy."

She grimaced again. "No ... I don't ..." She stopped and took a deep breath. "I don't like the beach."

"But your family is Hawaiian!" Everyone knew the Poppenhouses were Hawaiian. Poppenhouse pineapple and coconut cookies were one of the most popular cookies in the country and the back of the package featured a map of the islands. "How can someone from Hawaii not like the beach? That's impossible!"

Her gaze cooled instantly and I realized my error. Mentioning her family was obviously a no-no.

"You don't know anything about me," she said briskly.

"Okay." I held up my hands, privately bemoaning the wariness that had rushed back into her voice. "You're right. I don't know you."

She looked like she wanted to say more, but didn't.

"But I'd like to know you. And what better place for that to happen than the beach." I gave her my most innocent smile.

She snorted gently, torn somewhere between amusement and annoyance at my persistence. "I have things to do, Cadie."

This was going good. We were talking, not arguing, and she was tentatively smiling. I suspected she was tempted to take the day off and play, but I wasn't sure how far I could push her. I also had to be very careful or I was going to start flirting. And that was more dangerous than I was willing to accept.

"I have to buy my books," she went on, snuggling back into her pillow and looking like she wanted to do anything but that. She groaned a little. "And get ready for classes. Just, I dunno, stuff ..."

"Of course you do," I said reasonably. "And so do I. But we can do those things and still go to the beach." C'mon, Keilana, make my life easier. "We can't get to know each other if we don't spend any time together, right? If we're going to be roommates we might as well hang out a little. I want to be your friend."

And in that split second, our conversation came to a screeching halt. Every bit of progress I'd just made vanished like smoke in the wind. Her body stiffened and I knew I'd crossed some imaginary line in the sand.

"What makes you think I want to be yours?"

It was like being slapped in the face.

All of a sudden, I felt stupid for worrying about her the night before. This girl had claws just waiting to come out and play. "Jesus, I wasn't asking you to sleep with me, just go the Goddamned beach!" I sat up and scooted up the bed, putting a little more distance between us as I crossed my arms over my pajama-clad chest.

She looked away. "You'd have had better luck asking for the sex. That I can handle with no problem."

One more question answered.

"Is it just that you don't like me? Or do you have another reason for acting like such an asshole?"

Her eyes snapped up to meet mine and I saw a mosaic of anger, hurt, and resignation swirling there. My own eyes widened a little in response.

"Isn't that what you expect from me? I wouldn't want to disappoint you."

"I don't expect anything from you. I don't even know you!" But that was a lie. Knowing who her parents were *did* make me expect she'd be spoiled rotten. And after talking to Shauna's little group of she-devils, I expected her to be just as catty as they were. That might not have been fair, but life rarely was. The "asshole" part of the equation, however, Keilana was earning all by her lonesome.

I could see that I'd pushed her too far, but I'm only human and her outright rejection of me stung more than I cared to admit.

She climbed out of bed and with short, jerky movements dug through her dresser for a fresh set of clothes. She might have been pissed, but then so was I. Only I was angrier at myself than at Keilana. Russ had been right. I'd pushed things too far. But it was so hard to be patient. I'd been thinking about her for days, had met her family, had read everything I could find about her. I'd even tracked down some articles she'd written for her high school newspaper. I wish I'd bothered to hunt down a photograph. If I had, then yesterday's meeting would have been very different. She didn't feel like a stranger to me, even though she really was.

To Keilana, however, I was nothing more than that, and if she didn't want to spend the afternoon with me, well, I couldn't really blame her, could I?

I didn't try to stop her and make nice when she marched toward the bathroom. We both needed a few minutes to cool off. But something in the wastepaper basket caught her eye and she stopped dead in her tracks. Her eyes fluttered closed and her face turned red and I remembered what I'd thrown away.

"I smashed my face against the door," I said by way of an explanation.

She was staring at the bloodied washcloth from the day before. "I'm sorry," she said in a watery voice.

I thought she might start crying and my heart picked up a little. Please don't cry!

"I didn't want … I mean, I didn't think—" She ran into the bathroom, slamming the door behind her.

So she didn't want to be my friend? Fine. But at least a part of her did want to know me. I could just tell. I'd seen a glimmer of *something* in her smile earlier, something I didn't understand but that was drawing me forward, and making me want to learn all her secrets. And, one by one, I would.

God, I love my job.

Chapter Four

I was five minutes early to my first class, something I'd never managed in my own brief college career. I shuffled into class, feeling the weight of higher learning squarely on my back and thinking I would stick out like a sore thumb. I was wrong. No one looked twice at me except for some preppy kid with a short blond crew cut. He was wearing chinos, a blue blazer, and a white dress shirt with a bow tie. I suppose he thought he was making a statement. Of course, the statement was "I won't get laid till I turn forty or make my first million, whichever comes first," but I still managed to smile politely at him when he flopped down into the chair next to mine.

Madonna Del Mar didn't really have normal classrooms. The room looked more like the den in a rich guy's house, and was filled with leather love seats, chairs, and a few sofas arranged in a semi-circle. I pulled out a notebook and pen and doodled as the students filed in. Oh, goody, lookie who's here. Shauna.

She sneered at me, and I blew her a kiss and winked. She audibly gasped and I snickered, gallantly waving my arm, to offer her the empty seat to my right.

She didn't take it, of course. Instead, she threw her nose in the air and headed for the opposite side of the circle. Adios, bitch.

A few more minutes passed and every seat in the class filled but one. Keilana's. Exactly at eleven a.m. the instructor hurried into the room and plopped down on the tall stool that sat in the middle of the circle. Even though I had no intention of doing anything more than fill a chair during my time in class, my stomach fluttered nervously at her mere presence.

The instructor, Dr. Edith Gallop, began taking attendance. She was at least a hundred and ten years old, but still had garishly-dyed black hair. I shivered. When she said my name I half raised my hand and did my best to smile. She acknowledged me with a short nod and I shivered again, longing for the back row of a huge lecture bowl classroom.

When Dr. Gallop got to the last name on her list, she glanced around, then sighed. Loudly.

Just then, Keilana burst through the door, a book and a few pieces of paper clutched awkwardly in her hand.

"I see Miss Poppenhouse has decided to grace us with her presence. Too bad it appears that she's continuing last year's path to hell in a hand basket," Dr. Gallop said tartly as she lifted her jaw and gave Keilana a supremely disapproving look.

My eyebrows jumped. Hell seemed a slightly excessive punishment for being thirty seconds late to philosophy class.

"Sorry I'm late," Keilana murmured, taking the only available chair, which just so happened to be right next to me. Heh.

"Tardiness will not be tolerated."

Keilana's lips thinned but she remained polite. "Yes, Dr. Gallop."

"Good. It'll be a fresh start then." She nodded to herself. "I think it's best that we begin."

I looked at my watch. From my own brief college experience I remembered that the first class of the semester usually lasted all of about fifteen minutes. The professor would drone through a few moments of personal and then class information, pass out a syllabus, and then we'd be free until the next class. Apparently, however, that's not the way things worked at Madonna Del Mar.

Dr. Gallop turned a little to face me directly. "We have a new senior transfer student joining us this year." Now that she wasn't dealing with Keilana, her mood visibly brightened. "Welcome, Miss Blaisdell."

I smiled weakly. So much for quietly blending in.

"Let's start by discussing our assignment, the first forty-five pages of Foucault's *Madness and Civilization: A*

History of Insanity in the Age of Reason. Ms. Blaisdell, whenever you're ready."

My mouth shaped a tiny "O." There was an assignment the first day? The instructor sensed my confusion and pointed to the book in my lap. Then she did something I would have never in a million years suspected. She began speaking to me in tongues! Well, okay, it wasn't exactly tongues, but it was French and that was the same damn thing as far as I was concerned.

Eyes wide, I glanced around at the other students but everyone acted as though things were completely normal.

Was I in the wrong class? Totally bewildered, I stared at her blankly until she said, "Miss Blaisdell?" Ah, some words I understood.

"Yeah?" Some of the other students began to snicker. Keilana's expression, however, was fixed in stone.

"Ms. Blaisdell?" Dr. Gallop was losing patience. Her cheeks were just starting to turn pink. "I said, please stand up when I address you." She did her best to give me an encouraging smile. "It's tradition here at Madonna Del Mar to stand when being addressed."

I have a tradition too. It's puking when I'm nervous. I felt my stomach roil, but I forced myself to slowly stand. I am an adult, dammit!

"Let's focus first on the text from page twenty-seven, shall we?"

I hadn't as much as opened my book before class. I'd been busy trailing Keilana around campus the day before and hadn't even bought my books until just before the bookstore closed last night. Nobody has an assignment due the first day. Nobody! When I opened the book and peered at the text, my heart sank. The text was gibberish, more French. At least I thought it was French. Dr. Gallop was speaking so quickly the words sounded like one long string of babbling.

Now, I'm not a total novice at French. I took two years of it in high school and all I can say is a cheesy pickup line that asks my victim to go to bed with me. But somehow I was reluctant to use that phrase with our ancient professor.

Dr. Gallop was now pointedly staring at me and the class was growing restless. Worst of all, Shauna was snickering at me. Keilana wouldn't even look at me. The situation was eerily like a recurring nightmare I'd had all my life, where, to my horror, I had to take a final exam for a class I never actually attended. I glanced around to make sure that none of the other women were topless. Darn. That was always my favorite part of the dream.

I prayed my face wasn't as red as it felt and I opened my mouth to tell the professor I hadn't done the assignment when Keilana jumped to her feet and spoke calmly but passionately. In French, no less. I have no idea what she said but the students began shifting uncomfortably in their seats. My mouth dropped open when she changed back to English for the words "pole smoker."

What the hell?

Dr. Gallop gasped. "That issue will not be addressed in this class. Ever! And moreover, it's not relevant!" she snapped, in—thank God—English.

"Isn't it?" Keilana challenged. "Foucault was a homosexual and it's ridiculous to think that *that* didn't impact his opinions on the human psyche. Maybe you should have the guts to talk about *that* today." She smiled innocently to take the sting out of her words, a look that I was coming to associate with downright wickedness. "At least *that's* interesting," she continued.

Then the conversation exploded back into French with several other students rising to their feet and joining in an impassioned discussion. Suddenly, a squarely built guy with glasses told the skinny boy next to him, "I always did wonder about you!"

And there was pandemonium. The professor forgot that I even existed.

I watched Keilana in awe, wondering if that's what she'd intended all along.

After a few minutes of shouting, Dr. Gallop roared, "Class dismissed!" Flustered, she stormed from the room with the students hot on her heels. Keilana and I were the last two to leave the classroom.

Well, at least class hadn't been boring. "Why did you do that?" I asked, truly curious.

Her eyes twinkled a bit. "Because I wanted to."

"And that's the only reason?" I held the door open for her but she didn't walk through. "You sort of saved my butt though I'm sure it was unintentional."

Her eyebrows knitted as she looked me. "Before ... you said you wanted to be my friend, remember?

Huh? "Yesterday, you mean? Of course, I remember."

She licked her lips and I could see the tiny bit of nervousness she was trying to conceal. "Did you mean it?"

I answered honestly. "Sure."

Keilana looked right into my eyes and I felt her gaze to the bottom of my soul. She was standing so close that I could smell her skin and the faint trace of perfumed soap. "I'm sorry about your nose. I didn't mean for you to get hurt."

"My nose?" God, she smelled nice. I had no idea what she was talking about.

"It's a little bruised." She winced as she reached out cautiously and traced my nose with just the tip of her finger. "I didn't want you to get hurt. I want to back up things between us."

"Back up things?" I was cheering that she wanted to put our bad start behind us. But did she really think she could just rewind life as though it was a big DVD?

"I was wondering if you'd like to go to a movie or something tonight?" She quickly ran a hand through her hair, then stuck it into her back pocket as she awaited my answer. "The girls here are ... well, you've met them. You can't trust most of them." She must have seen the slight widening of my eyes because next she asked, "Can I trust you, Cadie?"

I froze at her words, unable to breathe as the little voice in my head screamed "No! I'm a spy!" But with my mouth the best that I could muster was, "I ... uh ... I mean—" Not more than a second or two could have passed, but that's all the time it took.

"I see," she said briskly, and she sped past me and through the door, disappointment coloring her words. "Never mind. I'm sure you'll be studying French tonight."

I closed my eyes. Shit. “Keilana!” I hurried after her and we emerged from the building into the hot sun. “You didn’t give me a chance to answer.” We trotted down the stairs. Damn but she had long legs. “You just surprised me is all.” I grabbed her arm, stopping her at the bottom step. “Hey, I’d love to go to the movies or something. Have I done anything that would make you distrust me?”

She sucked in a deep breath. “Not until just now.”

If she could always read people this well I was going to be in big trouble. I sighed. Who was I kidding? I was going to be in big trouble anyway.

It was nearly three weeks before we ended up making it to the movies and, oddly, I had settled into a fairly stable routine of being a retard in class, doing only as much homework as it took to get by, and being Keilana’s invisible shadow the rest of the time. Much to my frustration, she’d hung around campus or Santa Medina every night for the past two weeks, getting to bed by eleven each night.

Was she on to me? I was truly beginning to wonder. Nobody was that much of a homebody. And yet, if she knew who I was, why not confront me about it? True, she probably got a giggle out of my having to stand up in all our classes and look like I had shit for brains. But other than that, I couldn’t see what was in it for her.

While we weren’t exactly pals, we’d forged a sort of tenuous ... not exactly friendship, but a part-accepting, part-antagonistic relationship. We were starting to talk a little more and that strained feeling that had been there the first few days had faded.

A few guys on campus had come sniffing around her, but Keilana didn’t seem to care or notice. I hadn’t seen her with a girlfriend either. She truly seemed to enjoy her own company and I couldn’t really complain about that. What I *could* complain about was that so far, I hadn’t been able to figure out what in her life was pulling her away from her family.

That was about to change.

A couple of doors down from the movie theater was a coffee shop and we stepped inside to get a drink. We were greeted by a blast of some of the best smelling stuff on the planet—strong coffee, sizzling bacon, and grease.

"I can't believe you're hungry," I said to Keilana, truly amazed, even though I wouldn't have minded a french fry or thirty myself. "You eat twice as much as I do and you're as thin as a rail."

I had to watch what I was doing or I was going to fall victim to the freshman fifteen, fifteen years late. Keeping a covert eye on Keilana meant that I wasn't getting my normal amount of exercise.

"You're not fat," she said, reading my mind. Then we headed to a booth that had just been cleaned. The place was crowded and we were lucky not to have to wait. After we settled in, she plucked a menu from behind the saltshaker and began perusing it with predatory intent. "It's not like I can help it," she commented, picking up the trail of our conversation even after it was cold. She did that a lot and I was starting to get used to the fact that she needed a lot of time to process things before speaking. "I have a fast metabolism." Then her face lit up. "Ooo ... pie."

The corner of my mouth twitched upward. "You have the metabolism of six men."

She was reading the menu so intently, I'm not sure she realized she was speaking out loud. "You should hear my father. He hates the way I look and is always shoving food my way."

I tried to hide my surprise. This was the first time Keilana had mentioned her family at all. "Really?" I said lightly. "So he doesn't think thin is good?"

Keilana glanced up at me, slightly startled at herself for revealing that tidbit. "Never mind."

"C'mon." I smiled kindly. "Tell me."

She wrestled with herself for a moment before wrinkling her nose. "He thinks that mainlanders are obsessed with being thin and that I'm this way only to spite him and make myself less attractive within our social class."

"What class is that? Richer than God?"

"We prefer to say"—she threw her nose in the air for effect—"Hawaiian aristocracy."

I laughed, enjoying the rare moment of playfulness from her. "I'm sure your parents have your best interests at heart."

Her gaze clouded for a moment. "That makes one of us." Then she flipped the page of her menu and I knew that was the end of that particular line of conversation. There was a lot of hurt and resentment hiding behind Keilana's baby blues and not for the first time I wondered how much of it had been caused by my clients.

"So," she said quietly, after a few minutes. "Did you like the movie?"

I could accept a change of subject gracefully. "No, as a matter of fact, I did not."

She blinked, looking utterly bewildered. "But why? It was fantastic!"

"I'm no fan of the President, but Michael Moore is an obnoxious, slovenly, enormous Muppet. Now *Starsky and Hutch*"—I smiled unrepentantly—"*that* was a movie. Action, humor. It had it all."

Keilana looked at me as though I was an alien. "You have imbecilic tastes."

I crossed my arms over my chest defiantly. Just a couple of weeks ago her comment would have set me off. Keilana wasn't shy about offering her honest option, but I'd quickly learned that it was just part of her personality and not an attempt at meanness. "Right back at ya, sister." I pulled out a few sugar packets and began building a tower with them. "So what other movies do you like? Would I have heard of them? Or do they all have subtitles?"

She smiled tentatively and I was relieved that she wasn't bothered by my gentle return tease. "I like popular films too," she said wryly. "But only the good ones."

I arched a blond eyebrow. "Oh, really? Name one."

She arched an eyebrow right back. "New or old?"

"You choose."

"Rocky."

Beaming, I said, "That's one of my favorites!"

Her eyes lit up and her smile relaxed into something beautiful. "Really? Mine too. What's your favorite thing about the movie?"

This was more like it. "Same thing everyone likes, I guess. Kick-butt boxing. Good music. And best of all, Rocky made his dreams come true even if he didn't win the fight in the end."

"Mmm ..." Keilana leaned back in her seat.

"What about you?" I prompted.

She shrugged and grabbed a sugar packet of her own and focused on it. "I liked the dream part too. But what I liked the most is that he did it with no one, ya know?"

I wasn't sure I did, but I nodded, encouraging her to continue.

A weary bitterness, unbefitting someone Keilana's age, crept into her voice. "He didn't have any real friends who cared about him. Maybe that old guy, but that wasn't enough. And the people who acted like they were his friends really weren't. Adrian's brother, for example. He didn't care about him at all. He only cared about himself and was just using Rocky."

I visibly flinched, a sliver of guilt piercing my chest.

"Rocky was so lonely he was barely living," she said thoughtfully. "His heart was a wasteland. But somehow he dug down deep inside and made it. That's what I liked best."

I swallowed thickly, never having heard such a gloomy assessment of the crowd-pleasing film. Did she think she was all alone, her heart a wasteland?

Then, unexpectedly, she let loose with a hopeful smile. "Kind of makes you think anything is possible, doesn't it?"

I guess it did. But it was time to take things down a notch. We were supposed to be having fun. "You're not going to become a boxer, are you?" I pantomimed a few punches.

She snorted, then when I flopped back into my seat, pretending to take a hard punch on the chin, her chuckles turned into a full laugh. "Hardly." Her voice was soft and sweet. "Cadie, I'm much more of a lover than a fighter."

My mouth went bone dry. Was she flirting with me? The tips of her ears turned bright red at the same time mine did. She was! She was flirting with me, and I was loving every second of it. This wasn't Keilana admiring my ass. This was Keilana laughing and smiling and opening up just a tiny bit. And it was ten times as effective as her overt attention had been.

Just then, our waitress showed up and I turned over my coffee cup, which she silently filled. I hadn't taken out a menu so she focused on Keilana, who also turned over her cup. "Anything to eat?"

"Strawberry pie," Keilana said, giving a satisfied nod.

My eyebrows popped in surprise. Even for Keilana that was a fairly moderate choice.

"Good pick," the waitress murmured. She finished pouring Keilana's coffee and made a quick note on her pad. "Anything with that?"

The very tip of Keilana's tongue appeared as she thought. She looked like a little kid when she did it, and I privately thought it was endearing. "Yeah, a submarine sandwich and onion rings. The large size."

I smirked at the stunned look on the waitress's face. "I ... um ... I think she meant like ice cream or cool whip or something, Keilana."

She blinked. "Oh. Good idea. I'll take some ice cream." A pause. "But don't forget the sub."

"It's your funeral." The waitress, who was at least fifty pounds overweight, gave Keilana an envious look and headed back toward the kitchen.

I was about to try to steer things back to the topic of her family when I saw the expression on Keilana's face change. Her gaze was fixed over my shoulder and I turned my head to see just what had caused her radiant smile.

A tall, tanned woman with short, raven-colored hair and piercing green eyes strode into the coffee shop as quickly as her tight mini-skirt would allow.

Keilana stood up. "Billie!" She waved the woman over.

"Lana!" she screeched, causing my eardrums to bleed and everyone in the place to stare at us.

I judged the newcomer to be a few years older than me and even though she had the weathered look of someone who had been ridden hard and put away wet, something about her was undeniably attractive. Not to mention the fact that I was certain her breasts would arrive at our booth at least three seconds before the rest of her did.

When Billie sidled up to the table, she and Keilana shared a warm hug.

"I guess you two know each other," I said, trying not to look annoyed that they were both ignoring me.

"Where've you been keeping yourself, Lana?" Billie drew a pointy red fingernail down Keilana's cheek, then throat, in such a brazenly sensual fashion that I felt my cheeks heat.

Keilana grinned wildly. "I've been ..."—her voice cracked on the word—"around."

The tiny hairs on the back of my neck stood at attention.

Envy. That's what I was feeling at that moment. Billie was doing something I never could. I'm not a violent person by nature, but there was no doubting that I wanted to chop the interloper up into tiny bits and feed her to Smelly alongside his kibble.

Billie whispered something into Keilana's ear that I couldn't quite make out and I saw Keilana's eyes darken with what I was sure was desire.

I swallowed hard. Oh, yeah, at some point these two were lovers. The only question was, how current was their affair? If Billie didn't know that classes had started for Keilana it couldn't have been *too* recent, could it?

"I've been busy. School's started," Keilana finally said, putting just a tiny bit of distance between her and Billie as they both sat down. "I'm actually trying to do a little better this semester so I can graduate and get out of there."

Billie smiled at Keilana. "Ah, that makes sense. You're a smart cookie, so I know you'll graduate, Lana. But I admit that I've been missing you and wouldn't mind seeing you every now and then." The genuine fondness in her voice was mirrored by Keilana.

Shit.

Keilana gave Billie's hand an affectionate squeeze but slowly released it after she said, "Same here."

All right, I let out a relieved breath. "Billie and Keilana" were the recent past, but not exactly ancient history.

Keilana finally gestured toward me. “This is Cadie.”

“Hi Cadie,” Billie said inattentively, before scooting closer to Keilana. “How about we make up for lost time starting tonight?”

To my disgust, Keilana genuinely seemed to consider the suggestion.

Billie didn’t miss the torn look on Keilana’s face and her smile turned into a full-on, shit-eatin’ grin. Of all the nerve! What made her think that Keilana wasn’t *my* date tonight? I allowed all of the emotions thrumming through me to show plainly on my face.

My expression must have been a sight, because Billie backed away from Keilana as though her skin was on fire. If this was the mainlander scum after my roommate’s money, then it would be more than my pleasure to make quick work of her. Besides, she wore too much makeup and perfume, and the smell was starting to make me sick at my stomach.

Keilana glanced back and forth between me and Billie and gave us a confused look. “You’ll see me soon, Billie. I just need to get a handle on my classes first. I’ll call you.”

I frowned.

Billie screwed up her courage and moved close to Keilana again. “Unless you’ve already got plans, you can still come back to my place tonight. I won’t keep you up too late.” There was no missing the smoky timbre to her voice.

Keilana squirmed in her seat and I couldn’t even blame her. Billie could flip on the sex appeal like few women I’ve ever met. “I want to fuck your brains out” vibes literally oozed from her pores.

Keilana glanced up at me and licked her lips. “So I guess we’re done for the night, huh, Cadie?” She leaned forward a little, watching my face closely. I couldn’t tell if she wanted me to agree with her or not. Personally, I was leaning way toward “not.”

I wanted to shout out my frustration. How could I break this case if most of my encounters with Keilana were hit and runs? “I dunno,” I scrambled for an excuse for us to stay together for the rest of the evening. “I need a ride back to campus at least, and ... well ... I was sort of hoping you could help me with my French tonight before Dr. Gallop skewers me in front of the class again. I've been thinking about asking you to be my tutor." Not bad. I was pretty sure I wouldn't feel so proud of myself when I was roasting in hell for all this lying. But at the moment I was feeling pretty clever.

To my surprise, Keilana threw her head back and laughed, something that shaved several years off her appearance and made her look like a happy teenager. "Oh, man, and you need a tutor too. Dr. Gallop is killing you!"

I chuckled, then groaned. "I know. And that bitch Shauna is enjoying every minute of it. I think I can deal with the philosophy work. It's the French that is kicking my butt. I really need your help."

"You really need *me*?" Keilana asked, her forehead creased. "There are other students who are better at philosophy and French than I am."

Uh-oh. "Uh ... I'd rather have you."

Her gaze softened, but I doubted she was aware of it. Billie, however, who was watching her like a hawk, didn't miss a beat. She didn't look too happy. Heh. That's right, bitch. Keilana is coming home with me tonight.

Keilana drew in a deep breath. "Billie—"

"Lana—"

They shared slightly uncomfortable smiles as the waitress came by with the food.

Keilana looked truly sorry. "I'll take a rain check on getting together, Billie. See you around soon?"

"Oh yeah," Billie rolled her eyes and sighed. "I'm not going anywhere. And if you change your mind about coming 'round to my place"—she batted her eyelashes—"not just tonight but anytime—"

"I'll call first," Keilana assured her with a broad smile.

Billie stood and smoothed down her microscopic skirt. "Good." They hugged again. "That'll give me time to get Josh to a sitter."

My eyebrows rose. Billie didn't seem the mom type. Of course, Josh could be her poodle for all I knew.

Soon Keilana and I were alone again. Things felt a little awkward, but it also felt like we'd turned a corner in our nascent relationship.

"C'mon," Keilana said, shocking me by standing up, grabbing my hand, and tugging me out of the booth. "Let's go get this French lesson over with."

I looked back at the table as Keilana tossed a twenty-dollar bill onto the Formica. "But what about the food?"

Her eyes met and fiercely held mine, though her voice was feather soft. "That's not what I'm hungry for, Cadie."

My heart began to pound and I silently whimpered, praying she would stop looking at me that way … never? Nooo … That's not right. She needed to stop looking at me before we got back to campus and our cottage. Where we'd be alone together. All naked and sweaty.

Okay, that last part was just fantasy. But a woman cannot live on dreams of a water cooler alone!

A slow smile swept across Keilana's face.

God, I hate my job.

To my relief and disappointment, it turned out what Keilana was hungry for was chocolate. And we sat eating it, dressed in our pajamas, soft music playing in the background as I tried to decipher what she was saying. The lights were low and I found myself really relaxing for the first time since I moved in. It was nice. Keilana, when she wasn't wary of my every move, was surprisingly easy to be around.

She repositioned herself on the sofa by throwing one leg over the armrest. "C'mon, Cadie."

"I … I'm trying."

She blew out a frustrated breath and rolled her eyes. "I know you can do this."

"It's not like I don't want to!" It was painfully clear that I was lost. I repeated the French phrase, stumbling over several words that I was sure I should be able to easily pronounce.

She raised a suspicious eyebrow at me. "You don't speak French at all, do you?"

"Sure I do," I said, a touch defensively. "Sort of." I've always hated looking like an idiot and lately I did little else around my roommate.

She nodded slowly. "Okay." Then she plucked the book from my hands. "So make up your own sentence with more than four words in it." She set my book on the table and snagged a Hershey's Kiss from the candy bowl next to the book.

My mind raced for a way to exit this situation without looking like an even bigger loser, but I came up completely blank. "I don't wanna." Oh, that was mature.

She focused on the candy as she began to unwrap it. "I think you do."

I stared at her. It was either hate Keilana or do my best to like her as I stumbled through this job. Once I had made that decision to do my best to get along with her, I found that liking her was easier than I thought it would be. But God knows she didn't always make it easy. "I'm not kidding. I can't do this."

"You can."

Argh! Newman was back! "I can't!"

She popped the chocolate into her mouth. "You don't seem the type of woman who believes in excuses. You can do this. You just need to—"

"Fine!" I exploded. "Voulez-vous coucher avec moi?" Oops, I hadn't really meant to shout.

She began to choke on her chocolate and I had to slap her on the back a few times to dislodge it from her throat. "Wh-what did you say?" Keilana spluttered, her face splotchy and red from her near-death experience.

I knew it was stupid to care what she thought, but I did, and I covered my face with my hands, genuinely humiliated. "That's all I can say!" I wailed.

She tried to hold it for a few seconds, but she couldn't help but burst out laughing.

I narrowed my eyes at her. "It's not that funny."

She tossed her own book on the coffee table and smothered her laughter when she saw the angry glint flare up in my eyes. "Cadie, Dr. Gallop's class is the third in a series of classes that were all in French. The others were prerequisites for this one."

All I could think to say was, "Oh." God, I'm brilliant sometimes.

"Cadie," she said softly, "why are you in that class at all if you can't speak stinking French?"

I'd expected her to tease me, not honest curiosity, and I blinked a few times as I adjusted to another case of mental whiplash.

I wanted to say, "I can't spy on you from Pottery 101." Instead, I opted for something safer. "My ... uh ... my folks picked my classes. I didn't have much choice."

Her gaze darkened and she gave my leg a sympathetic pat. "That's happened to me before. It sucks."

"Well, they're paying for all this." I gestured to our undeniably comfortable surroundings. "So I guess it's not such a bad deal. If I don't flunk out, I'll have a degree when I'm finished and I won't have any debt." It had taken me several years to pay off my student loans for the measly amount of time I was in college. No degree and a pile of bills was not fun.

"It's not worth it," she said flatly. "It's only money."

I couldn't help it, I sniggered.

She sat up a little straighter. "What?"

"Nothing." She was glaring at me, but the fire in her eyes wasn't as hot as it had been last week. Still, I could tell I wasn't going to get off the hook until I gave her some sort of explanation for my comment. "Fine. It's easy to say 'it's only money' when you've never gone without. Not that I have," I quickly added. It was so hard to remember that I was supposed to be her peer. I might have looked the part I was playing, but I sure as hell didn't feel it. "I hear having to scrape to make ends meet can be really rough. I hear *some* kids live on Ramen noodles and Kool-Aid through college."

Keilana looked at me intently. "You're wrong, you know. Just because I haven't done without myself, doesn't mean I don't know the value of a dollar." Her gaze intensified as she spoke. "I understand just how far people are willing to go to make ends meet and to survive."

My ears perked. "You do?"

Somewhat reluctantly, she nodded. "Yeah. So don't think just because my parents have money that I don't know there's a real world out there where everything isn't as pretty and easy as this."

Ooo ... This was getting good. Talking to Keilana was like opening a can after the paper label had fallen off somewhere. I had no idea what I was going find when I finally pried off the lid.

"You don't see many students struggling here on campus." I picked up a piece of candy, being sure not to look at her directly as I spoke. "Everyone looks pretty privileged. Not getting a new designer dress whenever you want one isn't exactly what I'd call money troubles." Take the bait ...

"I'm not talking about the students here. I don't know a single student who even has a real job. Most of us live on allowances and Mommy and Daddy's credit cards."

"You don't?"

Suddenly she looked very uncomfortable.

My digging was pretty blatant, but I was too close to quit now. Hmm ... I wonder ... "You don't have to tell me, Keilana." I gave her an apologetic look. "I didn't mean to pry."

Her shoulders relaxed in obvious relief, the shuttered look on her face quickly evaporating. "I cut up the credit cards."

God, I'm a horrible, rotten, sneaky rat bastard. "Because they can track what you do with them?" I guessed.

"Yeah. And the allowance ... well, let's just say it gets put to better use than my buying expensive shoes and concert tickets."

"But how do you live? You need at least some cash for everyday things. Do you moonlight as a waitress or something?" I wadded up the silver foil candy wrapper and tossed it back into the bowl.

"No. I-I-I ..."

I looked up from my chocolate and waited. When she paused, I prompted her with a gentle, "Do you?"

"Not exactly." She glanced down. "Well, it's nothing you'd be interested in. But I guess that maybe I could show you sometime."

Cha-Ching! I was doing "the wave" on the inside even as a part of me was praying she wasn't going to take me to her meth lab where a truckload of illegal aliens were employed as her minion slaves. I forced myself to sound only mildly interested. “That’d be cool. How about we go now? It’s not that late.”

She smiled enigmatically. “Not tonight.”

Why the fuck not? “But—”

“Tonight you have to learn some French.”

I was dangerously near to pouting or crying. And I almost never cry. “But I don’t want to.”

Keilana seemed to struggle with herself for several seconds before coming to some internal decision. “I have an idea. Stand up.” When I didn’t move quick enough she reached down and took my hand, tugging me to my feet. She was a lot stronger than she looked. “Okay, close your eyes.”

“Why would I do that? I don’t want to cl—”

Keilana put her hands on her hips. “For fuck’s sake, Cadie, can’t you just play along? You’re the one who asked for my help, remember?”

My mouth clicked closed. I hated when she was right and I reminded myself that I really should do more to be a good sport. After all, if it hadn’t been for me, she and Billie would be probably be ... Well, I really didn’t want to think what she and Billie would be doing about now. But I was sure that moaning and the words “harder, baby!” would be involved.

“Good,” Keilana said, suddenly smiling again. “Now close your eyes.”

Dutifully, I did as she asked, turning my head to follow the soft sound of her bare feet on the floor as she moved behind me.

“Let’s start easy. You answer in French.” Her voice was velvety soft and she was standing so close to my back that goose bumps broke out across my shoulders. Her breath caressed my skin, causing it to tingle. “What color are my eyes?”

I sighed dreamily, hoping that it didn’t sound as dreamy to Keilana’s ears as it did to mine. “Beau bleu.”

She chuckled softly. “Thank you. How about a whole sentence next time? Now what about yours?”

“What about mine?”

“En français, s’il vous plait!”

I could hear the smile in her words as she mimicked Dr. Gallop.

I chewed my lip as I tried to remember the word for what I wanted to say. I'd been studying for the past couple of weeks and bits and pieces were starting to come back to me. Too bad it wasn't nearly enough. "Umm ... I think ... I mean ... Ils sont des boues."

"Tsk." She tugged a curl of hair that fell just above my ear. "They're not the color of mud. Vos yeux sont la couleur de caramel chaud ..."

This close I could smell the subtle, spicy scent of her perfume, and it was wonderfully distracting. I swallowed hard. "Huh?"

"Your eyes are the color of warm caramel," she purred directly into my ear.

"Yow!" I nearly jumped out of my skin. What the hell was she doing? "Keilana?" I squealed.

"Shh. We're not finished," she said matter of factly, but she wrapped a firm arm around my waist to hold me in place. "Eyes closed and stay still, okay?"

I was starting to get really turned on, but stupidly, I was more curious than cautious, and so I quickly nodded.

She didn't wait a single heartbeat before she molded her body to mine and rested her chin on my shoulder. Damn, that felt great. We were both wearing thin pajama tank tops and shorts, and I could feel her hard nipples pressing against my back and the sudden warmth of her naked thighs intimately touching mine. My heart began to thud wildly and my breathing quickened. But I did as she had asked, remaining stock still with my eyes closed tight.

"What's this?" She plucked at my hem of my shirt.

I was surprised when I heard myself say, "Chemise." The word had popped into my mind without thought.

"Mm-hm. See? You know more than you think you do. And what about this?" Warm fingers circled my wrist.

"Poignet."

"Very good. And now?" Her fingers moved to my palm and she gave it a little scratch.

"I ..." My tongue felt thick in my throat. "I have n-n-no idea."

"C'est votre paume."

My heart was beating so loudly I could barely hear what she was saying. “Paume,” I agreed absently. “Ri-right.”

She snuck her hand under my shirt and stroked my stomach with the tips of her fingers. I was sure she could feel the butterflies that were doing back flips there.

“Uhmm ...”

She pressed her cheek to mine. “Skin, Cadie. Soft skin. You know the words. Think.”

But I couldn’t think! She was seducing me and I was letting her. And when she attached her lips to the back of my neck, I forgot how to breathe. This should not be happening. She’s too young for me. It wasn’t right, but it was so good! And she’s, she’s ... so damn sizzling hot my entire body aches for her!

My knees nearly buckled and a low moan was torn from my chest when she used her teeth and tongue to stroke the length of my jugular. Her lips were so soft I melted under their attention. God, if only I could be myself. I would kiss her senseless! If only I wasn’t here to spy on her and lie to her and—*Liar. Spy.* The words were like having a bucket of ice water dumped on my head, and they snapped me out of my lust-induced haze with a near physical force.

I spun around to face my tormentor, whose skin was flushed and whose eyes were dark with passion. Oh, God. I began to stumble backward, mortified that I hadn’t put a stop to things sooner. “We ... we shouldn’t do this.” I scrubbed my face. Fuck!

“Why not?” Her face showed her hurt but she managed to keep her voice even. “Don’t tell me you don’t like girls. I know better.”

My mouth worked for a few seconds. I wasn’t even out to my parents and here I was about to tell her? “Well, I do but—”

“And don’t tell me you don’t want me.” Her eyes drilled into mine, and my temperature rose. “I’ve seen the way you watch me, Cadie. The way you look at me.”

Lord, take me now. Please.

"You want me. And I can tell you right now that I want you." She lowered her voice. "Badly." She took a step closer to me and I instantly took a step back.

Even though I was the one being chased, I felt like the fox in the hen house. All right, so I was more snake than fox, but it was still clear that I couldn't be trusted anywhere near her.

"So what's the problem?" She took another few steps forward, and I kept right on backing up until my back was against the wall, and we were standing toe to toe.

"We're roommates," I said lamely, the chilly wall doing little to cool my ardor.

Her eyes smiled. "I won't hold that against you."

"You won't?" I said weakly. "Are you sure? 'Cause you can if you want. I practically insist."

"We're both available and interested." She cocked her head to the side. "Why should we deny ourselves?"

I marveled at her confidence. And why was she being so reasonable? She was the most unreasonable woman I'd ever met! The third day in the cottage I accidentally used her toothpaste and she threatened to set my bed on fire. *Now* she was being all mature?

"We won't be hurting anyone," she continued.

Relief flooded me. Thank God she'd finally hit on something that wasn't true. We could both get hurt. "Listen, Keilana," I proceeded as carefully as I could. "If we sleep together and it doesn't work out, I would be uncomfortable living here."

She looked unconvinced by my statement.

"I'm too lazy to move!"

That made her smile. "Cadie?"

"If it doesn't work out things would be ... tense." Like they weren't already.

"If *what* doesn't work out?"

I gestured wildly and only just kept from pumping my hips for emphasis. "You know!"

She gave me an incredulous look. "Are you saying sleeping with me might suck?"

"No! Sleeping with you ..." I closed my eyes briefly in a bid for self-control. "I have no doubt that we'd be great in bed together." Truer words were never spoken. We generated enough heat and tension on a daily basis to run a power plant. We'd barely touched and every nerve in my body was singing. I'd be lucky not to spontaneously combust if she actually kissed me.

"Then I don't get it. I like you, but I don't want a girlfriend. I just want to have sex with you. In case you haven't noticed, we're both young, and healthy, and you're hot enough to have me dripping wet already."

My jaw dropped and my pussy clenched so tightly I thought I might come on the spot.

"So?"

So let's do it! I groaned. "I'm sorry, Keilana." My eyes conveyed true regret. In fact, the rest of my body would probably never forgive me. "I can't. "

She lifted her jaw and stepped back. She didn't say a word but I could tell that she was disappointed.

"I'm sorry."

"Don't be." But her words were stiff.

Keilana grabbed her car keys from the kitchen counter and slipped into a pair of sandals that were by the door. I didn't want her to leave mad, not to mention in her pajamas. We'd made real progress in the last couple of weeks and I wasn't about to throw that all away over a quick fuck. I blocked her path to the door.

"Move," she said crisply, visible holding back her emotions. "I mean it."

I wasn't sure whether she was really angry, but I was sure that I had hurt her feelings by rejecting her. "Not until we talk some more."

"There's nothing to talk about. I made you an offer." She forced a shrug. "You turned me down. It happens."

I gave her a small, knowing smile. "It doesn't happen to you though, does it?" Her eyes widened just a touch and I knew that I was right.

"I'm not sure why, but it never has before," she finally admitted a little sheepishly.

It was no mystery why to me, but I didn't interrupt.

"There's a first time for everything." She wrinkled her nose. "I guess ... well, I wouldn't have made such a fool of myself if I thought that you'd turn me down." She shook her head. "You seemed ... I mean, I thought—"

"I *am* very attracted to you. I'd be insane not to be." Didn't she know I'd be taking a thirty-minute cold shower tonight? "I'm also sorrier than I can say. But I don't want a quick lay and then nothing else. I really meant it when I said I wanted to be your friend. And sleeping together now would probably mess that up. Please, please don't be mad."

Her expression softened just a fraction and she pursed her lips.

"Please?" I gave her my best puppy dog eyes.

I could see the wheels in her head spinning. Her eyes still showed a combination of hurt and unspent lust and it was all I could do not to kiss it away.

"All right," she murmured after a moment. "But I reserve the right to try to ask you again at some future date."

I prayed she wouldn't, because I was very sure that I would not have the willpower to turn her down twice. "Deal."

She looked down at her feet and flexed her toes. "I don't have many friends, Cadie."

"Neither do I." It was true. I dated every once in a while, but nothing much seemed to come of it. Smelly, Russ, and a couple of the other dick draggers from my favorite beach were pretty much my entire social circle.

She glanced up from her feet to me. "And you want to be my friend more than you want to sleep with me?" She sounded skeptical and I guess I couldn't blame her.

"I'm clearly insane," I smiled, "but yeah."

"And you don't want any kind of a loan or to meet my father maybe?"

My heart ached for her. She'd obviously been hurt badly by some asshole who was using her. And I swore that I'd finish this job and get out of her life before she ever knew that I was basically doing the same thing. "I don't give a good Goddamn about your loot or the Poppenhouse Cookie dynasty. I don't even like cookies."

A tentative smile appeared on her face and it was as though a weight had toppled off my shoulders. "Everyone likes cookies."

I gave her a guilty look. "Yeah, I know."

"Are you hungry?" she suddenly asked. "'Cause I gave up my sandwich in hopes of something tastier tonight." She laughed softly when my cheeks colored.

I wasn't hungry in the least. In fact, I felt a little sick at my stomach after everything that had happened. Still, I managed to paste on a smile. "I'm starved."

Chapter Five

Another week passed before something big changed. It's not like I hadn't been waiting for something to break, but I was still a little surprised when it happened. We had our first round of college exams. I barely passed mine, but that was no shock.

Keilana, on the other hand, got all A's. I expected her to come home after her last class today, do a little homework, some reading for pleasure, and then we'd scare up a late supper together. It was what we did every night and I'd come to look forward to it.

I know it seems sappy, but I was so proud and happy for her! She'd worked damned hard and it had paid off in spades. I had picked up some wine and flowers at the grocery store in Santa Medina to celebrate her big accomplishment, but when I got back to our cottage all I found was a worthless note that made me want to tear my hair out by the roots.

> Cadie—
>
> Gone out for the evening. Don't wait up. I think there is some leftover shrimp & rice in the fridge. Help yourself to it all.
>
> K.

"Damn!" I dropped the bag of groceries on the counter in disgust. I couldn't believe that I'd let sloppy sentimentality send me to the store for celebration goodies when I should have been watching my quarry. What was wrong with me lately?

I read the note again. She didn't say where she was heading and I wondered what she was hiding and whether it was intentional or just a side effect of her very private personality. A kernel of worry exploded in my belly. Whatever she was doing had to be really bad. If not, why hide it?

Then I thought of Keilana's parking tickets. It was Friday night. Had she driven to San Diego?

It was warm, but rainy, and a staccato of drops bombarded the Jaguar's windshield as I pulled out of the campus parking lot. The car was fabulous, but would stick out like a sore thumb in the part of town where I was heading. Truth be told, I was glad for an excuse to go back to my apartment, if only for a few minutes.

I live on the third floor of an enormous, turn-of-the-century home that had been converted into four separate apartments during WWII. It's close to downtown and I have a private parking space in the alley behind the backyard. I've lived here for more than fourteen years and have seen a couple dozen other tenants come and go in that timeframe. I, however, haven't really had a reason to leave. The rent is reasonable, they allow me to keep Smelly, and I have a lot more privacy than I would in one of those enormous townhouse complexes on the other side of town.

Currently, I was the only resident not collecting Social Security so it was also deathly quiet there. Part of the reason I worked so much and spent so much time at the beach was that it allowed me to be around other people. Living alone can be ... well ... lonely. Not to mention boring as hell.

I pulled up next to my Mustang, a warm fuzzy feeling enveloping me, even though the car was, I fully admit, a heap of junk. But it wasn't just any car. It was my *first* car. I'd fended off several boyfriends in that car, and when I'd gotten older, given in to several girlfriends there. And even though I was sitting in a gem right now, I was looking forward to sliding behind the wheel of my own vehicle and sinking down into the seat that had perfectly molded to my butt over the years. It was *mine* and that's what I liked best about it.

But I wasn't going anywhere without the car keys, which were inside my apartment. Large trees shielded me from most of the rain as I trotted up the sandy path that bisected the backyard. As I unlocked the back door, I noticed the white paint on the house looked a little dingy and a few of the shutters were cracked. Why hadn't I seen that before? Had I gotten spoiled after only a few weeks at Madonna Del Mar? I thought of Shauna and frowned. If I believed I might start acting like her, I'd go jump off a bridge somewhere.

I was greeted with a blast of stale air when I opened my apartment door. And despite the rain, I threw open a window. The place was dark and drab compared to my new digs. And it was, I decided with a sigh, too quiet with Smelly gone. I snagged the keys from their usual resting place on my kitchen counter and noticed my answering machine blinking. Three messages.

The first was some dick-weed wanting to know if I wanted to switch my long distance carrier. The next was from my mom. She was wondering whether I was still alive and I made a mental note to call her back the next day. The last message was from Russ, pleading with me to toss him a crumb of information about my case. His workload was light at the moment and I guessed he was about ready to crawl up the walls with nothing to do.

I was just about to call him back when I heard a noise coming from my bathroom. I swallowed hard. Shit! I'd walked in on an intruder. The bum was probably hoping to find some nice prescription drugs in my medicine chest.

I didn't carry a big-ass gun in my purse like TV detectives. I didn't even have a baseball bat. I've always found running in the opposite direction of trouble to be a lot safer than direct confrontation. But tonight, for some reason, I didn't have the urge to flee. I had the urge to stay and fight.

I stood there, on a razor's edge, unsure of exactly what to do. Okay, that's not quite true. I knew what I *should* do, and I knew what I *wanted* to do. And as often happens with me, my emotions took control and common sense flew out the window. The thought that some skanky stranger might have pawed my most personal and prized possessions—Granny's locket, my mint condition first issue of *Surfing*, my collectible Wonder Woman lunch box—was more than I could bear.

Furious and with wild emotions pouring off me like the sparks from a firecracker, I crept over to the bathroom door and hid alongside it. It was mostly dark there and I left the lights off as I waited in the shadows. I heard the toilet flush and envisioned the lid being left up. "Bastard!" I seethed quietly. A nervous sweat beaded on my upper lip.

The door opened and I saw the shadow of a middle-sized man fill the doorway, drying his hands on my towels. He turned and tossed the towel back into the bathroom. Pig! My heart was beating so fast that I couldn't distinguish the beats. Adrenaline sang through my veins, making my limbs shake in anticipation.

I didn't give myself time to think or chicken out. Instead, I let out a primal roar and jumped in front of the door. The man jumped back when he saw me, but not in time to avoid my stunning kick to his groin. He fell to the ground with an inhuman wail, and I reared back to kick him again ... when Smelly scampered out of the bathroom, tromping over the writhing man's head in the process.

Uh-oh. I blinked. "Russ?"

All I heard was groaning.

I flicked on the hall light and there he was, curled up in a ball of misery, cursing me in-between his whimpers as he rocked back and forth.

"Russ! Oh, God." I dropped to my knees, petting Smelly with one hand and patting Russ on the back with the other. "I didn't know it was you." I didn't know where to touch him. It wasn't like I could comfort him *there*. "It was an accident, I swear!"

He bit his lip, a tortured look on his face. "Ugh ... You evil ... ugh ... damn, ughhhhh, fuckin'-A ... Jesus—"

Wow. I'd never seen a human being's face so red.

"I thought you were a burglar!" I cried. "Oh, please don't puke there, okay?" Smelly began to whine and lick Russ's face. Apparently, guys of all species have a special sort of empathy for each other in moments like these.

Russ was finally able to moan, "Do I look like a bu-burglar?"

I sighed, relieved that he'd stopped writhing. "You did in the dark. I didn't know you'd be here. What was I supposed to think?"

He didn't have a good answer for that, but he still managed to pose a very good question. "Since when do you attack burglars, Belinda?" He rolled over on his back and threw one arm over his eyes. "Are you trying to get yourself killed? Are you crazy? What if I'd had a gun or a knife?"

"I-I-I—" I couldn't think of a single reasonable explanation for what I'd just done. "The burglar's butt was on *my* toilet." I gestured frantically. "I couldn't think straight!"

He laughed even though I could tell it hurt when he did it. "Forget that I asked if you're crazy. I already know the answer."

Another moment passed before he sat up, his face a little pasty.

"Russ, do you need to go to the hospital?" I was horrified at the thought that I might have ruptured something that he, and presumably his wife, dearly loved. I'd threatened his balls many times over the years of our friendship, but I never intended to actually crush them.

"No way." He let out a painful breath. "No way am I going to explain to some nurse that my best friend"—he glanced at my T-shirt—"who is wearing pink today, I might add, beat me up."

"Do you want some ice or something?"

"So long as it's in a tall glass of scotch."

I nodded, relieved that I could do anything to help. Russ knew I didn't drink scotch, but I fetched two shockingly cold bottles of Sam Adams from the refrigerator and then hurried back to his side. I slid down the wall to join Russ, who was now sitting up and leaning against the wall in the hall. "What are you doing here anyway?" I passed him a bottle. "Did you and Sarah have another fight?"

"Yeah," his heavy brow furrowed. "A bad one."

I leaned my shoulder against his, and he rested his hand on my knee. Sometimes the best support you can offer a friend doesn't require any words at all.

He took a long pull of beer. "I crashed on your sofa last night and was going to do it again tonight." He inclined his head toward the dog. "Smelly missed you."

"I missed him, too." I petted my mutt again and he instantly rolled over so I could scratch his belly. I happily obliged, a smile blooming on my face.

"Why are *you* here?" Russ asked, his curiosity showing. We shared that sometimes-maddening trait. It was an occupational hazard. "You're supposed to be at that fancy-pants college, aren't you?"

"I'm picking up my car so I can trail Keilana."

Russ snorted. "Good luck. That girl has eyes in the back of her head. Hey, why didn't you just go with her when she left? Isn't that the point of living with her?"

I squirmed a little. "I wasn't invited, okay? She's got a life of her own. But at least I have an idea of where she's gone. Or at least the general vicinity."

He scratched his stubble-covered chin. Apparently being away from the wife means no shaving. "So you're going to go looking for her tonight instead of waiting till she comes home?"

I nodded. "I have to. Whatever it is she's up to, she does away from campus. I'm sure of that. Besides ..." My lips tensed. I hated to admit this for about a million different reasons. "She might never trust me enough to take me wherever it is she goes."

"Can I come too?" He finished off his beer in a few hurried swallows. "I'm ready." He snickered. "I've already been to the bathroom, Mom. I wouldn't go in there for a while, by the way."

Gross. "You can't come with me, Russ."

His eyes widened in disbelief. "Belinda!"

"The answer is no."

It was obvious that he was struggling not to raise his voice. "Why not?"

I knew he had to be bored here. Russ had the attention span of a three-year-old and was always full of restless energy. "Keilana already spotted you when you were following her earlier this year. If she sees you with me it'll blow my cover."

"Are you going to let her see you?"

I nearly spit out my drink. "Of course not! *I'm* not going to get made."

He narrowed his eyes at me.

"I'm going to spy on her and remain hidden. Alone."

He took my bottle from me and stole a sip. "Well ..." He licked the beer from his lips and passed me back the bottle. "If she won't see you, and I'm with you, then she won't see me either, right?"

"But—"

"Besides, back when I was following her she only saw me from a distance. And I was wearing a hat and dark glasses. I never even got out of the car. No way she could I.D. me after all this time."

I was about to say no again when he added, "Please?"

Shit. I was a sucker for him when he was polite. "Fine. But we need to go now. Can you walk?" I stood up and offered him a hand. Russ is only a few inches taller than me, with a thick neck and muscular body. I had to lean way back to help him to his feet. God, what did his wife feed him?

Wobbly, he stood, then drew in a deep breath and took a tentative step, nodding at the results. "I can walk. And I can sure as hell sit in your car. By the way you owe my injured 'boys'"—he pointed to his crotch—"a trip to Burger Boy later. And just so you know, I'm getting double of everything."

My face twisted in disgust. "Uck. I'll take you to Burger Boy every time we're together for a month if you swear to never mention your 'boys' in my presence ever, ever again."

"Deal." He grinned wildly. "Hey, Belinda, have we ever talked about my—"

"Don't even go there, Russ."

There was no single word that could describe this corner of San Diego's southeast side. The locals called the area El Vientre del Diablo. The Devil's Belly. And butted up against El Vientre del Diablo was one of the older parts of the city that had recently been the recipient of millions of dollars of redevelopment funds. It was an area in transition; an eclectic mix of grimy and dilapidated, glitzy and new. Right now, however, we were still in the part that was too salty and dangerous to be a tourist trap.

"God, Russ," I had to flick on my windshield wipers as the rain shifted from a sprinkle to a steady downpour. With twilight's rapid approach, the gray skies had taken on an amethyst hue. "I hope we don't find her hanging out here. But the area where Keilana got all those parking tickets is just few a streets over from here."

I stopped at an intersection so two tranny hookers could cross the street in front of my car. The wind and the rain had caused their once lofty hairstyles to fall into their faces, and they gave me a grateful wave as they scurried across the street, wearing shoes that looked like Dorothy's ruby red slippers from *The Wizard of Oz.* I grimaced. "Is that mascara pooling at their collars?" I mumbled, my eyes scanning both sides of the road for Keilana.

I barely heard his wistful sigh. "They remind me of my wife."

Good grief. Russ's wife is pretty, five feet, two inches tall, blond, and with a cupid-bow mouth. She reminded me of Betty Boop with an attitude.

The hookers had five o'clock shadows, were black, and tall enough to play for the NBA. "The resemblance is uncanny. How does Sarah resist your charm, Russ?"

"She manages."

I felt a twinge of pity for my friend. "Oh, fine. You don't have to sleep on the sofa at my place anymore." I'd always taken Russ in during his times of need. Which were many. But I'd always drawn the line at letting him use my bedroom.

His face lit up. "Really?"

I rolled my eyes at myself. "Yeah. You can have the bed, but only till I get home." I pointed at him. "And take the sheets with you when you leave."

"How long do you think that will be? 'Til you come home, I mean."

My lips tensed. I thought of collecting my big paycheck from the Poppenhouses, and then I thought of never seeing Keilana again. I wasn't sure which one of those thoughts made my stomach lurch, but it did. "It won't be long now." I prayed that would be true.

"Are you okay, Belinda? You've been sort of quiet tonight."

I hadn't been quiet at all. I'd told him all about living with Keilana and school and the college life from a new perspective. Then we'd talked for a while about the progress reports I was sending Keilana's father every three days. But he was right about one thing. I'd felt ... I don't know ... "off" for lack of a better word.

I was never very good at hiding my feelings and I smiled ruefully at Russ. "I'm ... I guess this job is starting to get to me. All the lying and spying. It's a lot easier when you don't know the person whose privacy you're invading."

He gave me a sympathetic look, then turned to glance out his window. "It's just a job. Money in your pocket, ya know? You can't let it tie you into knots. Besides, from what the parents said, the kid is hell on wheels. If someone is spying on her, it's because of her own doing."

My jaw clenched with sudden anger. "That's bullshit! Keilana doesn't *deserve* what I'm doing to her. Yeah, she can make me crazy and all, but she's also funny and smart and kind. She even laughs when I repeat the lousy jokes you've told me."

My blood pressure was still rising and I didn't try to stop it. "She smiles at me when I do something right in class. And last week, out of the blue, she bought me a quart of my favorite flavor of ice cream and put it in the freezer without saying a word. She's on some campus committee that collects used clothes for women and kids in battered women's shelters. Bet you didn't know that either?"

Russ didn't answer, but his eyes widened a bit.

I was on a roll, the words pouring out of me in an angry stream. "Of course you didn't. Nobody even thinks she'd do something that wasn't all about her. And I used to be just as ignorant. Oh, and she offered to help me pass my impossible fucking classes. For free." I left out the part about her wanting to get me naked since it didn't really help me get my point across.

"I guess I didn't know any of that," Russ admitted after a moment of worriedly staring at me. "But you make her sound like some goodie-two-shoes." He lifted a skeptical eyebrow. "I find that hard to believe, even with the way you've blabbered on all night about how great she is."

My mouth opened but no words came out. Had I really blabbered? "I do *not* blabber. And she's not some lame Girl Scout. But she's not some rotten rich bitch either. I've found out a lot of other good things about her that I'll bet her parents don't even know." I couldn't hide my disgust. It was hard enough hiding my distain in my progress reports I had to submit to the Poppenhouses. "I've been there for weeks and they haven't bothered to call her once."

He shrugged one shoulder. "They told me that she refuses to return their calls."

I slapped the steering wheel with my open hand. "They aren't even trying! They can't just give up. *They* are the parents. And they are the ones who hired us to spy on her. Of course Keilana is angry. Wouldn't you be?"

A tiny crease appeared between Russ's eyes. "The Poppenhouses aren't giving up on her. If they were, they wouldn't have hired you, Belinda."

I knew that was true even though my sympathy for Mr. and Mrs. Poppenhouse diminished every day I lived with their daughter. Nobody who hasn't been treated badly acted the way Keilana did. Nobody. And since they seemed to be as much to blame as Keilana for their sucky parent/child relationship, I refused to go out of my way to let them off the hook. "The parents probably made matters worse by hiring me. If Keilana ever finds out ..." My heart sped up a little at the mere thought. "She'll never trust them." Or me. "Ever again. And I mean *never*."

I was all wound up, but I didn't want to argue with Russ, so I forced my shoulders to relax and somehow managed a slow, calming breath. "Look," I said as I glanced sideways. "I've been with Keilana nearly twenty-four seven; she's not a bad person. She's not." My eyes begged him to believe me. I'm not sure why that was suddenly so important to me. It just was.

"And that reminds me"—my tone dared him to disagree—"she's not doing dope!" Oops, I was starting to get all crazy again.

"You think she's hooking?"

A prostitute? I gripped the steering wheel until my knuckles turned white and my hands hurt. I fought back the bitter taste of bile. "No way."

"What's going on with her then? It's gotta be something," Russ said, looking mildly startled by my vehemence.

"I-I ..." I just shook my head. "I don't know." A sigh escaped. I was still angry at myself for letting Keilana out of my sight in the first place. "I think she's just a regular, mixed-up young woman, who is really angry with her parents and is as mistrustful of everyone else as she is of them. I'll admit she's got a secret though. Or we wouldn't be driving around in the rain looking for her."

He smiled wickedly. "She won't have the secret for long."

I couldn't help but feel a tingle of anticipation in my belly. The chase was on.

We drove in silence for a few moments before he asked, "Do you think Keilana's attractive?"

"God, yes," I said a lot more quickly than I'd intended. I bit my tongue and briefly closed my eyes. Crap.

A relieved-looking smile broke out on Russ's face. "Belinda," he taunted with a chuckle. "You're hot for your roomie!" He slapped his knee, and laughed a little louder. "God, you had me worried there for a minute."

"Shut up." There was no way I could deny it and get away with it, so I didn't even bother trying. I wasn't just hot for Keilana. I was long past hot. About now I would fit nicely into the "smoldering piles of ashes" category. There were times when I was sure that everyone around me could see steam rising from my ears and other hotter, wetter parts of my body as I burned apart from within.

"She drives you to distraction, doesn't she?"

I swallowed my pride. “Yes. Yes. Yes! I can’t think anymore because I want her so badly! Happy?”

He clucked his tongue at me. “You do know that Kale Poppenhouse would probably hire a hit man to bury your ass in the Mexican desert if you as much as laid a finger on her, don’t you?” His expression turned serious. “You’re playing with fire.”

“I’m well aware of that, Russ.” I smiled a sickly-sweet smile. “But thanks so much for reminding me.”

“No problem.” He wiped mock sweat from his brow. “For a second I thought you had your head screwed on backwards and had ... I dunno ... a crush on her or something equally stupid. I should have known you wouldn’t go and do something so nuts. Wanting to bang her is dangerous, but completely understandable. Falling for her would be ... well, even you aren’t that crazy.”

My face heated as I considered his words. Falling for her? Was I? God above, I *knew* in my heart that I was *just* that crazy! I stopped for a red light and rubbed my temples with one hand. They were starting to throb.

A crush was way, *way* worse than just wanting to jump her bones. Sex I could deal with. A case of unrequited puppy love was something that I hadn’t had since the eighth grade. And come to think of it, it had ended badly then too.

I wasn’t anxious to repeat the experience.

The light turned green and I punched the gas pedal, slamming Russ back against his seat.

“Okay,” I said, gripping the steering wheel tightly. “I admit that I’m hot for her.”

He smiled smugly as he braced himself in his seat. “I knew it!”

“But that’s all you get out of me on the subject. At least for tonight. Oh, and Russ?” I turned my head to face him. “You really need to stop teasing me about this right now.”

He blinked. “I do?”

“Yes.” I slowed my Mustang down so that I could scan a small parking lot for Keilana’s car. “Because now that I know how easy it is to kick you in the balls, I’m much more likely to do it again. At any moment the mood strikes me, as a matter of fact.”

He gulped, and amazingly, that shut him up tighter than a clam … for all of five seconds.

He shook his head and gave me an envious look. “Belinda, you could have more pussy than the Humane Society if you’d only open your eyes to the women around you.”

I hung my head. “Jesus, Russ.”

“Just don’t let it be with a client’s daughter.”

“Do you always have to be so disgusting?” I wasn’t angry that he’d blown off my threat. He usually did.

He let out a low whistle as he shook his head. “I can’t blame you for sniffin’ after the Poppenhouse kid. There’s something sexy as hell about her.”

I ground my teeth together. That was the second time he’d called her a “kid” in the last five minutes. “She’s twenty-one years old, not twelve.” I would have knocked the smirk right off his face if I hadn’t been twice as obnoxious about the nineteen-year-old pet groomer’s assistant he’d briefly dated a few years ago. She still had braces on her teeth and talked about her senior prom incessantly.

“Okay, okay, she’s not jailbait,” he allowed good-naturedly. “You’re lucky there.” Then his jaw dropped the way it always did when he experienced an epiphany that he wasn’t particularly happy about. “She’s into chicks too?”

Reluctantly, I nodded. Normally, I wouldn’t share that sort of personal information about someone, but Keilana was totally out about her sexual orientation and Russ and I always talk about the women in our lives. The ones we’ve had, and the ones we only dream of having.

“Oh, man!” He couldn’t have looked more bereft if I’d told him that his beloved San Diego Chargers were moving to Calcutta. “Isn’t that always the way?” he cried. “Dammit all to hell. That blows!”

I flashed him an incredulous look. Why is it that when a guy finds out an attractive woman is a lesbian, he always takes it so personally? As though there will now be a shortage of women and that he, personally, will have to do without. “It’s not like you had a chance at her, you pervert!”

He pointed at his chest with his thumb. "Why am *I* the pervert?"

Thinking of Russ and Keilana together made my blood boil, but I couldn't very well say that. "Because ... umm ... because you're too old for her!"

His dark eyebrows rose. "You just made it very clear that she was a grownup. I'm only four years older than you." He poked me in the shoulder a little harder than necessary. "If I'm a pervert, you're one too."

Shit. Rule number one, perverts who live in glass houses really shouldn't throw stones. "I'm not married and you are." Hah! Take that.

"And I hope to be married for a long time. But that doesn't mean I'm blind." His gaze softened. "Living with her must be torture, huh?"

The lump in my throat rose so unexpectedly that I didn't answer for fear that my voice would crack. The road before us became a little blurrier.

Living with Keilana wasn't torture. It was astonishingly easy. And that made things even harder. What was torture was the knowledge that I was taking the nascent trust and friendship we shared and shredding it to bits on a daily basis with my endless lies and duplicity. I was using her.

I was worse than her parents, who, even though they were the sort who shouldn't have attempted to raise anything more complicated than a fern, were at least acting in part out of concern for their child. I was only in this for the money.

Russ must have noticed the sudden wave of melancholy that washed over me because he turned to face his side window again and gave me a tiny bit of privacy. He rubbed the fog that collected there with the back of his hand and peered out. I wasn't a scum-sucking pile of shit. I was the flea on the fly on the scum-sucking pile of shit.

I could tell that Russ wanted to say more on the subject and I wasn't sure what was holding him back. Still, I was grateful for the reprieve. He'd been peppering me with questions about my case and Keilana all night and I'd had about as much of the Curious George routine as I could handle.

A gust of wind shook my Mustang as I turned and rounded a sharp corner. Even in this lousy weather, the street I merged onto was busier than the one we'd just traveled, and pedestrians under umbrellas or baseball hats crowded the sidewalks as they waited to get into various dance clubs and bars. It was a rough and ready, young crowd that included a fair share of partying Marines.

Russ grabbed his enormous bag of cheeseburgers from the backseat. He carefully unwrapped a burger and passed it over to me, taking the time to wrap the paper around it so that I could hold the burger and not drip ketchup down my shirt as I drove. "Thanks," I said quietly.

Then he dug out a burger for himself. "Hey," he said around an enormous bite. He swallowed hastily. "Her BMW is white with a black bra and spoiler, right?"

"Yeah," my head snapped in the direction that he was looking. "I can't ... That might be it!" The headlights of a car in the parking lot illuminated what might be Keilana's car. But the light lasted only a couple of seconds and then it was gone. I swerved into a small, gravel lot that sat between a bar and a dance club. It was a pay lot, but the attendant, who had probably spent most of the evening locked in a tiny booth with a shotgun resting on his lap as he took money, was long gone by now.

The reflection of flashing neon from nearby signs off my wet windshield made it tough to see, but I was certain that the BMW was empty and that Keilana was nowhere in sight. I pulled up right behind what I thought was her car, and gave it another quick glance before I kept right on driving to the back of the parking lot.

There were no empty spots but I managed to fit my Mustang next to the last car in a row, though it meant two of my wheels were resting on the curb. Luckily, it was getting dark fast.

I killed the engine. "I tried, but I couldn't see whether the license plate matched."

"Christ, Belinda, how many white Beemers matching that description do you think are parked on the edge of The Devil's Belly? That's the one. Gotta be."

We both tossed our half-eaten burgers onto the dashboard. A tickle of excitement caused me to stop worrying about how I felt about Keilana and start focusing on why I was here.

"I'm gonna go check the plates just to be sure," I said.

Russ rolled his eyes. Then he nodded and pulled his baseball cap a little lower on his head. "I'll go check the plates. This the number?" He plucked a small, folded piece of paper from my ashtray.

I opened my mouth to protest and he held up a forestalling hand. "Let me," he said. "The girl—"

I glared at him.

"Errr ... I mean, Keilana, is already pissed at her parents. If she makes you, well, you already said it. It'll only make things worse. Not to mention the fact that it's bad to blow things with rich clients." He gave me a chagrined smile that made him look very much like a little boy. "I would know."

I let out an unhappy breath. "Russ—"

Just as he reached for the door handle his cell phone rang. Reluctantly, he dug it out of his pocket, then swallowed hard when he read the illuminated phone number of the caller.

"Go ahead answer it," I urged him. "The BMW will keep. I'm watching it. It's about time you and Sarah made up anyway."

"I don't know what to say to her."

The phone continued to ring.

I sighed. Men. "Answer it and apologize. I'll go check the plates."

"What if I make it worse?" The panic started in his eyes but spread to the rest of him in two seconds flat. "What if she starts to cry? What if—?"

"Just say you're sorry, for fuck's sake!" I grabbed his hands and pushed the phone toward his head. "Answer it. Answer it. Answer it!" If there is one thing I can't stand, it's a ringing phone.

"You talk to her!" And with that he pressed "talk" and thrust the phone in my hands, jumping out of the car before I could grab him.

"You pathetic, stinking coward," I hissed. "Come back ... umm ... hi, Sarah?"

"Is that you, Belinda?" she asked, sounding supremely annoyed.

I guess the plain fact is, nobody likes her husband being such close friends with another woman. Much less a former lover. Even though it worked for Russ and me, I knew it had to look a little unnatural to the rest of the world.

Sarah grumbled, "Why isn't Russ, that big chicken, answering his own phone?"

"Huh?" I barely heard what she said. Every ounce of my attention was on Russ as he approached the white BMW. Then to my horror, as if I needed further confirmation of existence of Murphy's Law, I saw someone who looked dangerously like Keilana approaching the parking lot out of Russ's line of vision.

My eyes bugged out of my head. Another woman was with her and they were huddled under a single, large umbrella together. "Oh, fuck me!"

"What?"

"Huh?"

"What is going on, Belinda?" Sarah demanded.

"Russ is sorry he was such an asshole. Gotta go." I pressed a random button on the phone and threw it onto the backseat. Then I climbed into Russ's seat to watch the horror unfold. Russ was crouched down, reading the license plate and Keilana was approaching him from the back. He glanced around, but so much water was pouring off his baseball cap, I doubted he could see more than a few feet.

Keilana was carrying something. A big purse? No, a backpack. Why would she be carrying her backpack away from school? Then I looked closer and realized this wasn't *her* school backpack, which was bright yellow. This one was dark, black or maybe navy blue.

A few more steps and the other woman came into better focus. It was Billie. I groaned as I clumsily climbed over the front seats and fell head first into the back seat. Like an excited puppy going on a car ride, I all but pressed my face to the glass as I watched.

The women stopped walking for a moment and Keilana glanced up at Billie and stroked her cheek with the back of her hand. Furiously, I rubbed the fog from my window so I could get a better look at them. I had no idea what they were saying, but their body language told me all I needed to know. Ugh.

Another gust of wind shook the car, and I watched as a strong gust tore the paper out of Russ's hand, sending it into the gravel a few feet from him. It instantly stuck to the ground and he tried to peel it up with wet, clumsy fingers. "Get out of there, Russ!" I whispered to myself. "Get out!" He kept fiddling with the paper as Keilana and Billie got closer and closer. "Oh no."

He finally gave up on it and started looking inside the car. He tried the door, and I could see him futilely yanking on the handle. It was locked and he was focusing his attention there and not on his surroundings.

"Shit!" Quietly, I snuck out of my car, blinking the rain back when it poured down my face. I stayed low to the ground as I crept between the parked cars. I had to warn Russ or everything would be ruined. The warm rain plastered my hair to my forehead and my clothes stuck uncomfortably to my body after just a few seconds.

I made it to Russ just ahead of Keilana and Billie. "Go. Get out of here!" I whispered as loudly as I dared.

Russ glanced in the direction I was hiding, confused by the disembodied voice. "Who's there?" He looked harder into the shadows. "Belinda?"

I managed to squeeze out, "Run!" a split second before it was too late.

"That's my car," Keilana said to Russ. Her mouth sounded cottony dry and she and Billie stopped well back from him as Keilana appraised Russ warily.

Like night and day, there stood Billie. Her entire body vibrated. Coiled, she was more than ready for a confrontation. Simply put, she looked like a hellcat with PMS. I had been too far away to see it before, but she was also sporting a white bandage on one cheek.

"Can I help you?" Keilana's voice quivered a little as she spoke, betraying her unease.

"Hi," Russ smiled and tried to stick his hands in his pocket, but his wet jeans had sucked themselves to his body and wouldn't cooperate. He ended up awkwardly hooking his thumbs in his belt loops and rocking back on his heels. "I don't need any help. But thanks. My … uh … best friend had his BMW stolen last week. We've been looking for it and I thought this might be it." He shrugged. "Guess I was wrong."

I nodded approvingly. A decent cover story.

Russ waggled his fingers at the women. He took a step forward. "Okay, I'll just be going now."

"You were trying to steal her car!" Billie accused, taking a menacing step forward. "You son of a bitch! I saw you looking inside the car and checking the doors. You were going to take it!"

"Billie," Keilana said worriedly, "for God's sake, he was leaving." She spoke through clenched teeth. "Let him go." She tried to restrain Billie without getting too close to Russ herself.

Good girl, I thought. She was smart to be cautious.

"You're mistaken," Russ said calmly. "I was just looking and since it's obviously not my friend's car, I'll be on my way." Once again, he started to walk away.

"Stay right here!" Billie ordered, blocking his path and holding her umbrella out like a sword.

Keilana shivered as the rain suddenly began pelting her.

Billie shook the umbrella at Russ. "I'm calling the cops." She pulled her cell phone from her pocket, and then cursed a blue streak when she discovered the battery was dead. In a fit of anger, she threw the phone to the ground, sending shards of plastic into a nearby puddle and against the BMW's bumper.

Even in the wan light, I could see the whites of Keilana's eyes grow. "Jesus, Billie. Calm down," she said. "The guy told us why he was checking out my car. What are you doing?" She put a calming hand on Billie's shoulder. "Let him leave."

Billie's face twisted in rage. "No way." Her eyes drilled holes in Russ as rivulets of water dripped from her chin and cheeks. Her bandage was soaked now and dark with what I guessed was rehydrating blood. "I'm sick of you bastards making it impossible to park here. I can't stand it!"

Then something inside Billie seemed to snap and she swung her umbrella at Russ over and over, connecting with a few powerful swipes. "You thieving asshole!" Another hit. "You think you can do anything you want?" Smack on the shoulder. "You think you can treat women this way?"

I winced as a particularly vicious blow landed on the top of his head. This really wasn't Russ's day.

"Billie!" Keilana screamed and tried to pull her friend off Russ, who was covering his head with his arms and hands and yelling for Billie to stop.

My hands balled into fists and released. My heart thudding loudly, I pressed my back against the quarter panel of an old Chevy truck, torn. I wanted to help Russ, but that would shoot my cover to hell. Still, he was my best friend. Crap, I whispered internally. I drew in a deep breath to stand and make my presence known when Billie tossed her umbrella aside, reached inside her purse, and pulled out a small pistol.

She pointed it right at Russ.

I swear to God I almost had a heart attack. I actually felt my chest seize up. Time stood still and for a fraction of a minute, everyone just stared at each other in shock and horror.

Billie seemed to be just as surprised as everyone else.

I glanced out at the street and although I could see people walking by, I realized that the streetlights were too far away for us to be visible to them.

"Holy shit!" Russ exclaimed, snapping out of his trance. "You're cr-cr-crazy!"

"Don't even think about going anywhere," Billie panted, waving the gun erratically. "Don't even think it!"

Russ, for once in his life, obeyed without comment. He held his hands up as though he was being robbed.

"Okay," Billie handed the gun to a stunned Keilana. "I'm going to that club"—she jerked her head sideways—"to call the cops. You watch him." She sneered in Russ's direction. "Shoot him if he tries to move, all right?"

Fuck. Fuck. Fuck! Why did Billie have to get Keilana more involved in this than she already was? But I felt a tiny measure of relief in the belief that Russ would be safer with Keilana holding the gun than Billie.

Still, Russ had to be peeing in his pants because I was fighting the urge myself.

"Okay," Keilana said evenly, her voice eerily calm. "I'll watch him."

A shiver chased its way down my spine and I wondered if I'd made a colossal miscalculation about Russ's chances with Keilana.

"You go call the police," she continued, coolly. "I think there is a pay phone in the very back by the ladies' room."

Billie flipped Russ the bird and took off toward the dance club.

I looked skyward in appeal. Please don't let her shoot me or Russ. Once again I was about to stand when Keilana's shoulders sagged dramatically and she moaned.

I froze.

She was soaked to the bone and she shuddered a little, even though the rain was warm. "I can't believe this night. I'm *so* sorry," she promised Russ. "My friend has had a horrible time of it. Some guy pawed her and hurt her pretty badly. I think she's in shock. She's not normally like this."

I don't know if Russ even heard what Keilana was saying. His eyes were trained on the gun in her hands. Keilana saw where he was looking and promptly turned the gun on herself, holding it by the barrel and pointing it at her own chest.

My eyes turned to saucers and for the second time tonight my heart felt like it was going to implode. Was she insane? What was she doing carrying a loaded gun like that?

Keilana smiled reassuringly. "Don't be afraid. It's not a real gun. It's just a very convincing toy. Billie keeps it to scare off the jerks, but she'd never really hurt anyone. See?" She pulled the trigger and both Russ and I both jerked at the movement and muted click.

But there was no gunshot and Keilana was still standing there.

I was so lightheaded with relief that I had to sit back on my heels and breathe deeply to keep from keeling over. For what had to be a full minute, stars danced in front of my eyes, tiny pinpoints of light on a sea of black velvet.

Salt stung my tongue and lips as the rain washed the sweat from my face.

But Russ still looked suspicious of Keilana. God, what more did he want her to do?

Keilana took a step closer to him, approaching him slowly, the way you would a skittish colt ... or someone your friend just beat with an umbrella and then threatened to shoot. "Are you okay?"

Her voice was soothing and warm and I could see Russ's body relax as he unconsciously responded to it. "She didn't hurt you with her umbrella, did she? God, I'm sorry. If she hurt you I can call a doctor or take you to the emergency room. Or—"

"No," Russ interrupted, lowering hands that were still shaking. I think he was finally gathering his wits and, to his credit, he didn't look like he was going to have a stroke anymore.

I was going to be buying him hamburgers for the next hundred years and he wasn't even going to have to ask.

"She scared about ten"—he chuckled somewhat frantically—"no, make that twenty years off my life, but I think I'm okay." He let out a ragged breath and nodded a few times, as if reassuring himself that what he'd just said was true.

"Thank goodness." Keilana's relief was just as evident. "You'd better get going then. I don't care if you *were* trying to steal my car, you've been through enough tonight."

"But I wasn't—"

Keilana shook her head. "It doesn't matter." She made a shooing motion. "Go before she gets back. And again, I'm really, really sorry." She stepped aside giving Russ a wide berth.

He didn't hesitate; he bolted out of the parking lot faster than I've ever seen him move, and in seconds, the street swallowed him up.

Keilana watched him go, then leaned against the trunk of her car and let her backpack drop gently to the ground. I knew I should be more curious about what was inside it. It was out of place here in The Devil's Belly, and in a case that sorely lacked clues, it was calling to me ... loudly. But even so, all I could really think about was her.

She lifted her face skyward and let the rain pound against it and after a moment she smoothed her long, dark hair back from her face. Her eyes were closed tight, her mouth open, and her throat working as she slowly drank in the water.

The sight was surprisingly erotic and I watched her for a long moment, holding my breath, my heart pounding the entire time.

She scrubbed her face with both hands and I wasn't sure whether she was washing away tears, nervous sweat, or just the incredible stress of the moment. But it seemed to work because it wasn't long before she repositioned herself into a slightly more relaxed stance.

The flashing neon lights made her normally pale skin glow an almost iridescent white, and for the first time tonight the frenzied strains of hard rock music coming from one of the clubs eased its way into my consciousness. Keilana looked almost otherworldly and I felt myself being drawn closer to her as if by magic. If I reached out, I could almost ... almost touch her.

With a soft sigh, she focused on the toy gun in her hands, flipping it over a few times as if deciding what to do. I was a little surprised when she dropped it to the ground and gave it a good stomp.

I heard the plastic crack just before Keilana kicked the gun and sent it sliding over the gravel and under a nearby van. I guess she was already too wet to bother coming in out of the rain or picking up the umbrella, so she just sat there on the trunk of her car, her arms wrapped around herself in mute comfort as she waited.

Billie was going to be livid, but I couldn't bring myself to care.

With every fiber of my being I longed to pull Keilana into a fierce embrace. I'd never felt anything as strong in my life and I honestly wasn't sure that I could clamp down on my desire to wrap her in my arms. I was so proud of how she'd handled things and how she'd been kind to Russ, even when she figured him for a thief.

I wanted to press my lips to her wet hair and murmur the sort of things you hear in mushy love songs that make you want to roll your eyes and burst out laughing. I craved the feeling of her warm body against mine and longed to gently stroke her back.

Now that I thought of it, selling my soul seemed like more than a fair price if that's what it took to make her smile again.

And in that instant I knew. Shaken, I plopped down onto the gravel, not even feeling the water I was sitting in. I didn't have a crush on Keilana Poppenhouse. Oh, man, it was so much worse than that.

I was falling in love with her.

Oh, boy.

When I'm right, I'm right. Billie was pissed when she got back to the car. It seems the police had declined her demand to come arrest someone for looking at Keilana's car, and now, not only had Keilana let the would-be thief escape, but she'd somehow lost Billie's fake gun in the process. Poor Billie.

The women argued vehemently for a few minutes, then, much to my disgust, the fuss ended with Billie bursting into tears and Keilana comforting her with a compassionate hug that went on far too long.

Sometime during the evil embrace, I retreated to the safety of my Mustang, determined not to lose them or the black backpack that Keilana had put into her trunk before leaving. Russ, I told myself, would want me to stick with the case no matter what. And more importantly, I wanted some answers and I was tired of waiting to get them.

I actually had to work hard to keep up with Keilana as she and Billie raced down the wet city streets. My mood had turned brighter and even the rain had shifted from a series of fitful downpours to a gentle sprinkle. Everyone I cared about was okay and even though I couldn't have gotten wetter if I jumped into a swimming pool, the chase was on again.

For the moment, life was good.

I was about three cars behind Keilana at a traffic light and had just taken a big bite of my wilted cheeseburger when Russ's cell phone rang. I decided it was fate that I wouldn't get any dinner tonight and I tossed my burger onto the passenger seat. It took some wrangling, but I was able to grab the phone from the back seat before traffic began moving again.

I pressed it to my ear, not needing to look to know who was calling. "Hello, Russ, you unlucky bastard."

"That bitch was crazy!"

"I can't disagree with that." I merged on the 5.

"Did you see what she did?"

"I was only about five feet away from the whole thing, Russ. Of course I saw it." I felt a pang of worry. "Are you okay?"

"Yeah, I'm fine," he said dismissively. "Did you see the backpack?"

I chuckled. "You're like a dog who's been teased with a whiff of a juicy bone."

"And just what are you doing at this very moment?"

I smiled. "Chasing the bone."

"Atta girl. Let me know what you find. I mean it. Don't make me wait too long."

"Will do, Russ. Take a cab back to my place and I'll pay you back for the fare, okay?"

"Don't lose them."

My smile turned feral. "Never."

About fifteen more minutes and Keilana and Billie pulled into the driveway of a surprisingly nice, if tiny, bungalow. Billie's house? I slowly drove past them, then killed my headlights and parked on the street a few houses away.

"Nooo!" I moaned. Keilana was digging in her trunk. "Not the backpack."

More digging.

"Not the backpack."

Keilana shut her truck and she and Billie headed toward the house.

"Oooooh." I sighed. "There goes the backpack." Well, at least I wouldn't be rooting around our campus cottage for it or picking the lock of Keilana's BMW. I'd be breaking into that red-haired bitch's house, instead.

The more I thought about that ... the more I liked it.

I decided not to bother stewing outside of Billie's house, in the pathetic hope that Keilana wouldn't decide to stay the night. So I drove back to campus, deep in thought. So much had happened so quickly that my head was still spinning.

It was well after two a.m. by the time I heard Keilana's key slide into the cottage door.

I looked up from the television program I'd been half-watching and tried to pretend not to be relieved to see her. "Hi." She wasn't, of course, carrying the backpack. I couldn't be that lucky.

She smiled weakly at me. "Hi." Then she glanced up at the clock and frowned. "You weren't waiting up for me, were you?" She tossed her keys on a small table near the door. "Didn't you get my note?"

"I got it. I wasn't waiting up for you. I was just watching ... um ..."—I glanced at the TV to see what was on and could only sigh—"an infomercial on Viagra for women." Fuck.

She shook her head and laughed softly. She walked into the bedroom, but continued talking, the words floating over the half wall that separated the two rooms. "What did you do tonight?"

I saw her blouse hit the floor and turned my head. Temptation, thy name is Keilana. "Not much. I met a friend and we drove around San Diego. You?"

There was a long pause.

"You remember my friend Billie?" she finally asked in a quiet voice.

My eyes turned to slits. "Yeah. I remember her."

"We spent the evening together."

"Are you sleeping with her?" I wanted to slap my hand over my mouth. Why, oh why, had I said that out loud?

Keilana poked her head into the living room and looked at me with wide eyes. "What?"

"Uhh ..." It was too late to suck the words back in now. Relentlessly, I picked the sofa, focusing on one teeny spot. "Is she, you know"—I glanced up, sure I looked as foolish as I felt—"your girlfriend?"

Keilana disappeared behind the wall again only to re-emerge a few seconds later wearing an oversized t-shirt and soft cotton boxers that were at least two sizes too big. Why did she always have to look so adorable?

She gave me a look I couldn't decipher. "I'm surprised you asked about Billie. You've made it clear that there can never be anything between you and me." She shrugged one shoulder. "Well, other than friendship." Then she cocked her head to the side like an interested puppy. "Have you changed your mind about that?" There was a hopeful lilt to her voice that tempted me like few things in my life had. God was cruel.

"I ... no." It felt like someone was sitting on my chest. "Keilana, we can't ..." Christ, I wanted to die.

She let out a deep breath and joined me on the sofa, but didn't sit too close. "What does that mean? We can't?"

I turned to her and prayed that my heart wasn't showing in every line of my face. "I think you know what it means."

She gave me a small, slightly guilty smile. "You can't blame me for trying."

I began to fidget. I had to change the subject or I was going to lean over and kiss her senseless. "Billie seemed interested in you. I, well, I just wondered if the feeling was mutual?"

She rested her head on the back of the sofa and closed her eyes. "I don't think that's any of your business. In fact, you know, Cadie, I don't think this is how friendship is supposed to go."

I blinked. "Whaddya mean?"

Keilana frowned, but kept her eyes closed. "You're always asking about me, but never telling me about you. Granted, I'm not used to the interest because most people hate me, but—"

"They do not!"

She merely raised an eyebrow at me. "Most people might hate me," she continued blithely, "but I'm pretty sure that real friends know stuff about each other."

"You know"—I waved my hands in the air—"stuff about me." Scintillating comebacks under pressure are my specialty.

"Nothing that matters," she disagreed pointedly.

She was right. God, I hated it when she was right. "Fine, you can ask me something about myself and then it's my turn. Deal?"

She made a sour face. "Just one question?"

There was a hint of challenge in her voice and I found myself unable to resist the bait. "How about three?"

One of her dark eyebrows edged upward again and it was all I could do not to reach out and run my fingertip over it. She hummed a little to herself. "Hmm ... And I can ask anything?"

I swallowed, a million things I did *not* want her to ask me running through my mind. "Anything."

"In that case I need a minute to think."

I rolled my eyes.

She turned sideways and tucked her feet underneath her. Then she proceeded to take her time about deciding what to say.

My nerves ratcheted up with every passing second, and yet I was surprised to find myself eager to share something about the real me. Even if it was only something small, a tiny bit of reality to assuage my guilt so that I could look her in the eye tomorrow—I sighed inwardly—just before I would work on another snitch report to her parents.

"Okay, is the reason you won't kiss me because you're interested in someone else?"

Whoa. That's not what I expected her to ask. "I ... no. There's no one else. There hasn't been anyone serious in my life for several years now."

"Wow. Years?" she mouthed silently, looking concerned.

Oops. I forgot that I was supposed to be twenty-one years old. I hadn't lived long enough to have too much emotional baggage. I smiled wryly. "Well, maybe it just seems like years. I work too much. Or at least I did before this fall. And I'm alone too much. I surf too much." God, I was starting to depress myself! "And none of those things are very conducive to finding someone special."

Her eyes narrowed suspiciously but she didn't say anything.

I licked my lips. "My turn yet?"

She gave me a reluctant nod. "Umm ... I guess."

"Good." I clapped my hands together, not bothering to hide my excitement. I had *carte blanche*, a nosy person's dream. But that didn't mean I could jump right in with both feet. No, I still had to be careful. If I aroused too much suspicion now, I would just be shooting myself in the foot for later. I nearly asked about Billie, but I decided to try to throw her off guard with another topic completely. "Why does Shauna hate you so much?"

Keilana didn't even hesitate. "Because sophomore year I had an affair with her roommate, who also happens to be her twin sister, and everyone found out about it."

I winced as I thought of this tiny school with all its gossipy cliques. "Oh, man. That sucks." No wonder she was a leper to Shauna and her friends. She'd violated a cardinal rule among the popular girls. She'd done something that showed plainly she wasn't a clone of the other girls. Well, that and eaten pussy.

Tiredly, she rubbed her eyes. "It was the one time I didn't look before I leapt and I've been paying for it ever since. I thought ..." Her jaw worked for a few seconds, but no sound came out. "I was stupid. I thought things would be different on the mainland. And they were. But just not different enough. Everyone has an agenda."

My heart sank.

"And after a while I stopped trying to convince people that I wasn't some sort of deviant predator and just let them think what they want about me."

"Predator?" That seemed a bit harsh. "You're no predator. I've been here for weeks now and I'm still the virgin I was when I got here."

She snorted softly and her mouth shaped a weak grin.

I scooted a little closer and bumped my arm against hers. "So Shauna blames you for her sister's wicked walk on the lesbian wild side, huh?"

"Of course." She mimicked Shauna's voice perfectly. "There aren't any dykes in the very distinguished Brewster family."

I couldn't help but snicker.

In her normal voice she grumbled, "I am a seducer of innocent women, after all. And to hear Shauna tell it, not even the nuns are safe around me."

I wasn't sure that if Keilana *really* turned on the sex appeal that *anyone* would be safe. I know I wasn't. The hard part to believe, though, was that she didn't seem to have a sense of how compelling she could be and how much power that gave her. At first I thought her apparent naiveté in this area was some sort of trick. But it wasn't. It was just Keilana.

"It was Shauna's sister, Misty, who seduced me, not the other way around." Her face took on a look that was a combination of anger, hurt, and embarrassment. "And it wasn't even me she was interested in. She wanted a job at the Poppenhouse Cookie headquarters in Honolulu and thought that she could convince me to sweet-talk Daddy into giving her a one-way ticket to her paradise."

My eyebrows rose further. "That's really lousy, Keilana. I'm sorry."

She forced a shrug and looked away. "I lived."

"You sure did. But that doesn't mean it didn't hurt."

She glanced back at me, her eyes holding no secrets and alive with panic. My stomach did a back flip. She needed comfort. She needed a real friend to lean on and tell her that everyone didn't use everyone else, someone she could count on no matter what.

In short, I was the absolute last thing she needed.

"So ..." I lightened my voice and did my best not to give in to my sudden urge to cry. "Did Shauna's sister get her ticket?"

She looked a little surprised by my question but she began to relax. After thirty seconds or so, the corner of her mouth quirked. "Oh, yeah, she got her ticket punched." Her smile broadened. "And so did I."

Our eyes met and we both dissolved into unexpected laughter over Keilana's suggestive tone. While she didn't seem to really be upset, there was just the barest hint of poorly-veiled hurt in her smile.

"Well," she said, sighing, suddenly aware at how closely I was watching her. "You sure picked weird questions." An evil twinkle invaded her eyes. "I still have two questions left, but I'm going to save them for when I'm not beat." She yawned.

My eyes saucered and my butt began to levitate off the couch. "That wasn't three questions! That was ..." Then I mentally replayed our conversation and wished I could kick my own ass. "You tricked me, *Newman.*"

Her brows contracted. "Why do you call me that sometimes?"

I covered my face with my hands, and cursed at how easily I'd gotten caught up in our conversation.

"And how did I trick you?" she asked in a voice so reasonable that I wanted to scream. She was teasing me and I knew it.

I glanced up and couldn't help it, I did something I hadn't done since I was six years old. I actually began to pout.

She smiled warmly and reached out very slowly to cup my cheek. I could have moved away. She made sure to give me plenty of time to escape. But I didn't. I wanted her touch as much as I'd wanted anything in my life and I bit back a gasp at the unexpected warmth of long fingers. It was the first time she'd touched me since my ill-fated French lesson that had left me hungry for her for days. My belly twisted all over again with the familiar craving.

"Thanks for making me laugh, Cadie." Her voice was as rich and sweet as honey and I felt it seep into my bones as she spoke. She stroked my check with her thumb. "Up until a few minutes ago, tonight had really sucked."

My tongue refused to work and all I could do was smile back.

She gave my cheek a final pat. "I'm going to take a quick shower to get the smoke out of my hair. I ..." Her eyes dropped to the small space between us. "It ..." She scrunched up her face, smiling just a little. "This is sort of hard. Okay, I just wanted to say that it felt good to tell someone about Misty. I never have." She glanced up, suddenly shy. "Thanks."

And then she was gone.

I sat there staring at the closed bathroom door, wondering how things had gotten away from me so easily. I nearly tripped over the ottoman as I ran to the bathroom. I banged loudly on the bathroom door, hearing a startled, disembodied, "Yeah?"

"Will you go to the beach and hang out with me tomorrow? I want to show you something that's really important to me. Please." I held my breath as I waited for her to shoot me down.

Finally, I heard what I was sure was a sigh. "Just the two of us?"

I exhaled, beaming a smile at the door. "Yeah, just us."

"Promise you won't laugh at me?"

Laugh at her? Who would be that rude? "Hell no. I'll take the first opportunity I can to laugh at you."

Playfully, Keilina growled through the bathroom door. "I knew you were going to say that." She opened the door and stuck her head out just far enough that I could see smooth skin, naked shoulders and endless back. I bit back a whimper.

She looked at me with eyes so beautiful and trusting that they broke my heart. "When do we leave?"

I jammed the end of my board into the sand and laughed as Keilana tried unsuccessfully to do the same thing with my spare board. "Here," I took the board from her and rammed it into the ground.

She frowned.

"Don't worry," I said with a smile. "It's not as easy as it looks."

We couldn't very well go to my usual haunt, Black's Beach. I didn't want someone to call me Belinda in front of Keilana. So we headed to Del Mar. The surfing wasn't as good here, but surfing was a lot like sex. Even when it was bad, it was still better than just about anything else you could do. Besides, this area held a special place in my heart and as silly as it sounded, I wanted to bring Keilana.

We walked a little north of the public beach and found a fairly secluded spot below the low, rocky cliffs at our back.

Keilana tilted her face skyward and spread her arms out wide. "It's still nighttime! What are we doing here at night?"

I blinked. "You haven't been to the beach at sunrise?" How did someone get to be twenty-one-years old and never once experience one of the most beautiful sights on the planet?

"There is no sun yet. And"—she shook her head—"well, our main house wasn't right on the water, just the guest quarters."

Oh, that made this even better. A puppy with two peters couldn't have been happier than I was at this moment. "This is the best time to be here!"

She gave me a skeptical look, her eyes a deep shade of violet in the gray, pre-dawn light.

I nudged her gently with my shoulder. "It's magic. You'll see."

Keilana looked around before spreading out a large beach blanket. I bent to help her, sneaking glances at her as we worked. She looked cute in her linen shorts and neatly pressed shirt and I couldn't help but look forward to seeing her in the swimsuit I knew she wore underneath. I was already in my shortie wetsuit and a thin black rash guard. We kicked off our shoes and sat down on the blanket.

It was going to be hot today and a balmy breeze tossed my hair around my face as I threw my feet off the edge of the blanket and dug my heels into the cool sand. The wet, lush smell of the water and vegetation was overwhelming and the salt from the spray stung the back of my tongue. Heaven.

Keilana leaned back on her hands. "Is it always this quiet here?" Only the sound of the surf punctuated her words. We couldn't see or hear another living soul. "Are you sure we're still in Southern California?"

"Ahh ... I'm sure. No screaming kids. No obnoxious punk teenagers. Why do you think I come so early?" I wrinkled my nose. "Later in the day it won't be like this."

She gave me a wry smile. "You, Cadie Blaisdell, are no more a people person than I am."

I gasped in mock horror, clutching my chest. "I'm not *that* terrible, am I?"

"Ha. Ha." She slapped my arm. "You're not at all shy and you have confidence to burn. So why do you look like you're going to throw up whenever any professor addresses you in class?"

I cringed. "There's a completely logical reason for that look."

"There is?"

"Of course. But it will cost you the second of your three questions to get the answer, *Newman*."

She bit her bottom lip. "You're still sore about that, huh?"

I merely smiled sweetly, holding her gaze.

She thought for a second. "No deal. I want to know something better than that."

I sighed. Except for *Clue*, which I still love to play, I've always sucked at games. This was no exception. Keilana, however, seemed to be the type that somehow managed to own Park Place and Boardwalk after only three turns, sending everyone else into the flames of pretend financial ruin.

Suddenly the shadows of Keilana's face looked just a little lighter. A hint of pink and yellow began to invade the atmosphere and I pressed the button to the light on my watch, then looked up at the brightening sky. A big grin split my face. "Okay, pay attention now."

Her eyebrows disappeared behind windblown bangs. "To what?"

"To everything." Just as I said the words, splashes of golden light shot across the water, illuminating the sea and its rolling waves in a divine glow, and the mist from dancing surf began to glitter like millions of radiant crystals infused with light.

"Wow," she breathed reverently, her eyes round. "It's beautiful."

I nodded, my focus trained on a world that was coming to life before my eyes. A sense of utter peace invaded me and I felt more centered than I had in weeks. "My dad used to take me to the beach every Saturday when I was a kid. It was our special time together. He was the one who taught me to surf."

"I ..." Keilana's face took on a faraway expression. "I have no idea what that must have felt like. I'll bet that was nice though."

I swallowed thickly, hurting for everything she'd clearly missed growing up and feeling my simmering anger toward her parents begin to bubble over. My hands shaped weak fists and I had to force myself to speak in a normal tone of voice. "It was nice. My dad worked all the time, but Saturday mornings were ours and it always made me feel special."

I vowed on the spot to phone my folks on Sunday. We hadn't spoken in well over a month and there was no reason for it other than we were all too caught up in our own lives to bother picking up the phone. As much as I hated to admit it, complacency was a two-way street.

More light poured down on the water, transforming it from an inky black, to a steel gray and finally a deep sapphire. In the distance, a small flock of birds came into view and they began swooping down to the sea in search of breakfast.

This time and place was important to me, and I wanted Keilana to understand that. It didn't matter that at any moment I would disappear from her life. What mattered was now ... this very second. "You know, for about five minutes every time I see the sun rise over the water, I'm certain there is a God. It just doesn't seem right that something so breathtaking could be an accident." I stretched out on the blanket, feeling the coolness of the sand soak through into my back. "The rest of the time, I'm not so sure." How's that for knowing something personal, Keilana? That's the real me.

She turned her head and flashed me a blinding smile. "Thanks for showing me this. You were right. It does seem sort of magic."

"I knew you'd think so too." I let out a satisfied breath and crossed my legs at the ankle. I looked up and lost myself in the endless sky. It wasn't nearly as blue as her eyes. It should be jealous. I turned my head. "This isn't all I want to show you."

She suddenly looked a little nervous. "It's not?"

I was too excited to sit still any longer "Nope." I jumped to my feet and offered her a hand up. "Let's paddle out and watch the sun coming up from the other direction. We can ride the surf in. You'll love it!"

She gulped so loud it had to be painful, but she reached for my extended hand.

I gripped her hand firmly. "It's easy," I promised, trying to erase the look on her face that had gone from nervous to outright fear in a blink of an eye. "You don't need to stand up on the board or anything. Just float and paddle. I'll show you how."

Stricken, she glanced back at the water, then at me.

Confused, I gentled my voice. "What is it?"

She kicked petulantly at the sand. "You'll laugh."

"Keilana"—I looked her dead in the eyes—"I won't." But she still didn't want to give it up. I squeezed her hand briefly before letting it go. Then I put my hands on my hips. "Okay, I'll start guessing if that's how you want it. You're allergic to salt water?"

No answer.

"No, huh? Okay, afraid of killer seals or floating debris from a passing cruise ship?"

A tiny smile appeared. "No. Not really."

"Worried about stepping on a fish hook?" I gestured toward the duffle bag I'd brought. "I have an extra pair of water shoes you can borrow."

She groaned a little, her hands twitching nervously. "It's not that simple, Cadie."

"Then what? Seaweed? Fish? Sharks?"

Her eyes popped wide open. "There are sharks here?" she screeched, scrambling back to the very edge of the blanket. Her head began moving like a bobblehead Jesus glued to the dashboard of a fast moving car. "Where? Where?"

I bit the inside of my cheek to keep from laughing. "They can't get you on land, you know."

She sensed my struggle not to chuckle and she stuck her tongue out at me in response. "It's not sharks. Though if we see any, I am leaving and you won't be able to stop me."

I nodded. "Don't worry, if we bump into any sharks, I'll be swimming so fast for shore all you'll see is my wake. So what's the problem?"

"*That's* the problem." She lowered her voice as if someone might hear her horrible confession. "You'll be swimming. I won't. I can't swim."

I just stared.

She pointed an accusing finger at me, her face turning pink with shame. "You said you wouldn't laugh!"

"I-I-I-" I love it when I sputter like a stalled engine. "Who's laughing?"

She let her hand drop and grumbled, "You can if you want."

I sat back down on the blanket. There would be no surfing today, but suddenly I didn't mind that so much. "Okay," I began slowly. "So we have to change our plans. That's no big deal. Lots of people can't swim." I didn't know any of them, of course. But I'm sure they're out there ... in Alaska or North Dakota or someplace.

"I'm sorry I didn't tell you sooner." She turned dismayed eyes out to the water. "We wouldn't have had to drive all the way here. But you wanted to come and I wanted to come with you and ... Well, it's just embarrassing and—"

"Whoa." I held up my hand to stop her rambling. "We're not leaving."

Her head snapped back and her jaw sagged a little. "We're not?"

"Of course not. I can teach you how to swim," I said gamely, only barely resisting the urge to tuck a strand of gently blowing hair behind Keilana's ear. The desire to touch her was getting stronger and stronger and I was growing less and less inclined to fight it. "It's easy. I was swimming before I was walking. If a little baby can do it, how hard could it be?"

She closed her eyes briefly, warring with herself.

I waited, wanting to push her but knowing it could damage our fragile relationship if I did.

"Fine," she finally said, her voice an octave higher than normal. She wasn't kidding. She was terrified.

Guilt assailed me. "Keilana—"

"I'm okay, really." She stripped off her shirt and shorts in record time and stood before me in just her bikini. Her string bikini. She pointed toward my bag. "Can I really borrow those shoes? I think my feet are bigger than yours."

My eyes drank her in and my mouth went bone dry.

She was wearing a sexy little belly button ring that I'd never seen before and the sight of it sent a skitter of unexpected excitement down my spine. Keilana didn't resemble your average Southern California Barbie Doll, which was more than fine by me. For one thing, her breasts were the perfect size, lovely and very real. And then there were her legs. They went on for days. Months maybe.

My heart beat a little faster as I took in her fair skin; it glowed in the morning light, looking as soft and inviting as warm silk. A scattering of a few freckles dotted her upper chest and torso and formed a random pattern down her long lean waist. She took my breath away.

God, I hadn't ever had it this bad!

Keilana glanced down at herself and crossed her arms in front of her. "Something wrong?"

"Hardly." I didn't bother to hide my appreciation as I pointed at her navel. Then I wriggled my eyebrows. "Is that new?"

She moaned a little and nodded. "It was Billie's idea and I wanted to cheer her up so I let her talk me into it. It hurts like a bitch!"

I laid a hand over my own bellybutton in empathy. "Well, *it* looks good." I grinned. "But *you* look great." More than great, actually. Please don't let that moisture on the corner of my mouth be drool.

"I've ... um ... put on a few pounds in the past couple of weeks." She laid a hand on her flat stomach, careful to avoid her navel, and smiled tentatively. “I think it’s helped.”

Dismayed, I moved closer to her. There wasn’t a lot I could do for Keilana, but I could do this one small thing. I needed to. She knew that other people found her attractive, but somehow she didn’t seem to believe it was true deep down inside. “Keilana, I didn’t say that because of a few pounds or a little piece of jewelry. *You’re* beautiful. Don’t let some crazy idea your father has make you think differently.”

“You’re right.” Her smile grew and I was delighted when she squared her shoulders, lifted her chin and said, “Thank you, Cadie. That means ...” She shook her head a little. “Just thanks.”

I did a little happy dance inside, feeling a joy all out of proportion with what I’d done. “You’re welcome.”

Our eyes met and held and the chemistry we shared flared to life, nearly blinding me. My belly tightened and I tried to think of something other than kissing her. Anything.

I glanced out at the ocean. “Now, how about learning something new? I won’t let you drown. You’ll be amazed at how simple it is. C’mon,” I coaxed gently, seeing her reluctance return with a vengeance.

She gave me a direct look and said, “I’m afraid to put my face in the water or go in any deeper than my knees.”

I unzipped my wetsuit. Okay, so teaching her to swim wouldn’t be simple. But since when did that stop me?

It took several hours and a dozen aborted attempts, but eventually, we were both standing in chest-deep water. The waves pushed us around a bit, but Keilana was doing her best to keep her footing and not let her fear get the better of her.

Her dark hair was slicked back, wet from several tumbles in the surf. She had some sand on her cheek and water droplets glistened on her chest and chin. “This isn’t s-so bad,” she stuttered.

I wasn't sure if the statement was meant to convince me or herself.

"You're doing great," I praised, really meaning it. Fear wasn't an easy thing to conquer and Keilana was doing her best to hold her own, despite flashes where it looked as though she might bolt at any minute.

My eyes roamed over her affectionately and I wondered when I'd turned into such a ball of useless mush. I hadn't thought of the case all day. Instead, I'd just enjoyed playing and laughing with this complex, interesting person who was standing in front of me and counting on me to keep her safe.

Keilana's shoulders were starting to turn pink and I gave in to the irresistible impulse to reach out and graze the soft skin with the tips of my fingers. "You need some more sunblock. Are you chilly?"

She shook her head. "I was earlier, but the sun is really hot now."

"The water feels great, doesn't it?" I was wearing just my rash guard and some swimsuit bottoms. I loved the feeling of the water against my skin.

She scraped her tongue against the roof of her mouth, making a face. "But it doesn't taste so hot."

"You're not supposed to drink it," I said wryly.

"I can't help it. I—Whoa!" A big wave shoved us violently toward shore. Keilana screamed and wrapped her arms around my neck as we surged forward.

"Put your feet down. You need to let me go!" I yelled, trying to pry her hands from me, knowing what was coming next. But she was too frightened to do more than grasp me in an iron grip far more powerful than anyone would have guessed she could muster. I coughed, stupidly swallowing a mouthful of salty water myself as I tried to dig my heels in sand. But it was no use. I was off balance and when the tide moved back out, the surge of water swept us both off our feet yanking us backward into water well over our heads.

Keilana panicked, her arms and legs flailing as she wrapped herself around me. "Cadie!" she half-screamed, half-sputtered, in a high-pitched voice that sent a rush of adrenaline tearing through me. Before I could react, we both were dragged beneath the water and it took every ounce of my will power not to panic myself and violently force Keilana off of me. I'd been in this situation dozens of times myself, but I'd never had anything but the ocean itself pulling me down.

I circled my arms around Keilana and squeezed hard, quelling some of her desperate flailing, then pushed off the bottom, sending both our heads blasting out of the surf. I opened my eyes to the bright blue sky and we both sucked in deep breaths of air. She began coughing and wildly thrashing as she fought to keep from going under.

"Stop." I pushed her slightly away from me. "Stop!" I shouted at the top of my lungs, and for a split second she froze. I grasped onto her arms and kicked only a few feet toward shore. "It's okay." I let out a shaky breath. "We can stand here, put your feet down."

She coughed a few more times and spat out what had to be a full mouth of seawater. Her face and neck were flushed, then she noticed that we were only a few paces from where we'd been playing all morning. Her cheeks grew even redder. "I'm sorry," she said softly.

"S'okay." I searched out her eyes when she dropped her gaze from mine. "I should have taught you what to do if that happens right off. That's my fault, not yours." And it really was. I'd been too busy having fun to notice that the waves had gotten progressively rougher. "Let's head back to our blanket and just relax for a while."

Her feet seemed to be rooted in the sand and the face that had been pink only a few seconds ago, now looked a little pale. Her fear was hitting home.

I felt horrible. "Are you okay?"

She licked her lips and nodded, doing her best to smile though her chin was trembling. "I'm okay."

I stepped forward and laid my palms on the sides of her face, stroking her cheekbones with my thumbs and glancing up into her eyes. They were vivid, tinged with anxiety and something else.

Neither one of us said anything, but everything about Keilana communicated volumes. I could see her pulse began to pound through the pale skin of her neck and knew her thoughts mirrored mine.

She trailed the backs of her fingers up my throat and over my chin, finally tangling them in my hair as she tugged me closer. "Cadie," she whispered breathily.

My gaze dropped to her lips, full and inviting, and I couldn't stop myself. I didn't want to stop myself. I leaned forward and kissed her, letting my mouth linger and losing myself in the utter sweetness of the moment.

Her hand tightened in my hair and she let out a moan that set my senses ablaze. I deepened the kiss, swirling my tongue around hers, tasting her, and feeling my nipples grow painfully, deliciously hard. We moved forward until our bodies were sliding tightly together all along their lengths. Heat exploded within me and chased away the chill of the water. Her skin was as soft as I'd remembered.

Keilana tenderly traced each of my lips with her tongue, giving the lower lip a gentle suck before kissing me hungrily. It was too much. My control snapped completely, and moaning with abandon, we began to devour each other the way I'd dreamt of doing for weeks.

"Whoo-hoo! Yeah, ladies! Can we play too?"

We were wrenched out of the moment by a couple of young guys carrying boogie boards, their dogs running up and down the beach. The men began to clap and hoot at us and regretfully I pulled away from Keilana. My senses were still reeling as I turned to face the assholes that had spoiled the perfect moment. "Show's over, you pubescent sons of bitches!" I growled, wanting to grab their snickering faces and hold them underwater.

The men hollered and laughed as they moved on up the beach.

They'd broken the spell I was under and the magnitude of what I'd just done crashed over me, more ferocious than any wave I've ever experienced. I'd started something I couldn't finish.

Keilana hadn't moved an inch. She was watching me intently, an utterly open look on her face. I swallowed hard, unable to meet her eyes. Oh, God. "Keil—" I had to swallow again before I could finish her name. "Keilana ..." I dared to glance up. Fuck. Fuck. Fuck! I hoped she could see my honest anguish. "I shouldn't have kissed you."

She blinked slowly, looking as though she wasn't processing what I was saying. "What? *What* did you just say?"

"Jesus, I'm sorry." I reached out for her arm but she jerked it way. "I'm so sorry. We can't. We—"

Her beautiful face had turned to stone before my eyes. "We can't be *that* to each other, right? Am I just some big game to you? Someone whose feelings you can screw around with for fun?"

"No!" I scrubbed my wet hair. "You're not a game. This is real." I closed my eyes and paused before ruthlessly adding, "But—"

"But kissing me was some horrible mistake," she ground out, saying the words before I could and stabbing me in the chest with every single one of them.

Tears welled in her eyes and I couldn't bear it.

Just then another wave pushed her forward a few paces from me and she went with it, practically running back to shore.

"Keilana! Wait!" I called, but I stayed where I was. I didn't trust myself to be close to her right now. I didn't trust myself to keep from spilling the beans about everything and dropping to my knees to beg her forgiveness.

She didn't look back at me as she snatched up her blanket and beach bag. The one with the cars keys in it. She was furious at me and I couldn't blame her.

When she was out of sight, I swam out into the ocean using powerful strokes to take me far from the beach. When I was so far out that the people looked like ants I tilted my head skyward and screamed until my throat was raw. I didn't have a clue about what to do, about what was best for us all, and for the first time I seriously wondered whether I'd be able to complete this job and still keep my sanity.

Loving Keilana was like quicksand. I'd been sucked in before I could stop myself and now I was floundering with no way out.

The best thing I'd ever experienced was killing me.

Chapter Six

Another week went by and in all that time Keilana barely spoke to me. Every bit of the warmth that had blossomed in our relationship had evaporated the moment my lips pressed against hers. Well, not with the kissing itself, which was fantastic, but with my rejection of her afterwards. I knew I'd stung her pride and self-esteem. But Keilana wasn't the only one hurting. I didn't want to eat. I didn't want to go to class. I just wanted to crawl into bed and pull the covers over my head and make the entire world go away.

Somehow I'd managed to fire off two more reports to the Poppenhouses, the last one recommending that they terminate their surveillance of their daughter. Keilana was attending class and she hadn't gone anywhere but Billie's house or the library after school all week.

If she was in a romantic relationship with Billie, I sure as hell wasn't going to be the one to out her to her parents. And, as much as I hated to admit it, if Billie and Keilana were lovers, it didn't seem to be hurting Keilana at the moment. There was no reason, other than the pathetic truth—that I wanted Keilana for myself—to mess up that relationship. Keilana's parents could go to hell if they didn't like it.

A low-level depression had settled over me, but an almost-desperate Russ had convinced me to get off my ass and finish what I'd started. He reminded me that Keilana might still need me. And while I doubted that was really true, I wasn't willing to let her down again.

I'd given up even trying to participate in class, and that had left me plenty of time to do some real detective work. But as with this entire case, the answers I got just led to more questions.

A guy named Jessie Albonianco owned the house where Keilana had left Billie and the black backpack. There was no marriage license or a filing for divorce for Jessie and Billie, but after some digging I found a birth certificate for a Joshua Albonianco, born in 1998. That had to be the Josh that Billie mentioned the night we met. Supposing that was true, that meant Billie's name wasn't Billie at all. The mother on Josh's birth certificate was listed as Hazel Jane Allen.

I'd been able to trace Billie's last place of employment to a bar in Ocean Beach. But it turned out that Billie hadn't worked there for over six months. After that, her employment trail went cold.

Suddenly, Keilana barreled through the front door of our cottage, and with a frown, I closed my case notebook. "Hi."

She gave me a quick nod of acknowledgment but no verbal answer.

She was wearing her workout clothes, her body covered in a thin sheen of perspiration. I'd given up watching her as she worked out. She always did the same thing and she never went anyplace until she'd come home and showered.

Keilana had seen me write in my notebook a time or two before and I'd simply explained it away as a journal. I was surprised when she didn't ask more about it, or exhibit any curiosity at all. But then I remembered that everyone isn't the meddling, prying person that I am.

"So," I said with forced cheerfulness, "what are you doing tonight?" We used to eat dinner together most evenings. We didn't do that anymore.

She didn't even look at me. Instead, she opened the refrigerator and pulled out a bottle of water.

My temper flared. "You can't ignore me forever, Keilana. You just ... you can't is all." I sat my casebook on the table next to my beer.

She turned and pinned me with a serious look. "I'm not ignoring you, Cadie. I just don't have anything to say to you." She turned back toward the fridge as she took a long drink of water, wiping her forehead with the back of her hand when she was finished.

"Well, I have something to say to you."

Her shoulders stiffened. “Don’t you always?”

My jaw tightened. “Listen, Newman, it wasn’t just my lips that were doing the kissing! You were there too!”

“But I’m not the one who started it and then immediately wanted to take it back!” she wailed.

That shut me up for several seconds and before I could come up with a suitable response she whirled around to face me.

“You were right, you know,” she said softly, now more genuinely sad than angry.

I blinked slowly. “I was?” This was the first time in my life where my being right sounded like a very, very bad thing.

She nodded. “You said that kissing me would be a mistake. That we might not be able to be friends afterward.”

A knot formed in my stomach. I didn’t like the direction this conversion was going, even though it was the most she’d said to me in days. “That’s not exactly what I said.”

“I think it’s close enough.”

Even now, even with her covered in sweat, being difficult, and pissed off at me, I wanted to kiss her, hold her, and tell her how much I cared for her. But my deceit, the enormous pink elephant that would always stand between us, kept me from doing anything at all.

Keilana looked as though she was either going to burst into tears or sock me in the face. I would have preferred the latter. “This last week has sucked,” she said plainly, sniffing a few times to control her emotions.

I could have sworn someone was sitting on my chest as I laughed humorlessly. “No kidding.”

“Just what is it about me that you find lacking?”

I closed my eyes, unable to look at her. “Aw, Keilana.” I sighed. “It’s not that. There’s nothing I find lacking about you. You’re smart, and funny, and pretty.” And I’m crazy about you!

“I know you probably think I’m being ridiculous, but it hurts to look at you and know that I want more from you than you want from me. In fact, it makes me feel like shit!”

I jumped to my feet, willing to say anything to make her stop looking at me like I was the female version of a prick tease. "Fucking isn't always the answer."

Her entire body jerked with my words. "I wasn't talking about fucking." She shot me a withering glare. "And you know it. Which is why I don't understand why you're doing this."

"You don't understand," I said quietly. "Things aren't as simple as you think they are." *Tell her the truth. Tell her. Tell her,* my mind chanted. But I bit my tongue. The fact that I refused to become romantically involved with her was for her own good, whether she knew it or not.

She moved closer to me, not stopping until we stood toe-to-toe. "I *do* understand!" Her eyes blazed. "I understand that you won't let us be lovers and I can't take us just being friends. So where does that leave us?"

The phone began to ring.

"Leave it," I said, gesturing toward the offending device with my middle finger. "We're not finished talking."

"Talking isn't going to change how I feel."

"Ugh!" My temper snapped. "Everything isn't about you. Must you be such an unreasonable brat?"

Keilana's blue eyes cooled several degrees as she picked up the phone from the kitchen counter. "It's what I do best, remember?"

"Not that again!" I slammed my palm down on the small kitchen table, making it vibrate and ring out loudly. "That bitchy princess act isn't going to work with me," I told her in no uncertain terms. "We're going to keep talking until we come to some sort of an understanding."

Ignoring me, she pressed the phone to her ear. "Hello."

"Goddammit, Keilana!"

"Oh, hi, Billie." Keilana leaned against the counter, pressing the cool water bottle to her flushed cheek.

"Fuck me," I mumbled, rolling my eyes in disgust. No matter where I tried to go, all roads led to Billie.

Keilana suddenly blanched. "I'm not sure I'm ready for that. I—" Then she saw that I was listening, and with an annoyed look, she marched into the bathroom, slamming the door shut behind her.

"Fine." I closed my eyes, and rubbed my temples, a helpless feeling enveloping me. "What am I gonna do? What am I gonna do?" If I told her the truth she would throw me out and never forgive me. If I continued to lie to her, I would never forgive myself. But that was my cross to bear, wasn't it? I'd sold my soul to the devil, so was it really right that now I was complaining about being in hell?

Deciding the only good thing left in my miserable excuse for a life was my business, I tried to listen to Keilana's conversation through the bathroom door. But she'd lowered her voice. All I could hear was a series of murmurs and finally the sound of the shower going.

Giving the bathroom door a good kick, I gave up. Rapidly approaching my breaking point, I locked my case notebook in my desk, grabbed my cell phone, and headed outside into the fresh evening air.

On the fourth ring, Russ picked up.

"Hey, Belinda!" he greeted, sounding happier than anyone should.

"Hey," I replied tonelessly. "I need your help tonight."

"You do? Excellent! What can I do?"

I looked back at our cottage. The automatic porch lights had just popped on, signaling dusk. The weather, right along with my relationship with Keilana had gotten colder all week. Absently, I rubbed the goose bumps on my arms, wishing I had on long sleeves. "I need you to babysit Keilana while I go see what I can find out about Billie."

"That's the crazy bitch who tried to shoot me, right?"

I didn't remind Russ that the gun had only been a toy and that she really hadn't tried to shoot him. His fear had been real and he'd undoubtedly gotten a lot of mileage out of his adventure with his pals from the office. "Yeah, that's her. I think she's part of whatever Keilana is doing."

"Her drug connection."

"No!" I exploded. "How many times do I have to tell you she's not a junkie?"

"Fine. Take it easy. Even if she's not her drug connection or madam ..."

"Russ," I warned.

"Confronting Billie might be dangerous."

I smiled coldly. "Don't you worry, I can handle Billie." In fact, I was looking forward to the prospect with childish glee.

"If she's not her connection, how does Billie fit into this other than being the Poppenhouse kid's nutcase friend?"

"It's likely that Keilana and Billie ..." I gripped the phone so hard my knuckles hurt. "They're probably sleeping together. And—"

Russ snorted derisively. "Keilana should have better taste."

I couldn't help but smile at that. "Be that as it may, there's something between them. It's more than them being girlfriends." I began moving down the small path toward the fountain, kicking pebbles out of my way as I went. "Call it women's intuition."

There was a small stretch of silence before Russ said, "If that's the case, shouldn't you stay with Keilana? I can case Billie's house. Hell, if she's not there, I'll break in and see if she still has that backpack. Just give me her address."

"No." My lips thinned. "I need to get away from this place tonight. I can't ... I just ..." I let out an unsteady breath. "If I don't get a break from this I'm going to go nuts, Russ. Please."

"I'll be there in twenty minutes."

It was more like forty-five minutes before Russ pulled into the visitor parking section at Madonna Del Mar College. I saw him select a spot, but I stayed where I was, on a well-lit stone bench with a good view of the area.

I called his cell phone. "You're late," I said flatly.

"Hey, don't get grumpy with me. It's not my fault you're in a piss-poor mood. I missed my dinner, I'm missing the Padres playoff game, and my wife wants both of our heads on a platter."

I sighed. "Sorry, Russ. I don't know what's wrong with me."

"Neither do I, Belinda. But I'm willing to bet that it's because something happened between you and Keilana."

Sometimes I was surprised at just how perceptive Russ could be. "What makes you think that?"

He chuckled softly. "You haven't gone on and on about her all week."

I scrubbed my chilly arms again, disgusted with myself for being so transparent. "Listen, I don't want to talk about it."

"Belinda, you'll feel better if you do."

"What's going to make me feel better is finishing this fucking case! If nothing breaks by the end of the weekend, I'm outta here. The Poppenhouses can have their money back if they don't like it." Wow. The decision was made that fast. And when I mulled over the words, I found, to my delight, that I meant every single one of them.

"What the hell? How are you going to pay rent on your office and apartment? How are you going to buy kibble for Smelly if you give back everything you've earned?"

I stood and headed for my car. "When I left Keilana she was in a pair of sweat pants, and reading in bed."

"Belinda—"

"Don't Belinda me. She's in for the night, Russ. Just make sure she doesn't get out without you following her. I'll pay your normal fee plus overtime."

I heard him let out a frustrated breath. "How are you going to pay me if you give back your fee!"

"I'll find a way." That would mean selling something, but whatever. I was past caring.

"I don't want your money."

I smiled bitterly to myself. "Sure you do. It's all about the money, isn't it? Just business. You told me so yourself."

"That's not—"

I hung up before I could say any more. It wasn't Russ's fault that my life was such a complicated mess, but I couldn't seem to keep from lashing out at people. I wasn't fit for human company or conversation. Hell, even my dog was lucky to be well away from me. Maybe something would break tonight, or maybe it wouldn't. Either way, a solitary stakeout where I could sit and think was what I needed.

Well, that and a little luck that wasn't all bad.

Chapter Seven

It was just before eight when a teenage girl knocked on Billie's bungalow door. I ducked down in my car and waited to see what would happen next. Thirty seconds later, Billie scampered out of her house, waving goodbye to a little boy and the girl that I assumed was his babysitter.

My mouth began to water. No, not at Billie, but at what she was carrying. The much-sought-after backpack.

It looked heavier than I'd remembered and I began to get a little nauseated as I considered the hideous, endless list of possibilities for what could be inside. Laundered money. Guns. Fake green cards. Body parts. Mary Kay products.

Billie climbed into a late-model Chevy Malibu and started down the street. I was hot on her tail, following her several cars back and singing to the song on the radio when my cell phone rang.

It was Russ.

"What's up?" I was bound and determined to make up for being such an asshole to him earlier.

"I lost her."

"What?" I roared, nearly steering myself into another car.

"A semi pulled between us on the 5 and right then she crossed two lanes and exited. I'm backtracking now but there's no way I'll find her. Wherever she was going, she was in a hurry."

"Goddammit, Russ, why didn't you call and tell me she was on the move?"

"I was going to call as soon as we got wherever she was going," he said, sounding contrite. "What do you want me to do now?"

I let out an unhappy breath. “You should go home to your wife and enjoy what’s left of the baseball game, Russ.”

“Belinda, I feel like a shithead. I can’t believe I lost her. I trail ten cheating husbands a week and I haven’t lost one in months.”

Following someone on the California highway system wasn’t as easy as the television shows made it appear. If Russ had gone months without losing someone, then he was a hell of a lot better at following by car than I was. “Don’t worry about it.”

“How come you’re not mad at me? You should be mad at me!”

I rolled my eyes as I merged into the left lane, continuing my pursuit of Billie. “Would it make you feel better if I were?” In truth, I was more than a little miffed, but I trusted that Russ had done his best and there was no guarantee that I could have done any better. Keilana drove like a bat out of hell.

“Yes,” he said bluntly. “It would make me feel way better.”

“Fine. You’re fired. And I’m not paying you for tonight either, you loser.”

“Thanks, Belinda.” I could hear the relief in his voice. “You’re the best.”

“God”—I laughed a little, despite my frustration—“we have a totally screwed up relationship.”

“If that ain’t the truth.” There was a long pause before he said, “You know I love you, no matter what, right?”

I nearly hit another car. “What?” Quickly, I straightened the wheel. Russ didn’t say things like that to me.

But the only sound in my ear was a dial tone.

I shook my head. The wiener did have a flare for the dramatic.

A few more turns and we were pulling into The Devil’s Belly. Oh, yeah. I knew it. I knew Billie was Keilana’s connection to this part of San Diego.

Billie pulled her Chevy Malibu into the same small parking lot where Keilana had parked her BMW. I scanned the area, taking in the names of the dance clubs and bars that were already pulsing with life, their neon signs lighting up the night.

I didn't park in the same lot as Billie. Instead, I parked on the street about a hundred feet from the lot. I kept my eyes peeled for Keilana. Were she and Billie meeting? Or was it just a coincidence that Billie had spoken to Keilana on the phone not long before I left the cottage?

Russ always said there were no coincidences in our line of work. Of course, Russ also said "Pull my finger" quite often. So it's not like I was going to engrave any of his little ditties on stone tablets.

I hid in the shadows as Billie and that black backpack went to the front door of a club called "Bottoms Up." She flashed the doorman / killer / bouncer a smile and he held open the door for her, a blast of music escaping as she hurried inside.

When I tried the same thing he stuck out his arm to block my way. "Ahem." He gave me a pointed look.

I stopped dead in my tracks. "Yes?"

"Fifteen dollars and"—he looked me over with a critical eye—"let's see some I.D."

"Gimme a break." I mumbled, "I'm older than you are, jackass," as I dug through the pockets of my jeans.

"What was that?" he asked sharply, taking a small wad of cash from a couple of sailors who were dressed like Popeye, and letting them inside. I couldn't help but notice that he didn't ask for their I.D. even though they looked like they were in their teens.

"Just a minute." I tried to look around them as they entered to see if I could spot Billie. But the Incredible Hulk blocked my view with his enormous body. He crossed his bulky arms over his chest.

I smiled brightly. "Here's a twenty and my driver's license. Keep the change."

He grunted as he reviewed my license, giving me a skeptical look.

Blue and red lights reflected off his shiny, bald head. "Next time you buy a fake, try getting one with an age somebody's gonna believe." But despite what he said, he stepped aside as he handed me back my license. I reached for the door but stopped with my hand on the handle. With my other hand, I dug out another twenty and held it under the bouncer's nose. "Does a woman named Billie work here? Tall, redhead."

He snatched the bill from my fingers so quickly that for a second I couldn't remember if I'd had one there at all.

"No."

I waited for more, but figured out pretty quickly that my twenty had only bought one word. Christ. Thank God I'd gone to the campus cash machine that morning. I peeled off another twenty.

"How about Hazel? Same description."

"Yep."

I shook my head. Only in California would someone use their real name to work in a bar on the edge of The Devil's Belly, but go by their fake name in everyday life.

"How about someone named Keilana?" I tried, hoping to make my money stretch.

He just stared at me.

I made a face and handed him another twenty, stuffing my few remaining bills back into my pocket along with my license.

"Never heard of him."

He clearly wasn't the sharpest tack in the box. "It's a her." I stepped aside as two young men and a women pretty enough to make me do a double take stepped up next to me, paid, and entered the club. Then I described Keilana in detail.

"She don't work here," he said finally. Unexpectedly, he winked and smiled, showing off several gold teeth. "But it sounds like she should."

What the hell did that mean? I frowned as I went inside.

The volume of the music on the outside of the club wasn't anything compared to what it was like on the inside. Deafening was putting it lightly. The large room was packed with people and smelled like a mixture of sweat, cologne, and alcohol. Yuck.

Near the door was a large sunken dance floor with what had to be two hundred sweating bodies pressed up against each other, writhing to the obnoxious music. Double yuck.

I caught sight of a waitress ... well, actually I caught sight of her breasts. Which was incredibly easy to do considering all that she had covering them were teensy pasties that made the girls at Hooters look positively Amish.

This was a titty bar? I glanced around again. This was, by far, the nicest titty bar I'd ever been in. Not that I'd been in many, mind you. It was relatively bright with lots of flashing lights illuminating a spattering of Halloween decorations that hung down from the ceiling. The place was clean too—my shoes weren't sticking to the floor with every step—and most of the patrons were dressed for a night on the town.

Have I ever mentioned how, on the right woman, a belly shirt is nothing short of a work of art? Yowsa.

The muted roar of applause drew my attention to the back of the enormous room. I waded my way through the mass of dancing bodies, my eardrums throbbing with every beat of the music. Just as I got far enough to see what was making the crowd cheer, the club went pitch black and the music came to an abrupt halt.

Muffled screams rippled through the place, and suddenly the air was electric with excitement. A velvety voice came over the loud speaker. "Gentlemen, and you very naughty ladies, are you ready to take a trip to the dark side ..."—his voice dropped to a whisper—"with Hazel?"

Oops. I guess Billie wasn't just a waitress.

The crowd went wild when they heard her name. I took a step forward, straining to see through the darkness, the dim exit lights in the corners of the club doing nothing to help me. I bumped into what I hoped was a chair, but said sorry just in case it was a really bony guy instead. I felt around for a second, *really* hoping it wasn't a guy, before gracelessly flopping down in the seat.

Just as my butt hit the wood, a spotlight lit a small stage and a hypnotic tune, all base and drums, filled the club. I looked around and realized I was in the middle of a section of the club filled with small tables. Almost every seat was taken, mostly by men, all with their eyes riveted on the wooden platform.

Okay, there was no pole on the stage. At least she wasn't a stripper. I was hoping for singer or comedian or something equally benign and unlikely.

People from the dance floor poured into the area where I was sitting, filling the small spaces between the tables, and leaving those who couldn't fit to dejectedly head back to the dance floor or to one of three bars around the perimeter. The music slowly got louder and louder and louder and, finally, when I thought it couldn't get any louder, it stopped altogether.

Then it started up again, much slower, the beat more sensual. Fog poured across the stage and out into the audience. It swirled around our tables and feet, making us part of whatever was going to happen. My belly tightened in anticipation of the unknown ...

Suddenly, as if by magic, a lone woman appeared out of the mist. She wore a glittering gold mask that covered only her eyes and nose and a full-length leather cape that was wrapped tightly around her and had a stiff collar that came up to her cheekbones. Other than her head, the only things exposed were her fishnet-covered ankles and black spike heels so high she looked like an Amazon.

I wasn't sure what exactly she was supposed to be dressed like, but whatever it was it did more than catch my eye. As soon as Billie moved, gas lamps along the edge of the stage exploded to life, providing a flickering, intimate light that replaced the flashing neon. More smoke flooded the stage, swirling around Billie's legs and giving the platform the appearance of a foggy London alleyway at midnight.

I was really starting to doubt that she was a comedian.

A hush fell over the crowd as we all waited with bated breath to see what would happen next. Patience is a cruel mistress, but, thankfully, we didn't have to wait long. The woman, who I was pretty sure was Billie, whipped open her cape to expose her flowing red hair and a body encased in a tight black bustier and a black thong so brief that it literally caused my mouth to drop open.

Oh, yeah, that was Billie and she was a stripper. The implications of that caused my stomach to fill with dread, but I had a hard time thinking of anything other than what was parading in front of me in barely nothing.

Billie's show did nothing if not command attention.

She snapped her cape closed, and there was a chorus of sighs, many of them female, as she strode to the end of the stage, her hips swaying dangerously with every step. When she got to the very edge of the stage she smiled a dangerous smile and began to dance for a man in the front row who was frantically waving a fistful of cash. I could see her body moving sensually beneath the cape and in perfect time with the music. The fact that I couldn't see exactly what she was doing only made it sexier.

She was good.

Only her gloved arms emerged from her cape as she moved in time with music that seemed to pulse with the beat of my heart. With agonizing slowness, she peeled off one elbow-length glove and my eyes got a little wider as she used it to stroke the man's cheek. He looked like he was about ready to pass out from the sheer ecstasy of Billie's touch, and his buddy had to reach out and grab him by the belt to keep him from crawling up on stage and mounting her.

She was better than good.

Somehow, in the middle of all that, Billie never missed a beat. She took his money, caressed his face with the tips of her long fingernails, then she drew her hand back and used her butter-soft leather glove to slap the man hard in the face.

A loud crack sounded as she hit him and I flinched.

More than a few members of the audience swooned.

There was a mixture of shouts and groans from the crowd. But the young man groaned as though getting bitch-slapped by a stripper was the greatest thing that had ever happened in his short life and threw his entire wad of bills on the stage. Smiling like a Cheshire cat, Billie turned her back to the crowd. She flipped her cape up off her bottom, locked her knees, and bent *deeply* to pick up the bills, giving her derriere a provocative little thrust then shake.

I saw ... well, everything. I didn't know a person could bend so deeply. By the way, Billie is a natural redhead.

I held in a nervous giggle as the name of the club came floating back to me. At least it was appropriate.

God only knew where Billie put the money she had collected. It disappeared in the blink of an eye and was nowhere to be seen. She straightened and spun around in one graceful move, flipping the cape over her shoulders and bringing her hands up to caress her chest as she strutted to the other side of the stage, her large breasts bobbing up and down with every step.

I felt a twinge of guilt at the wetness collecting between my legs. After all, I had good reason to hate Billie. But, God, I was only human!

She had a body to die for and when she had a "wardrobe malfunction" of her own, exposing a firm breast to the hot air of the club, and grabbed and twisted her own nipple, I gasped right along with the porky guy sitting next to me.

A waitress came by my table and gently inclined her head. The cocoa-colored skin covering her torso and hefty breasts was flawless, but I did my best to look her in the eye as I spoke. I held up another twenty-dollar bill. "A beer and a question?"

She nodded. "Make it quick."

"Does a women name Keilana work here? Young, five feet eight, long dark hair, amazing blue eyes." My gaze strayed to Billie who was now bare to the waist, her hips moving in a slow grind against her hand. Holy shit.

"Sorry. Never heard of her."

My head snapped back to the waitress. "Huh?"

"Never heard of her," she repeated tolerantly, a tiny smile shaping her mouth. She set my twenty on her tray. "Bud okay? It's what's on tap."

"Yeah," I said absently, dizzy with relief over her news. Maybe Keilana had only been picking up Billie from work the night Russ and I had tracked them down.

Oops. There went Billie's cape.

Yeah, maybe Keilana was just Billie's ride. I loved that thought, and like any person trying with all their might to delude themselves, I eagerly embraced it. I just began to smile when two more women joined Billie on stage.

The crowd cheered as the masked women, each clad in a slightly shorter version of Billie's cape, crawled across the stage like vixen pussycats, their backs arched high.

Billie turned only her head to look at them and commanded their movements with a bare flick of her hand or toss of her flaming hair.

I blinked. They were her slaves. Then I glanced around. So was the audience.

After stripping down to deep purple satin panties, the slaves bookended Billie and began to slide sensuously against her. She dug a hand into each of the women's hair and guided them together until they kissed each other. Hard.

God, I love my job.

The new zoning laws that the city council managed to get passed for this redevelopment area were something else! Was there anything that the performers couldn't do? I hoped not. Sometimes I'm such a pervert.

I swallowed dryly and squirmed a little in my seat, wishing that beer would hurry up already.

Billie placed a single finger under the platinum blonde's chin and lifted her face. The woman purred, reveling in complete control.

Have I mentioned that Billie was good at her job?

Then Billie kissed her slave softly, and with as much tenderness as I'd ever seen. The tip of her tongue appeared and she traced the woman's lips, pulling back just a little so the audience could see the thin line of glistening salvia that still connected them, only to be broken by a smoldering kiss where Billie dominated her minion completely, forcing her to lean way back as she devoured her.

A light sweat broke out across my forehead and I couldn't tear my eyes from the stage.

A shower of bills poured onto the stage from an enthusiastic patron who looked like a soccer mom out for the evening.

A fourth woman appeared out of the mist. Her cape was blood red and hooded and gleamed in the mysterious light. Her mask was a shimmering gold and Billie and her slaves recoiled at the sight of her.

I got lost in the show, holding my breath as the woman in red stormed over to Billie, her movements oozing with sensuality. Ooo ... she was already my favorite. The slaves cowered, but Billie faced her foe, standing tall and proud, though her chest heaved with fear.

Brazenly, the woman in red caressed Billie's throat, but Billie broke away. Billie danced around the woman, wantonly teasing her with her body, stripping as she went. In just a few minutes she wore nothing but garters and shoes.

The woman in red tried to fight it, but eventually it was Billie who was stronger, and who put her under her iniquitous spell.

Billie's slaves danced in delight, exposing more and more of their bodies as they moved to the edge of the stage and mercilessly worked the crowd, stuffing bills in their G-strings and capes.

Billie threw her head back and laughed wickedly, white teeth flashing. She hissed and tore back the woman's hood, causing a shock of dark hair to tumble forward.

A sense of foreboding hit me right in the gut.

More smoke flowed across the stage as she tore off the woman's cape, exposing a spectacular pale body covered in a scanty crimson bra and panties. I couldn't help but notice the woman's belly button was pierced.

And my stomach fell through the floor.

The spotlight focused on the woman in red as Billie's hand hovered over her breast, intent on ripping off a bra that fit so tight it was like a second skin.

My heart leapt into my throat.

The masked woman groaned in anguish, trying one last time to break Billie's sensual spell. They moved around the stage dancing and writhing. They finally came to an abrupt halt. Even the music stopped. And for one dramatic second they stood stock-still, until the women in red tore her gaze from Billie's and looked out into the crowd.

Right at me.

With incredible blue eyes.

My heart stopped beating and I flew to my feet. “Keilana?” I screamed, my voice rising above the throbbing beat of the music that had begun to play again.

Billie and the woman in red froze, then both their jaws dropped. It was her!

I don’t remember everything that happened next. All I knew was that Keilana did not belong up there in front of hundreds of prying eyes. And I was going to do everything in my power to get her off that stage.

Like a woman possessed, I rushed forward, forcing my way between the tables, and ignoring the outraged shouts of the patrons I shoved aside. I couldn’t get on stage from where I was because the slave girls were dancing in the front and a group of guys had clustered around them to stuff dollar bills in their panties.

I bolted for the side of the stage, seeing out of my peripheral vision another dancer holding a video recorder and taping the entire performance. Jesus, they were making a “Lezzy Stripper Gone Wild” video too? Could this *be* much worse?

I really should avoid asking that question in the future.

Just as I put my hands on the stage a beefy bouncer grabbed me by the collar. I whirled around and shoved him with all my might, sending him into a table of cheering college-aged men. He smashed into their drinks, sending several glasses to the ground.

During the commotion, the men tried to help the bouncer off their tiny table, and I turned, using my hands to push myself on stage. “Keilana?” I had barely gotten to my feet when two more bouncers tackled me. The wind rushed out of me and for a few seconds everything went black as they covered me.

“Keilana!” I gasped again when I was yanked up into the air, but she was gone and Billie and her slaves were dancing their hearts out on the other side of the stage, drawing attention away from me.

“Get off me!” Out of sheer instinct I began to kick and shout as I was whisked to a side door. I hated to be touched by strangers and not only were these gorillas rough about it, but one of them even copped a feel.

Suddenly there was a blast of cool air as the door to the alleyway was opened and I was unceremoniously tossed outside.

I smashed against a garbage can, seeing stars for a few seconds. Or was that neon? "Shit." It had rained while I was inside and I was sitting in a puddle again.

The man holding the door pointed an angry finger at me. "I don't feel like calling the cops this early in the night. Consider yourself lucky, bitch."

"I don't feel very lucky," I stupidly said, rubbing my head with a shaky hand.

He sneered at me. "Don't come back here again. Ever."

Then he slammed the door shut.

I sat there in the wet alleyway, stunned, the scent of rain and rotting garbage all around me. So my sort-of-girlfriend was a stripper? Great. Just great!

I was beside myself and, with a little effort, I was pretty sure I could chew through the metal door that separated me from her and steal her away from this skuzzy place. I know I thought it was sort of nice inside before. But that was *before*. Now it just seemed seedy and nasty and ... well, anything else bad I could think of.

I wanted to burn the place down.

There was no doubt that I was losing my mind. With a little grunt, I quickly pushed myself to my feet, wincing at my sore knees and wobbly legs. My jeans were torn at both knees and I felt the warm, sticky sensation of blood dripping from a couple of nasty scrapes.

Straightening my back, I brushed off my hands. I gasped at the sharp stinging sensation and turned them over to try and look at my palms. It was pretty dark back here, but I could tell by the pain and the rough feel of the skin that they were scratched up, tiny bits of rocks and broken glass still embedded. After another ruthless brushing against my torn jeans, they still hurt, but they no longer felt like they were on fire.

I gritted my teeth, drew in a deep breath, and ran as fast as I could for the front of the club. The bouncers had to wade through that crowd inside to the make it to the front and let the guy there know not to let me back in. If I was lucky, I could beat them there.

There was only one guy in front of me and I had my money ready when I got to the front of line. The bald bouncer looked at me a few seconds. He recognized me, but he was having trouble placing me.

"I was here last night," I lied, doing my best to smile. He didn't ask for I.D. this time, instead he just gave me a noncommittal grunt, took my money, and stepped aside. Maybe I look older when I'm wet, disheveled, and smell like garbage?

Once inside I headed straight for the ladies' room. I looked like crap. One of my eyes was already starting to poof up. I'd gotten a pretty good jostling when I was tossed out of the club—I touched the tender skin—but I didn't remember getting smacked in the eye. I didn't want to draw any more unwanted attention to myself so I used a few paper towels to clean off my knees and hands. Then I went back out in search of Keilana.

Billie was on stage again, dressed in a totally different outfit, and dancing to music with a sexy Latin beat. She was up there alone, so where was Keilana?

King Kong and Mighty Joe Young, aka the bouncers that kicked me out, were flanking the stage, making sure none of the customers wandered back where the strippers were. And that wouldn't do. I hated to do this, but …

I scanned the crowd standing around the bar and found a middle-aged man with his shirt unbuttoned to his belly, a cheesy "Hair Club for Men" toupee, and several gold chains around his neck. His jeans were three sizes too small and I could smell his cologne from here. Perfect.

I stood next to him and waited a few seconds until the crowd around us contained a couple more women, which wasn't easy in this mostly male audience. I waited until my first victim was close and then I discreetly gave her a hard pinch on the ass.

She screamed.

At the same time I pinched the second woman just as hard on the derriere then yelled myself, grabbing my butt in the process. Indignant, I pointed at the man next to us and screeched, "You pervert! I can't believe you did that. You pawed my ass!"

"Mine too!" the woman next to me immediately followed. She shoved the man hard. "Sick bastard!"

The man's jaw sagged and he blinked stupidly. "I … didn't … I—"

"You sicko!" the second woman exclaimed, taking the guy's own martini out of his hand and dumping it over his head. Good thing those Hair Club infomercials always show guys swimming and water skiing and such. "My girlfriend, Dusty, is going to kick"—she poked him in the chest with her finger—"your"—another poke—"ass!"

Uh-oh, time to go. I disappeared into the crowd just as the bouncers appeared and began peeling someone I figured was Dusty off the Hair Club guy. Sorry, man. I headed backstage as quickly as I could.

I'd never been backstage anything before and it was quieter than I expected. There were a few dancers milling around, but none of them were Keilana. "Keilana," I whispered loudly. "Keilana?" I came to a closed door on one side of the short hallway and just as I reached out to open it, a long arm appeared from nowhere and yanked me inside a tiny room on the opposite side of the hall.

I was whisked inside, and before I knew it, Keilana was locking the door. She whirled around and faced me, her eyes burning with anger. "Are you trying to get the shit beat out of you?"

I blinked. "I—I didn't … I—" Jesus, I sounded like the Hair Club guy.

"If the bouncers catch you back here after kicking you out there's no telling what they'll do." She ran her hands down my arms, checking me for injuries. When she saw my knees, she sighed. "I looked for you in the alleyway but you were already gone. I thought you might have come to your senses and gone home." Her eyes narrowed. "That reminds me. What the hell are you doing here?"

I pointed at myself with my thumb. "What am *I* doing here? What about you? Since when are you a Goddamned stripper!" I yelled, my emotions churning to the surface with surprising ease. "There is no way—!"

Keilana clamped her hand over my mouth. "Shut up," she said bluntly. "We can talk later. Thanks to you I've been asked to leave for the night."

I wrenched my head from her hand. “Tonight only?”

She nodded. “I’ll be back.”

The words tied my guts into a solid knot.

“And next time you won’t come and make trouble for me, got it?”

God, she’d certainly been pissed at me before, but now she practically had smoke coming out of her ears. I grabbed her biceps. I had to get through to her somehow. She wasn’t going to come back here and strip if I had to chain myself to her. This wasn’t about jealously or snobbery. Keilana was more than a pair of tits and a firm ass.

“You don’t have to be a stripper,” I said in a rush. I cast around for something to say that wouldn’t insult her or her friend Billie, but I didn’t have much luck. “Have you lost your mind?” I began to gesture wildly. “I don’t care how deep into trouble you think you are or whether or not your parents will help you out of it. I’ll help you. I’ll do whatever it takes. You don’t need to do this for the money.”

Her back stiffened. “Cadie—”

“Let me finish!” The music was deafening back here and I had to raise my voice even when I would have rather not.

I waited until her mouth snapped closed before I continued. “You’re too smart to waste yourself here. This is what you do when you can’t do anything else. This is what you do when you’re desperate. *You* don’t need this. Don’t you get it? You’re special!”

She lifted a single eyebrow. “Can I say something yet?”

“I guess.” I braced myself. This is where she told me her horrible secret. That she was a sex addict or that she had thirteen illegitimate children she was trying to support on the side. Or that she was the madam in a prostitution ring that worked out of this club. How many years in jail had Heidi Fleiss gotten?

“I’m not in trouble.”

I let go of her arms, stung to the core over her lie, and only barely stopped myself from shaking her. I closed my eyes in a bid for self-control. There was such a fine line between loving Keilana and wanting to kill her. “That can’t be true or you wouldn't be selling peeks at your naked body to a bunch of perverts!"

"You were in the audience."

"My point exactly. Christ, before I knew it was you in the red cape, I was hoping you'd dance closer to the front so I could get a good look at your nipples!"

"Are you saying you don't want to see my nipples now?"

"No! Yes! No! Ah!" I covered my face with my hands.

"I'm not a stripper, Cadie."

"I saw you on stage. I saw you dancing!" I didn't add that she'd been awesome.

She put her hands on her hips. "I gathered that when you rushed the stage, screaming like a madwoman."

I shook my head, and unable to do a better job of articulating what I was feeling or thinking, I blurted, "You can't be a stripper. You just can't."

Her gaze sharpened and her voice dropped to a dangerous purr. "Says who?"

"Says me! Me! Me! Me!" I don't spaz out often, but when I do I rarely go only halfway.

She pushed to her feet, using her slight height advantage as she glared down at me. "And who are you to tell me how to live my life?" She didn't seem like a twenty-one-year-old college student at that moment. She was a self-assured woman who knew exactly what she wanted. "Remember our game? Call this one of my questions, but I want the truth."

I took a step backward, needing a second to think. That really was the question, wasn't it? Who *was* I? "You know who I am. I—I'm your roommate."

"Try again," she demanded, stepping forward and giving me no relief.

I swallowed hard. "I'm your friend who doesn't want to see you debase yourself for a few dollars."

She shook her head. "Not good enough, not for how insane you're acting."

My eyes dropped to the floor and my hands shaped impotent fists. I looked up when I felt a warm hand come to rest on the side of my face.

Keilana's gaze softened. "I think you're someone who is in love with me, Cadie. Are you ever going to say it or are you going to make me wait forever?"

The music stopped and suddenly I could hear the pounding of my own heart thudding loudly in my ears. Astonished, I gaped at her. "You-you knew?" I finally spluttered.

"It's not like you hide it very well." She smiled cautiously. "So is it true? Even after seeing me on stage?" She gestured around the small room. "And here?"

I surged forward and kissed her with all my might.

She kissed me back like she wanted me more than anything on the planet and my knees went weak at the feeling.

When we finally separated there was a loud popping noise as the suction between our lips was broken. I felt a little dazed. "It's true," I whispered emotionally, thrilled to the core to finally be saying it. "Anyplace. Doesn't matter where."

And with that I knew this game had to end. I did love her and there would end the lies, even if that meant she'd never speak to me again. My nostrils flared with fear. "And how do you feel about me?"

She smiled a beautiful smile and took one of my hands in hers and cradled it softly. "You *are* the nosiest person I've ever met"—she laughed when the tips of my ears turned red—"but I'm falling in love with you anyway, Cadie. I have been since almost the beginning. I know I can trust you and to me that's the most important thing."

"It is?" My heart twisted in my chest.

"I don't just want to get you into bed. Well, I do," she said grinning, "but I want more than that too." A tiny bit of insecurity peeked through. "I want everything, I mean, if you do."

A lump grew in my throat and tears pooled in my eyes. My heart was soaring but at the same time I felt like I was going down in flames. She'd said everything I'd ever wanted to hear, well, I could have lived without the nosy part. But the rest was what I'd secretly longed for, even dreamt about. And yet it was all wrong.

She needed to fall in love with Belinda, not Cadie.

Then I noticed something near her feet. The damned black backpack! I hated that fucking thing the way I hated myself for betraying her trust.

She followed my gaze. "It's not a mouse, is it?" She began dancing around, looking at the floor. "I hate mice!"

"No mouse. What's inside that backpack?" My mouth was suddenly dry and I did my best to lick my lips. I knew in my heart that I'd forgive her damn near anything ... and that I'd help her out of whatever mess she was in. But I still had to know.

For me and no one else.

Her brows furrowed at my question and she bent to pick up the pack. "See for yourself."

I looked her right in the eyes and swore to myself that I wouldn't go crazy when she confirmed my suspicions. "It's where you keep your costumes for stripping, right?"

Puzzled, she just looked at me for a few seconds. "Weren't you listening?" She rolled her eyes. "I told you, I'm not a stripper."

I gritted my teeth. "Then what are you, Keilana? Because I know what I damn well saw!"

The sound of running footsteps pitter-patted down the hall.

"Shh!" Worriedly, she glanced at the door. "Keep your voice down. You're not supposed to be back here. I'm already going to be in trouble with the manager after your little freak attack out there."

I sighed. "Sorry."

She passed over the backpack. It was a little bigger and heavier than it had appeared at a distance and I held my breath as I grasped the zipper. It was cool to the touch and my hand froze. Was I ready for this?

"Is the zipper stuck?" Keilana started to reach for the pack, frowning. "I need a new bag."

"No, it's okay." I drew in a deep breath. Please, God, don't let there be body parts stored in Tupperware in here. As I unzipped the zipper and blindly stuck my hand inside, a flash of going to a nature center as a kid and reaching into a small hole in a wooden box to feel some sort of surprise, tore through my mind. It was always fur or antlers, by the way. Somehow I doubted that would be the case here.

I blinked. "Electronic equipment?" I flipped open the bag, exposing the mystery to the light. It was jammed with cameras, tiny video recorders, cords, a mini tape recorder, the smallest laptop I'd ever seen, and some loose batteries. What the hell was this? "You're making porn out of this pack?"

"No!" She looked at me like I was crazy. Which I'm not. I think. "Jesus Christ, Cadie, do you always imagine the most horrible situation possible and then put me in it?"

Of course. "Maybe," I said a touch defensively.

She hesitated for just a second, then let out a little breath, apparently having come to her decision. Her eyes blazed with sudden determination. "I want to be a documentarian and I'm making my first film. It's about strippers and Billie is pretty much my prime interview, though there are several other women in it too."

She scrunched up her face. "They were from some really seedy clubs down the road. The filming played havoc with my school schedule and nearly killed me. Thank God I finished it just before summer. Things here this semester have been a piece of cake in comparison."

"A filmmaker? That can't be true!" I shook my head wildly, unable to accept what she was saying.

"Shh! The manager lets me shoot back here, but at his discretion ... and after I bribe him on a regular basis. If he cuts me off this close to the end of production I'm screwed."

"But you were on stage. You weren't just filming. You were the woman in red!" My mind drifted back to Keilana appearing out of the mist. "The sizzling hot woman in red that I would still love to eat alive," I added, hoping that didn't sound as lecherous out loud as it had in my head.

This time it was her turn to blush. "Hold that thought, okay?"

I leaned forward and kissed her softly. She smelled incredible and I was still so keyed up from the show that I was about ready to explode. I don't know where I found the willpower to break that kiss. "Don't worry, I won't forget."

I held up the bag to remind Keilana I was still waiting for more of an explanation.

She quirked a grin and shook her finger at me. "Don't kiss me like that if you expect me to be able to think."

This time it was me that smiled. "Deal."

"Billie's been after me for months to learn one of the routines and perform so I'd really know what it feels like to be up on stage. I've been gathering my nerve and practicing the dancing. Tonight a couple of girls called off work so the club really needed someone to fill in. I umm ..." She paused to let out a shaky breath. "I wasn't going to get totally naked up there but my top was supposed to come off right at the end of the show."

I closed my eyes, half aroused by what she was telling me, the other half blessedly relieved that I stopped her in time. Keilana was too smart not to later regret something so stupid. I wanted to throttle Billie for even suggesting it.

"I got a taste of what Billie does up there everyday and I gotta tell you, it's a lot different being up on that stage than it is watching."

I squeezed her hand, wincing at the mild sting from my scrapes. "And?"

"And it was a lot scary and a little intoxicating and something I don't want to do again. It was a stupid idea that I should have never agreed to in the first place."

"True."

She crossed slender arms over her chest and lifted her chin. "You don't have to be so smug about it."

"How would you feel if I got up on that stage and did that same dance with Billie?"

The tiny, but instant, growl that exploded from her throat surprised me, but it wasn't an unhappy surprise. "Eww ... Okay, so I see your point."

I zipped the bag closed and handed it back to her, careful not to drop it. I'd have to sell a kidney to replace even one of those cameras.

I didn't know what to think about everything that had happened. I'd been expecting something horrible for so long that now that it hadn't happened, I wasn't sure how to act or how to feel.

"Are you okay?" she asked me, clearly concerned.

I blew my hair out of my eyes. "Yeah. I ... It's just been a long day."

"No kidding."

I still felt uneasy. "Why didn't you tell me what you were doing? There's nothing wrong with making a documentary. I still don't understand why you'd hide it?"

Dismayed, she trained her gaze on my dirty shoes. "My parents, Cadie, they aren't like most people's parents. They're control freaks. I mean *real* control freaks."

That was, unfortunately, completely true. I was living proof. "What does that have to do with me?"

Sadly, she glanced up at me. "They know I don't want to go back to Honolulu and work for Poppenhouse Cookies Charitable Giving Headquarters. That's the job my dad has all picked out for me."

My eyes went round. "You told them about this movie project?"

She gave me a lopsided grin. "Get real, okay? I told them I wanted to go to film school, and they said no. I told them I wanted to make documentaries. They said no. I told my mother I wouldn't marry Mr. Right, who they've had picked out for me since I was three years old, and they ignored me. They're selectively deaf! I wasn't far from graduating so I figured I'd do my best to get through school on their dime and then do whatever it is I want afterward."

"I still don't—"

She placed two fingers over my lips. "I'm still talking."

Contrite, I nodded.

"Last year my grades started to slip. I was out all hours of the night and some of the girls I was filming, well, let's just say they lived a little wilder life than I could keep up with." She smiled sheepishly. "Though for a while I gave it the good old college try. I kept what I was doing from my parents and used my allowance to finance my project. One day while I was on the phone with my mother, she let slip that she knew I was spending a lot of time in San Diego."

Uh-oh. "How did she know that?"

"That's a very good question. And the only answer that makes sense is that she paid some parasite to spy on me."

I felt like taking a bath in lye.

"I know it sounds crazy, but it's true! One day I realized that I was being followed."

All the blood drained from my face. "You were?" I managed weakly.

"Yeah, by some guy. Ever since then I've kept what I'm doing a total secret. My life at school and my work here never cross paths. I can't let them and hope to be able to keep doing what I'm doing.

I know it's stupid, especially since I was one of the parasites, but I still felt hurt that she didn't tell me what she was up to. She spoke with such passion about her project, this was something important to her, and so it was important to me too.

She caught my expression and gentled her voice, "Cadie, I've thought about telling you a dozen times, but you don't know my parents. If they wanted information out of you or believed you could be of some use to them, they'd make your life a living hell until they got it."

I forced a snort. "You make them sound like the mafia." Oh, crap. Please don't let them be the Hawaiian mob.

"They aren't the mafia," she said grimly. "They just get what they want, no matter who they hurt in the process."

They wouldn't get what they wanted this time. My knees started to shake. "Keilana, there's something I have to tell you."

"Keilana!" Billie began to bang on the door. "Are you in there?"

"Just a minute" Keilana called out. "Hide!" she said to me, and began pushing me toward the closet. "Billie's already jealous of you and she went out on a limb to get me on stage. If she sees you in here she's gonna go crazy and call the goons."

I dug in my heels. "So? They'll just tell me to go, no big deal." Okay, they'd probably toss me on my head this time, but that didn't mean I was going to give in.

"So I'll have to re-shoot weeks of film if she pulls out of this project," she hissed. "In the closet with you."

"But Keilana—"

She grasped my face and kissed me with purpose. It was short but smoking hot and I actually whimpered when she stopped. "That seems to be the best way to shut you up." Her grin took the sting from the words.

"You have a way to get home right?" she asked quickly. "And then you can tell me why *you're* hanging out in strip clubs. If you're in love with me shouldn't you be home knitting me dinner or something?"

A tiny laugh exploded from me, but my smile soon faded. "I promise to explain absolutely everything at home."

A crease appeared on her forehead and she touched my face with aching tenderness. "What's the matter?"

Billie was banging on the door again but I had Keilana's full attention. I could hardly keep from crying. "I always keep my promises."

She shook her head. "I don't understand."

Billie's banging grew even louder. "Keilana, c'mon. I need those gloves I lent you for my next number!"

"It's nothing," I said valiantly, doing my best to look like I wasn't dying inside.

"Okay, I gotta go start filming." She grabbed Billie's gloves from the small dressing room table. "I know they told me to go home, but Billie's trying a new G-string tonight."

My eyebrows jumped.

"Don't ask." She rolled her eyes. "Just be careful sneaking out of here, okay?" She smiled at me and my heart melted. Then she kissed her fingers and pressed them to the tip of my nose. "Until tonight."

I'd never hated my job so much.

Chapter Eight

Sneaking out wasn't as easy as I thought it'd be. In fact, it was nearly two hours before I could get out of that damn dressing room. One of the strippers decided to have a meltdown right outside the door and I was trapped there like the rat that I am. I didn't bother to drive back to my apartment and trade cars. Tonight I would tell Keilana everything and my days of driving around in snazzy Jaguars would be over.

It was nearly midnight by the time I made it back to campus. I pulled into the spot next to Keilana's BMW. She probably was wondering where I was. Even so, I couldn't bring myself to hurry. I leaned forward and rested my head on the steering wheel. The cool metal of the cross bars felt surprisingly good against my forehead, but did nothing to ease my nervous stomach.

What could I tell her that would keep her from hating me? I already hated myself so badly I could barely stand it.

For a moment I toyed with the idea of just not telling her at all. It's not too late, my evil side urged. But deep down I knew I couldn't do that. Besides, things were different now. I wanted to be with her and she wanted to be with me. A goofy grin interrupted my self-loathing. She was in love with me!

I felt fantastic and horrible all at the same time. Okay, she might have said she was *falling* in love with me. But I could work with that. She might not realize it now, but when I'm not being a disgusting, traitorous spy, I'm really a loyal, downright lovable person.

If she truly cared for me, surely I could convince her to forgive me, right? I was willing to accept her as a prostitute or druggie or whatever trouble she'd gotten herself into. If I could do that, this wouldn't be an impossible leap for her.

I nodded once, screwing up my courage as I exited the car and stood on Jell-O legs.

"Okay, Belinda, please don't fuck this up," I murmured into the breeze.

"Please."

Slowly, *very* slowly, I headed up the path toward our cottage. Most of the other residences were dark, but there was a golden light coming from the living room window. She'd waited up for me. I wasn't sure whether to be flattered or to turn around and run.

Since when had my feet grown so heavy? It felt as though I was slogging through a mud pit. Uphill.

I let out a few shaky breaths as I inserted my key into the lock, a little surprised to find that it wasn't locked.

"I'm home," I said quietly as I took a tentative step inside. I didn't turn on the lights in case she was asleep on the sofa and I had been granted a temporary reprieve. There were worse ways to spend a night than watching someone as special as Keilana sleep.

But my roomie was not only awake, she was sitting across the room on the sofa, holding something in her hands. Her head was down and the wan light cast long shadows across her face. Something was wrong. "Hi, Kei—"

She glanced up at me and I saw a glistening streak trail down her cheek. My stomach lurched.

"Hello, Belinda," she said softly, chilling me to the bone. "Or should I say Ms. Blaisdell?"

I felt as though I'd been shot in the chest. In her hands she held my case notebook.

"Oh my God." A cold sweat broke out across my body, causing me to tremble. "You weren't supposed to find … That's private." I hadn't left my notebook out! How had she found it?

From behind Keilana and out the shadows stepped her mountain of a mother. "I think you should go, Ms. Blaisdell." It wasn't a request. It was an order.

Incredulous, I blurted, "You just … what are you doing here?"

"Belinda." My head snapped sideways to see Russ standing in the kitchen. I could hardly breathe. "What the hell are *you* doing here?" My gaze flickered around the tiny cottage. Who else was going to pop out of nowhere? Was I the last person to be let in on some sick joke?

"C'mere. We need to talk." He cast uneasy eyes on Keilana and her mother and then took a few steps forward to reach out for me. "They need a few minutes to themselves."

Keilana had a vacant look in her eyes and Mrs. Poppenhouse laid a comforting hand on her shoulder. "Yes, we need another moment."

"No!" I jerked my arm away. "I'll deal with you later, Russ. I need to talk to Keilana now." I turned back toward her only to have Russ lift me off my feet and bodily haul me into the kitchen like I was a sack of potatoes. That was the second time that had happened tonight and this time pissed me off even more than the first. "Let the fuck go of me!" I screeched, elbowing him hard enough in the back to hear the air rush out of his lungs. "Dammit Russ! Let me go!"

"No," he grunted, sitting me down hard on the kitchen cabinet and out of sight of Keilana and her mother. "Did you need to hit me?" Scowling, he reached for his back. "Jesus! I have to tell you something before you go in there."

"Didn't you hear what I said?" I snapped angrily. "I can't talk to you now." I needed to go to her.

"Listen to me!" He grabbed both of my hands and held them hard.

I bared my teeth. Who did he think he was? First nosing incessantly in my business and now telling me what to do? He was pushing his luck even as my best friend. "Say what you have to say *fast* and then get out."

Hesitantly, he let go of my hands. "Just listen for a minute. Mrs. Poppenhouse showed up out of the blue tonight."

"Why were you here anyway?" I was instantly sorry that I'd ask the question. I didn't care nor have time to hear his answer. "Never mind. Tell me later." I could see the perspiration beading on his upper lip and felt my dread grow exponentially.

"I was in the house when she came through the front door. I didn't know she was coming," he said, rubbing his forehead, something he only did when he was very upset. "If I had I would have tried to stop her or warn you or something. I swear to God." The words were flying out of his mouth so quickly that I could barely understand him.

"You came in the house after you lost Keilana? I thought you were going home?"

He blew out a nervous breath and lifted his hand only to let it limply fall. "You don't understand. I never followed Keilana tonight. I was happy to have her out of the house so that it would be easier to break in. You guys hardly ever leave this place. You have no life!"

My mouth worked ineffectually for a few confused seconds as I tried desperately to put things together. "You lied to me and then broke into our house?"

Russ's voice was trembling. "Oh, Jesus, Belinda, I don't know how else to do this, so I'll just say it. I've been working for Mrs. Poppenhouse for weeks."

I gave him a part bewildered, part angry look. "They brought in a second P.I.?" Why hadn't he just told me? I was mad, but Russ was the least of my concerns at the moment. "You've been watching Keilana too and didn't bother to tell me? You suck, Russ. But I have to talk to her now. Go home."

His gaze dropped to the countertop. "No." He swallowed hard. "I've been watching you."

I just stared at him, knowing he couldn't have said what I thought he said. A painful silence thundered between us and he squirmed under the weight of my stare. "What ... what did you just say?"

He closed his eyes.

"Russ?" the urgency in my voice grew.

"Your reports to the Poppenhouses started to change after a couple of weeks. I saw them, Belinda. You all but told Mr. and Mrs. Poppenhouse to go to hell for being bad parents. And then you went on and on about what potential Keilana had and how she was such a good person. Mrs. Poppenhouse got worried and called me." He winced. "She thought you might be trying to take advantage of Keilana's vulnerable state."

"Take advantage?" Had everyone lost their mind? Wasn't I already taking advantage of our friendship to pump her for information? Did they think I was a rapist too? "What vulnerable state?"

He shrugged. "I dunno, but she was worried you two might become ..."—he lowered his voice as though this part was somehow worse than the rest—"involved with each other. Mr. Poppenhouse doesn't have a clue that his daughter is into girls and Mrs. Poppenhouse wants to keep it that way."

"What are you talking about!" I roared. My best friend was spying on me? None of this made any sense. I shook my head wildly, unable to process what he was saying. "Forget it. I don't give a shit right now." I jumped down off the counter. I couldn't think about him now anyway. I had to talk to Keilana. I had to explain things to her so she could move past this and forgive me.

"Please wait." He blocked my path. "There's more," he said quickly. "Your casebook. Or journal or whatever. I'm sorry, Belinda, I've been breaking in and making copies of the entries for Mrs. Poppenhouse since last month."

My feet froze and my mouth fell open.

Seeing the look on my face, he began to panic. "I didn't want to, but you mentioned the notebook in one of your reports and she insisted on seeing it! I tried to warn you not to get hooked on Keilana. I tried!" He threw his hands in the air. "I had no idea you'd put how you felt about her on paper. It was mixed in with everything else. I couldn't even erase the damn stuff." He grabbed his head as though it might somehow fly off his neck. "What were you thinking?"

"You son of a bitch," I hissed, the sour taste of betrayal erupting from my belly and making me ill. I looked him square in the eye, my breath coming in harsh pants. "You're supposed to be my best friend!"

My hurt and rage felt like a liquid heat, invading every pore of my body, and seeping into my blood with every furious beat of my heart. My voice was so deep and calm, that I didn't even recognize it. "Get out of my way right this fucking second, Russ. Or so help me, God"—I was shaking—"I will tear right through you."

I was deadly serious and his back straightened as my words registered. "Belinda, I'm sorry." He spread his hands out in entreaty. "I just need to explain. Please—"

I took a menacing step forward and his hands flew up to guard himself.

The desire to strangle him was growing into something more than I could bear. "Do you even know what you've done to me ... to Keilana?"

He looked at me with uncomprehending eyes. "But it's just a case," he said weakly. "Just a crush on a pretty girl." When I didn't answer, he paled. "Isn't it?"

"Where's my fucking dog?"

He started at my wild change in subjects. "Why do you want ... I mean, he's in the car. I took him with me tonight because he chewed a hole our carpet and Sarah—"

"Bring him back!" I demanded, taking a fistful of his shirt and then using it to shove him as far away as I could. "And then get as far away from me as you can!"

He stumbled back a few steps, looking stricken. "Just let me talk. Please." Stupidly, he moved back in front of me. "I can explain. There's more—"

I covered my ears with my hands and bent at the waist as I yelled, "I don't want to hear anymore!" Then I barreled into him with all of my strength, my shoulder impacting his mid-section with stunning force. We flew into the kitchen wall and his head hit hard, breaking an enormous hole in the plaster that our falling bodies made even bigger.

Stunned by the impact of the fall and what he'd just revealed, I scrambled off him and stumbled into the living room. Keilana was still sitting lifelessly on the sofa. She glanced up and then looked at me as though I were a stranger.

"You have to listen to me." I tried not to think about how Russ had just said the same thing and how I would just as soon kill him as comply. "You only *think* you don't know me." I dropped to my knees in front of her, ignoring Mrs. Poppenhouse, who was looking down at me in fear and shock. "But you *do* know me," I swore fervently. "Everything I said tonight was true. I *do* love you."

Keilana's mother audibly groaned.

"I promise I do," I continued desperately. Carefully, I took my case notebook out of Keilana's hands and held it up before her. "You know how I feel about you. You know how hard this has been. It's all in here. I started this to help the Poppenhouses ..." It was time for the brutal truth. "And for the money. But it hasn't been about getting paid in a long time."

Disgusted, Keilana looked away.

I'd never felt so small. "I thought you might need my help. It's all in here." Gently, I sat the notebook back in her lap.

Vaguely, I heard the front door open, then slam shut as Russ left.

"Cadie or—" she stopped and swallowed a few times. She was barely holding it together. "Or whoever you are."

That was a knife in my heart.

"I didn't read this." She picked up the notebook and threw it across the room in a fit of rage. "I couldn't read it and not go insane! When I came home tonight my wonderful mother," she said the last word as though it were a curse, "and her other little spy filled me in on who you really are. I already know more than enough, thank you."

My eyes jerked upward to Mrs. Poppenhouse. "Tell her why you hired me."

She just stared down at me with dark, wide eyes.

"Tell her!" I demanded when she didn't answer quickly enough.

"I told her," Mrs. Poppenhouse finally said. She shifted uncomfortably, looking as though she wanted to step farther away from me.

Was she actually afraid of me? Good.

"Your father and I were worried about you, Keilana. We couldn't just do nothing while you failed out of school and did God only knows what else."

Keilana shot to her feet, knocking me backward in the process. "Stop making excuses." Furious, she pointed at me. "You hired her so you could control my life just like always! How I act. Where I work. Who I marry. Who I sleep with. Where I live. You want to pick it all!"

Good for her. I was proud of her for sticking up to her mother. This was a good sign. Her anger was something I could deal with, something I deserved, and at least she was still talking.

"That's not true, Keilana," Mrs. Poppenhouse insisted, her face reddening with barely suppressed anger. "Despite what you think, you are still a child. And you don't always know what's best for you."

"What makes you"—blazing blue eyes swung down and bore into me with frightening intensity—"or *you*, think you know what's best for me? I won't be controlled or manipulated anymore." She fixed her stare on her mother. "It's my life and you can't have it."

"I'm your mother," Mrs. Poppenhouse said simply, as though that explained everything. "I'm staying at the Westgate Hotel. We'll talk tomorrow when you're able to be more reasonable and respectful."

Then she glanced down at me like I was a piece of garbage. "Kale needn't know about ..."—she gestured vaguely between Keilana and me—"the two of you."

Gee, how nice of her, seeing as how she's all about family unity and support.

Mrs. Poppenhouse's eyes narrowed. "Don't think that you'll be getting paid for your services after what you've done."

Happy to finally be saying it, I snarled, "You can keep every penny of your stinking money and kiss my sweet ass."

Keilana snorted derisively. "Looks like next time you hire a lap dog, Mother, you'd better find a more obedient one."

I winced.

Mrs. Poppenhouse puffed out her enormous chest. Luckily I was still sitting on my butt, reducing my chances at being blinded. "Give Keilana the keys to the cottage and the Jaguar and have your things out of here in the next half hour or I'll have the campus police arrest you." Then she marched out of our cottage as though she owned the place.

Come to think of it, she might.

In just a few seconds Keilana and I were alone.

I didn't know where to start, I only knew this might be my last chance and I couldn't waste it. Her breathing sounded abnormally loud and then I realized it was my own.

"Keilana," I began tentatively, wanting with all my heart to pull her into a hug and make every bit of the mess I'd caused vanish. "I made a mistake. A horrible mistake. I didn't know you when I took this job. I didn't do it to hurt you. I did it to help us both. I'm so, so sorry I wasn't honest with you. I-I don't know what else to say! Forgive me. Please."

Keilana laughed callously and it was like an Arctic blast rolling through the room. "Forgive you?" This close to her I could see how bloodshot and glassy her eyes were. She'd been crying. A lot. "You lied to me again and again. You *used* me!"

I wished with every ounce of my being that I could deny that. But I couldn't. "I know I did. I don't have an excuse. I got in so deep that there was no good way out. I was going to tell you everything tonight. I couldn't stand having this between us anymore." I searched for something else to say, for a way to redeem myself, but there wasn't one.

I studied Keilana for a long moment. Oh, God, she wasn't going to forgive me. I could see it in her eyes and I felt like throwing up. "I'm not a bad person. Please believe me. I'm so, so sorry." I wrapped my arms around myself, trying to ward off the pain that was making it hard to breathe or think or ...

"You betrayed me." She started to cry again and I felt like I wanted to die. "I trusted you."

"Keilana—"

The cries turned into sobs. "I believed you were my friend. I t-told you things. I confided in you and you tr-tricked me!"

Oh, Jesus, I really was going to be sick. I swallowed hard, then remembered my case notebook. Frantically, I crawled over to it and picked it up. "I know you don't believe anything I'm saying to you now. And I don't blame you." I held it up. "But I never thought you'd see this. It was locked away and meant for my eyes only. You have to believe this if nothing else! I wasn't lying to myself. Read it and you'll know everything."

She wiped her eyes with the back of her hand. "I already told you that I know enough."

Stunned and sick, I sat back on my heels. "Things don't have to end like this for us." Now I was crying too. "You can decide to forgive me."

Just then the front door opened and Smelly shot over to me like a bullet, flying into my arms. I hugged him tightly against me, letting him lick my salty face and drawing comfort from the only friend I had left. "You have to believe me."

She sniffed a few times and whispered, "Don't you get it? I do believe you." She smiled sadly and looked away. "I just can't trust you." She paused. "So what's the point?"

"*We* would be the point!"

"There is no we or us, Cad—Belinda." She let out an unsteady, but resolved breath, and looked at me with heartsick eyes. "There's only lies."

I blinked stupidly. This couldn't just be the end, could it?

She stood up and slowly walked to the bathroom. "Leave your keys on the table."

It was a chilly Sunday afternoon in November when I taped shut the last cardboard box and glumly looked around my office. It hadn't been impressive before, but I'd done my best to make it appear inviting and professional. Now, with everything packed up and its white walls naked, it looked downright depressing.

True to my word, I'd returned the Poppenhouses first couple of paychecks. I'd even paid them back for their expensive haircut and the designer clothes I hated. True to what Mrs. Poppenhouse had said, they hadn't paid me for my final couple weeks of work. That meant I couldn't make October or November's office rent.

So, with no jobs looming on the immediate horizon, Blaisdell Investigations was moving. Where? I still wasn't sure.

I sat down and dug a screwdriver out of my toolbox so that I could pry my nameplate from the placard outside the front door when someone came knocking. I'd glanced up and felt a sense of familiarity wash over me. I'd seen that shadowy silhouette through the privacy glass hundreds of times. But this was the first time it wasn't welcome.

"I know you're in there," Russ called out, rapping loudly. "Let me in, will ya?"

"Fuck off," I yelled back.

It had been weeks since I'd said more than that to him and I saw no reason to spoil my perfect streak now. My anger had cooled, but the hurt was still there. Keilana wouldn't talk to me and I wouldn't talk to Russ. All the rotten bastards I knew were getting just what they deserved.

Russ rapped sharply on the glass. So hard, in fact, I figured it would shatter at any moment. "I'm not the tenant anymore, Russ. You can break the glass for all I care."

"Belinda," he groaned, "enough with this horse shit. Just let me in. Please?"

I don't know what compelled me to open the door. I didn't want to talk to him. I didn't want to see him. I didn't want to have anything to do with the two-faced traitor. And yet, I found myself at my door, flicking open the deadbolt.

"Finally!" He rushed inside and wrapped me in a tight hug before I could move away. I bit my lower lip as I forced my arms to stay at my sides. I'm not one of those people who holds a grudge forever. My anger burns hot and then when I can think straight, I can usually forgive. But I wasn't ready to return Russ's hug.

He released me with a frustrated, slightly wounded look.

"Why are you here, Russ?"

He tilted his head to the side. "Why am I here? Why do you think? I want us to be friends again. I want us to hang out and surf and laugh and for you to come over to my house for dinner. I want you to forgive me."

"No."

"How can you say that? How can you stand there and be so unyielding when I'm asking less from you than you are from Keilana. I don't even want lesbian sex!" He gave me a sheepish grin. "Well, okay, I do, but I can live without it if I have to."

I didn't want to smile. I didn't.

"Aha! I saw that!" Beaming, he pointed at my face. "I saw that. You smiled."

I scowled. "You saw nothing."

"Did too." He let out a relieved breath. "You smiled. You're forgiving me even though you don't want to. I'm wearing you down with my groveling and charm."

I walked over and sat down on my desk, pulling my knees to my chest and wrapping my arms around them. "Just because I smiled, doesn't mean we're friends anymore. We're not. Friends, I mean."

He sat down next to me. "You're wrong," he said softly.

I blinked. "Are you saying I don't know who my own friends are?"

"Yeah." He nodded and shrugged broad shoulders. "Pretty much."

My eyes turned to slits. "I hate you."

"And sometimes I hate you. That's how it is with us. Doesn't mean we aren't friends. It just means we're twisted."

I socked him in the arm. Hard.

"Ow!" He made a face as he rubbed his bicep. "That hurt!"

"You spied on a friend! On *me.* How can I trust you after that? You screwed me for money!"

He looked stricken. "I didn't think I was screwing you. I thought it was an easy job and that I would be able to get you to see that what I'd done wasn't such a big deal. I thought that right now we'd be planning a trip to Australia to catch the perfect wave. I didn't mean to hurt you."

"And you say I'm wrong a lot?" I gestured crazily. "You're ... you're ... wronger than me!"

"Wronger?"

"Eat shit and die, Russ."

He turned to face me and gazed at me with puppy dog eyes, the soft sweet ones that I couldn't resist all those years ago. "See how much fun we're having?" he said. "Tell me you can live without this."

I had missed him. And I didn't want to live without our friendship. But still … he'd invaded my privacy and made a bad situation ten times worse. "Stop cracking jokes. This is serious."

"I know it's serious. But if I don't laugh, then I'll cry, and you'll call me a girly man again!" His gaze turned beseeching. "I'm desperate here, Belinda."

He did look on the verge of tears. And I would have called him a girly man.

"Just give me another chance not to screw up, okay?"

I rubbed my eyes with the back of my hand. "I don't think I can."

"You want Keilana to forgive you but you can't forgive me? Why is this so different?"

"I guess doing the forgiving is a helluva lot harder than asking for it. And this isn't like what happened with Keilana and me! You and I have been friends since I first started as a P.I. You weren't trying to help me by spying on me, you were trying to help yourself. You screwed a friend, not a stranger!"

"Fine." He held his hands up in a placating gesture. "I was trying to help myself. I know it sounds crazy, but I didn't think this was that big of a deal when I agreed to do it. It seemed more like harmless snooping for an obscene amount of money." He ran his hands through his short hair. "I'm sorry and I was wrong."

"I hope whatever you bought with the money breaks."

"I was trying to help you too."

My eyes widened. "Oh, sure you were," I said sarcastically. "How are you going to help me next? Shoot me in head?"

Russ began counting his fingers. "I was helping you keep your job, smartass. I was doing my best to keep Mrs. Poppenhouse off your back. I was trying to be there to remind you what a bad idea it would be to get involved with Keilana so you wouldn't get yourself into a mess you couldn't get out of. I—"

"You read my case notes! You knew I was in love with her."

"I didn't." He let out an exasperated groan. "I tried to tell you all this that night, but you were so hell-bent on talking to Keilana that you wouldn't give me a chance. I checked out your notes the first time I copied them and then not again until the night Mrs. Poppenhouse showed up. The first time I looked at them there were one or two personal comments and that's it. It was no big deal and all businesslike. I didn't think you were going to add some sort of weird running narrative!"

I rested my head against my knees. "Looks like you were wrong again."

"I think we covered that."

"Not enough, Russ."

He scrubbed his face and sighed. "I messed up bad. I hurt you. I'm sorry. I love you and don't want to lose you." All traces of teasing were gone. "You can trust me."

I snickered.

"You can! I know what I did was wrong and it won't ever happen again. I've learned my lesson. Being without my best friend sucks."

I studied him intently, and despite not wanting to, I found myself believing his words. Russ wasn't a complicated guy and even though he had horrible judgment at times, he tried his best to be honest. "It's going to take some time, Russ. No promises."

His face lit up like a Christmas tree. "I understand. And I'm going to work to make things up to you. Thanks."

"Don't thank me yet. I'm still pissed."

He tried to smile. "I know." He reached into the pocket of his leather jacket and pulled out a white envelope. "But I'm going to earn back your trust and make things right. And this is how I want to start." He handed it over. "Here."

I looked at the envelope, and then back at him. "What's this?"

"Two things. First, inside is a receipt for three months rent for this place. You're paid through New Year's." He glanced around. "Sorry I didn't catch you before you took down your pictures."

"Russ!" I started to jump off the desk but he held me back.

"Don't bother saying you can't accept it, because it's already done and I can't get the money back now anyway. The place is yours."

Dumbfounded, I just stared at what was in my hands. "You can't afford to help me." Three months' rent was close to ten thousand dollars. My office was small but the location was choice and brought in business all on its own. "You're saving for a house."

"I can't afford not to do this," he said seriously. "Besides, even though I messed up, I do know the right thing to do when I see it. And this is it. You're like a sister to me, Belinda. Family sticks together when it rains shit."

My back stiffened as a nasty thought crossed my mind. "I won't take the money the Poppenhouses paid you." My eyes glinted dangerously.

The corner of his mouth shot upward. "Stubborn to the end, eh? This isn't their money. I know how you'd feel about that."

My jaw worked. Russ knew how much my business meant to me. He also knew that my brother was just scraping by and that my parents were retired and living on a very modest fixed income. I didn't have anywhere else to turn. "What does Sarah think about this?" I turned the envelope over in my hands. "This is a lot of money."

"It was her idea." He waggled a finger at me. "But I get credit for being married to her and having the sense to agree with her."

I snorted. "She called me last week and begged me to take you back." I smiled a little. "Apparently you're spending way too much time at home on the weekends and in the evenings, and she's about ready to drink poison."

"The women in my life are all evil," he muttered, rolling his eyes.

"I dunno, Russ. I'm not even sure I should be speaking to you, much less taking your money."

"If the positions were reversed would you do it for me?"

"You know I would. But—"

He took my hand in his and squeezed. "Please don't be too proud or angry to accept my help. You'll always be my best friend, even if I'm not always as good a friend as you deserve."

I didn't know what to say so I settled on a hoarse, "Thanks." I cleared my throat a little and focused on the envelope. "You said there were two things in here? Is the other a pony? 'Cause I've always wanted a pony."

"Go on." He nudged my foot with his. "Open it."

I did, blinking slowly when I saw what was inside. "A plane ticket?"

"Uh-huh. To Hawaii."

My heart lurched. *Keilana.*

"She's there visiting her grandmother while she's on Thanksgiving break."

I shot him a look and he braced himself as though I might take a swing at him.

"Don't go crazy, Jesus! I'm not spying on her or anything. I went to Madonna Del Mar and knocked on her door like a regular person. She's got a new roommate, by the way, ugliest girl I've ever seen, and that's who told me where she was."

I closed my eyes. "She won't talk to me, Russ." I wanted to cry, something I hadn't done in what? Hours? "I've tried a dozen times. I've emailed, I've called, and I've shown up at her door only to have it slammed in my face again and again. The campus police know my car and towed it last time!"

He looked surprised and just a little disappointed. "So you're giving up on her then?"

My expression sobered. "No way. I'm just ... just ..."

He bumped my shoulder with his and looked straight ahead to give me a little privacy as my eyes teared up. "Regrouping?"

"Floundering!" God, it felt good to be talking to him again. It would take some time, but we'd be okay. We always were. "I'm miserable without her."

"So don't be without her."

I blew out an annoyed breath. "It's not that easy. You know that."

"Of course it's not. But it's not getting any easier with you here and her hundreds of miles away." He paused.

I could tell he wanted to say something but was holding back. I would probably be sorry I asked, but as usual, I couldn't help myself. "What?"

"Is she the one?"

He didn't have to say more for me to know exactly what he meant. Sarah was the *one* for him. Anyone who knew him could see that that was true. They fought like cats and dogs, but in a way that most people really couldn't understand, they completed each other.

Was Keilana Poppenhouse, that willful, guarded, intelligent, witty, kind young woman the *one* for me? I thought about the sort of person she was deep down inside and the way I felt just being near her. I turned to look at Russ. "I think she might be, but I never got the chance to find out."

"Well, then." He jumped down from my desk and brushed his hands off on his jeans. "What are you waiting for?"

Good question.

A warm, fragrant breeze blew off the water and ruffled my hair as I approached Keilana's grandmother's house. It had taken me two plane trips and a short boat trip to get to this tiny island, whose name I'd already forgotten. The boat driver had given me simple directions to stop at the first house I found, and I was finally here.

The house itself was at least seventy years old and the grounds were lush and beautiful. They overflowed with colorful flowers and plants that were a dozen shades of green. It wasn't as opulent as I'd expected though. There were no gates or servants manning the driveway or guard dogs. It was just a charming old house that was clearly well-maintained and loved.

To be honest, I hadn't expected this level of moderation from anyone in the Poppenhouse family, even Keilana.

I held my breath as I knocked at the door. I hadn't eaten anything since the day before because I was so nervous I wasn't sure I'd be able to keep it down. Now, however, I was a little lightheaded and hadn't even seen her yet!

The door opened and I found myself looking at a white-haired woman with weathered dark skin and lively eyes as black as coal. She was old but it was impossible to tell just how old. "Hello," she said.

She couldn't have been more than five feet tall! "How in the world did you have a baby that huge?" I exclaimed. Then I froze, mortified that my thoughts tumbled from my brain to my mouth with no stops in-between. I felt my face heat and I clamped my hand over my mouth before I could humiliate myself again. "Oh, God," I said through my fingers. Carefully, I peeled away my hand. "I'm so sorry. I—"

But to my relief, she just laughed. "I guess you've met my son Kale. And, yes, it wasn't easy, he was nearly eleven pounds!" She smiled at me, warm but cautious. "You must be Ms. Blaisdell."

I shifted uncomfortably from one foot to the next. "You know about me?" I glanced behind her in case I was wrong about the guard dogs and I was about to become breakfast.

"I do indeed." She stepped aside. "Keilana mentioned that she had a falling out with her roommate."

Whew. "Yes, that's what's happened." I hesitated even though I desperately wanted to talk to Keilana. I knew my unannounced visit was rude. "I apologize for coming by so early."

"Nonsense. Besides, you've already been sitting at the foot of my driveway for three hours. I was starting to wonder if you'd ever come up."

I wanted to crawl under a rock.

"You two must have had some argument. Especially if it brought you all the way to my tiny island."

"That's an understatement." She was being so polite and understanding and so unlike Kale Poppenhouse or his wife. Maybe she was adopted too?

I set my small travel bag on the porch and stepped just inside the doorway. The house smelled like coffee and toast. Yum. "Mrs. Poppenhouse—"

"You can call me Malipeloku."

My eyes went a little wide with panic. "Umm ... I don't think I can!"

She laughed heartily. "Keilana said you were funny."

I licked my lips, covertly glancing around. "Speaking of Keilana, is she here? I'd like to speak with her, please."

She gave me a thorough once over before deciding what to tell me. "She's reading on the beach. Would you like to have some coffee and bring Keilana hers? I just made a fresh pot and was about to walk it down to the beach myself."

Relief washed over me. "Yes. I'd be glad to bring her some coffee."

I followed Mrs. Poppenhouse into the kitchen and sat down at a small breakfast bar while she carefully took three large cups from the cupboard. She filled them in silence and passed two of them over to me.

I took the cups, hoping my hands weren't twitching as badly as I feared. "Which way do I go?"

She opened the kitchen door, allowing the bright sunlight to pour over me. "Turn left and keep walking until you see her."

Gingerly, I took a sip of my hot coffee so I'd have less chance of spilling it down my shirt as I stepped out onto the sand.

"Ms. Blaisdell?"

I turned back and raised my eyebrows in question.

"Don't blow it."

Our eyes met and I got the distinct impression that she was holding out on me. "I won't."

I can't.

The beach was deserted and I began to think that when Keilana's grandmother had said "my" island, she'd really meant it. The fresh air felt nice against my bare legs and arms and the wind fluttered my T-shirt. I pushed off my shoes after a few hundred feet, wanting the comforting feeling of the sand between my toes.

It was at least fifteen minutes before I saw her, sitting under a short palm tree on a soft blanket in the sand. She was beautiful and I drank in the sight of her, my heart racing with fear and anticipation. I guess it wasn't broken after all. I'd known I was missing her. How could I not? But it wasn't until that very moment that I realized just how much.

I got within twenty feet of her before she glanced up at me. She did a double take, and startled, she dropped her book.

"Hi," I said softly, joining her on her blanket without waiting for an invitation.

"Cad— I mean, Ms., I mean Belin ... ugh." Confused, she finally gave up stumbling over my name. "What are you doing here? How did you find me?"

"I didn't do anything shady." I nearly tacked on "I promise" but I suspected my promises wouldn't mean much to her at the moment. "Your roommate told my friend where you'd gone for Thanksgiving break and then he told me. But it was your Granny who gave me directions to this spot on the beach, if that's what you mean."

I took in our surroundings, giving her a few minutes to adjust to my presence. She still looked shocked. "This is beautiful."

"It is."

When I turned back to her, I caught her staring right at me and she quickly looked away. "You're growing out your hair. It looks pretty," she murmured, a little embarrassed.

A kernel of hope ignited inside me. "Thanks. This is for you." I held up her cup that was now lukewarm at best, the aroma of the beans mingling with the fresh scent of the ocean.

Gingerly, she took it, still unwilling to look me in the eye. "Thanks." She took a sip and then set it back down on the sand next to mine, the glass clinking gently.

Well, at least she hadn't told me to go to hell yet. That was an improvement over the first dozen times I'd tried to talk to her since that night.

She gazed out at the water and I couldn't help but think of our trip to the beach at Del Mar and how close I'd felt to her that day, and how awkward things felt now. I had more regrets than I knew what to do with.

"When are you going to give up?" she asked, unconsciously wringing long fingers.

I examined her profile, strong and angry. She looked tired, the dark circles under her eyes more prominent than I'd ever seen them. "Never," I said simply. "I'm never going to give up."

Her forehead creased. "Nobody means that when they say it. Not really."

"That's exactly what I mean." I longed to touch her and had to sit on my hands to keep from reaching out. "I understand that if you're going to trust me again—and I pray that you are—that it's going to take some time. I'll wait as long as I have to."

"What it if never happens?"

"Then I guess I've got a long wait ahead of me." She wanted me to say that I'd bail on her when I didn't get what I wanted fast enough, but I wouldn't do it. I wanted to be in this for the long haul, if she'd only let me.

She swallowed a few times and looked like she might actually start to talk to me.

I leaned forward in anticipation.

Then, abruptly, she picked up her book and started searching for the spot she'd stopped reading. "You're wasting your time. Go home and back to your slimeball spying."

I grabbed the book and tossed it over her head before she could use it as a prop in her latest production of *Let's Ignore Belinda.*

"Hey! Give it back!" she said through clenched teeth, her eyes sparking.

"No." I gentled my voice, which was threatening to rise. "We need to talk."

"You've got some nerve!" She looked like she wanted to scream. "I already have enough people in my life who don't care what I think and who want to control me. I don't need you joining the party."

"Stop it." My anger flared. "Stop being such a Goddamn baby. I don't want to control you and I sure as hell care what you think or I wouldn't be here at all. You might not ever love me. You might not even ever like me again or come close to accepting my apology, but at least listen to it! I've been crafting it for weeks and have come twenty-five hundred miles to give it."

She ground her teeth together but I could see that she was teetering on the edge.

"Will you just listen to me? Please, Keilana." I wasn't above begging. "Please?"

Reluctantly, she nodded.

I could feel my heart pounding painfully and I drew in a nervous breath. Failure wasn't an option. Okay, I told myself, here goes everything. No pressure or anything. "My name is Belinda Blaisdell."

She blinked a few times and I could tell she was surprised by how I'd started, but that was okay. At least she was listening. Besides, I was more concerned that we ended up in the same place than whether we agreed on the road we took to get there.

"My middle name is Cadie. My mom used to call me that when I was teensy tiny, but my dad didn't like it much and so she stopped after a while. I'd forgotten that I liked it until you started using it. You can call me Belinda, like everyone else does, but you aren't like everyone else to me. So you can call me Cadie if you want."

Bewildered, she slowly said, "Okay," and I guessed that she was wondering why she'd have to use my name at all if she decided never to speak to me again.

I had to admit, she had a point.

"You'll want to have a name to use when you curse me at least, right?" I ventured, hoping I'd guessed right.

She sighed, both sadness and frustration leaking into the sound. "I don't want to curse you. Well, actually I do. But I'm trying to get over wanting that and ..." her voice dropped to a whisper, "a lot more."

I struggled not to fall into those beautiful eyes that had somehow grown more intense in the weeks we'd been apart. "So long as you don't get over me," I said in a rush, my anxiety rising. "At least not until I'm done talking. Promise?"

Her eyes flashed. "I can't promise you any—"

"Promise?" I asked frantically. "Or I swear to God I'll do something horrible like ... like ... I'll start singing a wretched love song at the top of my lungs, humiliating myself, and scaring the birds, and sickening you in the process. I'm not bluffing, I'll really do it! I will!"

Somehow, a tiny smile cracked through her stony veneer. "In that case, and because I've heard you sing in the shower, I promise."

That was better. I took a calming breath. "Okay, you already know that I'm a private investigator." I got up and sat down in front of her so that she didn't have to turn her head to look at me. That put me off the blanket and onto the damp sand. My butt was wet again, but I was actually getting used to that. "I have my own tiny business that was doing okay up until a few months ago, but I'll be back on my feet again soon."

She tried not to look concerned. "The job my parents hired you for ruined your business?"

"No. *I* ruined my business. But that doesn't matter now."

"I'm a California native, a college drop-out, and Russ, you remember him, the other slimeball spy? He's my best friend. I haven't forgiven him for his part in this, but we're talking again and I'm trying my best not to hold a grudge or want to kill him every second."

She was looking at me funny. "What?" I asked, allowing her expression to derail me.

"I don't understand what you're doing. Why are you telling me these things?"

"I'm telling you about myself." I swallowed hard. "Keilana, there are a thousand lies between us and I can't take them all back or change what I've done. You deserved the whole truth. And so you're getting it now." I smiled bravely. This didn't sound nearly so cheesy when I was rehearsing it on the airplane. "Even though it's long overdue."

I let out a little groan. "I messed up already, I think. Because I should have started off by telling you that I love you."

Her nostrils flared.

"You haven't gotten to hear me say that nearly as much as you should have, but that doesn't mean it's not true. I also need to tell you that from the very bottom of my heart, I'm so, *so* sorry that I deceived you." My eyes begged her to believe me.

Her chin began to quiver.

"Oh, God, please don't cry," I said helplessly. "I can't stand to see you cry. It'll make me cry and then I'll never get through this." I didn't think I had any tears left, but I'd been wrong every one of the twenty-one days I'd thought that for the past three weeks.

She nodded and I could see she was struggling with her composure. I wanted to help her, but I couldn't force her to open her heart to me or to forgive. All I could do is ask her to take a chance on me. On us.

"What I felt for you ... what I still feel, is *real.* No matter what, you have to know that." My chest still felt like a fat guy was sitting on it and I let out a shuddering breath. "I'm sorry. I'll do my best to be honest with you from now on if you'll give me the chance."

She opened her mouth but I didn't give her an opportunity to contradict me. If I did, and she told me to get lost again, then what would I do? I had no ideas left! "What else should you know about me?" I was babbling but I didn't care. "Oh, right, there is one thing that I was faking the entire time we lived together."

"That you speak French?

Her voice startled me a little. Then I realized what she'd said and my eyes narrowed for a split second. "Okay, there were *two* things I was faking the entire time we lived together."

Her expression filled with dread and her entire body tensed. "What?"

"I'm not neat. I'm a messy pig who was only pretending to be neat so that you wouldn't be repulsed by me."

She gasped. "That was you being neat?"

I nodded gravely. "My neatest. Oh, and I have a dog named Smelly and instead of being twenty-one I just turned thirty-three years old."

"Shut up!" Her eyes nearly popped out of her head. "That can't be true!"

"I know, I know. Cats are way less work."

This time the smile stretched her cheeks, even if it was brief. I was getting to her, I could tell. She wanted to hate me the way I wanted to hate Russ, but hating someone you really cared about did nothing but suck out every bit of your energy and make you miserable. It was hard, horrible work and I hoped, in the end, Keilana would risk happiness instead.

"You said before that all we had between us was lies." Unable to stop myself, I reached out and stroked her cheek with my hand. Her skin was smooth and warm from the morning sun and I was thrilled when she closed her eyes and leaned into my touch. "You were so wrong. Everything I said about you, and how special you are, was true. Everything I felt was true. Everything you felt between us, the attraction, the affection ... it was all real, Keilana. Every bit of it."

Dismayed, she peeled my hand from her face but held it in hers as she looked into my eyes all the way down to the bottom of my soul. "How can I believe you after you tricked and used me?"

Nothing hurts like the bitter truth. Nothing. "I don't know," I said with brutal honesty. "What I did was unforgivable. But I'm asking ... I'm begging you to forgive me anyway."

She bit her lower lip, and didn't say anything else, leaving me to wonder what she was thinking and feeling. I wasn't sure which I'd do first—pass out, or go insane. Keilana was still so much of a mystery to me, maddening and fascinating at the same time.

My worry was somewhere in the stratosphere by the time she finally started to speak. "I've missed you. I've missed cooking dinner with you and talking with you after we've both gone to bed. I've missed playing with you. I've even missed arguing with you." She licked her lips. "I've missed my friend."

"Oh, Keilana," I had to clear my throat to be able to speak. "I've missed you too."

She wiped at her teary eyes. "Umm ... After you left, I read your notebook. It was hard to see what you really thought of me at the beginning, but harder to read how you kept up your lies even after you knew how it would hurt me when I found out the truth."

Looking at Keilana's pain-filled face, I wasn't sure whether it was possible to hate yourself more than I did at that moment. I was relieved that things were all the way out in the open now, but it made me feel vulnerable too, like I was stripped to the bone.

She knew everything, even the ugliest, most unflattering details of my deception. She knew about my self-doubts, indecision, and endless mistakes when it came to her. My empty stomach twisted. How can you ever apologize enough for shattering a fragile trust?

"Keilana,"—I lifted a handful of sand and let it trickle through my fingers, willing something brilliant to come to mind and help save me from myself. It didn't of course; all I had was the inadequate truth—"I didn't know how to put an end to things and not hurt you. Once I took that damn job and started to care about you, there was no good way out."

I glanced up at her and our gazes locked. "I couldn't stop myself from falling in love with you no matter how hard I tried. I didn't mean for it to happen. And to be honest, I'm not sorry that it did, I'm just sorry that I disappointed and hurt you."

Her chest jerked and she started to cry in earnest. "I couldn't have stopped myself either," she said miserably.

Fuck it. I pulled her into a hug, unwilling to clamp down on my urge to comfort her any longer. We both needed it desperately and if we could help each other, even for just a few seconds, it would be worth the pain that would surely follow when she pushed me away.

But she didn't push me away. She held me closer.

"Forgive me," I whispered emotionally, my cheek pressed tightly against hers. "You won't be sorry. I think we can make each other happy, if you'll just give us a chance. If you'll just be brave and crazy and stick your heart out on the line one more time. I'll guard it with everything I have."

She felt so good in my arms, her heart thudding against my chest, her soft skin melded to mine, that I never wanted to let her go.

She sniffed a few times and let out a long breath that brought us even closer together. "No more lies?" she said directly into my ear, her lips tickling the sensitive skin.

I felt lightheaded. "Never. I swear."

She pulled back from me and wiped her cheeks with shaky fingers. Her eyes were brimming with something I hadn't seen since that night at the strip club. Hope. And I knew mine reflected the same thing.

I threaded my fingers with hers. "Can we have a do-over?"

She smiled and I was sure she was remembering when she'd asked me that same thing weeks ago. At the time, her request had seemed unrealistic and childish. Now, I clung to the words, to the hope for a second chance, like a lifeline.

She sighed. "I don't think I have a choice about the do-over. I want to be with you more than I want to stay angry or afraid." She smiled a determined smile and her bravery took my breath away. "Even though you make me crazy, the chance to be together is worth the risk. I don't want to walk away from what we could have."

"Thank God!" I flopped back on the sand, grinning like an idiot.

Keilana laughed gently, sweet and low, and the weight of the world tumbled off my shoulders and into the sea. Then a soft pair of lips covered mine, and I was in heaven.

Stolen Souls

KG MacGregor

"Welcome to the Denver International Airport. Please keep a close watch on your belongings at all times. Unattended bags will be ..."

From her vinyl-covered chair near the exit, Lorna watched as the throng of passengers arriving from San Francisco walked stiffly toward the baggage claim area. Mentally, she crossed off her list those who were greeted by family or friends, along with the businesspeople who carried briefcases or hanging garment bags. That left a handful of stragglers, one of whom was her quarry.

This run to town, which Lorna made twice a week, usually took her to the bus station or along the highways in search of hitchhikers. Those lost souls were what Astrid called the "low-hanging fruit," people down on their luck, looking for friendship and a way to get by. Lorna herself had come to Sky Ranch after hitching west to Denver from Chicago four years ago. But people arriving via the airport were a different breed, smarter and emotionally stronger, and they tended to have more access to cash than those coming to the ranch by other means. They were trickier to score, but worth it in the long run. Quality over quantity, Astrid said.

Lorna kept her vigil as passengers plucked their bags from the carousel. When the crowd began to thin, she zeroed in on a woman in her mid-thirties dressed in tight jeans, a blazer, and boots. Her straight auburn hair was cut short and tucked behind her ears, and she was without makeup. It was a no-nonsense look that said she couldn't care less about styles of the day. She hefted a large blue duffle bag on her shoulder like it weighed nothing at all and marched toward the exit with a confident gait. Astrid was right—this kind of person was quality.

Careful not to arouse suspicions, Lorna hung back, watching through the window as her target waited on the curb. Again and again, the woman checked her watch, her growing impatience apparent. The Copper J Ranch shuttle bus was now thirty minutes late. The bus would not be coming at all, Lorna knew—because there was no Copper J Ranch. *Heh.*

Finally, the woman gave up her wait, pulling a few printed pages from her pocket as she trudged back inside the baggage claim area to a payphone.

Lorna smiled to herself as she noted the exasperated look. *The number you are calling is not in service at this time.*

After slamming the receiver down, the woman dropped her bag and stomped angrily over to the monitor that announced departing flights.

That was Lorna's cue. She rose from her seat and approached the flustered traveler. "Excuse me, miss. Your name wouldn't happen to be Hickman, would it?"

"No," the woman answered gruffly, walking back to her bag.

"Sorry. I just thought for a minute you might be the woman I was supposed to meet. She signed up to spend a couple of weeks on our ranch. You looked—"

"Wait! Are you with the Copper J Ranch?"

"Oh, no! Not another one for the Copper J." Lorna shook her head. "I thought the state had finally closed them down."

"What do you mean?"

"I hate to be the one to tell you this, but they're a scam. I bet you found them on the Internet, right?"

The woman nodded.

"Then I guess they're still at it. Bet you paid by check, too."

"Yeah ... and they already cashed it." The woman scowled and glanced back at the monitor. "So they're not even for real?"

"Afraid not."

"Goddamnit! How could I have been so stupid?" The woman slapped the phony documents against her palm and spun around to check the monitor again. "And the flight back to San Francisco just left."

Lorna let her fume for a few more seconds before extending her offer. "Look, if you're still up for working on a ranch for a couple of weeks, it looks like this

Hickman woman isn't going to show. She already paid, and we're short three hands this week. You can have her spot if you want it."

The woman looked at her skeptically. "What kind of work you got?"

"Whatever you want. Range work ... corral ... mess hall. Do you ride?"

She shook her head. "Not much. But I'd be willing to give it a shot."

"I think we can find you something, and we'll be sure to get you some time in the saddle too."

The woman sighed in resignation. "How much will it cost me? I already paid those assholes almost three thousand dollars."

Lorna shook her head. "You'd be in Hickman's spot, and like I said, she paid already. Besides, we sometimes have to pick up extras from town when we're short of hands. We have to pay them a salary, so it works out for both of us if you want to just come along."

"You sure it's okay?"

Lorna held out her hand for a shake. "Anybody who's willing to work is welcome at Sky Ranch. I'm Lorna Pierce."

The woman took it with a firm grip. "Vonne Maglio."

Lorna stole another glance at her brooding passenger. They had been riding deeper into the canyons west of the flatirons for almost an hour and she had barely said a word. "You might as well get over it, Vonne. You were snookered, but at least you landed on your feet."

Her passenger snorted.

"Besides, I think you're going to like Sky Ranch even better than you would have a place like the Copper J. We're not like those other ranches." The elaborate ruse was necessary, Astrid said, so the new hands would arrive without expectations ... and so no one on the outside would be able to track them, at least not easily.

"How so?"

"Most of the others cater to tourists. They let you sleep in while the real hands do all the hard work, and they have these big barbecue cookouts at the end of the day. It's phony."

"So now you're telling me that there's no barbecue? How bad does this get?"

Lorna laughed. "We're a real working ranch, and everybody at Sky has to pull their own weight. Some people grumble about it at first, but when their time's up, they feel good about it because they've worked so hard."

"I can handle the work ... but the barbecue would have been a nice touch."

"Sorry. But I think you'll like us anyway. You look like somebody that's not afraid of a little work." Sky Ranch could use more hands like Vonne Maglio, Lorna thought. "Some people like it so much they hire on for good. They don't want to go back to wearing a tie or high heels, and sitting behind a desk all day."

"They just stay there?"

"Some of them do. Of course, not everybody gets to stay—just those that work hard and contribute."

"I'll do my share, but you don't have to worry about me wanting a job when my two weeks are up. I'm just here to get away from the city for a while ... take some time to think about what I want to do with my life."

"They all say that at first," Lorna answered with a chuckle. "What kind of work do you do now?" She already knew this from the application form Vonne had filled out on the Internet for the fictitious Copper J Ranch. Astrid used the information to pick which ones she wanted. She looked for people who lived alone, who worked at dead-end jobs, and especially who had money to drop on a trip like this.

"I'm sort of between jobs right now. I got out of the navy not long ago."

"Ready to have your feet on dry land, eh?"

"I'll say."

Lorna pointed to a turn up ahead, a narrow dirt road that disappeared into the trees. "This is where the ranch starts." A few hundred yards down the road, they reached a gate plastered with warning signs about trespassing and the dangers of the electric fence. She fingered a remote hooked above her visor and the gate opened automatically, closing behind them once they drove through.

"Is that really an electric fence?"

"You want me to stop so you can go find out?" That was her standard answer, and she had yet to have any takers.

"I guess I'll take your word for it."

"We've had a little trouble with teenagers coming out here looking for places to drink and smoke dope."

Vonne chuckled. "Looks like the perfect spot."

"We don't allow any illegal drugs on the property. That won't be a problem, will it?"

Vonne backpedaled immediately. "No, of course not. I had my fill of all that in the navy ... drinking too. I was just thinking back to when I was a teenager. I would have been looking for a place like this too."

"Yeah, I guess we all had those years. By the way, we don't allow cell phones or laptops or things like that either. If you brought that kind of stuff, we'll check it for you and give it back when you leave." The phony Copper J website had spelled out those restrictions as well.

"No, I came out here to get away from that shit."

"I hear you."

After another mile, they came to a pasture, where a few hundred head of cattle grazed as a half dozen hands milled around on horseback.

"How big is the herd?"

"Couple of thousand ... pretty big for a ranch like this. It brings a good dollar out of the slaughterhouse, and we eat well. We also sell a lot of breeding stock."

Vonne nodded as they drove past. The road ended at the mouth of a canyon, where several buildings were clustered beneath two towering walls of rock.

"This is beautiful," Vonne said.

"The property runs way back into those canyons. We've got about forty working hands. Six of them are women on their own like you, but we have a few families too," Lorna explained. "Right now, we've got four visitors, counting you, but one of them has already asked about staying on." She parked the van beside the large barn and they both got out. "Let's stow your gear and I'll give you a quick tour."

They stopped at one of the smaller buildings, designated as the women's bunkhouse, and dropped off Vonne's duffle bag and blazer. Despite the open windows and doors, the room felt stuffy. When they stepped back outside, Lorna then pointed out the larger bunkhouse for the men, and the shared bathhouse out back. Vonne excused herself for a quick trip to the women's latrine, which was attached to the bathhouse but opened to the outside near the women's bunkhouse. When she returned, they continued on past several smaller cabins set aside for the families on the ranch, and then around the main house, easily the largest building on the property.

"Back here is the mess hall," Lorna said, indicating a side door. Inside the large room were five long tables with a dozen chairs each, and a pass-through to the kitchen. Several women ranging in age from late teens to fifties were working, tending ovens and stovetops. The smell of dinner already filled the air. "Most of the women on the ranch work here in the kitchen or in the main house."

Vonne looked from one woman to another, smiling her greeting. "What do they do in the main house?"

"Laundry, teaching ... taking care of the kids. I think one of them is Astrid's housekeeper."

"Who's Astrid?"

"Astrid Becker. She owns the place. Sky Ranch has been in her family for generations, but she's the last of the line. You'll meet her tonight at dinner."

Vonne nodded. Keeping her voice low, she said, "I don't think I could stand working in the kitchen all day. You got any jobs outside?"

"Most of the range work means riding every day, but there's a lot to do around the yard."

They exited the mess hall on the other side, where a dusty courtyard led to the barn and an adjacent corral. A wiry woman a couple of inches shorter than Vonne was unloading feedbags from a pickup truck, stacking them neatly just inside the barn door.

"This is Liza. She works the yard."

The woman looked up and nodded in their direction before turning back to her work. Like Vonne, she was dressed in tight jeans and boots. Her sleeveless denim shirt bore a sweat stain down the center of her back, and a tan Stetson hid most of her curly brown hair from the sun.

"She doesn't talk much," Lorna whispered as they walked past the woman into the barn. "There's a lot to be done out here every day. Liza sees to the supplies for the whole ranch ... keeps the kitchen and the barn stocked ... runs lunch out to the range hands, that kind of stuff. She could sure use some help if you're up for heavy lifting." She looked back at the subject of their conversation. "Don't know how she'd take to working with somebody, though. She seems to like being by herself."

"I could do that kind of work, I guess. Better than peeling potatoes."

"Or there's always working in the barn."

They stopped just past where Liza had stacked the supplies. Vonne's eyes went immediately to a scruffy-looking man who emerged from a stall, his pants covered to his knees with horse manure. Tobacco spittle dribbled off his chin onto a western shirt that probably had been white at one time.

"That's Clint. He handles the horses. He has a couple of helpers, but he's about to lose one of them ... Dominick is the one I told you about that wants to stay on, but only if he can get out of the barn and do some real ranch work."

Lorna waited as though watching the wheels turn inside Vonne's head. The new arrival looked first at Clint, then back over her shoulder at Liza, who had stopped working to watch them. The women's eyes held for several seconds before Liza turned back toward the truck, stretching to pull a large burlap sack from the bed.

"I think I'll take my chances with Liza." Vonne said as she hurried back to the barn entrance. She reached alongside her into the truck, grasping the other end of the sack. Together, they carried it into the barn and heaved it onto the neat pile.

"Thanks," Liza muttered.

"No problem."

Pleased at Vonne's choice, Lorna joined them. "Liza, this is Vonne. She's going to be working with you for a couple of weeks. Think you can show her the ropes?"

Liza pushed the brim of her hat up to get a good look at the new hire. "Sure," she answered, her voice flat but not unwelcoming.

"Vonne Maglio," she said, holding out her hand.

Liza took it in a dusty grip. "Liza Wingate."

Lorna smiled with satisfaction. "Don't kill her on the first day, all right?"

"You should have told me there were three more truckloads like this before I took this job." Vonne stopped to massage her aching shoulder.

"You can always go back and work in the horseshit." Liza had loosened up practically the minute Lorna disappeared.

"I'd feel better if you didn't act like you enjoyed my misery so much."

"Too bad. That sympathy train left the station—along with your ride back to town."

Vonne snorted. "And I distinctly remember Lorna telling you not to kill me on my first day."

"I won't. But all bets are off tomorrow."

Vonne shook her head and grabbed another sack. After just a few hours, she realized she was in for an interesting two weeks. From only their brief conversations, it was obvious Liza was well-spoken and smart, and she had a wicked—if not downright evil—sense of humor. They had already fallen into a playful rapport, surprising since Lorna had described her as a loner.

As they were hauling the last of their load into the barn, Vonne looked up to see a column of men on horseback emerging from the woods behind the main house. Clint and a man Liza said was Dominick met them to lead the horses into the barn. "That's a big job, taking care of all those horses."

"Yeah, Lorna's trying to hire some more help. I think she was hoping you would do it." She looked at Vonne with a smirk. "One more load of dry goods to the kitchen and we're done for the day. Then you can west your poor wittle muscles."

"Lorna told me you were the quiet type."

Liza huffed. "That's because I don't talk to her."

Vonne wanted to ask why, but figured it would be a pretty nosy question coming from someone who had been there all of four hours. "I'll have to ask her how she got you to do that."

Rest couldn't come soon enough for Vonne, and after their last load they finally headed back to the bunkhouse. Liza pointed out the top bunk next to the window.

"You'll thank me tonight."

Vonne reached into her duffle bag and pulled out shorts and a T-shirt. "What's the shower schedule?"

"The men have it before dinner, we get it after. But the toilets on the right side are ours all the time."

"Yeah, I found those earlier." Vonne spread out a blanket and crawled up onto her bed, relishing the chance to finally relax.

"Don't get too comfortable. Dinner's in about ten minutes."

For an instant, Vonne entertained the idea of skipping dinner and getting some rest. But she wanted to meet this Astrid Becker, the owner of Sky Ranch.

"That one's Astrid—the woman in the gold shirt."

Vonne would have known that anyway, even without Liza pointing it out. Astrid Becker was a handsome woman, tall and muscular, with graying curls held back on both sides with barrettes. She easily commanded the room with a manner that was almost regal. And if that weren't evidence enough, everyone in the room came to their feet until she was seated at the center of the head table.

"Wow! Do people always stand up when she comes in?"

"Just at dinner," Liza explained. "She doesn't require it or anything. I think it's just to show respect for her."

The buffet dinner—pot roast, stewed vegetables, and bread—was filling, but a poor substitute for barbecue, Vonne thought. She ate heartily, though, knowing the next day's work would require all the energy she could muster.

"Where's our new hand?"

Vonne looked up to see Astrid standing and scanning the room.

"Right here." Vonne stood slowly and smiled. "Vonne Maglio."

"Welcome to Sky Ranch, Vonne. I hope you enjoy your time here. Lorna says you were looking for a working vacation, and I have a hunch you've found it."

Vonne chuckled along with everyone else.

"If there's anything we can do to make your stay more uncomfortable ..."

They laughed again, louder this time.

"But for tonight, why don't you sit back down and relax. We always finish dinner with a lively discussion, just to make sure our brains get a workout too."

Vonne sat mesmerized for the next thirty minutes as Astrid tossed out philosophical questions to generate mild debate and discussion among the hands as they all finished their meal. It was clear she was held in high regard—perhaps even reverence—by the men and women of Sky Ranch. As the evening progressed, Vonne began to see why they found her so gripping. She obviously was very intelligent, and she had a way with people that seemed to make them strive to please her.

Finally, Astrid stood and cleared her throat. At that time, the room fell quiet and she excused the temporary workers—Vonne, Dominick, and a man and woman who Liza said were husband and wife—saying she had business to discuss with the permanent help. She wished them all a good night's rest.

"I guess this means we get a head start on going to sleep," Vonne said casually to Dominick as they walked outside. The married couple were walking together ahead toward the bunkhouses.

"Don't worry, Vonne. The first couple of days are the hardest, but then on the third day you wake up and can't wait to get started. And it's like that every day after."

"Then I sure am looking forward to Monday."

"Except Mondays are usually pretty tough because there's extra to do."

"Then Tuesday."

"That's the day we load up for the slaughterhouse."

"Level with me, Dominick."

"Okay, you're going to feel like this every night, and you're always going to dread getting up." He laughed at his own joke.

"That's what I was afraid of."

"But you're going to love it here, Vonne. Wait and see." He bid her goodnight and disappeared in the shadows toward the men's bunkhouse.

She reached the women's bunkhouse, walking in to find the married woman, Crystal, getting ready for the shower.

"It's good she lets us go early sometimes," Crystal said. "I like having a little privacy in the bathhouse instead of being in there with everybody at once."

Vonne had peeked in the bathhouse earlier this afternoon and knew it consisted of three small changing rooms, one private shower, and a large communal shower. "Do you want me to wait here while you go?"

Crystal shook her head. "No, that's all right."

"You like Sky Ranch?" Vonne made conversation as they walked to the bathhouse.

"Not me. We just came here to work for a little while so we could earn the money to get all the way to Ohio. Our bus ticket ran out in Denver and Lorna picked us up. I'm ready to move on as soon as we get enough money, but Philip—he's my husband—he likes it here and wants to stay."

"How come you don't like it?"

"I don't like sleeping in a bunkhouse with a bunch of women!" She said it as though it was the most ridiculous question ever asked. "And besides, there ain't no way for us to get to church on Sunday. Astrid don't have no use for church."

"How long before you have enough money?"

"Should be any day now. I sure will be glad to get back on that bus." They entered the bathhouse together and Crystal went straight for the private shower and pulled the curtain closed.

Vonne continued into the larger room, stopping at the showerhead closest to the door. After a few minutes, the hot water reached the muscles in her shoulders and neck, and she knew she had found the one thing she needed more than sleep. It took all the willpower she could muster to turn it off after she rinsed, figuring there would be hell to pay if the others ended up taking cold showers.

She and Crystal returned to the bunkhouse just as the other women were coming back from the after-dinner meeting. Vonne stowed her gear and climbed up to stretch out while the others went off to bathe. Liza lagged behind in the bunkhouse for a few minutes, leaving for the showers as the other women began to return. She came back a full half hour after the others had turned in for the night.

As a gentle breeze wafted through the bunkhouse, Vonne said a silent thanks for the tip about sleeping next to the window. Liza slept directly beneath her and the other five women—four of them kitchen workers, and one who she learned handled all of the laundry—occupied bunks at the far end of the room. The bunkhouse clusters seemed more practical than cliquish, since only a few of the beds were adjacent to windows. Vonne supposed they all shifted near the big stone fireplace in the winter.

These women led an interesting life, she thought. Working from dawn to sundown and sharing a bunkhouse and showers with others was a lot like being in the navy. She wondered if the hands at Sky Ranch got anything like shore leave. She doubted it.

She rolled her head from side to side, still trying to loosen the knots in her neck. Getting up at dawn wasn't going to be easy, especially with the one-hour time difference from the west coast. Despite her fatigue, she had lain awake for forty-five minutes, listening as her bunkmates fell asleep. She envied their soft snores and deep breathing. She would join them soon in Dreamland—but not yet.

Careful not to make a sound, she swung her legs over the side of the bed and slid quietly to the floor. Checking one last time to make sure everyone was asleep, she tiptoed to the door and pushed the screen softly. Holding it so it wouldn't slam, she allowed it to close before stepping off the porch in the direction of the bathhouse.

As she approached the latrine, the odor of disinfectant grew stronger. That explained why Liza had come back a half hour after the other women had turned in. She had probably been the one who stayed behind and cleaned up. Once inside the dark latrine, Vonne closed and locked the door with the barrel bolt. Carefully, she climbed onto the toilet seat to retrieve the cell phone she had stashed in the eaves when she first arrived at Sky Ranch. Her suspicions had paid off, since someone—probably Lorna—had searched her bag while she was out working with Liza. She turned on the phone and waited for it to come to life. With her speed dial, she was connected at once.

"Hey, Jerry. I'm in ... but it's not the Copper J. They pulled a switch at the airport ... Yeah, she's here. And your buddy was right—it's Astrid Becker." Vonne unlocked and cracked the door so she could peer out at the women's bunkhouse. "This place is called Sky Ranch." She could see a woman emerge from the bunkhouse and start toward the bathhouse. "I don't know yet. Find out what you can on your end ... I'll call you when I figure out what she's doing to these people. I gotta go."

Vonne turned off the phone and stepped onto the toilet seat to set it in the corner out of sight. It was too risky to keep it in the bunkhouse. She flushed the toilet and walked outside in time to greet the woman, one of the ones she had met earlier in the kitchen. Then she continued back to her bunk where she quietly climbed into bed. Sleep came instantly.

Liza backed the pickup truck up to the door of the kitchen. "Everything should be ready by now. We just have to load it and haul it out to the range hands."

Vonne hopped out and joined Liza at the rear of the truck, where they lowered the tailgate in anticipation of their load. Inside, they found the kitchen crew hard at work on dinner. Four large insulated containers—lunch for the thirty-some range hands—were stacked by the door.

"These all go out to the pasture?"

"No, just the green one. We have to take the others up to the canyon. That's where most of the hands are."

Vonne stepped over to help with the load and was surprised to see Liza hoist a packed container on her own. For someone so lithe, she was deceptively strong. Vonne had noticed the muscle definition in her upper arms. That was only one of the many things she noticed on pretty women.

"Ungh!" Vonne grunted as she lifted one by herself.

"Let me help."

"No way! You think I'm going to let you show me up?"

Liza laughed. "I hope this means you'll be too proud to whine tonight."

"You're evil all the way through, aren't you?"

"Hey! This is me being nice," Liza countered.

"Now you're scaring me."

In only a few minutes, they loaded the truck and set out on a rutted dirt road that zigzagged up the hillside. Periodically, a trail crossed the road and continued on up.

"What's that trail I keep seeing?"

"That's the horse trail. The hands go straight up from the back of the house on horseback, but it's too steep for us to go that way."

When they reached a level clearing near the top of the ridge, Liza stopped and killed the engine. In the center of the clearing sat a wooden frame building with a wide covered porch. Several picnic tables were positioned underneath the awning. The women got out and hauled three of the containers to the porch.

"What's in there?" Vonne nodded toward the building.

"Supplies, I guess. It's always closed up."

And the windows are covered so no one can peek inside.

"We just unload it and leave it here," Liza said.

"Where is everybody?"

Liza pointed toward a continuation of the horse trail that led into more rugged terrain. "Through that pass. We can't get the truck any farther, so they have to come down here to eat. We just leave it and come back in a few hours to pick up the empties."

"So you don't even see them?"

"Nope."

Peculiar.

Two rifle shots pierced the air, causing Vonne to jump. "What was that?"

Liza shrugged, seemingly impervious to the noise. "Coyote or something, I guess. You hear a lot of that up here." She got back into the truck and started it up. "Now we have to drop this one off at the pasture."

"What's back up there in the canyon?"

"I think it's a big herd, because most of the hands go up there every day."

The herd in the lower pasture numbered about three or four hundred and took only six hands to manage, Vonne remembered. Lorna had said there were a couple of thousand head, so most of them had to be in the canyon.

They followed the zigzag road back down the way they came, and twenty minutes later pulled up to a second building similar to the one near the canyon but not as large. Here, the half dozen hands who managed the lower herd were already gathered on the front porch waiting for their lunch. Vonne recognized one as Philip, the temporary helper who was married to Crystal.

"I can get this one. Just sit here and rest your tired old bones," Liza said. When she returned, she set a smaller cooler on the seat between them. "This is for us. I usually stop down at the creek and eat."

"Good! Or is it considered whining if I act like I'm hungry?"

"Nah, you've worked hard this morning. I won't begrudge you a bite to eat."

"Wow, a compliment from Miss Hard Ass! I'm all misty-eyed."

Liza chuckled. "Yeah, me too."

In a few minutes, Liza pulled the truck under a stand of trees where a small creek trickled down from the canyon pass. She grabbed the cooler and walked to a seat on a boulder near the water. "This is my favorite part of the whole day."

"I can see why." Vonne followed, soaking up the sensation of being so close to nature—and so far from the commotion of the city. A part of her wished this wasn't a job, but a real vacation instead. It was easy to understand why some people came to a place like this and didn't want to leave.

All morning, Vonne had peppered Liza with questions about life on the ranch. At first, she had been interested in learning more about Astrid, but the more she talked with Liza, the more she wanted to understand why she had chosen a life like this. "How long have you worked at Sky Ranch?"

"About six months."

"So what's it like here in the winter?"

Liza chuckled. "You don't want to know."

"That bad, huh?"

"Nothing changes as far as the work's concerned. The range hands go out every day, and all the supplies still have to move."

"Wow. I guess I never thought of it that way."

"Just because there's two feet of snow on the ground doesn't mean the animals or the hands don't have to eat."

"That must be hard work."

"It's all right. You just do it."

"Do you like it here?"

Liza shrugged noncommittally. "It's as good a place as any, I guess." She picked up her sandwich and walked downstream, crossing the creek to take a seat on a sunny ledge.

Vonne followed her, stripping down to her tank top so she could soak up the sun. From behind her sunglasses, she saw Liza watching her intently, and it was a look that Vonne recognized. She flipped up her glasses to look Liza in the eye. "So where are you from?"

Liza hurriedly looked away, obviously embarrassed about being caught checking Vonne out. "Orange County."

"Disneyland."

Liza snorted. "Now you see why I don't want to go back." She poured cold water from a thermos and handed a cup to Vonne. "What about you?"

"I'm from the Bay Area ... Sausalito."

"It's pretty up there."

"Yeah, but not like this." Vonne leaned back against the warm rock. "Lorna might be right. She said two weeks up here and I wouldn't want to go back."

"Sure beats ledgers and spreadsheets."

"So you're a number cruncher?"

"Used to be. But I'm not going back to that. I'd rather be homeless." Liza finished off her sandwich with one last bite.

"That would be pretty boring compared to this."

"Not to mention crooked," Liza mumbled before swallowing. "What kind of work do you do?"

"I just got out of the navy. Hard to say what I'll do next. Something where I get to be outside a lot, I guess."

"I hear you." Liza began to gather their trash, her signal that their break was over. "It's time to go back and pick up the empties. You ready?"

Vonne nodded and pulled on her denim shirt. She assumed most of the hands at Sky Ranch were as cynical as Liza about the world outside. What she wanted to know was why, and what Astrid Becker was offering them instead.

"So ... let's see, where is the greenhorn?" Astrid looked around the room from her seat at the head table, finally spotting Vonne at the table farthest away. "Vonne, how was your first full day?"

"It was great, thanks. My blisters have already started to turn into calluses."

The other hands laughed in unison, nodding in understanding.

"I'm glad to hear it," Astrid said, smiling. "Why don't you start us off with the discussion tonight? I think these folks get a little tired of listening to me"—she looked around the room and smirked—"but they're all too polite to say so."

Vonne laughed along with the others, already racking her brain to come up with something to talk about.

Astrid saw her hesitation and rescued her. "I'll make it easy. Here's a question to get the ball rolling."

Vonne glanced briefly at Liza, who gave her an encouraging nod.

"Why don't you tell us what you think is the most important thing a government should do for its people?"

Vonne set down her knife and fork and swallowed the last of her roast beef. Astrid's question was in the vein of those she had tossed out last evening, but as a newcomer, she hadn't been asked to participate in that debate. Her grace period was over, it seemed, and she stood to address the leader.

"Provide justice, I think."

"Why is that?" Astrid frowned, as though disappointed with the answer.

"Justice gives us a set of common rules to live by. It's what separates us from barbarians and anarchists." Vonne was sure she saw Astrid flinch.

"But what if justice isn't fair?" Astrid barked. "What if it favors one race over another? Or one class over another? What if it favors men over women?"

"Justice isn't perfect. Few things are. But that doesn't diminish its importance, since without it none of the other contributions of government would matter. People wouldn't be safe to come and go, or to keep what they earn. Families wouldn't be secure ... and the people who take advantage of others would do so with impunity."

"I think you make a mistake to assume that only the government can hold people accountable for violations of acceptable behavior." Astrid looked around the room and softened her tone. "Maybe we should go back to the days of the Old West, when justice was worn on the hip."

The other hands laughed and nodded again, mumbling to one another in agreement. Vonne decided it was all in fun and joined in.

<>

"Don't be too bothered about Astrid's questions tonight," Liza said as they returned to the bunkhouse. "You held your own. She respects that."

"I don't know about holding my own. She had some pretty good points about justice being uneven."

"Yeah, but you had good points too. Astrid doesn't challenge people to put them down. She wants to make people think. That's one of the things I really like about her."

Vonne knew there was more to it than that. In just two days at Sky Ranch, she could tell Astrid's sway over these people was powerful, much stronger than she had suspected at first. That could be dangerous if Astrid ever asked them to do something illegal, or something that put them at risk.

When they reached the bunkhouse, Liza pulled off her boots and stretched out on her bed.

Vonne opened her duffle bag and took out clean underwear, a fresh T-shirt and the shorts she usually slept in. "Aren't you going to the showers?"

"I usually wait until the others are finishing up so I can clean the bathhouse."

"Yeah, I noticed when I got up last night that the place had been disinfected. You should have told me. I would have helped."

Liza waved her hand in dismissal. "Not a big deal. It's not my favorite job, but it has to be done. It doesn't take that long. Besides, you whined so much I hated to ask."

"If I really thought whining would help, I would do it more." Vonne sat down on the empty lower bunk across from Liza's. "But I don't mind helping. I came here to work, and if I pitch in, it'll go even quicker."

"Okay, thanks." Liza sat up and pulled her shorts and T-shirt out from under her pillow. "What I was trying to say about Astrid is that she's really good at getting people to understand complex things. I mean, look at some of the people here." She lowered her voice as the last of the women left for the showers. "Most of them are drifters, dropouts ... people who can't hold a job somewhere else. And she's got them thinking about things like the

Constitution and the structure of a republic. The other night, she read from Thomas Paine and got everybody to talk about it."

"Why does she do that?"

"She likes that stuff. She says living out here away from everybody and working together the way we do, we have to be our own government. She wants us to understand the right principles, because we all have responsibilities to each other. In a place as small as this, we can't afford to have problems like the ones they have everywhere else, like drugs or crime ... or people using too much of something."

"That's interesting."

"It really is, especially when you get to see it played out on a small scale like here on the ranch. She's got some books in the house if you ever want to read something." Liza reached under the bed and pulled out a tattered paperback. "I've been reading this one, but it took me awhile to get through it."

"John Locke."

"Yeah, it's a bunch of essays about things like religion, taxes ... stuff like that."

Vonne recognized the title as one she had read in a political science class during her freshman year at Annapolis. "You're finished with it?"

Liza nodded. "But I've been hanging on to it because as soon as I turn it in, Astrid will ask me to talk about it at dinner. I don't want to do that until I know it cold. You know what I mean?"

Vonne nodded, astounded to realize just how much Astrid's opinion mattered to Liza, and probably to all the others. "Why don't you practice on me? You can tell me all about Locke when we're cleaning up."

"Sure you don't mind?"

"Nah, it'll be interesting."

When the other women began to return from the bathhouse, Liza put her book away, indicating it was time to go clean. They walked over to the bathhouse and she showed Vonne the storage closet where the supplies were kept and they started on the latrines. As they worked, Liza explained as much as she could remember and understand from Locke's book, while Vonne interjected questions and comments to mimic how Astrid might respond.

"I actually think all this talk is helping," Liza proclaimed as they finished up by mopping the communal shower. "Who knew you'd turn out to be so useful?"

"Always the smartass."

Liza gave Vonne a genuine smile and held out her hand for the mop, which she stowed back in the closet. "Now comes the best part. We get to be the first ones to use the clean bathhouse."

"I've been looking forward to this all day, ever since you handed me that sack with the horseshit all over it." Vonne pulled off her shirt and tossed it onto the bench next to her clean clothes.

Liza too began to get undressed. "I didn't know it had horseshit on it. It was just on that one side."

"Yeah, my side." By this time, Vonne was naked and headed into the shower room. "Which one of these is the best?" she asked, looking at the eight showerheads that protruded from the concrete block wall.

"This one," Liza answered, arriving just in time to claim the space in the right-hand corner.

"That wasn't very nice." Vonne tested each of the showerheads for pressure, settling on one two spaces down from Liza. "God, this feels good."

"Yeah, that's another thing about waiting until last. There's more water pressure and the water heats up again while we're cleaning."

"You know all the tricks, don't you?" Vonne began to massage her head with shampoo from one of the dispensers. From the corner of her eye, she could see Liza watching her ... studying her body as the steamy water poured over it. She didn't mind—except that with Liza watching her, it was hard to watch Liza.

When they finished, they toweled off and got dressed, their discussion of Locke apparently done for the night. The long day of hard work was catching up with both of them.

"I don't know about you, but I'm beat," Liza said as they walked out of the bathhouse.

"If you're beat, you can imagine how I feel ... being a tenderfoot and all." Vonne laughed, looking up just in time to see a dark figure exit the bunkhouse and disappear into the shadows by the main house. "Who was that?"

"Where?"

"Somebody just came out of the bunkhouse and went around the corner."

"It was probably Lorna," Liza answered, her voice giving away her irritation.

"What would she be doing in the bunkhouse? I thought she had a room of her own in the main house."

"She does, but she comes in to spy on everybody."

"What kind of stuff is she looking for?"

"Who knows? I don't have anything to hide. I just don't like her being so sneaky all the time."

"I guess Astrid feels like she needs another set of eyes to keep up with everyone." Paranoia was a common characteristic of cults—and with every new piece of information, that's what Sky Ranch was beginning to look like.

"She doesn't have to worry about any of us. I just think Lorna likes to be nosy, and she uses her position with Astrid to justify it."

"Some people are like that." Vonne was tempted to mention her suspicions that Lorna had searched her bags, but she didn't want anyone to know that she knew. It was becoming obvious Lorna was a major player in whatever Astrid was doing at Sky Ranch.

All in all, Vonne was pleased with how much she already had learned about the workings of this place. The more details she could put together about Astrid and the ranch, the easier Jerry's job would be. Whatever was going on in the canyon was probably the key, and she was relieved that Liza didn't seem to be a part of it—at least not knowingly. From what Vonne could gather, only a couple of dozen hands were involved in the canyon activities, and that was a manageable number if Jerry needed to call in help to head off any problems.

No matter what happened in the end, Vonne was committed to making sure innocent people like Liza didn't get hurt. There were probably lots of people at the ranch like her, workers who were unwittingly caught in a web of manipulation.

Vonne stood in the breakfast line behind Liza, barely aware she was studying a threadbare patch beneath the back pocket of Liza's jeans. She had gotten a sneak peek at the whole picture last night in the shower, but that wasn't nearly as tantalizing as seeing this naked sliver of skin. She hadn't meant to let her thoughts wander down that path, but ever since she caught Liza checking her out, she couldn't seem to get it out of her mind.

Of course, Jerry would tear her a new asshole if she didn't behave herself.

"You should try one of these," Liza said, interrupting her prurient thoughts. They were last in line after making an early morning run to the supply shed so they could stock the vegetable bins.

"What are they?"

"Fruit turnovers. I think these have blackberries inside."

Vonne put one on her plate. "How come Astrid doesn't eat breakfast with us?" After their talk in the bathhouse last night, Liza seemed more eager to talk about the ranch's owner. Vonne was careful to frame her questions so they sounded casual rather than like an investigation—which is precisely what they were.

"I don't know. She just never does." Liza looked around to see if anyone was listening. "I heard somebody say that she takes breakfast early in her library."

"What does she do all day?"

"She usually rides out to the pasture first. Then she goes up to the canyon around ten o'clock. She spends a lot of time up there."

Vonne didn't bother to press for more about the canyon. Liza was convinced it held another herd, and there was no need to arouse her suspicions about what else could be going on up there. The last thing she wanted was for Liza to call attention to herself by asking around.

Vonne needed to find a way to investigate without raising suspicions, and she also wanted to have a look at that library Liza had talked about. "So what are we doing today?"

"Mondays are pretty busy. We need to go around to the bunkhouses and pick up the laundry bags. Then we take lunch out to the hands and come back. Lorna should be back by then with the fuel truck."

"Fuel truck?"

"Yeah, she goes into Denver once a week to get fuel. We have to fill up all the generators and vehicles, then drive the truck up to the canyon."

"What do they need gas for up there? Aren't they all on horseback?"

"Yeah, but I guess maybe they have generators up there too." Liza shrugged. "Maybe that's what's in that building. I just know that I leave it out there on Monday and pick it up on Tuesday. Clint used to follow me up there in the pickup so I could ride back with him. He'll be glad you're doing it instead because he'd rather stay in the barn. And I'll be glad because you smell better."

"I won't if you keep handing me horseshit."

"Hey, here comes Astrid now. I hardly ever see her in here in the morning."

"Her ears must have been burning."

All conversations stopped as the hands turned their attention to their leader.

"Good morning, everyone. I have two announcements to make before we all head out today." She nodded in the direction of the couple who had stopped at Sky Ranch on their way to Ohio. "First, Philip and Crystal will be leaving us today, continuing on their journey. We wish them well and thank them for sharing the last three weeks with us. Let's give them a big sendoff, shall we?"

All the hands stood and applauded in the direction of the departing couple.

"And the other announcement is one I'm sure you'll think is good news. Dominick will be staying on here at Sky Ranch and joining us today up in the canyon. He said to tell you that he's not going to handle your horses up there, so don't even think about it."

The canyon hands chuckled and Dominick smiled. It was obvious he was a welcome addition to the permanent staff, and Vonne wanted to know how he had gotten into Astrid's inner circle in only two months.

Vonne reached into the truck bed for the last hay bale and lugged it to the stack just inside the barn door. Liza was right about Mondays—they were murder! Skipping dinner and going straight to her bunk had a lot of appeal.

"Hey, here come the guys," Liza said. "Looks like Dominick went through some sort of initiation."

Vonne looked up to see the men riding toward the barn on horseback, laughing raucously at the newest canyon hand, who was covered in mud from head to toe and laughing along with his tormentors.

Clint walked out of the barn to greet the horses. "What the hell happened to you?"

"These guys thought it would be funny to roll me in the mud on my first day," Dominick explained.

Vonne looked at the others and made a startling observation—they were clean. Not just cleaner than Dominick, but clean as though they hadn't worked all day. At first she thought she must be imagining it, but she watched them all as they dismounted and turned their horses over to Clint.

Whatever it was these guys did in the canyon all day, it didn't have anything to do with ranching.

As the first week wore on, Vonne settled into the routine of the ranch, and her back and neck became accustomed to the physical labor. The work went faster, which gave her and Liza more time to relax and talk as they went about their chores. There were plenty of chances for Vonne to ask about Astrid and life at Sky Ranch, but it was growing clear she had gotten just about all the information Liza had to give. Though she had been accepted as a permanent hand, Liza wasn't privy to the secrets of this place, so the only chance Vonne had to interact with the hands who knew about the canyon was at dinner. Since it was obvious that the canyon's activities were meant to be secret, no one would be talking about it, and she might even call unwanted attention to herself by asking questions.

Also during that week, Vonne had found herself enjoying Liza's company more than she liked to admit, and it wasn't just because her hormones were flying off the scale. Liza was fun to work with and she could talk about practically anything and sound intelligent. The only bit that bothered Vonne was Liza's almost unconditional deference to Astrid, and all the beliefs she espoused. She had seen that sort of over-the-top devotion before, and knew it could be dangerous under the wrong influence.

"You ready for dinner?"

"Sure," Vonne answered, hopping down from her bunk. "You nervous?"

"What do you think?"

After two more days of talking about the Locke book, Liza had finally gotten the nerve to return it to Astrid. The rancher had been pleased, and indicated she was looking forward to discussing Locke at dinner.

"Don't worry about it. You know it. And I'd say you're right about the main theme being natural law. I think that's why Astrid wanted you to read it."

They went through the line and filled their plates. Liza expected the questions to begin as soon as everyone was settled with their food. Suddenly, all eyes turned to the head table, where Astrid abruptly stood and tossed her napkin onto her plate.

"We do not discuss private matters here!" Astrid retreated immediately into the main area of the house, with the canyon hand who had come to her table close on her heels. A few moments later, a woman stood with her toddler and followed.

"What was that all about?" Vonne whispered. The room was deathly quiet.

Liza frowned and shook her head. Like the other hands, she kept her face down as she hurried to finish her meal. One by one, the workers rose and returned their trays to the kitchen, seemingly eager to leave the uncomfortable silence.

Not a soul had spoken of the events from last night's dinner. In fact, the whole ranch had taken on a pall, as though Astrid's outburst had them all afraid to speak.

At the side of the main house, Vonne and Liza loaded the pickup with laundry and clean linens bound for the men's bunkhouse. From their position, it was impossible to avoid the scene in the courtyard, where Lorna was helping load suitcases for the family that had created the commotion at dinner the night before.

"Looks like they're leaving," Vonne said.

"Don't stare, Vonne." Liza handed her a stack of sheets from the large pile. "Astrid says we shouldn't stick our noses in people's business. She says we all deserve our privacy."

Despite the warning, Vonne continued to steal glances at the courtyard. One of the range hands, a burly man named Ray who usually sat beside Astrid at dinner, had joined them to finish loading the van as the couple climbed in with their child. "I was just—"

"Eyes here—now!" Liza said sharply. "You need to stay out of stuff that doesn't concern you."

All day, the scene played over and over in Vonne's head, but she held back from asking more. Liza was barely talking and she didn't want to make things worse. If her hunches about Sky Ranch were true—that it was a cult in every sense of the word, and that something sinister was going on in the canyon—it was indeed extraordinary that people were being sent away or simply allowed to leave. It was different with Philip and Crystal. They were just temporaries like Vonne, and they apparently didn't fit into Astrid's plans. Letting them go wasn't a risk, since they weren't privy to the secrets of Sky Ranch. But that wasn't the case with this couple, since the man worked up in the canyon.

Vonne had experience with dangerous cults. Last year in Florida, she had kidnapped a teenage boy from a religious cult, only to discover that he was wired with explosives. The bomb was dismantled, but the leader had to be taken down in order to break his psychological hold on the boy and others.

"I'm sorry I yelled at you earlier," Liza offered out of the blue as they stopped for lunch at the creek. "I just didn't want you to get into trouble."

"Who would I get in trouble with?" Her question was met with silence. "Astrid?"

Liza sighed. "Not trouble, really. Just ... she can really make you feel bad about stuff like that. One time, I went into the main house because I heard somebody crying. I just wanted to see if there was something wrong and if I could help." She frowned and looked down at her hands, obviously upset by the memory.

"What happened?"

"Astrid came in right when I did and yelled at me to leave. She said I had no right to interfere, that people didn't want others to see them cry."

"But you were only trying to help."

"I shouldn't have, though. We're always told to ask for help only when we really need it. Astrid says it makes us try harder to do things on our own, and that makes us stronger."

Astrid says ... Vonne wanted to speak her mind, to say that Astrid's behavior was bizarre and even abusive, but she figured Liza would only defend her.

"Anyway, I felt bad for what I did, and I didn't want the same thing to happen to you."

Astrid seemed to have a firm grip on all of the hands, easily controlling their behavior through guilt and manipulation. She hated to think what that couple who left had gone through.

"I appreciate you looking out for me, Liza. I'll try not to do anything that Astrid won't like." Vonne could almost see the tension drain from Liza's face. "So what's for lunch today?"

It was early afternoon when the van returned to the ranch and the truth came to light, as least for Vonne. She watched from behind the pickup as Lorna got out with the small child and Ray began to unload all of the suitcases they had packed just this morning. The man and woman who left had probably met an unfortunate fate.

Vonne watched the bunkhouse through the crack in the door. From her vantage point in the latrine, she could also see the lights on upstairs in the main house. That was uncommon for this late hour, but everything about today had been different.

There was none of the usual discussion at dinner tonight. Instead, Astrid had stood to announce that Greg, one of the canyon hands, and Susan, a kitchen worker who lived in the women's bunkhouse, would be married the next evening and would take up residence in the small house vacated by the other family. A ceremony would take place in the courtyard after dinner, with a reception in the main house to follow. When dinner was over, Vonne, who was now the only temporary worker remaining on the ranch, was excused. The others remained for a meeting.

Liza hadn't shed much light on things today, keeping to herself, seemingly lost in her thoughts. Only when they were finishing in the shower that night did she loosen up, breaking her solemn mood with a genuine laugh when Vonne discovered a field mouse in her towel. The tension finally broken, they began to talk again, but as though the day's incident hadn't happened at all. Liza fell asleep right away and that gave Vonne the chance to get away and make her call.

"Hey ... I'm fine. As far as I can tell, nobody suspects a thing." She kept her voice low. "I'm starting to think this place is really bad news, Jerry. Something creepy happened today." She went on to describe the events of the day, underscoring her suspicions that the couple in question had been taken out and killed. "There's something going on up in the canyon near here, but I haven't had a chance to check it out. Give me a few more days ... No, I'll be okay. But right now, I need to hit the sack. This ranching is hard work ... Talk to you later."

Vonne returned the phone to its hiding place. She had nine days left before her scheduled time at Sky Ranch was up. If she didn't get to the bottom of what was going on by then, she would have to ask to stay, at least for a couple more weeks. That might at least get her more access to the ranch and to the meetings, but in light of today's tragic events, she didn't want to risk letting this drag out. Astrid Becker needed to be stopped before this got even more out of hand.

Vonne stood back from the crowd, intrigued by the change that had taken place in the last twenty-four hours. Gone was the group's somber mood, the departed couple seemingly forgotten. Instead, the ranch was abuzz with the typical cheerfulness that surrounded wedding festivities.

Astrid took her place on the third step of the front porch and spread her arms in invitation. Greg and Susan moved forward and joined hands. After solemn vows of faithfulness to family and one another, she pronounced them united and opened the large double doors to the main house.

"That didn't take long," Vonne remarked to Liza, mindful to hide her cynicism. They were back to their easy camaraderie, the discomfort of yesterday's events now in the past. She followed Liza through the double doors for her first look at the inside of the main house.

"It was just like the last one, when David and Ann got married."

"Are they the ones that are having the baby?"

"Yeah. They got married the first week I was here."

Vonne wondered what had happened then to trigger a vacancy in family housing, but she knew such a question would sound facetious. No one here seemed to think the timing of these events was bizarre.

As they walked into the now-crowded living room, the toddler who had returned with Lorna the day before ran past. Hot on his heels was Ann, the pregnant woman they were just talking about.

"Say, Liza?" Vonne kept her voice low so no one else would hear above the din of the crowd. "I know I'm not supposed to ask questions, but that little boy there ... his mom and dad were the ones who left yesterday. How come he's still here?"

Liza's eyes darted about nervously to see if anyone had heard. "I'll tell you later. Just don't ... don't say anymore to anyone, okay?"

Vonne nodded. She was startled by the urgency in Liza's voice, as though she truly feared being overheard.

"So Vonne, what do you think of ranching?" Lorna appeared out of nowhere, prompting Liza to excuse herself suddenly and skitter through the crowd to the other side of the room.

"You were right about Sky Ranch. It's definitely not a tourist resort." Vonne fought hard to remain casual. Her natural inclination was to retreat from people like Lorna, just as Liza had. Despite Lorna's calm and friendly manner, Vonne was sure she was involved in the disappearance of that couple, and that made her someone to fear.

"I told you so. That Hickson woman doesn't know what she's missing."

Hickman. "Did you ever hear from her?"

Lorna shook her head. "Nah, she'll probably call in a week or so saying that she had it marked wrong on her calendar. We'll work something out for her."

"Make sure it includes cleaning the latrines. You never told me about that part."

Lorna laughed. "If I had, would you have stayed?"

"No."

"Well, there you go."

"So that bit about getting some saddle time ... was that one of your tricks too?"

"We still might be able to work that out. Let me talk with Astrid and see what we can do."

"Thanks."

"But don't come crying to me the next day because you're too sore to walk."

"I won't. I promise." Vonne watched as Lorna returned to take her place alongside Astrid and the newlyweds. Just past where they stood was a tall door that was slightly ajar, enough so Vonne could see bookshelves—the library Liza had told her about. She had been eager to get a glimpse of Astrid's collection, thinking it might reveal more about her philosophies and objectives.

Vonne scooted around the clusters of revelers, finally reaching the door. She stepped inside and pushed it closed. A quick perusal of titles revealed nothing out of the ordinary, just the primers of democracy one might read in college, including the Locke book Liza had returned. But as Vonne walked the length of the room, the titles became more radical in nature, from the revolutionary writings of the Bolsheviks to works by Emma Goldman to an historical account of the Haymarket Affair. Vonne wasn't familiar with all of the texts, but those she recognized had a common theme—anarchy, a rejection of governmental authority.

"Find anything interesting?"

Vonne whirled around to find herself face-to-face with the ranch's matriarch.

"I wanted to peek at your library. I hope you don't mind."

"Were you looking for something in particular? Maybe I can help you."

"You have quite a collection. Liza was telling me about the book she just finished, the one about religion and taxes."

"John Locke."

"Right. I remember studying about him in college. He was one of the writers they say helped shape our democracy."

"Our republic," Astrid countered. "The United States is a republic, not a democracy."

"Right … because we have branches, and …"

"And we're led by elites who call themselves representatives. The real truth is they represent only themselves," she said, her tone bitter. "Are you interested in government, Vonne?"

"Mmmm … a little," she said, careful not to give away how much she knew. "I enjoy the talks we have at dinner."

"The best part of the day, if you ask me. It's nice to be surrounded by people who are eager to learn about the principles that rule their lives." She plucked a book from one of the shelves, eyeing the spine. "Do you know anything about the Levelers?"

Vonne shook her head as she reached out and took the offered book. She vaguely recalled the Levelers as British agitators, a thorn in Cromwell's side.

"You might find this interesting," Astrid said. "And thanks for reminding me about Locke. I'll have to remember to have Liza talk to us at dinner about what she read."

Astrid held the door open and waited, a clear indication she wished for Vonne to leave.

"Thanks for the book."

"You're welcome. Perhaps we can sit and discuss it when you're finished."

Vonne sat leaning against the side of the house, one knee bent, the other dangling off the front porch. Her long-neck beer was warm, but she didn't know when she would get another one, so she vowed to drink it anyway.

The party inside was starting to break up, the hands heading on to the bunkhouse because, as Liza had pointed out, the work on a ranch never stopped. Vonne hoped to catch her on the way out, thinking it would be a good place to ask her again about that toddler before they got back to the bunkhouse with everyone else around. Just then, the object of her thoughts emerged.

"Hey!"

Liza turned toward her voice, her eyes not yet adjusted to the darkness.

"It's just little ol' me."

Liza walked over.

"Want a sip of beer? It's nice and warm," she joked.

"I think I'll pass. What are you sitting out here for?"

Vonne shrugged. "No reason."

"What's that you've got?"

Vonne held up her book. "Oh, Astrid caught me snooping in her library and she gave me homework."

Liza chuckled. "Serves you right."

Vonne pushed up from her seat. "Want to take a walk?"

"That's not always a good idea in these parts. There are coyotes and mountain lions out there. And even bears."

"You should be all right if you stick close to me."

"What are you ... like Grizzly Adams or something?"

"No, but I'm sweeter than you, so they'll eat me instead and give you time to get away."

"Ha ha." They stepped down from the porch. "I guess we can walk if we don't go too far."

When they reached a safe distance from the house, Vonne asked her earlier question again. "You were going to tell me something about that little boy."

Liza nervously looked over her shoulder. "We're not supposed to talk about things, Vonne. That's why Astrid sent you out at dinner last night."

"So you're not going to tell me?"

"When your time's up, you leave. Astrid wouldn't want somebody going and giving people the wrong idea about Sky Ranch."

"So what's the right idea?"

"The couple that left ... they weren't good parents. She explained it all at dinner last night after you left."

"Do you know that for sure? Did you ever see it?"

"I didn't, but Lorna said she did. Besides, why would Astrid lie about something like that?" she said defensively. "Last night, she talked to us about our responsibilities. She said we're all supposed to act like good parents because the children we raise are going to have a voice in our future."

"I'll buy that, but why the secrecy?"

"Because there are laws against just giving your child to someone else, but that's what needed to be done. Astrid was afraid they wouldn't take care of their little boy when they left so she talked them into letting him stay."

Vonne was completely sure Liza believed every word she was saying. Even though she wanted to believe it too, it didn't explain why the boy had left in the van with his parents if they were giving him up. Nor did it answer why Ray and Lorna returned with all of the family's suitcases, something she bet Liza didn't know.

"I thought it was probably something like that, but I wasn't sure." They were past the barn, out of sight of the house. "Thanks for telling me."

"Sure ... just don't say anything, okay? You're not supposed to know."

"Okay." They stopped when they reached the corral and leaned on the fence. Their sudden presence sent the horses closest to them scurrying to the other side. "You don't seem to like Lorna very much. Is that my imagination?"

"No, probably not." Liza looked away for a second, then back. "I don't dislike her. I just ... I don't know. Like I said the other night, I don't like that she checks up on everybody so she can report back to Astrid. The people here would do anything Astrid wanted. They don't need Lorna looking over their shoulder."

Anything Astrid wanted. Liza was probably right about that, and that's what made Astrid Becker so dangerous.

"Astrid must feel like she needs that. She seems to trust Lorna ... and that guy named Ray. Why do you think that is?" Vonne knew she was pushing it, but she needed to take advantage of Liza's willingness to talk. And while she felt guilty for her deception, there was probably much more at stake than hands like Liza realized.

"I don't know. But I guess that's how she found out those people weren't taking care of their kid, so something good came from it."

This was the pattern Vonne had come to expect—Liza would somehow justify Astrid's decisions and the way things were done. Few people in places like this were capable of seeing it any other way. She decided not to press her luck further by asking more questions. The last thing she wanted was for Liza to get defensive, so she changed to a more benign topic.

"That beer went straight to my head. I can't believe I got buzzed on just two."

"It's the altitude. The same thing happened to me when I went to that other wedding I told you about."

"You guys are lucky I didn't try to karaoke."

Liza laughed. "I would have paid to see that. Your navy pals must have had a good time with you."

"I didn't drink much with my shipmates. One stumble and you're in the ocean."

"I guess the equivalent on a ranch would be one stumble and you're in horseshit."

"Save me from myself," Vonne said with a chuckle. She really enjoyed Liza's humorous side. "By the way, I told Lorna I wanted to do some riding while I was here. She said tonight she'd try to set it up."

"Who's going to do all the work while you're out playing Calamity Jane?"

"Smarty pants." Vonne chucked her hip playfully into Liza's side. "I'll get up really, really early and do my work first. Do you ever ride?"

"No, I missed my chance by not asking about it when I first got here. I got settled into this job and I hate to bring it up now. I don't want Astrid to think I'm just goofing off."

Everything's about Astrid. "Too bad. Because if I fall off and bust my ass, you won't be there to see it, and that's a loss you'll really regret."

"No, but I'll get to poke the bruises on your butt," Liza answered with a sneer. "That would be better than watching you fall."

"You're in an awfully good humor tonight. How many beers did you have?"

"Two. But look who's talking! You've finally stopped asking a million questions and checking everything out. It's like you're writing a report for school or something."

Liza's tone was teasing but Vonne's stomach dropped with panic. All along she had been careful to ease off when she thought she was pushing for too many details, but obviously she had gone to the well too many times with Liza. Now she needed to back off completely or risk exposure. "As a matter of fact, I am writing a report. How do you spell impudent?"

"Use cheeky instead."

"Good idea. That describes you perfectly tonight." She looked at Liza and grinned. "Can I ask you one more question for my report?"

"Sure."

"How come you don't really talk to anyone else, but with me, you hardly shut up? What did I do to deserve that?"

Liza punched her arm. "I like you better, smartass. Though I don't know why."

Vonne rubbed her arm as though mortally wounded. "I wasn't complaining. I like you too." She suddenly felt the urge to blurt out everything she knew and plead with Liza to leave tonight. She had enough information for Jerry, and Liza definitely wasn't a part of the sinister happenings at Sky Ranch. The most important thing was getting out without getting hurt.

"I really don't have all that much in common with the other women here. They're nice enough, but they're all like Susan—all they want is to marry a cowboy."

"No cowboys for you, huh?" Vonne grinned. "Why's that?"

"I think it's my turn for a question," Liza said.

"Okay, but I'm not finished with the stuff for my book." She folded her arms on the top rail of the corral so their shoulders were touching.

"How come you don't ever talk about yourself?"

"Not much to say, I guess."

"Don't you have a life back in Sausalito? Friends? Somebody special?"

"Yes, yes ... and no." Vonne turned, bringing them face-to-face. "Now you, same question."

"I have no life back in Sausalito—"

Now it was Vonne delivering the punch. "And you call me a smartass!"

"Okay, okay ... the answers are not anymore, no, and no."

"You just left everything for good?"

"Nothing to go back for," she answered without emotion. "But I want to hear more about you. Tell me about life in Sausalito."

"All right." Vonne called up the bare bones version, but with enough meat to make it credible. "I grew up there. My dad was in the navy, too. When he got out, he and mom bought a sailboat and took off. They fell in love with the Caribbean, so if I want to see them, that's where I have to go. But they left me a nice house."

"And why is it you don't have someone special? Are you defective?"

Vonne chuckled at the gentle, almost flirtatious, teasing. "I don't think so, but maybe I'm not the best judge about something like that."

"What else could it be?" Liza asked as though she dared Vonne to answer.

"Maybe I just haven't met the right girl yet."

A satisfied smile crossed Liza's face. "What's that going to take?"

"That's too many questions for you. It should be my turn again." She ducked her head to make sure she had eye contact. "How come you don't have someone special?"

"Because I'm defective."

Vonne smiled slowly. "If you have a defect, I sure haven't found it."

"You just haven't been looking close enough." Their voices had dropped to barely a whisper and their faces were moving closer.

"Oh, I've been looking, believe me." Vonne leaned forward to meet Liza's lips for a gentle kiss. "I've definitely been looking."

"Something tells me hooking up with Vonne Maglio might be more than I can handle."

"There's only one way you're going to find out."

Vonne relaxed in the truck's passenger seat, her elbow resting on the door so it hung out the open window. "You really think you could be satisfied with a life like this?"

"Probably not in the long run," Liza admitted, jamming the truck into low gear for the climb back up to the mouth of the canyon to collect the lunch containers. "I just needed some time away from life, and Sky Ranch is a pretty good refuge. I'm sure I'll go back out there eventually and start acting like an adult again."

"Things must have gotten pretty bad back home."

Liza nodded. "Yeah, kind of all the way around. I was working at my father's company and saw some things I didn't like ... things about the business, and things about him. I didn't want to be a part of it."

"The company or your father?"

"Both. You hate to admit that your own father's a crook, but when you're the one doing the books, it's pretty hard to miss. My mom would roll over in her grave if she knew what I knew." They pulled into the clearing and stopped.

"So your mom's gone?" This wasn't Vonne pumping Liza for information anymore. This was genuine interest, a rush of emotion to catch up with all the feelings that had made her want to kiss Liza last night. She felt overwhelming compassion at a loss of faith in family so great that it drove Liza to leave them all behind. Too often, that was how people ended up in places like this.

"Yeah, she died about four years ago. The company still had a conscience back then, before they went public and started doing everything to please the analysts and stockholders." As they talked, they hopped out of the truck and grabbed the empty containers. "Are you going to put all this in your report?"

Vonne didn't answer, distracted now by something that lay beneath one of the picnic tables.

"What is it?"

"Where did this come from?" She reached down and picked up a camouflage cap. "I thought all of the hands wore hats like yours." She indicated the Stetson.

Liza walked over to look at it. "I don't know. I've never seen anybody here wear one of those."

Para-military activity in the canyon was the worst-case scenario, as far as she was concerned. But if these guys were changing into uniforms every morning, that sure explained how they managed to keep their clothes clean. Vonne looked inside the cap. "It says Collins."

"That's Billy."

"Which one is he?"

“He’s the one that got all flustered the other night when Astrid was asking him questions about one of the books she gave him. He didn’t understand it. Remember?”

“Oh, yeah. I know which one he is.” From what Vonne could gather, he wasn’t held in high regard by Astrid.

She looked around for more clues. Besides the hat, there was nothing unusual. The containers had been left in a stack, as always, and the area policed for trash. She set the cap on the table and started to walk back to the truck.

“Wait. Maybe you should put it back where it was under the table.”

“Why? If I leave it out here, he’ll see it and pick it up on the way back to the barn.”

“I know. But they already give Billy a hard time about stuff. If somebody else sees it first, they’ll just tease him even more about losing his hat. This way, maybe he’ll remember it and pick it up before somebody else finds it.”

Vonne nodded and dropped the cap back underneath the table. Liza was probably right—Billy would catch hell if the others realized she had found his cap—but the consequences might be more severe than just teasing.

She climbed into the passenger seat and closed the door, shooting one last look at the cap under the table. What other sorts of paramilitary gear did these ranch hands have? And why? All the more reason to find out what was in that canyon.

“You did all right,” Vonne said, slapping Liza on the back as they walked out of the dining hall. Astrid had grilled her for almost thirty minutes after dinner about Locke’s essays.

“It’s a good thing you helped me practice. I was hoping she had forgotten about it though.”

Vonne looked away sheepishly, knowing it was her mention of the book to Astrid that had triggered the rancher’s memory. “Look at it this way—it’s behind you now, and I think you really impressed her.”

"Hey, Vonne!" Lorna caught up with them just outside the door. "You still want to do some riding?"

"Sure!"

"Great. Come to the barn tomorrow morning at nine-thirty. I'll have Clint saddle you up a mount."

"Thanks. I look forward to it." Vonne turned back to Liza as Lorna walked away. "Sure you don't want to take a ride? Maybe we can get lost in the woods again or something." After lunch, they had walked along the creek until they were obscured by the thick summer foliage. There, they had picked up where they left off the night before, with kisses that started slowly at first, but quickly grew deeper and more intense. Things heated up so fast it was all they do to keep themselves under control.

"I don't think you'll want me to tag along for this one. If you're going at nine-thirty, you're probably going with Astrid."

Vonne stepped under the spray and soaked her hair, simultaneously rinsing away the soap from her freshly-washed body. With her eyes closed, she jabbed at the shampoo dispenser until the liquid trickled into her hand. In no time, she turned it into a rich lather.

She could hear Liza turn on the shower in the corner. There was a different atmosphere in the bathhouse tonight, at least in her mind, and probably in Liza's too. Now that they had kissed, they weren't just friends sharing a communal shower anymore. They were two women attracted to one another and they were naked and alone—an electric combination.

Vonne rinsed her hair and pushed it straight back, finally opening her eyes. She looked to her right, not surprised to find Liza facing away. Finally, she had the chance to gaze without trepidation at Liza's naked body.

Suddenly, Liza looked over her shoulder, boldly returning Vonne's gesture with a lust-filled look of her own.

That was all the encouragement Vonne needed. She released a dollop of the liquid soap and rubbed it into her hands. Then she closed the distance between them and pressed both hands against Liza's shoulder blades. She felt Liza stiffen then relax as she flattened her palms and swirled the soap generously all over her back. She marveled at the strong muscles, hardened by the physical labor of the ranch. Up and down, she gently stroked, finally sliding her hands lower over the round cheeks. She cupped Liza's bottom and leaned closer.

"If you want me to stop, you're going to have to tell me," she whispered from behind.

Liza started to turn, but Vonne brought one arm around her waist to hold her in place. Her other hand continued its gentle massage, dipping lower into the slippery crack. Over and over, she stroked it softly with her fingers, from its Y-shaped top to the tender flesh between Liza's legs.

Vonne could feel Liza begin to lose her equilibrium. "Put your hands on the wall."

Liza did, gradually opening her legs to encourage more of Vonne's touch. The water sprayed unnoticed, a constant lubricant for Vonne's explorations.

She pushed one, then two fingers inside, moving closer to press her center against Liza's hip. With her other hand, she found a breast, where her pinch of a nipple elicited a greedy moan.

She thrust harder, spurred on by the rhythm of Liza jerking up and down against the fingers inside her. Vonne squeezed the breast one last time and swept her palm across Liza's stomach, into the hair at the top of her legs, and finally onto her center. Her fingers found the hard clitoris, prompting a new jolt as Liza gripped the showerhead.

Vonne intensified her touch, hearing her own ragged breaths as she drew closer to climax from the friction of her body grinding against the wet skin. She came just as she felt the velvet walls clench. Liza's weight fell into her arms and Vonne dropped to one knee, carefully guiding her to the concrete floor.

Liza rolled over and looked into her face. "You should at least kiss me now," she said breathlessly.

Vonne surged forward and crushed the eager lips, her mouth open as if to devour. Far from sated, her fingers once again found the pulsing clitoris, and she teased it to a second climax and a third.

"I think this is where I'm supposed to tell you to stop," Liza rasped.

The water had gone tepid and Liza was physically spent. Vonne helped her to her feet and they turned off the spray. Soon, they were dressed and sitting side by side on the bench outside the showers.

It was Liza who spoke first. "That was ..." She waved her hand in the air, finding no words to finish.

"Oh, it was way better than that." Vonne nodded and rubbed her hand along Liza's thigh. "I can't wait to do it again."

"No, it's my turn next, so don't think you're going to come back from that ride tomorrow and whine about being sore. There will be no mercy."

"You've got yourself a deal." Vonne leaned over for one last kiss before standing up and holding out her hand. "Let me walk you home, little girl."

From her upper bunk that night, Vonne listened as Liza's breathing slowed. Her head was filled with erotic images, her body overflowing with warm sensations. For the first time in over a week, she fell asleep without thinking of Jerry, or of Astrid and the strange goings-on at Sky Ranch.

"Don't let him get away with that," Astrid said sharply. "You have to show him who's boss."

Vonne jerked the reins to the left and dug her heels into the stubborn horse's ribs, putting a stop to his grazing spree.

"I think Clint gave you the rowdiest horse in the barn. He'll test your patience, but he can sure run."

"You say that like it's a good thing."

Astrid laughed. "There's a flat stretch up here where you can push him a little. You've got insurance, right?"

"Just catastrophic."

"Let's hope it doesn't come to that."

Vonne leaned forward in the saddle as they started up a steep hill. She was curious about how far they would ride, fairly certain she would be turned back before they reached the canyon. But she figured that would give her about half an hour to double back and see if she could learn more about what lay beyond the narrow pass. There were all sorts of side trails, and she could always claim she got lost if she were discovered. If she was gone longer than a half hour, though, she might be missed.

"Lorna tells me you spent some time in the navy."

"I got my six years in."

"And now I suppose you're ready for that great career they promised."

Vonne wasn't surprised by the sarcasm in the rancher's voice. She seemed to be skeptical about most things having to do with the U.S. government. "Yeah, but there doesn't seem to be much demand for someone who knows how to catch a plane on a carrier deck."

"Typical. Empty promises from Uncle Sam." They reached a washed-out gulley, where the trail widened in a slight grade for a quarter-mile. "Here we go. Give him a kick and hold on!"

Vonne slapped the stirrups into the horse's belly and he took off, pulling even with Astrid's mare when they reached the crest of the next hill. The painful bouncing when the horse trotted now became a comfortable glide.

"Good job, Vonne," Astrid said, obviously pleased that a beginning rider would show such poise in the saddle. They brought the horses to stop.

"That was easier than I thought it would be." Vonne smiled with satisfaction and patted the horse's neck. Looking around, she tried to get her bearings. This was the same view they got on the last turn toward the lunch site, so that meant they would cross the road soon.

"So you aren't working right now?"

"That's right. I'll need to get off my ass and get a job when I get back, though."

"Any idea what you'll do?"

"Not really. I have a friend at one of those overnight shipping places. He said he might be able to get me on there." Vonne had expected questions like these, sure this ride had been orchestrated to give Astrid an opportunity to find out where she stood. She hoped her answers would set up an invitation to stay on at Sky Ranch.

"You strike me as somebody who likes that sort of thing ... the physical work."

"Yeah, I can't imagine sitting behind a desk all day. I like to be outside. That's what's so nice about being here at Sky Ranch."

Astrid looked straight ahead as they started up what Vonne thought would be the last hill before they reached the lunch site. "A lot of people come here and fall in love with this place."

"Easy to see why. It's beautiful."

"It is that." Astrid pulled ahead to lead her horse through a narrow part of the trail. "What about the rest of it? Do you enjoy the other hands? Do you like working with Liza?"

"Liza's great. I don't really see much of the others except at dinner." That was the segue Vonne had been hoping for. "But I like the dinner discussions a lot. You really know a lot about that kind of stuff. And you always make it so interesting." *Stroke that ego.*

Astrid turned in the saddle to face her, their horses still plodding up the hill. "What do you find interesting about it?"

"Practically everything. I was sitting there the other night trying to imagine talking about that kind of stuff with my shipmates and I almost laughed out loud."

Astrid snorted. "You probably wouldn't have gotten much debate in a place like that anyway. Everyone in the military is told *what* to think. Nobody learns *how* to think."

That's what Liza had said was different about Astrid and Sky Ranch, almost verbatim. But Astrid's trick was even better—she knew how to get people to think what she wanted them to think.

"I can't argue with that," Vonne said. "I think I was different because I went to college for a couple of years first. And I've always liked to read."

"How are you coming on that book?"

"I'm about halfway through it. I'm starting to think the Levelers got a bum rap."

"How so?"

"Well, a lot of people just considered them troublemakers. But if you look at what they stood for—things like natural rights that we're all born with—those are some of the principles our government is founded on."

"Pffft! Hardly." Astrid shook her head in disgust.

"What? Am I reading it wrong?"

"No, you're not reading the Levelers wrong at all. But you're mistaken if you think our government here respects principles of natural law. We're worse than any monarchy could ever be. At least you can kill the king and be done with the line."

They finally crested the last hill, emerging into the clearing that served as the lunch site. Vonne was frustrated to see a hand sitting at one of the tables on the porch, his horse tied nearby. Obviously, he was here to escort her back to the barn.

"You're very good at that," Vonne said, pulling Liza up from the floor to straddle her lap on the bench in the dressing room.

"I skipped dessert tonight"—Liza kissed her, her lips soft and moist from what she had been doing—"because you told me you were sweet."

"Was I right?"

"I'll say."

Vonne hugged her tightly around the waist. "I've been thinking about you all day. How about coming back with me to Sausalito?" Astrid's persistent secrecy this morning about the canyon underscored the likelihood that Sky Ranch was not only a cult, but a volatile one at that. Vonne wanted Liza out of here, along with all of the innocents. *Make this easy, please.*

"I have a better idea. How about you staying here?"

Vonne sighed. If she appeared too desperate, Liza might get spooked enough to pull away. "I can't just stay. I'm only here on vacation."

"So was I when I first got here. But I liked it, and I asked Astrid if I could stay and work and she let me. I bet she'd let you too. There's plenty to do, and I know she likes you."

"I don't know, Liza. I like it here, but I don't think ranching is what I want to do with my life."

"Nobody says you have to do it your whole life. But we could do it for a couple of years. I'm just not ready to leave yet."

Vonne sighed and put her head on Liza's shoulder. "I know. But I don't want to leave you."

"Then stay for a while longer."

"For what? Sex in the bathhouse? We deserve better than that."

"You weren't complaining a few minutes ago," Liza said, her feelings obviously hurt.

"Liza—" Vonne squeezed her shoulders and groaned in frustration.

"I know what you're saying, and you're right. We do deserve better." Liza kissed the tip of Vonne's nose. "I just ... I can't leave right now. Astrid took me in when I had no place else to go, and it wouldn't be right just to walk out on her. Nobody else here knows how to do my job."

Vonne sighed. "I guess I could talk to her about staying a while longer."

"Now that's what I wanted to hear!"

"But we're going to have to find a place a little more romantic than this."

"How about near the creek where we eat lunch?"

"A nooner?"

"Yeah."

"Then we better get to bed. I think I have a very important luncheon engagement tomorrow."

"Hey, Jerry. What did you find out?" It was almost three a.m. and Vonne was dead on her feet. Liza had tossed and turned before falling asleep, no doubt replaying the conversation from the bathhouse, and Vonne had no choice but to wait her out.

"Can you get one of your pals to fly over and get some pictures? The canyon is about three miles northeast of here. You got the phone signal, right? ... I think they might be running some kind of military games up there." She told him about finding the hat.

"Look, I might have to stay on a few more days to make sure everybody gets out that should ... I know it's not, but I can't just leave these people here. Not all of them are part of this—they're just caught up in it."

Vonne stifled a yawn.

"Okay, I'll call you in a couple of days. Try to get the pictures during the daytime. That's when they're all up there."

"Damn! I forgot we have to drive the fuel truck back today," Vonne said as they reached the clearing and spotted the small tanker. "There go my lunch plans."

Liza chuckled. "I forgot about it too. That's because you're distracting me from my work, you know."

"Yeah, I know. But I don't care." Vonne hopped out of the truck and leaned into the bed for one of the containers, which she hefted effortlessly. She was pleased at the strength she had gained from only one week of strenuous labor. "But don't think I'm going to forget that we have an appointment."

The sound of horses coming down the trail from the canyon pass startled them. Astrid emerged into the clearing, followed by Ray, who led a horse with a body draped over its saddle.

"There's been an accident," she declared, sliding down from her mare.

"Oh, my God! What happened?" Liza rushed over as the body was removed from its perch and rolled over. The white shirt was covered with blood. "It's Billy."

Vonne pushed past and leaned down, pressing her fingers to the man's neck in a futile attempt to locate a pulse.

"He's dead," Astrid said, her voice giving away no emotion. "We were chasing a mountain lion up a ridge and he caught a stray bullet."

Right in the heart. The blood stains covered his chest, but the shirt wasn't pierced, Vonne noticed. Someone had taken the time to change his clothes as he lay dying.

"Take him back to the ranch in the truck. Ray, you ride on ahead and tell Lorna to get the van ready. Go with her to take care of this."

As Ray disappeared down the steep horse trail, Vonne moved behind the dead man and lifted his shoulders, gesturing for Liza to grab his feet. Together, they carried him to the truck and set him on the tailgate. Vonne climbed into the bed and dragged him forward, while Liza closed the gate.

Astrid mounted up and turned back into the canyon without another word.

"Let's go," Liza said quietly.

Vonne tamped down her anger and jumped over the side of the bed. She felt sick that she hadn't moved quickly enough in her investigation of Sky Ranch to save Billy Collins. That was because she had let her feelings for Liza distract her. She couldn't afford to make that mistake again.

Dinner was a quiet affair. One of the women had made the poignant gesture of setting an empty place at Billy's usual seat.

As they finished eating, Astrid stood and cleared her throat. One by one, the ranch hands set down their utensils and turned to face her.

"I know we're all feeling very sad tonight. These tragedies, unfortunately, are a part of any family. But we'll see one another through this terrible loss."

Vonne could hear sniffling from a few of the women around her. The men who had been in the canyon were impassive, not giving away what they knew about Billy's fate.

"But it would be even more tragic if we didn't take a lesson to heart from this horrible accident." She looked into the eyes of her workers, her family. "Billy Collins was a fine young man. He enjoyed his work here, and he tried very hard to do his best. Sadly, his enthusiasm worked against him sometimes. Billy often got caught up in things and became careless."

She shook her head vehemently as if both angry and frustrated. "Ladies and gentlemen ... my family"—her voice softened—"this is a dangerous way of life we've chosen for ourselves. We must make good decisions—smart decisions. We can't afford these sorts of tragic errors in judgment."

Vonne felt a chill up her spine, even before Astrid's final words.

"Please take care that nothing so unfortunate befalls one of you."

Vonne eased out of her bunk to the floor, leaning over to check on Liza, who was finally asleep. Everyone was still upset about Billy, and some of the women in the bunkhouse had continued to cry softly after going to bed.

It was time for answers, and Vonne knew Jerry was on the case because she had caught a glimpse early this afternoon of a private plane turning over the canyon. With any luck, the chaos of the day had squelched any curiosity about who might have been flying over.

She tiptoed to the bathhouse and entered the latrine, where she stood on the toilet to retrieve her phone. When the phone came to life, she dialed and was connected right away.

"Jerry, we need to move soon. I don't think I'm going to be able to wait this out." She told the story of Billy's death and how she suspected he had been killed for too many screw-ups. "Could you see what was in the canyon?" She listened as he described the results of the flyover.

"That's what I was afraid of ... You need to get some people in here to take this woman down, and soon!"

Vonne reached to open the door to the latrine so she could keep an eye on the bunkhouse. The instant her hand touched the handle the door was flung open, banging hard into her shoulder. She was momentarily blinded when the light switch was thrown.

Liza stood in the doorway, her face contorted in fury. "Who are you talking to?" she demanded.

Vonne pulled the phone back and held up her other hand to stop Liza's advance. "Something's going on here, Liza ... something dangerous."

Liza shoved her hard, causing her head to slam against the concrete wall of the small room. Immediately, a gash opened behind her ear and blood began to pour down her neck.

"I heard what you said. You came here to hurt Astrid. And I'm not going to let you do it." Liza grabbed the phone from her hand and flung it onto the concrete floor, shattering it into small pieces.

"I didn't come here for Astrid!" Vonne pressed the heel of her hand against the gaping wound and leaned into the wall to steady herself, finally looking up to meet Liza's steely eyes. "I came here ... to get you."

"We can't just sit here, Liza. Jerry's working with somebody in the FBI and he probably called them already to get out here and see what's going on."

"Shut up!" Liza perched on the bench of the changing room, fully in command of the situation, as Vonne sat at her feet on the concrete floor holding a towel to her still-throbbing head.

Vonne had known all along that Liza would feel betrayed—most cult members did once they discovered why she was there. They resisted deprogramming efforts out of both anger at being taken away and loyalty to the cult. But Liza wasn't brainwashed, at least not in the classic sense. She had merely fallen victim to her own naïveté and need for escape.

"You have no idea how dangerous this is, Liza." Vonne's biggest concern was that Liza would hand her over to Astrid, who would deal with her the same way she had with other threats to her plans.

"So how much did my father pay you to come here and fuck me?"

"It's not like that."

"Then why don't you tell me what it's like, Vonne? Fill my pretty head with more of your lies."

"Your father's dead." Vonne saw a flash of disbelief, then shock in Liza's angry eyes. "It was stomach cancer ... it happened very fast."

Liza didn't say anything for several long moments; then her face finally returned to its cold, dispassionate state. "Figures the bastard would find one last way to cheat his investors."

"Your brother's cooperating with the SEC. He wants to make things right, but he needs your help to do that."

"Now I know you're lying. All Robb ever thinks about is himself, just like Dad. He probably can't get his inheritance until I show up for the reading of the will."

"That's not how it is. He knows you're the one who turned your father in. He didn't believe what you said at first, but then he found all the information on your computer after you disappeared." Vonne checked the towel again and was relieved to see the bleeding had finally stopped. "Besides, when the SEC gets finished, there probably won't be any inheritance. He knows that, and so do you."

"Who were you were talking to on the phone?"

"My friend Jerry. He runs a clinic in San Francisco. We worked together in the navy as psychologists. Jerry helps people who have been ... who are being unduly influenced by other people."

"So Robb hired a couple of shrinks because he thinks I'm being brainwashed." It wasn't a question, just a resigned statement of fact.

"I don't have anything to do with that part. I teach psychology at a college in San Francisco. I'm here because Jerry asked me to help get you out safely."

"And you had to lie to me to do that?"

"I couldn't tell you the truth. I needed to know what kind of place this was."

"So your friend could fix my brain in case I was under some kind of spell."

"So I wouldn't get myself killed, Liza. I never know what kind of situation I'm going to find when I go in."

"All of this is ridiculous." Liza waved her hand dismissively. "I'm not being held against my will. I'm just here to work on a ranch. I don't need my father's money or my—"

"Listen to me! You're not working on just any old ranch. Surely you can see that. Most of the men spend all day up in that canyon. Jerry flew over it today. He saw tents—military tents, Liza—and a firing range. And all the horses were corralled. There isn't any livestock up there, so no way this is just a ranch."

"That still doesn't prove anything."

"What about Billy? Do you honestly think someone accidentally shot him right here?" She pointed to the center of her chest. "I've seen bullet wounds before, and that one came from close range. His shirt didn't even have a hole in it, because he was probably wearing military fatigues when it happened."

Vonne could see Liza was finally starting to listen, giving at least some credence to her version of events. She went on to relate her suspicions that the couple who left had been killed, citing the fact that the van had returned with their suitcases.

"It's still just innuendo. Besides, how can you expect me to believe any of what you say when everything about you is a lie?"

Vonne shook her head and sighed. "It isn't a lie that I care about you."

"Don't you dare say that!" She clenched her teeth and glared at Vonne with a look that bordered on disgust.

"I do. And no matter what happens here, what I want most of all is for you to get out of this without getting hurt." It was obvious Liza was too furious to consider any of Vonne's personal reasons. She would have to appeal to her sense of logic and concern for the others. "The authorities are going to come—they're probably on the way right now. No matter what you decide to do, they want to talk to Astrid. You and I need to find a way out of here first." She knew Liza well enough by now to know she didn't want to see anyone get hurt. She just had to convince her it would happen.

"I don't want to leave!"

"Neither did the people at Waco! Do you remember those pictures? That building burning with all those people inside? Everybody died—women, children, even little babies."

"Astrid wouldn't let something like that happen."

"You don't know how she'll act if they back her into a corner. She may feel like she has nothing left to lose."

"You don't know her at all! She cares about us."

"She cares about herself."

"You're wrong. She's made Sky Ranch into a place where things are fair, where right and wrong isn't decided by the almighty dollar."

"No, because right and wrong is decided by Astrid Becker."

"Why not Astrid Becker? We all have a better life here because of her. She takes care of us and teaches us to think for ourselves."

"No, she doesn't. She manipulates you," Vonne argued. "What happens when you give an opinion that's different from hers? I've seen it—she withholds her approval. And you feel awful because you've disappointed her. So you work harder to adjust your thoughts, and the next time, you try to give her what she wants. That's not teaching people to think, Liza. That's called brainwashing."

Liza bristled and slumped back against the wall, her arms folded defiantly across her chest.

"Astrid is an anarchist. You know what that means, don't you?" Liza gave her an uncertain nod. "She's anti-government. Lots of people feel that way, and there's nothing wrong with it—except when they carry it too far. Then you end up with people like Timothy McVeigh and the Unabomber."

"Astrid isn't like that."

"She's raising a militia that trains up in the canyon. And she's killed people—that couple who tried to leave, and Billy, who didn't measure up."

"You don't know that for sure."

"How did you end up at Sky Ranch?" Before she could respond, Vonne continued. "Let me answer that, because it's the same way I got here. Robb found the Copper J Ranch on your computer. We couldn't locate it anywhere, so I filled out the same questionnaire you did and sent it back. I said I was single, between jobs, and I was willing to pay money up front. She tricked us both into coming here."

"So what!" But it was clear the circumstances were adding up and Liza was having difficulty explaining it all away in her head. "I know she isn't like those other people."

Vonne put her hand on Liza's knee. "You aren't like those people either. That's why you turned your father in. You knew people were going to get hurt. Now you need to help me see that these people don't get hurt." She could see the anguish in Liza's face as she finally faced the truth. "We have to stop them now—tonight."

It was several agonizing minutes before Liza finally spoke, her voice low and weak. "How?"

Relieved beyond measure, Vonne pushed herself up off the floor. "The first thing we need to do is get you out of here. If I know Jerry, the shit could hit the fan at any minute. We should walk down to the gate right now and meet them so we can tell them where everyone is ... and who's not involved in this. Maybe they can come in fast and it will over before anybody knows—"

"You won't be going anywhere."

Both women jumped as Astrid stepped into the doorway of the bathhouse, flanked by Lorna and Ray, both of whom held automatic rifles.

"At least Liza's not going anywhere." Astrid looked at her coldly. "I'm very disappointed that you'd let someone turn you against me so easily."

"Astrid ..." Liza's face showed her devastation. "I didn't want anyone to be hurt."

"You know I won't let that happen. It's my job to take care of all of you, and I intend to do that." She turned to glower at Vonne. "But since you're the one bringing this fight to our doorstep, I'm not all that concerned about what happens to you."

"I didn't bring this fight, Astrid. You brought it to yourself with your twisted ideas and your Messiah complex."

"That's enough out of you." She jerked her head to the door. "Take her for a ride. Then meet us up at the canyon."

"I'll be sure and say hi to Billy ... and to all the others that didn't buy into your crap." Vonne looked one last time at Liza and saw the terror in her eyes.

Vonne wriggled in vain against the plastic tie that bound her wrists together behind her back. Lorna was driving the van. Ray rode beside her in the front seat, his rifle butt resting on the floor.

"You're not going to outrun these guys. You're better off if you just give up now before anyone else gets hurt." *Especially me.*

"We always knew this day would come, Vonne," Lorna said calmly. "We're ready for it."

"Are you ready for a hundred agents storming that gate?"

Ray chuckled. "Anyone storming that gate's going to get what they deserve."

Lorna drove to the end of a dirt side road and stopped. Ray hopped out and opened the sliding door to the back seat. "End of the line," he announced sardonically.

"For you, Ray," a male voice answered.

As Ray's gun aimed upward at the voice from the back of the van, three bullets thumped into his chest and he fell. Lorna scrambled in the front seat for her gun.

"No, Lorna!"

She ignored the command and was dropped with two bullets before she could get off a shot.

Vonne whirled around to see a familiar face rising from the row of seats behind her. "Dominick!"

"Special Agent Dominick Haynes, FBI. At your service."

"God, am I ever glad to see you!" Vonne stepped over Ray's body as she stumbled out of the van.

"Here, let me get those cuffs off." Dominick pulled out a pocketknife and cut the plastic. "We have to hurry. Those guys should be getting to the gate any minute, and I don't want them finding Ray's surprise."

Vonne ran around to the driver's seat and pulled Lorna's body out, dumping it unceremoniously on the ground. "How did you know?"

"I got a vibrating text message about an hour ago. We've been watching Astrid Becker for almost a year, ever since she started collecting munitions."

"She's probably up in the canyon preparing an ambush." Vonne spun the van around and headed back down the dusty road. At the end, she took a left toward the gate.

"I doubt she's there yet. I turned all the horses out to pasture before I left."

"Then they'll take the truck."

"Not on four flat tires."

"Damn, you're good!" She could see several sets of headlights gathered at the gate. "I'm going to let you out here and head back. I think Liza's in for trouble."

"All right. Take that last cutoff before you get to the barn. There's a horse tied behind the bathhouse, saddled and ready." Dominick took the automatic pistol from his belt and replaced the clip. "And take this, Lieutenant."

Vonne smiled at the address, one she hadn't heard for several years. "Thanks. And be careful with that gate."

"You be careful. Astrid Becker's crazy."

"Is ... that ... all you ... know ... how ... to do?" Vonne groaned as the horse bounced her mercilessly in a trot up the path to the supply shed. A quick look around the ranch had confirmed all of the hands were gone, most likely headed on foot to the canyon, where Astrid would make her stand. She had to get to Liza, no matter what.

Vonne brought the obstinate beast to a stop when she crossed the zigzag road for the third time. She was less than two hundred yards from the shed, but it would be suicide to continue on this path. She had to find another way into the canyon, and the best bet was the stream that crossed the road about fifty yards from where she was now stopped.

"You get to stay in the woods and eat all the weeds you want." She tethered the reins and hurried as quietly as she could along the road, entering the woods again at the stream to start her trek uphill.

After fifteen minutes of steep climbing, she crested the ridge. From this vantage point, she could see lights moving about, as though people were carrying flashlights or lanterns. She heard shouting, including one voice that was unmistakably Astrid's. Carefully, she picked her way down the rocky slope into the thick brush that lined the canyon wall. She could make out the shapes of vehicles, probably jeeps and trucks, moving into a broad semi-circle around the mouth of the canyon. This was where they would stage their ambush.

Vonne crept closer, straining her eyes in the dark to find Liza. She spotted a lone figure sitting at the base of a large boulder near the entrance. Several hands worked nearby, positioning two 55-gallon drums on either side. *Gasoline bombs.* Astrid intended to blow up the agents as they stormed the canyon, and Liza would be right at the center of the explosions.

Vonne scrambled back up the ridge and down the path by the stream, frantic to stop the assault. When she reached the road, she could see the caravan zigzagging up the hillside. She waited in the woods until they reached her, six four-wheel drive vehicles, each carrying four or five agents. Then she jumped into the center of the road and waved her arms wildly.

"You can't go through the pass. She's got it rigged to blow up."

Dominick nodded and looked to his chief, who was driving the lead vehicle. "Is there another way in?"

"Follow me. You might want to drive a couple of these vehicles up that way so she won't get suspicious. But get the hell out of there when you reach the shed."

The senior agent pulled to the side of the road and relayed their strategy to two of the trailing vehicles, which continued on to the shed. Then, two dozen armed agents set out on foot behind Vonne. When they reached the top of the ridge, she showed them the lay of the land. Dominick added more information from his brief stint working in the canyon on Astrid's military drills.

"We'll take it from here," said the agent in charge. "You should go on back down to the road and wait."

"You can do whatever you want," Vonne answered. "But I'm going for Liza. It's my fault she's down there, and I'm not even sure whose side she's on. I just hope I can get her to trust me."

Dominick spoke up. "We'll cover you if we can, but look out, because things are going to get pretty wild."

"You guys too." And with a final nod, Vonne was gone, slinking through the brush around the perimeter, stopping within only a few yards of Liza's position. Even in the dim light, she could see that the woman was bound and gagged, left as bait for the would-be rescuers. "Psssstt ... Liza!"

Their eyes met, and Vonne could see her fear and desperation.

"Are you wired?"

Liza shook her head, and Vonne scrambled forward and pulled the duct tape from her mouth.

"The barrels are full of gas," Liza whispered. "Astrid's going to blow them up when somebody tries to get through."

"We need to get you out of here fast!" She worked hard to pull the ropes from Liza's wrists.

"You're clever, Vonne. I'll give you that."

Both women turned to find Astrid emerging from the shadows, her pistol aimed directly at Vonne.

"We're not part of your war, Astrid. Let us go." As she locked eyes with her assailant, Vonne reached slowly behind her for the pistol she had tucked into her belt.

"Your kind is the whole reason for this war," she practically growled. "Get away from her."

Vonne took a step backward and drew her gun. "Run, Liza!"

Her words were drowned by the retort from Astrid's pistol, a shot to Vonne's shoulder that knocked her to the ground and caused her to drop her gun. Astrid drew closer as Liza cowered, but Vonne's long leg swept her off her feet. She fell backward, striking her head against a rock.

"We have to hurry," Vonne grunted, pressing hard against her bleeding wound.

Liza worked her ropes and finally shook her hands free.

Astrid struggled to sit up, her hand going immediately to the knot on the back of her head. Liza jumped up and kicked the gun out of her reach. "Let's go!" She helped Vonne to her feet and they hobbled quickly toward the perimeter.

"Stop them," Astrid gasped, her voice not strong enough to reach the ranch hands, who were in position deeper into the canyon. "Stop them ... Now!" she shouted.

From a hundred yards away, the two hands heard the command they had been instructed to wait for. One nodded to the other, who touched the two wires together, igniting the massive fireball that would claim Astrid Becker.

Vonne opened her eyes suddenly and blinked, aware she wasn't alone in the dark room.

"Hey." It was a warm voice ... from someone sitting in the chair by her right shoulder.

"Liza?"

"Yeah, it's me." She stood and took a step closer to the bed. "How do you feel?"

"Sore." Vonne squirmed in her bed to loosen up her stiff joints. "What time is it?"

"Almost ten. You've been in and out of it all day."

"I don't remember coming here."

"You lost a lot of blood." Liza sat down on the edge of the bed. "They said you'd be all right, but it scared us all anyway." She rattled a vial. "Did anyone show you this? It's your bullet."

Vonne took the vial and turned it in her hand. "Was anybody else ...?"

"No, just you ... and Astrid, of course. The agents got the drop on the others when the bombs went off. Those guys never had a clue they were surrounded."

"I'm sorry about Astrid. I didn't want that to happen."

Liza took a deep breath and sighed. "Ironic ... she got caught in her own trap. I can't help but feel like it was my fault."

"Why? You couldn't have stopped her."

Liza shrugged. "I should have realized it, though. So many secrets ... I just didn't want to see it so I tuned it out. They're never going to believe my statement."

"Yes, they will. I'll tell them the same thing."

"But you didn't let Astrid manipulate you the way I did."

"She wasn't wrong about everything, Liza. She was a smart woman, and some of the things she believed in would make this country a better place. She just carried things too far."

"And we all helped her, whether we knew it or not."

"I always knew you weren't part of it."

An uncomfortable silence reigned as each woman gathered her thoughts about what else needed to be said. Liza scooted closer, resting her hand on Vonne's leg. "I met your friend Jerry."

"You didn't kill him, did you?"

Liza chuckled slightly. "No, he was in here with you most of the day. I felt sorry for him and let him live. But I'm not letting him inside my head."

Vonne reached up and cradled Liza's cheek with her palm. "There's nothing wrong with your head."

Liza took her hand and intertwined their fingers. "I guess I'll be heading back to Orange County day after tomorrow."

"What are you going to do?"

"I need to help Robb sort out the company's mess. We'll meet with the board and probably file for bankruptcy."

"Then what?"

Liza shrugged. "Then I'll have to start looking for a job ... or run away again to another ranch." She said the last bit with a wry smile.

"Come to Sausalito."

Liza shook her head. "I don't think I should."

"Why not?"

"Because ... I don't trust where we stand, Vonne. I don't know what parts are real for either of us."

"Everything I felt about you was real." Vonne struggled to sit up. "I admit that I took advantage ... When I asked you that night to leave with me, I thought it would be the easiest way for both of us to walk out. But everything I said about wanting you to come back to Sausalito with me was true."

Liza pulled their joined hands to her chest. "It was real for me too."

"Then give us a chance."

Soft white light flooded the room as the door was pushed open by a uniformed nurse. "You'll need to be going soon. Our patient needs her rest."

Liza nodded and looked back at Vonne. "There's something else. When Ray and Lorna took you away ..."

"Dominick—"

"I know. He told me. But ..." She shook her head and sighed.

"What is it?" Vonne took her hand and tenderly rubbed her thumb across the knuckles, finally pulling them to her lips for a soft kiss.

"How do I live with knowing that I almost got you killed?"

"You let it go because it didn't happen." Vonne's words had no effect on Liza's look of guilt. "When I saw you tied up at the canyon pass between those two barrels, I knew I was the one who had put you there. We're both going to have to live with regrets about things ... but they didn't happen, Liza."

Liza nodded solemnly.

"And it will be easier for me to forgive myself if I can look up and be reminded by your smile that everything turned out all right."

The mention of a smile was enough to soften Liza's worried look. "I'll come back tomorrow." She lowered her head and they shared a gentle kiss. As she started to leave Vonne grabbed her hand.

"Thanks for being here."

Liza squeezed her hand and dropped one more kiss on her brow. Then she was gone.

Vonne lay still for almost an hour, her mind bombarded by the brutal images from the past couple of weeks—the young couple that disappeared, Billy's lifeless body, and Astrid shrieking as she burned to death. She envisioned Liza, captive between the two deadly bombs, and imagined her screaming as the barrels blew.

Each time, she calmed herself with the memory of Liza's warm hand, her soft lips, and her promise to return tomorrow. And finally, she drifted off to a peaceful sleep.

Narc Redux

SX Meagher

The Set-Up

I started to walk toward the restaurant as usual, trying to put on my game face. It shouldn't be that hard to look like a slightly used, morally flexible waitress, but it was kind of a stretch for me. It probably sounds silly, but it actually takes the whole ten-minute walk to get into character. I was so intent on putting the wiggle in my hips that I almost made a big error, a very big error. Luckily, I put on the brakes before anyone spotted me. Anyone that I could see, that is. I'm sure someone's on his radio right now, ready to wet his pants, saying, "Detective Grady's approaching Sergeant Randolph! Please instruct!"

Calm down, fellas. I'm not gonna wave and cry out, "Hi, Sergeant! Ready for the big bust?" It's not my fault you guys scheduled this for half an hour before my shift starts. Of course, I assume no one bothered to check to see when my shift starts, but if you're gonna stick a girl in this dump for six months, it might be nice to make sure she's on duty when the payoff hits.

I was just about to make a hard left to go into the service entrance of Taverna Ptomaine when I paused just long enough to check her out. I'd only seen her once before, but I had to admit I had what could unkindly be called a schoolgirl's crush on Sergeant Randolph.

Yes, it's childish, but she's the kind of cop I'd like to grow up to be. She's probably in her mid-thirties, and everyone knows she'll make lieutenant this year ... even if this bust doesn't go down. She's one of those women that people don't fuck with. But looking at her up close, all you notice is her cool professionalism. She looks like she really owns that sweet BMW she's driving. And that suit looks like it cost two thousand dollars. It's a good return on investment though, 'cause it makes her look like a million bucks. She looks exactly like a big time drug dealer who never touches the stuff. All business.

I looked away, not wanting to take the chance of her seeing me. Not like she'd know me if she did. As I said, I'd only seen her once, and she was addressing a crowd big enough that it could have started its own slow-pitch softball league. It must be nice to get a hot car, a great wardrobe, and enough manpower to fill an articulated bus; and I intend to find out for myself ... eventually.

But before I can convince people I'm a high-level drug dealer I've got to start looking more like an important woman and less like a cheap whore.

I've got a few special outfits to match my cover. My bra is far too small, but it makes my boobs look like they're going to escape at any minute. The guys here love that. And I always wear a blouse that might have fit me in grade school. If you're in the market for a lot of attention to be paid to your boobs, The Gap makes the perfect blouse. It's a cotton/poly blend, short sleeved, tailored, and it has a bit of stretch in it. I bought it in pink, lime, and orange, and I always leave two buttons undone. Thank God my husband never sees me leave for work. He's up and gone by seven, so I have time for a leisurely breakfast before I have to get into my strumpet clothes. It's barely spring, so I've been able to wear a long coat home every night. Tim's aware of my comings and goings, but we've been married for three years and we're past the point where he jumps up and follows me into the bedroom just to watch me undress. Still, it's for sure that he'd notice the makeup, so I bought some of those makeup remover pads and keep them in my purse. I get a few looks on the El when I'm cleaning my face like a twelve-year-old girl going home to her overprotective parents, but even at that, I'm far from being the strangest sight on the El.

Tim knows about my assignment, of course. It's just that he knows Sonny and the types of goons who hang around him. No man would like to know that his wife is trying to get a bunch of perverts to hit on her so she might be able to squeeze a little info out of them.

Actually, even though I've done my best to keep Tim in the dark about my daily activities, I've been amazed that he hasn't noticed most of the bruises on my butt and thighs. Luckily, I'm a bit of a klutz, so I was able to explain away the one lurid bruise he noticed when we were making love in the shower. Since then, I've tried to lure him into bed, where we keep the lights nice and low or, even better, off.

You might wonder why Tim knows anything about Sonny. That's because we're a two-cop family. Tim's a legacy. His dad and his uncle were both cops. I'd deny having said this, but even though it was a natural choice for him, Tim doesn't have police work in his blood. Not like I do. He'd be just as happy, and just as successful, as a mortgage banker or a teacher or in the Vatican. He likes being in charge, and he's good at managing people and projects. That's why he's a lieutenant, heading for captain, and he's only thirty-six.

I, on the other hand, just want to be a detective. I want to work on ridding the streets of rats. I know there will always be more than we can catch, but I have a real need to pick them off ... one after another.

We've had some problems with our different views of the job. Tim, as I said, has been very successful, and he doesn't understand why I don't model my career after his. But I don't have any interest in playing the political game. I want to be on the street, working leads, interviewing people. It's not going to get my name in the papers and it's not going to put any gold braid on my dress hat, but it's what makes me happy.

If I were to model my career after anyone, it might be Sergeant Randolph. I've never heard of a person worth his badge who didn't respect her. No one was surprised when she was given this assignment, and not too many people complained. That alone is cause for celebration. Officers are not known for wishing other people good luck when they get a prime assignment. We're a catty bunch.

What did surprise me was that Tim didn't have much to say about the sergeant when I asked about her. He didn't say anything bad ... he just damned her with faint praise. That puzzled the heck out of me. It wasn't until I went to a meeting of everyone assigned to the sting that I figured out what Tim's problem was. I think I mentioned that the task force for this sting was huge, so huge that the meeting was held in the auditorium at police headquarters.

I found a seat next to a buddy from the academy. When Sergeant Randolph took the stage, Jim Krakowiecki leaned over and said, "Can you believe she's a dyke? What a waste!"

Mystery solved! Tim didn't have a problem with her police work; he didn't like her choice of bed partners. Too damn bad she wasn't dumpy and ugly. That might have helped ... me, at least. She probably preferred being tall and beautifully built and gorgeous. I'm sure it's easier getting dates that way.

There's one little thing I haven't told you, and it's key to Tim's dislike of gorgeous lesbians. When I was in college, I had a year-long love affair with a woman. I don't regret it, even though she broke my heart into a billion pieces. What I do regret, and I'll regret to my dying day, is telling Tim about it. I know now that you should never tell your husband about any of your past dates. Heck, you shouldn't let him know you think heartthrob movie stars are good-looking. But I was just twenty-two when Tim and I met. I was a fresh-faced girl from Charleston, Illinois, just out of the police academy. A good-looking, mature, cool, calm, low-key guy and I start dating and he asked about my past experiences. No one told me I should have told him I'd never noticed a man before him.

How was I to know that his substantial self-confidence would be shaken to the core by my having loved a woman? I still don't get it. I don't think I ever will. But I honestly think he'd rather I'd slept with the entire roster of the Bears than with that one woman. It's been six years since I've kissed a woman, and Charlotte was the only woman I've ever kissed, much less had sex with. But Tim still has a nagging suspicion that I'm secretly eyeing every pair of boobs pointed in my direction.

Now, don't get the wrong idea. He doesn't give me a hard time about it; I can just tell that it bothers him. He's not the type to bitch at me about things. I couldn't stand that. I wouldn't stand for it. But sometimes he'll sneak a quick look at me if a beautiful woman's on TV or in a movie. It's like he's expecting to find my tongue hanging out and my eyes popping out of my head, like they do in cartoons.

The truth is that even though I loved Charlotte, the sex wasn't great. Dang, I might as well be honest. It wasn't even good. We both wound up with men. Actually, Charlotte dumped me for a guy. It was more … a romantic friendship, if you know what I mean. We touched each other sweetly, carefully, gently … infrequently. But sweet and infrequent aren't the adjectives I want to use for my sex life.

It wasn't all her fault. I was slow to mature and hadn't done much of anything in high school. I looked very, very young in high school. Guys thought of me as a pal … a little sister type. But when I was nearly seventeen I grew into my body, and things started to turn around.

Charlotte was my roommate freshman year in college, and near the end of the year we started to … go to another level. I wasn't sure what was happening, but I thought about her constantly that summer while I was working on my grandfather's farm. As soon as we got back together we started to sleep in the same bed, and eventually we started to kiss. After months of kissing and holding each other, we finally had sex, but it was never a red-hot love affair. Heck, she didn't even want to call it sex. One time I told her I wanted to talk about our sex life and she laughed at me! She said we couldn't *really* have sex. We just touched each other because we loved each other. I was stumped. It felt like sex to me, but she was quite sure it wasn't, and who was I to argue? So we snuggled in a twin bed, hugged and spooned and kissed. And every once in a while our hands would stray, and we'd have what I was pretty sure was sex. Not hot, wet, messy sex, but we gave each other orgasms … and that felt pretty darned good to me.

The problem was that Charlotte would get a little distant after we did that, so I started waiting for her to make the first move. One day, she did. She started going out with a guy named Jeff. She was honestly puzzled that I didn't want to sleep with her anymore. I don't know what went on in her head, but she thought she could have me as her best friend, cuddle-buddy while she was dating and probably sleeping with Jeff. After a few heated, pointless arguments, I found a new roommate, and spent months trying to figure out what I'd done wrong. I finally decided that romantic friendships weren't for me. I wanted sex. Good sex. Great sex. And I found it with a guy who knew how to make me hot ... and he knew how to cool me off.

Three boyfriends later, I found Tim, and I'm darned glad I did. He's not my best friend, but I've found I don't need that from a man. Women are better at being best friends. Tim's a man I respect and admire, and I'm very, very hot for him. Thank God he feels the same about me. I know he'll never be the person I get everything from, but he doesn't get everything from me, either. That's why we each have friends. My girlfriends understand me in a way that no man probably ever could. I listen to them and they listen to me. Sometimes my friends go to things with me that Tim *would* go to, but only under protest. But that's not a big deal. He loves me and he satisfies me and I know he'll be a wonderful father to our kids.

Before we can be parents, we have to figure out a way to make our marriage as strong as it can be. I don't want him supervising me, but I also don't want to upset him. So I withhold little things from him. Nothing huge ... really. But there aren't many men who'd want to know the little details of their wife's day when she's working for a bunch of slimy drug dealers.

I've seen some things in the past six months that have opened my eyes to a whole side of the world I wish didn't exist. But it does exist, and I do my best to put a dent in the sleaze. I know it's a losing battle, but every little bit helps.

I've never told Tim that Chris invariably sticks a generous tip into my cleavage, rooting around in my bra like a pig in slop. It gives me the creeps, but telling Tim wouldn't make it less creepy; it would just worry him and piss him off.

Which brings me to my big lie. Yesterday my sergeant told me that Sergeant Randolph was going to make the bust today. I'm sure Tim found out as soon as he got to work this morning, and he's not gonna be happy if he finds out I knew about it yesterday. I know I should have told him, but I wanted to save myself the lecture about being safe and staying out of the line of fire, and all of the other things I do instinctively. I wish I could have shared my excitement with him, but sometimes he doesn't treat me like a fellow cop. He treats me like his wife—someone he loves and wants to protect. There's nothing wrong with that, but it takes some of the fun out of it. I know it sounds silly to someone who isn't in this kind of work, but this part of my job is equivalent to a huge, noisy, scary roller coaster, and I'm so excited I'm ready to jump out of my skin. I guess I need a girlfriend on the force. No, not that kind of girlfriend. Just the kind who'd understand what it's like to do this for a living, and be happy for me.

The rats began to scamper as I turned into the alley. One of the bolder ones was standing right behind the door, and he slapped me on the butt when I crossed the threshold. "Hi, sweetcheeks," he oozed.

"Hi, Chris." I managed a smile, not caring that it couldn't have looked sincere. I'd learned that Chris didn't care about sincerity as much as he did about tight clothes. As my wardrobe went from a size ten to an eight, my tips went up significantly. Today I had on a size six skirt that would have prevented me from taking a full step if it hadn't been so short. Thank God my parents have never seen me at work. Pop would have a stroke and Mom would be too busy whipping me to give him CPR.

Spiro, another swell fella, walked into the kitchen and snapped his fingers at Chris. "Let's go," he said.

Without another word to me, Chris nearly ran after him. Huh. I usually get a goodbye pinch. I guess they know something big is going on today. They must not be as in the dark about Sonny's business as they should be ... given that they're both morons.

Yet another of my fans, Sonya, slapped down an order on the pass-through and narrowed her eyes at me. "Don't even think about trying to take any of my tips. You're due at eleven, and not a minute before."

"I won't," I said. "My bus was early. I had to go somewhere."

"You can stick your thumb up your ass, for all I care. Just keep your mitts off my tables."

I held up my hands, hoping Sonya understood sign language better than English. “I won’t touch your tables. I’ll just fill condiments until your tables clear.”

She turned, muttering, “That little whore better not steal my tips.”

Now that was just uncalled for. She didn’t know whether or not I was a whore. I’m not, by the way. But it’s darned annoying when a woman assumes you’re loose just because you dress like a slut, wear too much makeup, let sleazy guys paw you, and make good tips.

I put on my change apron and went to the booth closest to the kitchen, the one where a cook or a busboy or a waitress is usually reading the paper or eating. Maybe I’ve been going to the wrong kinds of restaurants, but if I were the owner, I’d frown on that kind of behavior. Especially since we have such a nice combination break room/coat closet. Granted, there weren’t cameras and microphones trained on the booth, and no one had been threatened to within an inch of her life to stay out of the booth when any of the big guns were there, but still, I thought it was bad business to be sitting down filling salt shakers when there were customers being ignored.

My idea of customer service and Sonny’s—he’s the owner of this fine establishment and a major drug importer—clearly differed. He didn’t care that the place was often empty, or that many of the customers seemed like relatives or relatives of relatives. It was almost like working at someone’s home ... if their home was a dirty, health code-violating Greek diner.

I’d been dying to sneak a peek at Sonny’s special table, but I didn’t want Sonya to see me. But as she went to the pass-through to pick up an order, I caught sight of the sergeant, making small talk with the Great Triumvirate. Everything looked like it was going just fine, and for no reason at all, I found my confidence soaring. We were trying to pull off a major drug buy from a major dealer, and we were doing it inside his place of business. I still don’t know how this whole thing was arranged, but I was impressed. Guys didn’t usually allow deals to go down in a public place. But from what Tim tells me, Sonny has enough cops on his payroll to field one entire team in our imaginary softball league.

Yes, it's sad, but true: cops get dirty. I'm not sure if it's because they're already slime when they first start, or it comes over them over time, but they are slime. They don't belong in my family. And, yes, I mean family. There are people I've worked with who I could learn to hate, but they're still members of my family and I'd do anything to keep them safe. It's just like at home. My great-uncle Charlie is a drunk, and he's tried to grope every girl in the family as soon as she starts to grow boobs. But everyone keeps an eye on him, and we've all been instructed to never be alone with him. Even though he's a sloppy letch, we'd all give him a kidney if he needed one. He's family. Just make sure you turn your head when he kisses you goodbye or you're gonna regret it.

The Bust

I'd been watching Sonny's table out of the corner of my eye, and not much was happening. Sonny was a big talker, and I figured he'd bore her for a while before they got down to business. I wasn't carrying, but when Spiro abruptly grabbed Sergeant Randolph's suit jacket and yanked it hard, I instinctively reached for my weapon. When Sonny slapped Spiro's big meat hook away, my heart rate slowed down a little bit.

I'd done the salt and pepper shakers, so I started to fill the Heinz ketchup bottles with the watery sludge they bought from some third-rate supplier. I was so intent on not making a mess that I almost missed seeing Spiro stand up and gesture for the sergeant to walk in front of him. What in the hell? They were heading for the break-room, but I couldn't figure out why. Damn! I couldn't decide if I should make up a reason to go into the room, or just wait until I heard a shot. I could claim I didn't know there was anyone in there, but I'd been warned in no uncertain terms that I was never to go in there if Sonny or the boys were in the restaurant.

Sonny moved to Spiro's seat and stood a menu in front of the napkin dispenser. I'd never been allowed to touch anything on Sonny's special table, but it didn't take a genius to figure out he had a camera in the break room and a monitor hooked up in the napkin dispenser. Napkins just aren't that interesting. I've never seen a man's eyes widen at the sight of napkins, either. Sonny grabbed Chris and snapped, "Go stop that idiot!"

Dang, I hope Spiro isn't doing anything awful to the sergeant, 'cause there's nothing I can do to stop him. My heart was racing again, and my hands were shaking so badly that I spilled the watery ketchup all over the table. I was making plans to run for the front door to call in the troops *after* Spiro shot the sergeant ... not the ideal time to come to the aid of a fellow officer. Don't let anyone tell you police work isn't nerve-wracking. The problem is that it's nerve-wracking for three minutes, then boring for hours upon hours. But those three minutes really do drag on.

My intestines were in a knot by the time the door opened and the sergeant walked out, bracketed by both thugs. I'd never been so glad to see anyone, and I didn't know her from Adam ... or Eve.

Before Spiro could even sit, Sonny slapped him across the face. I could see Spiro struggle to keep the anger he felt from showing. It must have been hard to let a man slap you and not even be allowed to look pissed-off. I didn't feel a bit guilty about the pleasure I took at seeing him humiliated. I couldn't count the times he'd "dropped" something and asked me to pick it up. He didn't usually paw me, but it was still degrading to be forced to show a creep your butt.

I have no idea what had pissed Sonny off, but he was plenty angry. He slapped Spiro again, much harder this time. I could see the big lug hold on to the table, probably to keep himself from snapping Sonny's neck with his bare hands.

Whatever happened, they must have made up, because Sonny started talking again. Sonya eventually told me to get off my ass and wait on a table. Gosh, she was nice! I was in the kitchen, trying to explain to the cook that the eggs he'd given me weren't dry enough when the sergeant and Chris disappeared. I figured they were in the break room, since Sonny was watching the napkin dispenser again. Now what?

This time I wasn't as nervous, since it would have been Spiro who killed her if there was killing to be done. Chris was rumored to be relatively clean since he was engaged to Sonny's daughter. But everyone stepped aside when Spiro walked into the room, and I didn't think that was just because of his cologne ... although it could have been. The guy reeked!

Sergeant Randolph and Chris were back before I could get too anxious, but she didn't look right. I don't know what he did to her, but she looked ... a little vacant. I didn't have long to consider her, because I heard a loud snap and I looked up like the trained pet I was. "You," Sonny said, pointing right at me.

Numbly, I put down my tray and approached the table, feeling like I was stepping into a pit of vipers. What if she'd told Chris something?

But Sonny looked strangely friendly as I drew near. "What's your name, honey?"

"Brittany." No, that's not my real name, but my sergeant thought it was funny to name me after Britney Spears. I changed the spelling just for a little revenge.

Sonny smiled at the other men. "That's a nice name, isn't it?"

Chris and Spiro nodded, something they did a lot.

"Why are you working here, honey?"

"To make money," I said, hoping that wasn't the wrong answer.

Sonny laughed. "There are thousands of restaurants in Chicago. Do you live around here?"

"Uhm ... not too far. Near Printer's Row."

"Restaurants over there pay a lot more than I do."

I nodded, even though I had no idea how much restaurants paid. "But I go to school at UIC. I was in the neighborhood one day and saw a sign in your window saying you had a job available. I thought it made sense to be closer to school than home."

"And how do you like it here?" Sonny asked. "You've been here a while, right?"

"Six months. It's fine. Nice people. Regular crowd."

"Notice anything funny?" His dark eyes fixed on mine like magnets to iron.

I had no idea what to say! What was the right answer? "Uhm ... like what?"

"Oh, I don't know. You look like a smart girl. Perceptive. A young girl like you would probably only work here if she wanted something."

"Wanted something?"

"Yeah. Like an introduction into the business, or to meet a guy with a load of cash or to ... get information."

I had to admit to something or look like I was blind and stupid. A guy didn't intimate you were spying on him and not expect an answer. "I, uhm ... I ... guess I did notice some funny things going on."

"Like what?" He was talking to me like my grandfather did when I visited his farm.

"Like ..." Figuring that he was already in trouble, I looked at Spiro. "I've seen Spiro grab a towel and put ice in it and wrap it around his hand. He looked like he'd been in a fight or something."

"Uh-huh. What else?"

"Well ... like you said ... some of the guys have a lot of money on 'em. Sometimes they'll give me a really big tip, even when I haven't waited on 'em." I didn't mean to, but I shot Chris a look. It was just a reaction. I swear.

"So ... men in fights ... lots of cash ... big tips. What do you think? Is this just a regular restaurant?"

"Probably not," I said. "I think it's a front."

Sonny laughed and slapped both Chris and me on the arm. "A front!"

I nodded, hoping his laugh was genuine.

"What kinda front?"

"Probably drugs or some other kinda crime."

"But you'd still rather work here than near Printer's Row."

I nodded again. I hadn't been shot yet, so I figured I might as well stick with my stock response.

"Why is that? Shouldn't a nice girl like you wanna work someplace full of young lawyers and legitimate businessmen?"

Time to look as tough as I felt when I was carrying my weapon. "I wanna have money. Sometimes you've gotta take risks to get it."

"Ah-ha!" Sonny cried. "Look what we have here! A little entrepreneur."

"I spent a few months stripping," I said, just for fun. Might as well look like I'd been around the block. "The money isn't as good here, but I don't get pawed as much."

He started at my feet and let his eyes roam up my body. I immediately regretted my lie about stripping. There was no way I looked sexy enough to make a living with my body. "You get pawed here?"

Relieved, I muttered, "Not much. Some guys pat my ass or put tips down my blouse."

Sonny shot a glare at Chris. "I'd better never find you doing anything like that. I'll cut your nuts off."

Deciding I needed all of the friends I could get, I interrupted. "Chris has always been a perfect gentleman."

Sonny kept his eyes on Chris, and it was clear he knew I was lying, but he let it pass. "Well, Brittany," he said, turning to me, looking friendly and cheerful, "how would you like to make a quick thou?"

"A thousand dollars?" I gasped, not because of the money—I wouldn't get to keep it anyway. But I knew he wouldn't offer me a thousand dollars for flaming a plate of saganaki.

"Yep. And I bet it won't take you more than fifteen minutes. Twenty, tops."

I hoped my blouse wasn't so tight that he could see my heart beating. "What do I have to do?"

"All you have to do," he said, speaking softly so I had to lean in to hear, "is to take my lady friend here into the back room and make her come. Any way you want."

I stood up so fast I got a little dizzy. "Make her come?"

"Yeah. Give her a little head. Finger-fuck her. Whatever you want. You ever muff-dived?"

I shook my head until I saw stars. Damn, hadn't I learned anything at the academy? Cool down! "Never," I said, hoping that I wasn't as red as a beet.

"Well," Sonny said, "you don't have to do it. But if you don't, you don't need to come back. If I'm gonna have a good-looking young girl around here, she's gotta be willing to do me some favors."

I couldn't help it. I gave Sonya a sideways look. She wasn't good-looking, young, or competent. "She's the wife of a former associate," Sonny said. "Her husband screwed up, but that wasn't her fault. I'm not gonna throw money at her, but I don't want her or her kids to starve."

Maybe Sonya wasn't such a bad egg. I probably wouldn't be in a good mood very often if I had to wait tables for slime just because I'd married the wrong guy.

"Why?" Sergeant Randolph said. She had to be ready to wet her pants, but she sounded as cool as a tall glass of lemonade. "I've told you I'm a dyke. Why waste money trying to make me prove it?"

Well! They'd been having an interesting talk while I was filling salt shakers. I'd missed all the fun!

"The drugs are making you stupid," he said, smirking. "This isn't to prove that you're a dyke. Who would lie about that? This is insurance in case you're a cop. I know you're not gonna want everybody in the department to know you're a bulldagger. And if you don't care about that, you're not gonna want the tape put on the Internet."

Dang! She was high! I tried to think, quickly realizing that I had to step in ... even though I might be destroying my marriage and my career. She couldn't be thinking straight, so I had to think for her. It's part of the deal. Police work sucks. I cleared my throat. "I'll do it. Cash, right?" I asked, just to show I was only doing it for the money.

He patted his jacket, and I could see the bulge that was probably a combination of a weapon and a wad of dough. "Yep. It's right here."

I looked at the sergeant, trying to give the impression that I did this kind of thing all the time. "Let's go."

She stood, and I was very glad I'd agreed. She didn't look dizzy, but she certainly didn't look like she was all there. Her eyes were barely focusing and she was far too happy, given the circumstances.

I led the way, and when I opened the door I saw her look around. That was a relief. At least she was acting like a cop. She stood so that the cameras were at her back and mouthed, "I'm sorry."

I was facing the camera, so I couldn't acknowledge her apology. But even if I could have, I wouldn't have. If she hadn't taken drugs, I might not have had to do this. Even though I assumed they'd made her do whatever she'd done, I was still ticked off.

I decided to get down to business, partially to get it over with and partially because I knew we were being watched ... carefully. "How do you wanna do this?"

"Uhm ..." She smiled like a sixteen-year-old boy who was getting lucky for the first time. "Sonny said something about ... uhm ... going down on me ..."

"Fine." I'd been hoping the idiot would ask me to use my hand on her. I had experience with that. Even more annoyed, I asked, "Where do you wanna be, fuck-head? You wanna stand up, sit down, lie down? How ... do ... you ... come?" I swear that I usually don't speak like this, but I had to keep up my ex-stripper attitude.

"Oh! Right!"

She took so long looking around the room that I snapped at her, "Make up your fucking mind!"

"I'm trying," she said, looking confused and very indecisive.

I wasn't sure what she was on, so I decided to ask. "Are you high?"

"Very. Crystal."

"That'll help." I knew she'd be easy to do on meth. I always paid close attention in the drug seminars. "Are you turned on?"

"Not really," she said, but she looked like she was lying. Maybe I was better looking than I thought.

"Let's take care of that first. I'd like to spend as little time as possible between your legs."

She giggled. "That's not the best seduction line I've ever heard."

She sure was calm. Either she loved the danger, or the drugs really helped. That made me mad that I didn't get any drugs! I took off her lovely jacket and hung it on a chair. Very nice material. Facing her, I ran my hands down her back. They told us she was going in naked, but I didn't want to find out the hard way that she'd changed her mind. I started to unbutton her shirt. I didn't want to take off more than I had to, but Sonny said to make her come and I wasn't gonna screw up. If I was gonna get shot, it wasn't gonna be because I couldn't make a woman come. That's just not what I want in my obituary.

I knew the only way I could get through this was to take the offensive. This was new for me, but the sergeant looked just slightly more stable than a bowl of Jell-O. Reaching behind her head I pulled her down, kissing her the way Tim kisses me when he's really ready to go. Tim always grasps one of my breasts when he's wound up, so I thought I'd try that, too.

Wow! Charlotte's nipples never got that hard that fast! Meth must make me darned hot! Maybe I should have given some to Charlotte.

I've been honest so far, so there's no sense in lying now. Having a gorgeous woman respond to me so quickly was a turn-on. I wouldn't have admitted it to Tim, even if there was a gun to my head, but it's the truth.

Responding to the animal instincts surging through me, I grasped her head with both of my hands and really let her have it. I kissed her so hungrily that I felt like I could eat her. I was acting ... but I wasn't acting, if that makes any sense. Actors always say that they don't get aroused during love scenes. That's always made sense to me. But this wasn't a love scene, and those weren't directors sitting outside. They were mean guys with big guns who wanted to embarrass Sergeant Randolph. They didn't just want us playing patty-cake. They wanted an orgasm ... and I didn't know about them, but Tim could always tell when I'd had one. I was bound and determined to leave the sergeant with every sign I'd ever seen—splotchy chest, flushed skin, maybe even a little sweat.

I decided we were on the right track when she groaned and grabbed my butt. I don't know why, but that seemed too intimate. Being in control felt better to me, and letting her touch me felt like an invasion. I took her wrists and pinned them behind her back, holding them as tightly as I would a suspect's.

We were pressed up against each other, my boobs rubbing against her tummy. She was doing her best to move her shoulders so her breasts would press harder against me. She obviously needed some stimulation there, so I figured I'd better give her some. God knows I like a little attention on my breasts, so ... fair's fair.

I let Randolph kiss me while I put my free hand between us and played with her boobs, still holding her wrists behind her back. One of the things I'd most loved about touching Charlotte was playing with her breasts. I always touched her gently, nuzzling and mouthing her soft skin like a kitten nursing, but it had taken all my control to behave that way with her. I'd wanted to really let go and lose myself ... show her how hot it made me to touch her ... but I hadn't had the nerve.

This wasn't the ideal place to finally get my wish, but I had to make this woman come. I pinched Sergeant Randolph's nipples until I heard her begin to scream. She was practically licking my face, something I didn't think I'd like, but it was amazingly exciting.

My back was starting to get stiff from pushing against the sergeant, so I leaned back a little. She was right with me, kissing me and probing at my mouth with her tongue. I opened my mouth to let her tongue in, and in that split second I stopped caring that people were watching. I stopped caring that we were being forced to do this. I just cared about that hot, wet tongue in my mouth, and the way her breast filled my hand. I ran my thumb over her nipple and she sucked my tongue so hard that I got chills. Damn! My animal instinct was in charge, and I was getting hot ... really hot. It wasn't part of the deal but I wondered briefly if Sonny would mind if I came too.

We started to pass the power back and forth, something I love to do with Tim. But no matter how much Tim lets me play, he's always the more powerful one. It wasn't like that with the sergeant. I was easily as strong as she was, and I could toy with her ... play with her. It was exciting in a way I never would have imagined.

I envied Sergeant Randolph. She had a good excuse for acting like we were all alone in a cheap motel—she was out of her mind on meth, and a lesbian to boot. I couldn't claim either of those reasons, but I was as hot as I've ever been. I should have at least been worried about having this all over the Internet, but I knew the sergeant wouldn't screw up. She'd make the bust and we'd get the tape. One way or the other.

I know it sounds crazy, but I let my barriers down. This was my only chance to have sex with a woman the way I'd dreamed. All of those nights that I went to sleep frustrated out of my mind because Charlotte fell asleep just when I was getting turned on could be erased in just a few minutes. Ten years from now, when Tim and I have a couple of kids, I can pull this experience from my memory bank and get a thrill. I knew it made no rational sense, but I lost myself. I pushed everything else out of my mind and just had sex.

I grabbed the sergeant's head and kissed her hard while undoing the button on her slacks. Drugged as she was, she reached up and helped me, obviously anxious to get down to business.

As her pants fell, I slipped my hands into her shirt and filled my hands with the incredibly soft resiliency of her butt. There's something wonderful about having warm, smooth flesh that conforms to your hands and moves just enough to make your knees weak. The sexy panties didn't hurt, either. Very nice panties, sergeant. If you don't have a girlfriend, it's not because you can't get one, that's for sure. If you'd been my roommate in college, I think I would have flunked out ... but it would have been worth it.

The panties were white and lacy. They fit her like a second skin and showed off her cocoa-colored flesh. But as nice as they were, they had to come off. Immediately. I put my fingers into the waistband and slipped them down her long legs. She reached down and kicked off her shoes and removed her socks while tossing the panties aside.

Looking at her, half-naked with her shirt partly open and her soft, curly hair all mussed, I needed to kiss her again. I wrapped her in my arms and held her tight, kissing her so hard all I could hear were the short, quick breaths she managed to take. Ooo, she was turned on ... and I was the one who'd turned her on. Me and a huge hit of meth were apparently a good combination.

Roughly, I shoved her onto the table, sat on one of the chairs and said, "Spread 'em." I was amazed at how calm and sure my voice sounded, 'cause I was neither.

She leaned back on her hands and let her legs drop open. I couldn't see her, so I undid the bottom buttons on her shirt and pushed it aside. Having her right there in front of me, so open, so vulnerable, made me light-headed. I barely knew where to start, so I tried to toughen up and sound like the woman I was impersonating.

"Do you need to be fucked?"

I could see her clit jump. That must have been a good question.

"Optional," she said, her voice thin and weak.

My hands were shaking a little, but I spread her open and got close, staring at the intricate beauty of her body. It made me laugh a little, thinking of all of the opportunities I'd missed with Charlotte. The sergeant was so lovely and so obviously aroused that I knew this wouldn't take long. I held her open and used my thumbs to spread moisture around her clitoris. I wanted to drop my head and lick her until she screamed, but sitting here looking right at her felt so natural ... like there was nothing wrong with what we were doing. It was strangely freeing, even with the remarkably strange circumstances. Oddly, if I'd done this with Charlotte, it would have been easier to handle our breakup. I'd always thought that I was just a dud. Sex always seemed like something we did only when we couldn't stand being turned on any more. But this felt ... natural. We were touching and kissing and were naturally turned on. Why wouldn't I put my mouth on her and make her come?

Sergeant Randolph's head was dropped back against her shoulder and she was staring at the ceiling like she was on drugs ... which she was.

She looked like she wanted me to tell her what to do. It felt so damned good to be in charge, and I found I had a knack for it. "Put your legs over my shoulders," I said, something I hadn't realized I'd always wanted to say.

I took in a breath, trying to see if I could pick up her scent. It was everything I thought it would be and I couldn't resist. I kissed her gently, more gently than I'd kissed her mouth. I was nearly reverent with her, so amazed at the sensations that I was experiencing. I opened my mouth, and let my tongue touch her tentatively. She shivered roughly, making me lean in and nuzzle against her.

Her scent filled my lungs, and her delicate taste infused my senses. I had no idea what I was doing, but it didn't seem to matter. Everywhere I touched her made her jerk and whimper. I started to feel like I really was in control and I loved it in a way that was almost frightening. My own body felt like a jolt of electricity was passing through it. I knew I was ridiculously wet, and if I'd had a free hand Sonny would have gotten two for the price of one. But I needed both of my hands to take care of the sergeant. I didn't want to miss a thing.

Every time I kissed her vulva she spread her legs wider apart, begging me to touch her again. I made my tongue as soft as I could and licked her—long, slow swipes with my tongue. Her hips bucked up off the table, then thudded back down so hard I was afraid she'd break something.

She was reacting so forcefully that I knew I didn't have long to investigate. And since this would be my last time doing this, I decided to go for it. I pointed my tongue and worked it in and around and over every part of her. I'd never been so enthralled while having sex. Normally I could just relax and let Tim please me; I could put my mind on hold and let sensation take over. But today, I was the one with the power. I was the one who was gonna make this woman come ... with just the power of my tongue.

I was so mesmerized, that I was totally stunned when the sergeant froze for a split second and came. She didn't make a sound, but her knees were locked around my head like a vise. I sat, stunned, watching her whole vulva pulse and twitch. "Fuck," she murmured, breathless.

What the hell. The boys wanted a show, and we were in this as deep as we were gonna get. They wanted her to come ... let 'em hear her this time. I spread her legs apart while they were still shaking and started to lick her again. She twitched a little when I started, and I'm sure she was surprised, but she certainly didn't argue. It took a little longer this time, maybe two minutes, and I could tell when she was close. It was so thrilling to hear her start to breathe heavily, then feel her vulva twitch, then hear her moan and tell me to keep doing what I was doing. She made me feel like I had the whole world in my power. Watching the flush climb up her chest as she came was deeply thrilling and my vulva was so sensitive that I could have pressed my legs together a few times and gotten off.

But I couldn't divert my attention for a second. The sergeant was rigid, all of her muscles tense and hard. But her vagina was twitching and throbbing and it called to me. I had to know what it felt like to put my fingers inside of her. She hadn't relaxed from her last orgasm, so I played around her opening until I could just manage to slip a finger into her unbelievably hot and wet skin. It conformed to my finger like a glove, and I grinned with pleasure when she dropped to the table and let me fuck her, her hips dancing around as I slid in and out and in and out.

I couldn't stop. She could have given me a direct order and I would have kept going ... the urge was just too strong. She seemed to want it hard, so I gave her everything I had, watching her squirm, holding on to my arm with both of her hands, helping me fuck her into a frenzy. When she came, her flesh clamped down on my fingers so tightly that I began to understand why Tim wants to be inside me when he comes. If it feels that good to fingers ... wow. Just wow. Now I know why men think about it every moment.

I desperately wanted to rest my cheek against her and feel her juices on my face, but the spell was broken. Time to be the ex-stripper looking for dough. I sat up and waited for a few seconds so the sergeant could consider releasing my fingers. It took longer than I thought it would, and I was secretly pleased that I'd done her so well she couldn't relax. But there was finally enough room for me to pull out. Just to act tough, I walked to the corner and held my fingers up to the camera. I knew they were loaded and when I turned them upside down, a big drop of the sergeant's juices slid off. Take that, you perverts!

By the time I walked into the bathroom, my whole body was shaking. The enormity of what I'd done and what a fantastic time I'd had doing it, finally hit me. I washed my hands and my face with the harsh soap, then tried to dry my skin with the cheap, wood-pulp paper towels.

When I went back into the room, Sergeant Randolph was collecting her clothes. Now it didn't feel like we'd just had a hell of a good time; it felt like I'd just gone down on a higher ranking officer and there was a tape of it.

When I passed by the table, Sonny stuffed ten hundred dollar bills into my hand, his eyes glazed and remarkably wide. I went into the kitchen and tried to look like I had some purpose being there, but I clearly didn't. Eva, the other lunch waitress, was trying to serve the whole restaurant, and she dashed into the kitchen to curse at me and tell me to get to work.

I followed her out into the restaurant, and saw that the sergeant was still absent. I figured she was cleaning up, but Chris was gone, too. Now what? Then she walked back into the restaurant with Chris and shook both Sonny and Spiro's hands. She didn't sit down, but it was clear Sonny was trying to get her to stay.

I knew where she was going and I knew what she was going to do … so I did what I had to do.

Moments later, the door was knocked off its hinges and people started to scream and curse. Most of the screams were from the customers, but the old man sitting at one of my tables stared right at the officers streaming in and started calling them names I'm embarrassed to repeat. Must have had a few run-ins with Chicago's finest when he was a lad.

A uniformed officer grabbed me and whirled me around so fast I didn't know what hit me. Good technique. He'd started to pat me down when Sergeant Randolph strolled by. Spiro was turned in my direction, so for his benefit I filled my mouth and spit everything I had right in her face. I've never spit on anyone, and it felt weird, but it was the only weapon I had at the moment, and I wanted to make sure Spiro saw me. The uniform turned me around and got me cuffed fast. He looked like he was gonna give me a swift hit with his nightstick, but the sergeant pulled him off. "Leave her alone," she said. "She's had a tough day."

After the Bust

I went directly home. No, that's not what I should have done. But this had been an extraordinary day, and I needed a little time to myself. I'm not particularly proud to admit this, but I stripped off my clothes, lay down on the sofa and masturbated until I was sore. I knew I'd feel too guilty to fantasize about my afternoon when I was making love to Tim, but I had to get this energy out. I just had to.

When I was finished, I covered up with a throw and lay there to think. I had so many things going through my mind that it seemed like I was looking at my day through a kaleidoscope. Images came at me from everywhere: Sonny and his cold eyes, Chris and the way he'd slapped my ass, Spiro's face when Sonny slapped him, the moment when the door was knocked off its hinges like a piece of balsawood. But the image that kept coming back was that of Sergeant Randolph's body. I know it's odd, but I'd never gotten to really look at Charlotte, and I'm not the kind of woman who'd use a hand mirror to look at herself. There was something so profoundly beautiful about a woman's body ... something that I'm not able to put words to.

There might be fallout from today ... terrible fallout. But I'm glad I did what I did. If Tim finds out and can't get over it ... better to know that now than when we have kids. But I don't think that's gonna happen ... on either front. I don't think he'll find out, and I can't tell him. If this comes out, I've got to take my lumps, but if it doesn't I can't tell because I'd be ratting out the sergeant. And I'm not going to do that. You don't do that to another cop. You just don't.

But even if he finds out, I think we'll be able to work through it. He loves me very much, and I love him just as much. He's not dumb, and he wouldn't want to give up something great just because of something I had to do to save my own life and the life of a fellow officer. He's my husband, but he's also a cop. An accountant might not understand, but a cop would. That doesn't mean he'd be happy about it, but I think he'd understand.

And now ... remarkably ... I think I could explain what happened. I'd never tell him that I got so hot I had to masturbate for a half hour. But I could honestly say that Sergeant Randolph didn't make me hot ... even though I was sizzling. I wasn't having sex with her ... even though I would have leapt at the chance at one point in my life. I was doing what I had to do as a cop ... and getting rid of some bad memories at the same time. No, I wouldn't tell him that, either. But I could honestly say that the experience didn't make me want to do it again. I'd had a fantastic sexual experience ... devoid of love and caring and emotional connection. It was wild and exciting and reckless, but that's not how I want to experience sex on a regular basis. I want to be loved and cared for and cherished by my lover ... not act on pure animal lust. Yes, lust is part of it, but I don't want it to be all of it. I want Tim. I know that now, more than ever.

Resolved, I got up and took a long, hot shower. I flossed, used mouthwash, brushed, used more mouthwash and brushed again. I just wished my sister lived close. I'd trust her to tell me if my breath smelled like a woman. But I didn't have the luxury of having a friend nearby who wouldn't judge me for what I'd had to do. So I got dressed, went to work, and started filling out paperwork. I was always in a hurry to divest myself of the tips I received, but today I needed to get that thousand dollars off me. It felt like blood money, and I can honestly say I've never been happier to lose a thousand bucks.

I slept surprisingly well. Partly because Tim was so effusive in his praise for the bust. I think there will always be a part of me that wants his approval. He made some overtures about making love, but I pled exhaustion, which was true. I didn't mention the fact that I couldn't stand to have another orgasm, but that was my business. He's not much of a cuddler, but I snuggled up to him and he put his arm around me.

"You did some very good police work on this sting," he murmured, kissing my head. "I know you didn't get the most exciting assignment, but you'll get there. I know you will."

"Thanks," I said. I kissed his bare chest, not even slightly disappointed to find flat, hard muscle. He's the man I love, and he'd look plain silly with a pair of boobs.

We didn't work in the same building, so I had to invent an excuse to sneak over to her desk. I didn't know many people on her floor, so I just glided by and dropped a note, not turning to see if she'd even noticed it fall onto her lap.

A few moments later, she walked into the restroom and stood there a little uncertainly. "Uhm ... hi," she said.

I put a manila envelope on the sink. "I know I committed a crime, but I can't afford to have this ruin my career."

"You took the tape?" She looked tremendously happy, and my heart started to beat harder.

"I had to learn something in six months. Other than the fact that I never wanna be a waitress."

She picked up the envelope. "Are you giving this to me?"

I took a breath, hoping against hope that she'd view the situation the same way I did. "Yeah. It's your decision. You're the lead officer. If you want to turn me in ... it's your call." I noted that she was unable to look me in the eyes, but I wasn't really in a hurry to lock gazes with her, either.

"I can't do that to you," she said. "I could just say I found it. It happens."

My heart was thudding so loudly, I swear I could hear it. "Will you turn it in? If you do, I've gotta do some damage control."

"At home?"

"Yeah. My husband wasn't wild about my going into narcotics. I don't think this'll change his mind."

"He might not find out."

"He's a lieutenant in the police commissioner's office. He finds out everything." I was on the verge of crying, just thinking about the look on Tim's face if he saw the tape, but there was no way I was gonna let her see me cry. I had to maintain my self-respect.

"My girlfriend wouldn't be happy, either."

Something about the casual tone she used made me mad. I looked right at her. "Would she divorce you?"

"I don't think so. But I guess I'm not sure. It wouldn't help our relationship."

It was a little late to be all coy, so I told the truth. "I had an affair with a woman in college. Biggest mistake I ever made was telling my husband about it."

I thought I saw her wince. She looked at the envelope in her hand, knowing how much it could hurt both of us. She met my eyes, holding my gaze for a moment. "If I was the only one on this tape, I'd turn it in. I follow the rules. That's the only thing that keeps us from being like Sonny."

I nodded, hoping against hope that there was a big "but" coming.

"Anything else on here?"

"Nothing," I said quickly. "They must have put in a new tape."

"Hmm ..." She looked thoughtful. "How bad was it working there?"

Odd question. "Bad," I said. "I think I've got Chris' fingerprints permanently branded on my butt," I said, feeling the sense of shame that always overcame me when he touched me. "That bastard never walked by me that he didn't manhandle me."

"Sometimes it sucks being a woman on the force. I've dressed up like a hooker more times than I can count." She laughed softly. "Sometimes I think the force would still be all male if they didn't need us for prostitution busts."

She said it with such good grace that I had to laugh, too.

Slapping the envelope against her hand, a little line formed between her brows. "What about the buy? It's on here, isn't it?"

"No." I shook my head quickly. "Spiro got up and turned the recorder off when you and Chris went into the back room." I smiled at her. "They're not dumb enough to record a big sale."

She waited for a second, her gaze flickering over my face. "Wanna go out for breakfast?"

I blinked. Oh, God, don't tell me she wants a repeat performance! "Uhm ... why?"

The sergeant gave me such a warm, friendly smile that my heart resumed its normal beat. "I wanna go to the hardware store down the street and buy a magnet. Then I wanna pull this tape out and run that magnet over it. Then I thought we could burn it, and then ..."

I practically squealed. "Can I put the ashes in the river?"

"With a lead weight."

I could be wrong, but I think I've found a girlfriend on the force.

Books by Blayne Cooper

Available at StarCrossed Productions, Inc, http://www.scp-inc.biz/, Amazon.com, www.blaynecooper.com, *and fine bookstores everywhere.*

Unbreakable

From their earliest years, five very different girls were as close as sisters—sharing everything, even secrets and lies—until their friendship and their lives were ripped apart by a devastating act of betrayal from one of their own.

Twenty years have gone by, and one woman has more cause to regret her estrangement from the group than the rest. An old promise leads to a reunion, which unearths memories, mistrust, and hidden agendas as the former friends—grown up and grown apart—reconnect and realize the impact they've had on each other's lives. Real and perceived betrayals jeopardize the entire event … as well as the hopes of a rekindled romance.

The bonds of love and friendship can be as strong as steel. But are they unbreakable?

The Last Train Home

One cold winter's night in Manhattan's Lower East side, tragedy strikes the Chisholm family. Thrown together by fate and disaster, Virginia "Ginny" Chisholm meets Lindsay Killian, a street-smart drifter who spends her days picking pockets and riding the rails. Together, the young women embark on a desperate journey that spans from the slums of New York City to the Western Frontier, as Ginny tries to reunite her family, regardless of the cost. In this dramatic saga a solid friendship is forged, one strong enough to endure the trials of an impoverished existence in 1890s America and a quest from which neither woman will back down. It's those same bonds that form the basis of a tender, and very unexpected, romance.

Cobb Island

Cobb Island offers not one but three romances in this novel set off the coast of Virginia. Marcy and Doug have had only sporadic contact since Marcy's family moved away a year ago. Their older sisters agree to supervise the lovesick teens during a week-long stay in an eerie island house that has been in Marcy's family since the late 1600s. But who will chaperone the chaperones? Sparks fly between them almost from the beginning, growing into lightning-size bolts when Liv notices that Kayla is answering her questions before she has even voiced them. It is Liv's training in translating foreign languages, however that proves to be the key that unlocks the house's secret history—and the story of a tragic love begun and ended four centuries earlier.

Echoes From the Mist

In this sequel to Cobb Island, paranormal researchers Kayla Redding and Olivia Hazelwood begin their professional and personal partnership as they tackle their first case together in the world's most haunted city—Edinburgh, Scotland. While in Edinburgh, the women visit the Cobb family ancestral home. The Cobb family historian takes the women on a journey back through time to 17th Century Colonial Virginia. He weaves the tale of Faylinn Cobb, explaining what happened to her and her family after her sister-in-law, Bridget Redding, was branded a witch.

The Story of Me

*written using the pen name Advocate

Randi is just trying to make sense of it all as she sits in the park, pouring out her woes to a pair of bemused squirrels. The first thing she determines is that she sucks at thinking up snappy titles. Hence, the prosaic name for this classic farce that might best be described as a free fall into insanity.

In truth, it would be hard to find something better to call this screwball comedy, featuring the misadventures of a tall, dark driving instructor and the blonde nurse who's stalking her. Mac is intent on drawing Randi into a madcap plot to exact revenge upon a common enemy; the two-timing wench who dumped Mac for her brother, the doctor - and who, years earlier, deprived Randi of academic fame and a college scholarship. The ill-conceived plan takes them across America to Las Vegas. It's a 'road trip from Hell' that features a wild array of occurrences, ranging from mere mishap to outright disaster. Inexorably - delightfully - the women slide into an endearing, nutty relationship that was simply meant to be.

Castaway, Second Ed.
Co-written by Ryan Daly and only available at www.scp-inc.biz

Where "Survivor" meets "Gilligan's Island" in "The Twilight Zone." Sixteen men and women are stranded on a tropical island-with an intrusive camera crew and a psychotic producer, where they fight for survival, TV ratings, and a million dollar prize. The winner is anyone who loves thrill-a-minute misadventures, gut-busting laughs, and 'broad'-minded women.

The premise may be familiar, though the contestants are anything but, when a desperate network owner is hell-bent on blockbuster ratings and casts the show accordingly. Shannon, a budding novelist and former network employee, falls deeply in lust with tall, dark, paranoid Ryan, a Kentucky survivalist who is determined to win. "The course of true love never did run smooth," Shakespeare said. Even he couldn't have imagined the road bumps Shannon and Ryan will encounter en route to love and hot monkey sex.

The women are not only star-crossed, but insect infested and sand crab bitten. In this irreverent spoof, which focuses on an industry where nothing is as it seems, and no one can be trusted, Shannon and Ryan pull out all the stops to 'get the girl' - and win the prize. Join them as they discover the best thing about 'Paradise' is each other.

Blayne Cooper is also the author of ***Madam President***, ***First Lady***, and ***The Road to Glory*** (all co-written by T. Novan).

Books by KG MacGregor

Coming soon from Bella Books
http://www.kgmacgregor.com

Just This Once (2006)

Wynne Connelly is a marketing manager from Baltimore who travels regularly to her company's headquarters in Orlando. Paula McKenzie is the night manager at the luxurious Weller Regent, the downtown business hotel where Wynne stays. When their flirtations spiral out of control, they share a scorching night together that awakens for both women what passion should be. But physical and emotional scars from a near-fatal accident keep Wynne from thinking she can be the lover Paula deserves.

Mulligan (2006)

The days are long and lonely for Louise Stevens, whose retirement plans did not include facing the sudden loss of her life partner. Nor did she anticipate meeting sixty-year-old Marty Beck, a fun-loving golf pro with no experience in making relationships last. Too bad they didn't hit it off.

Shaken (2007)

When a powerful earthquake strikes LA, two strangers are trapped in a crumbled shopping mall. Luxury car dealer Anna Kaklis and family attorney Lily Stewart join forces to escape the rubble; and the friendship that follows grows into the strongest connection either has ever known. *Shaken* is a story of chance and courage, loss and triumph, strength and family.

Books by SX Meagher

Available at StarCrossed Productions, Inc.
http://www.scp-inc.biz/
www.sxmeagher.com

The Milk of Human Kindness
Anthology edited by Lori L. Lake

That Way is the story of a little girl and the women in her life—her mother and grandmother—and their differing opinions about her developing personality.

Intimate Pleasures
Anthology edited by Stacia Seaman and Nann Dunne

What happens in *Vegas* stays in Vegas … sometimes.

Telltale Kisses
Anthology edited by Stephanie Solomon-Lopez and Medora MacDougall

Take a look behind the scenes of a professional golfer in *Water Hazard*.

I Found My Heart in San Francisco (2006)

If you always hate to have a novel end, and are often left wanting to know just a little more about the characters, this is the series for you!

A work-in-progress, the twenty-six books of *I Found My Heart In San Francisco* focus on two young women from the San Francisco Bay area. You'll get to know them, their families, friends, hobbies, habits and quirks as thoroughly as those of your close friends.

Arbor Vitae (2006)

Clancy O'Connor is a young landscape architect, just starting her own business. One of her first important clients, Abby Graham, is a woman who seems to have very little in common with the rough-and-tumble landscaper. But opposites can and do attract, as both women come to learn.